The Se

Marty Shaver

July / 2010

The Second Verdict

Mark E. Shaver

Copyright © 2007 Mark E. Shaver
All rights reserved.
ISBN: 1-4196-6743-2
ISBN-13: 978-1419667435

Visit www.booksurge.com to order additional copies.

The Second Verdict

Acknowledgements

My undying gratitude and heartfelt appreciation goes to my wife, Brenda. Her encouragement and support are truly without bounds.

A special thanks to Will Dunn, whose creativity and artistic talents came together perfectly in the cover of this book. (welldun@msn.com)

Back cover photo by Country Park Portraits. Thanks Sam. (www.countryparkportraits.com)

For Florence Hotson,
through whose warmth and hospitality
this story began.

CHAPTER ONE

Beads of sweat trickled down Ryan Edloe's face as he stood in the shadow of what simply had to be a bad dream; a nightmare, but it was not. As the silhouette edged ever closer to him, a voice that whispered, yet uttered its words as if it were growling, pierced the silence.

"It has been written that vengeance belongs to the Lord. Those words had meaning where you came from, but they mean nothing here."

A thick mist of steam accompanied the words leaving a foul odor in the frigid air.

"Vengeance can be yours if you so choose."

"Vengeance for what?" Ryan stuttered, not knowing where he was or how he got here.

The voice grew louder. "Don't you know what place this is?"

Ryan tried to look around, but instead closed his eyes tightly and began to chant aloud, "This is just a dream. It's not real. I'm going to wake up and it will all be over. It's just a dream."

As he spoke, he felt something tearing at the flesh of his right forearm. He looked down to see his shirt torn and blood quickly soaking the tattered fabric.

"Tell me Edloe" the voice spoke mockingly, "is that your imagination or your blood running down your arm?"

Ryan's eyes watched as blood began to drip from his hand. Then, as if no longer under his control, his eyes slowly drifted upwards towards the shadow. As he watched, a figure began to emerge from the darkness. He was unable to identify it. It had the legs of a wild animal, but stood upright as a man. Its skin appeared weathered and wrinkled, but it had the muscles and posture of a youth. But more than anything else Ryan noticed the horns. The head of the beast had at least ten of them, and one appeared to have its own eye.

Ryan was frozen with fear at the sight of the beast. Its eyes pierced his flesh and penetrated his soul.

"I am offering you that which only I can offer; true revenge. I'm offering you the opportunity to exact your pound of flesh, to make the person responsible for your being here pay. I'm offering you the opportunity to watch his fear and savor his pain, and to witness the transformation by your own hand, from sanity to utter madness. And all I ask in return is the pleasure of your company as my guest."

Before Ryan could answer, his vision became blurred, and the image of the beast began to fade as if he were moving rapidly away from it.

"This time it was not to be." the beast roared angrily. "But rest assured our paths will cross again."

The image of what he had just seen melted into a sea of bright light. As his eyes began to focus, the white coat of a medical attendant came into view.

"He's back." were the only words Ryan could make out as a siren screamed in the background.

Ryan's heart pounded in his chest. He looked up with indescribable relief at the paramedic.

"How did we miss that?" the paramedic asked, pointing to a wound on Ryan's arm.

"I don't know" a voice answered from behind him, "but it's bleeding like a son of a bitch. Better put a few butterflies on it and wrap it up before we lose him again."

Ryan's eyes nervously crept downward until they saw the gashes on his forearm. For a second his body felt a distant chill and he could smell the stench as his mind unwillingly replayed the last few moments of a memory that would haunt him for the rest of his life.

The ambulance screamed past the window in a small examining room on its way to the ER entrance. Brad Martin listened as the siren faded into the cold January air.

"Take a deep breath and hold it, or would you rather turn your head and cough?" The doctor was trying to be funny, but Brad found no humor in his remarks. Brad sat, his shirt unbuttoned, on the edge of the examination table with a cold stethoscope pressed to his chest. It was Tuesday, and Tuesday meant the first of a twice-weekly visit to the hospital for treatment. Although Brad seemed a normal, healthy man of some thirty three years, his body was fighting a disease which had, thanks to the experimental program in which he was participating, gone into remission. It was his intention as it was the intention of those treating him that it stayed that way.

"So far, so good." the doctor commented as he made his notes in what looked like a foreign language on the chart. "I feel guardedly optimistic about your condition."

"Guardedly optimistic" Brad repeated. "Did someone write that for you guys or did you make it up on your own?"

The doctor looked at him not knowing if he were serious or just kidding.

"That must be the most used line in the medical profession." Brad scoffed as he slid down off the examination table and began to button his shirt.

"No, you're wrong," the doctor argued. "That is by no means the most commonly used phrase in the medical profession."

Bred turned and faced the doctor. "Then what is?"

"Do you have insurance or are you paying for this yourself?" The doctor smiled, realizing that it was all in fun, or at least partly so. "You can go back out to the lounge for a bit. If everyone gets here on time, we'll start the treatments in about twenty minutes."

Brad tucked his shirt in. He was very conscious of his appearance. It was important to him. He believed it said a lot about a person, the way they kept themselves. Feeling sufficiently presentable, he walked over to the door and through it into the adjoining room.

The room was quite large and impressively appointed. It was constructed for the purpose of socializing, sort of a lounge where the patients could sit and talk while they waited for their treatments to begin. It was divided with furniture into sections. Couches and chairs were arranged in squares, and it was within one of these squares that four people, whose paths otherwise would never have crossed, became friends, and later much more.

Despite the size of the room, it was never occupied by more than a few people at a time. Although the original purpose of this facility was to provide a very specialized experimental treatment to a large number of patients, numerous unforeseen budget cuts reduced the number of participants to a small handful. Consequently the room remained silent much of the time.

Brad took his usual seat in a small cluster of chairs next to a couch by the treatment room door. He was always the first one there, the first of the four in his treatment group. He hated to be late. It was just his nature. The therapy offered by the center was a welcome alternative to accepting his condition and facing its consequences.

Brad was a writer and had been for most of his adult life. His accomplishments consisted mainly of novels and short stories. Although he had been reasonably successful, he was still waiting for that one thought, that one idea that would spark a best seller, and put him on top. His affliction, contrary to what many might think, did not hamper his ability to write. If anything, it enhanced it. He looked at life from a different perspective because of it. It had become his mission to write something so unique, so spectacular, that it would live on far beyond his limited years. And as he sat in the lounge of the treatment center this particular morning, he had no idea how close he was to actually living something that was more incredible and more outrageous, than anything he could have ever imagined.

Brad was an exceptionally cautious individual in every aspect of his life except his stock trading. He took risks and long shots in the market more frequently than most would, and almost without fail they paid off for him. This was the only area of his life he allowed any risk. Every other action was carefully planned and thoughtfully executed. He did very little spontaneously and nothing impulsively. This made him a more prudent individual, but it also made him a little boring at times.

But Brad was happy with his life, or what he had left of it. He had been involved in several short, uneventful relationships with a couple of different women. None of them, to this point, had impressed him much past the invitation of a second date. I guess he wasn't really looking for a long-term relationship. Nonetheless, his drive and determination to change his perception of his own 'long term' were the reasons he found himself sitting in the lounge of the treatment center this and every Tuesday and Thursday afternoon.

The same picture greeted Arthur Jensen each time he arrived for treatment; Brad sitting in the same place, with his feet propped up on the chair in front of him reading a newspaper. Arthur would always arrive shortly after Brad. He was a stock broker and since Brad invested in the stock market as heavily as his book royalties would allow, he and Brad always had something to talk about.

Arthur was the much-envied 'happily married man' with a beautiful wife and two children. His visits to the center were more in his mind more for his wife's benefit than his own. Being ex-military and a combat veteran afforded him a certain toughness, but deep down inside he knew he was doing the right thing by coming here. That was very important to Arthur, doing the right thing. He saw so much around him that was unfair and many times despaired over his inability to do anything about it. All of that was about to change.

Of Arthur's two children, one was as close to being the perfect child as any parent could hope for, and the other was as far from it as any parent could imagine. The younger of the two, his son, was a typical five year old and responsible for nowhere near as many headaches for his dad as was his sister. Angie was sixteen, a very dangerous age indeed. With all the confidence in the world, she was as outspoken as Arthur was steadfast.

Despite the ongoing dissension with Angie, Arthur and his family were living the American dream. The only dark side to this dream was the reason Arthur was in the lounge this morning with Brad.

"What's the temperature on Wall Street this week, Arthur?" Brad asked as Arthur took his place on the couch.

"Don't ever have a daughter." Arthur snapped. "I'm telling you, you'll live to regret it!"

"I take it this has nothing to do with the stock market." Brad muttered under his breath as he shuffled through some papers, trying his best to keep a straight face.

"Purple hair, she wants purple hair."

"I've seen that before." Brad recalled, staring pretentiously into the air. "I saw a skinny girl in a long white coat with purple hair. She looked just like a grape tootsie roll pop!"

"That doesn't make me feel any better, Brad." Arthur peered at him over the top of his reading glasses. "How the hell do you deal with purple hair? When I was young we had long hair, but that's the way it grew. It was perfectly natural; hair grows, but purple hair?"

"Look Arthur, she's probably doing all this to be attractive to her peers. Don't you have any high school kids working part time at your office that you could introduce her to? Somebody from the mail room or something"

"I doubt she'd go for anyone that conservative. Besides, she's too young. Anyway, the last guy she brought home had three earrings in each ear."

"You have a tattoo." Brad countered.

"It's from the Marine Corps. Quit siding with her, you're supposed to be an adult."

The conversation paused as the two exchanged some papers. "This is what I want to invest this time." Brad stated with confidence, handing a cashier's check to Arthur. "This is my gambling money for the quarter, and I've picked a company that I want to invest in. I've done the research."

Brad handed Arthur a copy of the stock page from the newspaper with a circle around his choice.

"You could lose it all!" Arthur warned. "It's a start up company with a lot of debt, not to mention some well established competition."

"I'm willing to take that chance." Brad said confidently.

"Do you know something that I don't?" Arthur asked.

"I always side with the underdog." Brad admitted.

"I hope you know what you're doing." Arthur shook his head as he tucked Brad's check away in his brief case.

The conversation was interrupted by the sound of the wind howling through one of the main entry doors as it opened.

Derek Williams was perhaps the only member of the group who led anything close to an average life style, at least by today's standards. He was also the youngest. It seemed so unfair that a young man of twenty-five should be dealing with a life threatening disease, but he persevered. He and his wife enjoyed a modest existence. Derek worked in a local iron works plant. His wife Katie, worked for one of the city's newspapers, and was pregnant with their first child.

Derek was a positive, optimistic person despite his condition. He was running a race not only against time, but also against life itself; the life of his unborn child. No matter what, he knew he would experience at least some of the joys of being a father. His drive and determination were a testimony to that.

Money was always a concern, or at least a serious consideration with Derek and Katie. It seemed there were always as many bills as there was income. They always made ends meet, although those ends never did get to know each other very well. Money though had never been the driving force in their relationship.

Derek viewed Arthur as a sort of father figure, and Brad as an older brother. Despite the fact that their lots in life were significantly different, once inside the treatment center, the playing field became enigmatically level and each of them viewed one another in those terms.

"How's that beautiful wife of yours, Derek?' Brad asked as Derek took his seat in the chair adjacent to Arthur.

"Pregnant and beautiful as ever!" was always his answer.

"Ya, there's something about a pregnant woman." Arthur spoke with a certain reminiscent conviction. Brad sat back and listened with a distant smile. Never having been married, he could only imagine what it must be like.

"So how are things at the plant?" Arthur asked.

"We're still working, so I guess everything's alright. But you two guys couldn't relate to that concept could you?" Derek remarked with some degree of false sarcasm.

"Hey, I was young and struggling once too!" Arthur spoke in his own defense.

Before the conversation could go any further, the unmistakable footsteps of the technician became audible as he made his way down the flight of stairs and into the lounge. He pushed open the doors, as the rustling sound of the pages on his clipboard signaled the treatments were about to begin.

"Where is the other one?" he inquired without looking up from his notes. Somehow he knew one of them was absent. There was a brief moment of silence that was soon broken by Derek.

"Well you know how rich folks are." He was referring to Evan Marshall. He really was rich. His father made sure of that. Dear old dad was very wealthy and never gave his son a chance to make anything of himself. Despite the intentions of his father, Evan turned out alright. His dedication to the institute and his treatments occasionally became side tracked by more immediate concerns, usually women. Most were just after his money, and usually got enough to make it an even trade, or at best a modest compromise. Today's absence indicated there was a compromise in the works, or at least there was last night.

Brad leaned over to Arthur, "I'd rather be getting laid than be in here myself!"

"Especially if she's one of Evan's girlfriends" Arthur whispered.

"I thought you were a happily married man?" Brad added in an artificially surprised voice.

"Hey, I can look, can't I?" Arthur argued as they walked through the doors into the treatment room.

"Sure, but it would be like a dog chasing a car. What would you do if you caught her? Brad questioned.

"Not a damned thing." Arthur replied without even thinking. "Not a damned thing."

The doors closed slowly behind them leaving an echo that faded away into the silence of the empty room.

Two and a half sobering hours later, the three men made their way down the corridor to the parking garage. The conversation was usually a bit more guarded and restrained after the treatment session.

"You've been kind of quiet today Derek." Arthur noticed, "Anything wrong?"

"Nothing that I can't handle." he answered.

"Anything we can do to help?" Brad asked.

"No, it's no big deal."

"No, come on. What's wrong?" Brad insisted

"The plant discontinued its monthly production bonuses." Derek explained. "I had planned to do something special for Katie this month, just to show her how special she is to me. But by the time we pay the bills and my share of these treatment costs, there's nothing left. And I have to pass up most of my over-time to make these sessions. Sometimes I feel like quitting these treatments and spending what ever time I have left living a normal life."

"Wrong!" Brad snapped, almost shouting. "These treatments are our only chance. You owe it to her to do everything you can do to grow old together"

"You're right, I know. Sometimes I get to feeling sorry for myself, that's all."

As the three men buttoned up their coats and prepared to face the frigid January weather, Brad slipped something into Derek's shirt pocket.

"Isn't it your birthday today?" he asked.

"No, not until June, why?"

"Didn't your parents ever teach you not to argue with your elders?" Brad slapped him on the back before he could answer. "You're never too old to learn. We'll see you on Thursday."

Arthur smiled, knowing what Brad had done.

Brad and Arthur left Derek zipping up his coat. After the doors had completely closed, he reached into his pocket. In his fingers was a fifty-dollar bill. In a way he felt bad for taking it, though he knew he shouldn't.

The trip home that night found Derek making a mental list of restaurants and movies that he and his wife had talked about. Should they do dinner and a movie or a dinner and some shopping? Should he bring her flowers, or should he surprise her with a gift? Before he was able to make any decisions, he was turning onto a quiet street lined with modest wood frame houses.

As he approached his house something seemed different. There were no lights on. Katie usually met him at the door on treatment days. He pulled into the driveway and turned off his headlights, waiting for the motion light on the front of the garage to come on. It didn't. He was sure now that something was wrong. Opening the car door, he ran across the yard and up the porch steps. He threw open the front door, paying little attention to the splintered and broken wood as he called out Katie's name. There was no reply.

A dim line of light under the bedroom door was the only light in the house. He made his way down the dark hall and opened the door. Inside he found Katie, lying on the bed, her head facing the wall. He touched her arm thinking she was sleeping. She tensed to his touch. He took her by the arm and turned her around to face him. His eyes widened and his heart began to pound at what he saw. Her eyes were both swollen almost completely shut. A large bruise had risen on her left cheek. Several cuts on her arms had left trails of dried blood to her hands.

"What happened?" Derek asked trying to control his hysteria. "Who did this?"

A single teardrop trickled down Katie's cheek. "I tried to get away, but I just can't move very fast any more."

"Come on!" Derek picked her up from the bed and carried her through the house to the car. As they passed through the living room, he noticed the absence of his TV and stereo. He carried her down the steps and over to the passenger side of the car. Opening the door, he carefully sat her in the seat, doing his best to maintain his composure. He fastened the seat belt around her and assured her that everything would be alright. They backed out of the driveway and sped off into the night, and the house was once again silent.

The floor of the waiting area in the emergency room looks the same no matter where you walk. Derek knew this to be true because he had paced every square inch of it. In light of Katie's condition he was not allowed to go with her into the ER. The fact that she was pregnant was the cause of great concern to the attending physician. She was placed in a wheelchair and taken through the automatic doors. That was forty-five minutes ago. Derek came to hate those doors. He hated the sound they made, that high-pitched electric whine. Each time the doors opened, another helpless victim passed through, entering into a place to which he was denied entry. One by one they passed through those doors, dozens of them. They all went in, but no one ever came out, nor would anyone for another thirty minutes.

When the doors opened again a lone figure in a white coat emerged and entered the waiting room.

"Are you Mr. Williams?"

"Yes, how is my wife?"

"Have you notified the police?"

"No" Derek snapped, "I was more concerned about getting my wife to the hospital."

"Well, we have. The assault on your wife has caused a complication. Do you know how far along is she exactly?"

"Almost seven and a half months, why? What kind of complication are you talking about?"

"Your wife was struck at least once in her stomach. This has caused the protective environment that surrounds the baby to rupture. In other words, her water has broken. We have no choice but to take the baby now. I know it's almost two months premature, but we have all the facilities here to deal with a situation like this."

"What are the chances the baby will be okay?"

"Right now, fifty-fifty" Derek's face turned white as he dropped back into the chair behind him. The doctor knelt down in front of him.

"I'm needed back in there. I just wanted you to know what was going on and to tell you that we are doing everything we can. I'll come back when we know a little more."

The doctor stood up and the doors opened, as if they knew he was coming. Before he could pass through, a stretcher emerged. On it Katie laid motionless. A nurse followed along side carrying an I.V. bag. Derek jumped to his feet and ran to her. As she passed by, he took her hand.

"Everything's going to be alright, I promise."

Her eyes gave a brief glimpse of comfort. He held her hand tightly as she was pushed down the corridor. Their hands were separated as she entered the elevator. The doors slowly closed leaving Derek alone in the silence of the empty hallway.

An overwhelming feeling of helplessness began to overtake him. He needed to talk to someone. He slid his hand into his pocket as he walked toward the phones. He pulled his hand from his pocket. In it was a fifty-dollar bill.

The only light that was on in Brad's apartment was for the lamp next to his computer. He was working on the final chapter of his latest project. The phone was on its fourth ring as he hit the last few keys to complete his thought. He picked it up and a cup of coffee at the same time. Derek's voice was shaky as he identified himself.

"You're supposed to be out to dinner" Brad told him sarcastically as he sipped his coffee.

"I'm at Mid Town Memorial."

"What's wrong?" Brad put his cup down, splashing the hot coffee on his hand.

"It's Katie. Someone broke into our house. She got beat up pretty bad. They have to take the baby tonight."

Before Derek could say any more, Brad interrupted. "I'll be there in fifteen minutes."

Derek was checking his watch for the forth time when Brad burst through the waiting room doors.

"Have you heard anything more since we talked?"

"No. No one has even been in here." The two men sat down next to each other. Brad looked at Derek. "You know, no news is usually good news."

"Of all the houses in this city, why did he have to pick ours? We don't have anything worth stealing. Why not rob some rich person?

"Anybody that would do something like this can't be too smart to begin with. Besides, it could have been worse. He could have had a gun."

Brad reached into his pocket and pulled out a pack of gum. He took a piece, and then offered a piece to Derek. Before he could get it unwrapped, the doctor came into the waiting room and sat down on the other side of him.

"How is she?" Derek asked eagerly.

"Well, first I want to congratulate you on the birth of your son!" The doctor smiled as he took off his glasses.

"My son" Derek turned to Brad. "I have a son." He turned back to the doctor. "How is he, and how is Katie?"

"He is very premature and because of that he has a very low birth weight. What that means is he has not had sufficient time to completely develop."

"But he's alright?" Derek kept pressing the doctor for the answer he wanted.

"His condition is serious. We're by no means out of the woods. We anticipated these complications and we are one of the best equipped facilities in the city to deal with premature births."

Derek seemed to be somewhat relieved by the doctor's words. "How's my wife?" he repeated.

"She is still sedated. She will be coming down to her room soon. If you ask at the nurse's station, they can give you a room number. You can wait for her there."

"Is the baby in an incubator?" Brad inquired as the doctor stood up.

"Yes. He will remain there until he has developed to the point that he can better deal with our environment, probably three or four weeks."

Brad thanked the doctor as he left the room, then led Derek to the nurse's station and soon they were waiting for Katie in her room. They had been there only a few minutes when someone knocked lightly on the door. As the two turned to see who it was, a police officer opened the door to the room and identified himself.

"I'm Officer George Grant, Mid Town police. The hospital reported to us that there was an assault tonight."

"That's right" Derek answered, "my wife."

"I'll need to ask you some questions." He turned to Brad. "Would you excuse us for a few minutes please?"

Brad looked at Derek, waiting for his unspoken response before leaving him.

"It's okay." Derek assured him.

"I'll be just outside the door if you need me."

Brad left the room, taking his cell phone from his pocket.

The ringing phone in Arthur's kitchen interrupted his daughter's pleadings to stay out an extra hour. Brad counted the rings. Arthur was still talking to his daughter as he picked up the phone. "The answer is still no......hello."

"Arthur it's me."

"What's up Brad?"

"I'm here at Mid Town Memorial. Someone broke into Derek's house and beat the hell out of Katie."

"What? How is she?"

"They had to take the baby. They're both doing as well as can be expected."

How is Derek taking it?"

"Not too well. There is a cop talking to him now."

"Do you need me to come down there?" Arthur asked.

"Not tonight. But if you and Sandy could come tomorrow morning it would probably be a good idea."

"We'll be there."

Brad slipped the phone back into his pocket just as the door began to open. As the officer stepped into the hallway, Brad stopped him.

"What are the chances of finding the guy that did this?"

"Well, I'll need to talk to his wife and see if we can get a description. Then we'll get her to look at some mug shots, and if he has ever been arrested before maybe she'll be able to pick him out. Then it will be up to us to find him."

"What if he doesn't have a record?"

"Then we get his description and start from there."

"Since no one was killed, will this case be given very much attention?" Brad asked.

"Lots of crime in this city. We just take them as they come." With that the officer excused himself and continued down the hall.

Brad rejoined Derek in the room. "How did it go?"

"He said they'd do their best to find the guy, but I'll be surprised if they do." Derek's concerns were for his wife. As he spoke, the door was pushed open. Slowly Katie was wheeled in. Derek's expression changed as he saw his wife. She looked much better than she did at their house. He took her hand. Her eyes were still closed, but her fingers softly tightened around his.

"I'm going to leave you two alone." Brad said as he picked up his coat. "If you need anything, anything at all, you call me. I'll be back in the morning." Brad left the room.

Arthur tucked his son into bed and gave him a kiss on his forehead. He walked back downstairs to his den and began putting some papers he had been working on back in his brief case. As he closed the case, his thoughts drifted to Derek. His concern for his friend began to turn to anger. He found himself fighting to keep his rage from consuming him as it had a tendency to do. That rage was forced to take second place to Derek and Katie's needs, although it would not hold that position for long.

CHAPTER TWO

Arthur and his wife weaved their way down the corridor as carts carrying the remnants of breakfast were being wheeled away. Approaching Katie's room, they noticed the door to be slightly ajar. Sandy gently knocked on the open door then peeked into the room. The bed was empty as was the chair next to it. Arthur took a step backwards to the center of the corridor and looked in both directions. At the far end of the corridor, Derek and Katie were slowly making their way back towards the room, Derek pushing her in a wheel chair. Arthur tapped Sandy on her shoulder and motioned for her to follow him. They walked down the corridor and met Derek and Katie half way.

"We have just seen the most beautiful baby." Derek's eyes were gleaming with the pride as he spoke about his son.

"He's tiny, but the doctor seems to think he'll be just fine." Katie added.

Sandy embraced Katie and the four of them walked back towards Katie's room.

Arthur bent down to give Katy a hug and quickly felt the rage building within him as he saw the cuts and bruises on her face. He did his best to mask it.

"When do we get to see this beautiful baby?" she asked.

"For now they're only letting family members into the ICU. But they should be moving him out in a few days."

"We can't wait to see him." Arthur added.

When the four made it back to Katie's room, the fatigue from the trip was evident on her face. Derek helped her back into bed and after a short visit, Arthur and Sandy excused themselves. Katie needed to rest and Arthur had to get to work.

"Is there anything you need, anything we can bring either of you?" Sandy asked on her way out the door.

"No" Derek said as he took Katie's hand, "I've got everything I need right here."

"We'll come back tonight." Sandy promised as she and Arthur left the room.

The next treatment session once again found Brad and Arthur sitting, as they usually do, alone in the lounge. The order of rotation as it were, was broken this day by Evan's presence. Evan Marshall truly enjoyed the pleasures of life, but he would never miss more than one treatment because of them. He was, to a certain degree, the stereotypical 'rich kid', although he was in his early thirties.

Evan's father was a very successful business man. His success though, did not come without a price. He and Evan were much more distant than any father and son should be. In fact, he rarely ever saw his father, especially since his mother died.

Evan's life was by no means empty. He lived on one of his father's estates, a large rambling place, much too excessive for just one person. But the house was paid for as were all of the bills, not to mention all of the trappings that go along with that degree of wealth. Evan's father had also set up a trust which disbursed funds to Evan on a monthly basis. The amount of money he received each month was more than the average family of six would need to survive for a year, but he always managed to find a way to spend it.

"Where's Derek?" Evan asked as he took a seat opposite Arthur.

"Someone robbed his house and put Katie in the hospital in the process."

"What? Is the baby okay?"

"They had to take the baby. He is in an incubator for the next few weeks, but the doctors say he'll be alright."

"Why didn't anybody call me? We're all family, remember."

Before the conversation was finished, Derek entered the lounge.

"How's Katie and.....hey, what did you name you're son anyway?" Brad felt embarrassed for asking.

"We've got it narrowed down to three." Derek said proudly. "I'll let you know what we decide. We didn't count on having to come up with a name so soon, but I'm not complaining."

Derek took his place in a large winged back chair.

"By the way" Derek added as he got comfortable in the chair, "the police called and told me they made an arrest. Katie's going to identify him this afternoon."

Brad and Arthur were stunned. "When did this happen?" Arthur asked.

"Yesterday they brought some pictures for Katie to look at. She picked the guy out right away. Seems he pawned some of our stuff. The pawn shop got busted and the owner gave the guy up to make things easier on himself. Now I'm glad I took the time to put my driver's license number on everything."

"So Katie picked his picture out? She knew what he looked like?" Arthur seemed surprised.

"She picked him out, so I guess she did."

"When does the case go to court?" Evan inquired.

"About four weeks, according to the cops, why?"

"We'll be there!" Arthur stated rather matter of factually, almost angrily. The others looked at him, surprised by his tone. Arthur shrugged his shoulders. "I just want to get a look at this guy, that's all." Then he turned to Brad. "So do you, don't you?"

Brad looked at Arthur as if waiting for an explanation. But before the conversation could continue, the technician appeared, and soon after the treatments began.

The four weeks passed very quickly. The baby grew stronger, Katie's injuries had almost healed and things were getting back to normal. It was eleven fifteen when Brad checked his watch. He, Arthur and Evan were sitting side by side in a very crowded court room. There were many cases to be heard and the judge was going through them very quickly. The three men were somewhat surprised at the whole process, never having been directly involved in the legal system themselves.

"He sure doesn't take much time with each case does he?" Evan remarked.

"Well, they got this guy dead to rights." Arthur whispered confidently, "He'll do some time for what he did."

The gavel sounded. The next case was Katie's. A man was led into the courtroom in hand cuffs. He was a relatively young man, in his late twenties, and unshaven for several days. He had a total look of contempt on his face. It was almost as if he knew he was going to get off.

The man stood behind a table next to his court appointed attorney. The judge took a few moments to look over the papers that he was handed regarding this case. After what seemed an eternity of silence, the judge took off his glasses and laid them down on the file in front of him.

"Young man" he began, "you stand accused of some very serious crimes. You robbed and assaulted a pregnant woman causing the premature birth of her child. And if I understand it correctly, some of the stolen property was in your possession at the time of your arrest. Your obvious lack of remorse only strengthens my suspicions that you are a predator."

Arthur nodded in agreement. Derek and Katie were sitting several rows in front of him. He was sure their hearts were pounding as hard as his.

How do you plead?"

The man's attorney answered, "Guilty, your honor."

"Then I am prepared to pass sentence." The judge put his glasses on and looked down at the accused and his lawyer.

"This is not the first time you have been charged and convicted of a crime such as this. It is clear to me that you pose a very real threat to society. Unfortunately" he continued, "there are many people out there who pose an even greater threat to society than do you. In order to accommodate those persons in our prison system, I am sentencing you to five years probation and one hundred twenty hours of community service."

"What?" Arthur said aloud. "This is bullshit!" Arthur's words were loud enough to be heard by most of the court room.

As he began to stand up, Brad grabbed his sleeve and pulled him back down to his seat.

"What are you doing?" Brad whispered angrily. "Do you want to get yourself thrown in jail?"

"Are you kidding?" Arthur's voice was thick with contempt. "This son of a bitch obviously doesn't lock anybody up."

"Bailiff, next case" With that, the judge's gavel sounded, and it was over.

Derek and Katie got up and made their way towards the doors at the rear of the court room as the prisoner, soon to be set free, was led away. Arthur, Brad and Evan also made their way to the doors and met with Derek and Katie in the hallway. The judge watched from the corners of his eyes as the doors slowly closed behind them, looking helplessly remorseful.

"I can't believe he can do something like this and get away with it!" Katie said. She had gone through a lot for it all to end like this.

"Well, it's over. The best thing we can do now is to try and put all of this behind us and move on." Brad said, doing his best to keep a bad situation from getting worse.

"You're right." Derek agreed. "Katie is getting back to normal, and our son is getting stronger every day. I guess we have a lot to be thankful for."

"Besides" Evan added, "he'll probably screw up again and somebody will fix his wagon!" Arthur had been silent throughout the conversation. Evan's comments didn't seem to help much.

"That's right." Arthur added, "It's over and let's just move on and leave all of this in the past." Arthur's comments surprised Brad who, only moments earlier had to restrain him.

"It's also lunch time" Evan announced, "and lunch is on me for anybody that's hungry!"

"Sounds good to us" Derek said eagerly, "let's go."

Several days passed before the next treatment. Brad had hoped that time would help to heal the whole unfortunate incident. He was concerned about Arthur. He had never seen him act so impetuously, almost to the point of recklessness, as he did that day in the courtroom. As he locked his car and walked briskly through the crisp winter air to the treatment center doors, he hoped his concerns would be nothing more than that.

When he entered the lounge, he saw Arthur sitting alone in his usual place. In all of the eleven months of treatments, Arthur had never arrived before Brad. He stopped to check his watch, thinking he might be late. His watch and the clock on the wall were three minutes apart.

"This is a switch! Did you get fired or something?" Brad's voice echoed as he walked across the empty room.

"No, I wanted to talk to you before anyone else got here." Arthur leaned forward as Brad sat down in the chair in front of him. Before he had a chance to begin, the lounge doors opened and Evan entered the room.

"What the hell is this?" Brad looked at Evan. "What are you doing here so early?"

"I had no idea the woman was married!" Evan confessed. "Besides, Arthur asked me to get here a little earlier today"

"I'm glad you're here." Arthur remarked. "Now I can discuss this with both of you."

Evan took his seat, looking as puzzled as Brad.

"We're a very close group here." Arthur began. "You all are the best friends I've have ever had. We're like family, and we have to look out for each other like family. When something happens to one of us, it happens to all of us. Something happened to one of us and nothing got done about it."

It was becoming clear where this conversation was going. Brad leaned forward in his chair. "I know what you're getting at Arthur, but the judge passed sentence. It's over."

Arthur sat back in his seat, his face showing only a trace of his indignation. "You're right; the judge did pass his sentence." Arthur paused for a moment. "Now I'm going to pass mine!"

Brad's eyes widened and his jaw dropped at Arthur's comments. "What are you talking about? Do you really think you can take the law into you're own hands. You're not a vigilante. You were in the Marines for God's sake."

"Somebody has to." Arthur argued. Besides, what can they do to us? We've already got a death sentence. And you know what they say; a dying man has nothing to lose."

"I hate to admit it" Evan confessed, "but the man is right."

"Oh not you too" Brad pleaded, "you're talking about breaking the law here. We're all professionals, not criminals."

"That's exactly right." Arthur replied, "We're all professionals. We have the skill and the ability to do this without getting caught."

"To do what?" Brad demanded, his voice growing louder. "What do you want to do, kill him?"

"Of course not" Arthur scoffed, "I got enough of that in combat. He needs a dose of his own medicine. Let's just say a more creative form of retribution."

"Count me in." Evan said, bringing his fist down on the arm of the chair.

"Thanks." Arthur nodded before shifting his attention to Brad. "Can I count on you?"

Brad sat silent for a moment, fielding a battle between his emotions and common sense. He was passive by nature, but even he had been angered by this whole incident. In the end, when push came to shove, he really didn't believe Arthur would do it. So he conceded.

"Alright, alright, I'll do it. You guys will probably screw it up if I'm not there to help you anyway!"

"Oh, listen to him." Evan laughed.

"Derek can't know anything about this." Brad warned, "He's not a good liar and if he was ever asked, he would probably tell."

Arthur stood up. "It's not safe to talk here." He looked over at Evan. "Why don't we get together at your place, say sometime within the next couple of weeks? That work for you guys?"

Both men agreed. Their acknowledgment came at the same moment as Derek pushed open the doors to the lounge. As he approached the three, they seemed different than each of them normally did. He couldn't put his finger on it, but his three friends all looked like the cats that had eaten the canary.

As he slowly sat down, Brad asked about his son and things soon seemed normal.

Three hours later, Brad was making his way through the icy streets to his apartment. His radio, which usually played all the time, was turned off. He was uncomfortable with the decision he had made, but his sense of loyalty to his friends left him with no other choice. He remembered reading in the Bible who it was that vengeance belonged to. He felt as if he was breaking more than a few rules here, but maybe the reasons would count for something. After all, one could conclude they were just carrying out a sentence that the system was unable or unwilling to carry out itself. *That's it*, he thought to himself, *we are just making our contribution to the judicial system.* Brad was so immersed in his thoughts that he drove through a red light. A car approaching him from the cross street slammed on its brakes and slid sideways through the intersection, missing Brad's car by only inches and quickly snapping him back to reality.

Brad drove a block then pulled over to the curb to catch his breath. "This stuff is not my cup of tea." he said aloud. He regained his composure and continued his journey home.

Several days passed with no mention of the conversation that had been weighing heavily on Brad's mind. The days soon turned into a week. Brad began to think that it may have been just a bunch of talk to make Arthur feel better, and that was fine with him. But the ringing telephone in Brad's apartment that cold, winter night dispelled his hopes that this would all disappear like the snow in spring time. Brad was sipping a cup of tea and watching a TV sitcom, something he rarely did. He reached for the phone that lay on the arm of his chair. It was Evan.

"Got any plans for this Wednesday night?"

"None that I can think of" Brad answered.

"Well, you do now. Arthur says he has all of the details worked out and wants us all to get together. Eight o'clock work for you?"

"What details? What are you talking about?" Brad had put the whole thing out of his mind in the hopes that it would just go away, but deep down he knew it wouldn't.

"You know" Evan prompted, "the court room, the injustice? I think Judge Arthur is about to pass sentence!"

"Damn." Brad winced as he straightened up in his chair. "I was hoping he had forgotten about all that." He ran his fingers through his hair in frustration.

"No chance." Evan quickly answered. "He has been working it out ever since we talked about it a week ago. He's called me nearly every night."

Brad stood up and walked across the floor. This whole business was against his grain. He really didn't want any part of it, but he had committed himself.

"Alright" he conceded, "I'll be there." As he hung up the phone, he wondered how great a mistake he was making.

Wednesday was a day like any other for Arthur, managing a team of stock traders. His was a very fast paced line of work. He had little time to pause and think about what they were planning to do, nor did he have any idea that this one act would so dramatically change their lives. Charting profitability, calculating return on investment; it seemed just another day at the office. Being in a management position, he was responsible for the actions and decisions of a number of stock traders within his department. Everything was running smoothly as it usually did. Indeed, it was just another day.

Life was beginning to get back to normal for Derek and Katie. Their son, who they decided to name Derek Jr., was out of ICU and growing stronger every day. There was barely any evidence of what had happened all those weeks ago on Katie's face. Her wounds had healed. Somehow the entire incident made them even closer to each other. They were both looking forward to bringing the new baby home. Most of Derek's free time, when he wasn't at the hospital with his son, was spent getting the baby's room finished; new paint and wallpaper, curtains, and all those things hanging from the ceiling that babies seem to love. Life had indeed, returned to normal.

Wednesday night found Brad and Arthur sitting at the bar in Evan's den sipping something that neither one of them had ever heard of before.

"What is this stuff?" Arthur asked, looking at the pinkish colored liquid in his glass. "It's pretty good."

"It ought to be!" Evan touted, "It costs a hundred and eighty dollars a bottle!"

"A hundred and eighty dollars" Brad almost choked on the swallow he had just taken. "I don't drink a hundred and eighty dollars worth of liquor a year."

"How can you spend so much for one bottle?" Arthur asked.

"I didn't. It's just something from the wine cellar. Dad has expensive taste."

Arthur picked up his drink and walked over to what seemed an entire wall of electronic gadgetry. He stood shaking his head as he looked at it all. There were flashing lights, lights that stayed on all the time and lights that only came on when something was wrong. The house that Evan lived in was one of five that his father owned. The den was the nerve center for the security system. There were cameras constantly scanning the grounds, the main gate and the entrances. The house was protected by an alarm system second to none. There were sensors and motion detectors everywhere, not to mention pressure sensitive areas in the floor that could detect the presence of the most methodical intruder. There was also a state-of-the-art audio and video system occupying the same space which made it all look terribly complicated.

"I just can't get over all these knobs and switches." Arthur was the practical type and could not understand why anyone would want something like this.

"I bet there's a switch here somewhere that wipes your ass!"

"Third row down" Evan replied casually. "But use the bathroom, its so much more sanitary."

Brad sat tapping his fingers impatiently on the bar. "Can we get on with this?" His discomfort with this whole affair was becoming evident.

"Okay Brad." Arthur walked back to the bar and poured himself another drink.

"I've given this a great deal of thought over the past week. I have worked out every detail very carefully to afford us total protection. I guarantee you there is no way anyone will ever find out who did it."

Brad was somewhat surprised. He came here expecting to discuss whether or not they should even try to do something. Arthur apparently had arrived at that decision some time ago and was proceeding at a much faster pace than Brad expected.

Over the course of the next hour, Arthur laid out every detail of his plan. It was obvious he had spent a great deal of time working this all out. And he was right; it seemed no one could possibly tie them to it.

By the time Arthur was finished, everyone's glass was empty, as was the bottle, and the hour was late. A date had been decided upon. Justice would be served this coming Friday. Arthur directed all of them to review their individual tasks in their minds until they could perform them blind folded, then he and Brad left leaving Evan washing the glasses in the sink behind the bar.

Evan sat the wet glasses upside down on a towel next to the sink and poured himself one more drink. He turned the lights off as he left the den and went down the hall to a formal living room.

In this room there was hung a large portrait of his father. Evan sat down in a chair directly in front of it. The small light above the portrait was the only light in the room. As he sat staring at the portrait, he began to reminisce about the times he did spend with his father. Evan never really became what his father wanted him to be. Sometimes that bothered him more than others. This was one of those times.

"I hope you understand why we're doing this." he spoke aloud as he gazed at the portrait hanging on the wall. "Your interpretation of right and wrong has always been a little different from mine. That always seemed to keep some distance between us. I never intended it to be that way. Despite our differences, I really do love you dad. I just wish I could say it to your face."

By this time, Evan's eyes had drifted downwards until he was looking at the floor. *It's funny* he thought, *how everyone thinks I have it all when I would gladly trade all of it for the one thing I don't have.* He stood up, raising his glass to his father, and bid him good night. Then, turning off the light, he left the room.

Arthur's finger pressed against the button on the garage door opener as he approached his driveway. The door rose as he rolled up the driveway and into the garage. Once inside, he turned the car's engine off and closed the garage door. He sat momentarily in the silence, his mind drifting back to a small village in a remote Middle Eastern country. Gun and rocket fire were being hurled back and forth. The small village was caught in the cross fire.

Arthur and his platoon were dug in and shooting out of a long trench. The villagers, caught off guard, were running and hiding for their lives. There comes a point when the aggressiveness with which one fights is overtaken by the instinct of survival. Arthur had reached that point. He was no longer aggressively fighting as much as he was just defending himself. In the midst of the gunfire and the shelling, a young child, unnerved by the noise and the panic, broke free from his mother and ran screaming into the line of fire. He was struck several times. The child's mother in desperation ran to retrieve her injured child. The soldier next to Arthur took aim and shot the woman, killing her instantly. Arthur saw the woman drop and passed it off as a misfortune of war. At that moment, the soldier next to Arthur nudged him.

"Got her." he boasted. "She won't be making any more little enemies!"

Arthur looked at the man in disbelief. "You son of a bitch!" he yelled, "She was a woman!"

Arthur dropped his rifle and grabbed him by the front of his uniform with both hands. The soldier raised his rifle and pointed it at Arthur's throat.

"She was the enemy!" he shouted. "And this is damned near treason."

"She was a civilian. She was unarmed." Arthur ignored the weapon pointed at his throat, his sense of reason blinded by rage.

"She was the enemy. You were brought over here to kill the enemy. She'd have killed you in a heartbeat if you gave her half a chance." The exchange of words was barely audible over the shooting, but both knew what the other had said.

Arthur could have easily killed him right there for what he had done. That memory haunted Arthur to this day.

The garage light came on and popped Arthur back to reality. Sandy opened the door into the house and the aroma of a late dinner embraced him, his thoughts becoming temporarily diverted.

Brad hurriedly unlocked the door to his apartment hoping to catch the ringing phone before his answering machine picked it up. It was his publisher in Denver.

"Brad, any chance you could come down here Friday? I have a client that's interested in talking to you about a re-write of one of your books for a movie, but I can't get hold of anyone from your agent's office. Can I tell them you're interested?"

Brad paused momentarily, searching for a reason to say no that didn't make him feel as if he were a criminal.

"I've got another commitment Friday. Could we set up a conference call and work out the details? If not, I'd be glad to come down next week." Brad's voice was growing shaky.

"Sure. I guess that would work." The voice on the phone hesitated. "Are you alright Brad?"

"Ya, I'm fine. Just got a lot going on right now. Call me back when you have it set up."

The voice on the other end agreed and Brad hung up the phone, heaving a sigh of relief. He wasn't sure if he should feel relieved or threatened. *'Just my damned luck'*, he thought to himself. Despite his indifference, this had been a dream of Brad's for years, but at this particular moment and under these circumstances, he gave it little consideration.

Brad put on a kettle of water for tea. He thought about Derek and Katie. What would they think if they knew what was going to happen? Would they even believe it? He still wasn't convinced that what they were about to do was right. Then he thought about Derek Jr. Was it right that he had to come into this world under the circumstances that he did? A smile that could have been a sigh crept across Brad's face as he thought about the baby, but soon the persistent scream of the boiling kettle brought him back from the place his thoughts had taken him.

CHAPTER THREE

Friday came as it inevitably would, despite the better wishes of Brad, who by now regretted ever getting involved in the whole affair in the first place. The bitter February air greeted him as he left the security of his warm apartment. Fumbling with the key, he locked the door. The frozen snow crackled under his feet as he made his way down the stairs to his car. The plan was to meet in the parking lot of a local mall. Their cars would be inconspicuous there as the mall was always very crowded. It was only a ten minute drive. His car barely had a chance to warm up before he pulled into the mall parking lot. Brad parked in a secluded spot away from the light.

After locking his car and setting the alarm, he walked across the frigid parking lot to the mall entrance. He entered the mall and headed for a book store where he had purchased a number of books in the past. Almost arbitrarily he selected one from the closest display to the front of the store without even looking at the title. The plan was to purchase it with a charge card. This would provide him with proof that he had been shopping if they came under suspicion.

As he stood in the check-out line, he looked at the faces of those around him. He felt profoundly conspicuous, considering himself to be the only person whose purchase was nothing more than an alibi. Nonetheless, he was now the proud owner of 'The History of Modern Atomic Principals', a subject to which he had given little if any consideration in his lifetime.

At precisely six o'clock, as planned, Arthur and Evan pulled up in front of the main entrance to the mall. Brad was waiting for them inside. Seeing them, he walked outside and across the sidewalk. Evan reached behind him and opened the rear passenger door. Brad got into the back seat, and the three sped away.

"Whose car is this?" Brad asked, knowing it wasn't Arthur's.

"I rented it."

"You what? Oh that's just great, Arthur." Brad was surprised he would do something so foolish. "If something happens, they will trace this car right back to you."

"No chance" Arthur argued, "I rented it under another name."

"Who, John Smith?" Brad asked sarcastically.

"No, Myron Schwartz actually. I've even got a fake driver's license with that name on it, see." Arthur passed it back to Brad. After looking at it, he burst out laughing. He passed it up to Evan who also got a good laugh out of it.

"Myron Schwartz?" he heckled, "You look about as Jewish as the Pope!" Their laughter was short lived.

"Did you confirm Derek's alibi?" Arthur asked, looking at Brad in the mirror.

"Ya, I called him last night. He got the tickets to the dinner show in the mail three days ago. They're taking Katie's parents with them." Brad seemed to have his end under control.

"Where did you mail the tickets from?"

"I gave them to a friend who mailed them from a small town in South Carolina as he was passing through."

So far, miraculously enough, everything seemed to be going according to plan.

Katie was applying the last of her make-up as Derek checked his watch for the third time.

"Are you almost ready? Your parents will be here any minute!"

Katie smiled as she looked at Derek in the mirror. "I lived with them for twenty one years. Daddy knows I'm never ready on time. Besides, he thrives on consistency. It would upset him if I were ready when they got here."

Derek, realizing that he was dealing with something he had absolutely no control over, left the bedroom and walked down the hall. The door bell rang before he reached the living room. "If he thrives on consistency, he won't be disappointed tonight." he mumbled to himself. Derek unlocked the door and opened it.

"Where's that darling baby?" his mother-in-law asked as she rushed past him towards the baby's room.

"Wait for me!" her husband said, briefly greeting Derek with a nod as he passed by him. Derek closed the door and smiled. He had heard it would be like this. It seems when you are the parents of a newborn, you become temporarily an 'un-person' to the new grandparents. But that was okay. He was living a dream himself, and the cloud he was riding on felt as if it would last forever. *Maybe my luck is changing*, he thought to himself; maybe indeed.

The street light outside the bar provided just enough light for Arthur to attach the device to the valve stem on the right rear tire of the older model sedan. He returned quickly to the car where Brad and Evan were waiting.

"Explain to me again how that thing works." Brad was not at all mechanically inclined.

Evan rolled his eyes. "It works on the basis of centrifugal force. As the wheel turns, the centrifugal force pushes outward and forces open a valve which, in turn, begins to let the air out of the tire. The faster the wheel turns, the faster the air will come out." This was his third attempt to explain it to Brad.

"Where did you get that thing?"

"I made it" Evan replied, much to Brad's surprise, "it's kind of a hobby."

"You know, I never thought you'd have a hobby like that", Brad admitted, "Your hobbies are usually more....."

"We all know what his hobbies are!" Arthur interrupted. He had been paying very little attention to the conversation up to this point. Suddenly he leaned forward in his seat, his eyes fixed on a figure across the street. A lone man walked out of the bar and headed towards the parking lot. It was the man they had seen in the court room. He had the same look on his face that he did back then. He felt he had the world by the tail. He had no idea how wrong he was.

A cloud of bluish gray smoke billowed from the car as it left the parking space. Arthur turned the key and started the rental car. He pulled away from the curb, driving several hundred feet down the street before turning on his headlights. He kept a reasonable distance between himself and the car they were following as they disappeared into the darkness.

"When is that thing going to start working?" Brad asked, still confused about its function.

"It's working now!" Arthur snapped impatiently. "In about another two minutes, the tire will be flat and he'll have to pull off the road."

Arthur allowed a little more distance between the two cars. Sure enough, within a couple of minutes, the car slowed down and pulled off the road. Arthur passed the car then pulled off the road in front of it so what they were about to do would not be done in their car's head lights. The three got out and walked back to find the man kneeling next to a very flat tire.

"Need some help buddy?" Arthur asked.

"No, I got it." the man replied, paying little attention to him.

"You sure?" Arthur asked as he reached into his pocket. His eyes moved towards Evan. Evan nodded. And in an instant, Brad and Evan were on top of the man, holding him down while Arthur held a wet cloth over his face. In a matter of seconds the man's body went limp. Arthur removed the device from the valve stem, while Brad and Evan quickly drug him back to their car and pushed him into the back seat. Brad slid in next to him. Arthur jumped back into the car almost at the same moment as Evan and put the car into drive. Evan pulled his door closed, and as quickly as it all happened, they were gone, leaving the man's disabled car in the darkness.

Just as each man had a task in the preparation of this exercise, each had a task in its deployment. As Arthur made a

U-turn and headed back into town, Evan reached under the seat and handed Brad a brown paper bag. Brad removed its contents.

"Where did you get this anyway? It isn't yours I hope!" Brad's eyes showed his concern as he unfolded a white shiny robe and odd looking pointed hat.

"Hell no, it's not mine!" Evan replied. "My dad is a major share holder in a production company. It's just a stage prop, but it looks real, doesn't it?" It most certainly did look real to Brad. "You don't really think I'd be associated with those assholes do you?"

"No, I know you wouldn't." Brad said as he slipped the white robe, hat and face mask onto the man. "I guess this is my first encounter with the KKK!" Brad announced as he strapped the limp figure back into the seat belt. The man could have passed for the grand wizard himself. His appearance epitomized everyone's perceptions of the Ku Klux Klan and then some.

Brad, having completed the man's transformation, looked out the window to find row after row of run down apartment buildings. Amongst the rubble a car sat up on blocks, its wheels and doors removed. This was a part of town he had never been in before, and hopefully after this would never have occasion to visit again. Arthur slowed the car down and began looking intently up ahead. As they drove on, they passed a large vacant lot. The remnants of an old building were strewn across the property. Great chunks of graffiti covered concrete were scattered among the debris. It all looked surprisingly enough like it belonged here.

Arthur slowed down once again then leaned forward, straining his eyes to see through the darkness. The figures of three black men standing under a street light could be seen a couple of blocks ahead.

"Get ready!" Arthur warned. The three of them put on ski masks and black gloves. Arthur crossed the center line of the empty street and stopped in front of the three men. A faint electric hum could be heard as he lowered his window. The two men on the curb looked in amazement as Arthur spoke.

"Look what we found!" At that moment he lowered the rear window, exposing the man in the KKK garb, who by this time was beginning to regain consciousness.

"You want him?"

"Shit ya. Turn that home boy loose. We'll take him!" The largest of the three men stepped towards the car. Brad unfastened his seat belt, as Arthur reached behind him into the back seat and opened the door. The man looked down at what he was wearing just as two very large hands pulled him from the car.

"Hey, what's going on here!" the man demanded.

"You about to get your ass kicked!" one of the other men on the curb laughed.

"No, wait....."

Arthur pushed the gas peddle to the floor. The tires squealed and the rear door closed by itself from the acceleration. Brad looked back to see the man being drug into an alley by the men on the curb. As he turned around, he removed the ski mask and gloves. "You don't suppose they'll kill him do you?"

"No." Arthur spoke, in a more relaxed voice. "But they'll probably beat the living shit out of him."

"Well, you were right, Arthur." Evan observed, "He got what he deserved, and somebody else did it!"

"We're not out of the woods yet!" Brad warned.

"You worry too much Brad." Arthur complained, looking at Brad again in the rear view mirror. "The chloroform will blur his memory of what happened at his car, and the beating he's getting right now will blur his memory of us."

Brad did not share Arthur's optimism.

The three eventually made their way back to the mall. Arthur pulled up once again to the mall entrance. "Don't forget to buy something else." he reminded Brad, "That will seal your alibi."

"What are you two going to do?" Brad asked.

"I'm going to follow Arthur across the state line." Evan answered.

"That's where I'm dropping the car off." Arthur added. "We'll be in touch in the morning."

"Drive carefully." Brad cautioned as he closed the door and walked back towards the mall. Arthur and Evan drove out of the parking lot and disappeared once again into the frigid night air. Brad made one final credit card purchase then went home. As he drove, he thought about what they had done. Maybe it wasn't as bad as he had imagined it would be. But he was uncomfortable with it nonetheless. He was glad it was over, and he swore to himself that he would never be a part of anything like this again.

The following morning Arthur and his family were sitting around the breakfast table. The scene was a familiar one, his daughter pleading her case to set a new standard in outrageous clothing, and his wife putting up a gallant, but losing battle to change her mind.

"But mom, everybody wears tee shirts with things written on them. Why can't I?"

"Do you mean to tell me that every girl in school wears a tee shirt that reads 'Man Handler'? I can't believe you bought that thing in the first place."

"Well, not exactly every girl, just sort of the cool ones."

"Well, not exactly, but sort of get upstairs and kind of change into something else. You're not setting foot outside this house with that on."

Her mom's words seemed to be final. But the battle was never over until both her parents concurred.

Arthur leafed through the newspaper as he sipped his coffee, oblivious to the conversation going on across the table from him. He found what he was looking for in the metropolitan section. 'Man in KKK Garb Attacked in Housing Project', the headline read. According to the article, a man wandered into the project and made threats to several black tenants who, fearing for their lives, were compelled to defend themselves. The man was in the hospital with multiple fractures, abrasions and broken bones. No mention was made of anyone else. Arthur smiled, then put the paper down and stood up. As he took one last sip of coffee, Angie asked him the question.

"So what do you think?" She waited impatiently for his answer.

"About what?" he asked as he grabbed his suit jacket and brushed by Sandy, giving her a quick peck on the cheek. "See you tonight honey." he said, then headed towards the garage door. Angie stood with her hands on her hips, blocking his path and fully exposing her 'Man Handler' tee shirt, her actions begging a response.

"Nice outfit!" he commented casually as he made his way around her, giving her a similar peck on her cheek. Angie was stunned by his remark. Was this the same man, who only last week, told her that her clothes looked like they belonged in the circus? *'Grown-ups'*, she thought to herself.

A thin trickle of smoke rose from the circuit board as Evan soldered the final connection. The phone rang as he carefully returned the soldering gun to its holder, burning himself in the process. The ringing phone was buried under several layers of electrical schematics and as many pages of handwritten notes. Holding his burned finger in a glass of orange juice, he threw aside the papers to expose a phone wedged between a phone book and an empty soda can. He picked it up. It was Arthur.

"Read the paper yet this morning?"

"No not yet." Evan answered.

"Well, let me tell you what I read." Arthur continued in a sarcastic tone. "Seems some stupid son of a bitch in a Klan get-up wandered into the wrong part of town and made some threats which initiated a confrontation for which he was ill prepared."

"Was there any mention of how he got there, or his car or the flat tire?" Evan questioned.

"Not a word. He was probably considered to be drunk when he left the bar so nothing he says will carry much weight. I knew we could do it. It was just a question of working through all the details."

By this time Evan's phone was clicking, signaling another call was coming in. He said good bye to Arthur and pushed the button to answer the other call. The voice on the other end was unfamiliar to him. It was the voice of an older man. His tone was very clear and his words exacting.

"I know what you did." There was a pause.

"Who is this?" Evan demanded.

"That's not important right now." the voice replied. "What is important is that you understand. I know what you and your friends did last night."

"I don't know what you're talking about." Evan replied nervously.

"You know exactly what I'm talking about." The man's voice was precise and confident while Evan's grew anxious.

"So what do you want?" he asked.

"We'll discuss that when next we speak."

The line went dead. Evan hung up the phone and sat in the silence.

Son of a bitch, he thought to himself.

He began going over last night's activities in his mind. Who could have seen them? Everything went off so well. He picked up the phone and began to punch in a number, but quickly changed his mind and slammed it down.

Beads of perspiration formed on his forehead as he left the room and walked down the hall to the closet. He pulled on his coat and buttoned it up as he hurried out of the house to his car.

The buildings passed by quickly as Evan weaved through the morning traffic to a large office building with dark glass windows. He pulled into the parking garage, his tires gently squealing as he came to a stop in the closest space. His pace quickened as he walked through the garage to the lobby of the building and into an open elevator. His foot tapped nervously while the bell sounded the passing of each floor. The doors opened after it had rang seventeen times. Evan quickly regained his pace, passing through the double doors of 'Atweiler and Fisk Investments'. The girl at the front desk had no opportunity to stop him as he rushed past her to a door at the end of the corridor. He threw the door open. Behind a desk in the office Arthur sat still holding the receiver of his phone in his hand.

"I got a phone call this morning." Evan barked, but before he could say any more, Arthur interrupted.

"So did I, just now." Arthur placed the receiver slowly back down on the phone.

"Who the hell is this guy?" Evan asked as he closed the door and sat down in a chair in front of Arthur's desk.

"Damned if I know."

"Well, what do you suppose he wants? Did he ask you for anything?"

"No, he talked to me for less than a minute." Arthur thought for a moment. "If he knows us well enough to call us like he did, he must know that you could probably lay your hands on some cash if you needed to."

"But he didn't ask me for money. He didn't ask for anything. That's what makes it so weird."

Arthur leaned forward in his chair. "What exactly did he say to you?"

"He told me that he knew what we did and that he would call again. Said he wanted to talk some more."

Arthur leaned back in his chair and ran his fingers through his hair. "If he calls Brad we may have a problem. He really didn't want anything to do with this in the first place. Now I feel bad that I got him involved."

"Well, maybe Brad's not at home this morning. Maybe he's out." Evan too was concerned.

The boiling water made the kettle scream a little longer than it normally did as Brad finished the sentence he was writing. As he made his way from his computer into the kitchen, the noise from the kettle was joined by the ringing telephone. Brad grabbed the receiver on his way to the stove.

"Brad!" The voice on the other end of the phone sounded excited.

"That's me!" he replied.

"This is Lenny. Remember me? I helped you out with some one-liners in a book you were writing last year. Remember?"

Brad thought for a moment. "Of course I remember you, Lenny. You're the funniest guy I ever met, how could I forget you?"

Lenny was a very funny guy. Brad ran into him at a comedy club last year while working on a book with some humorous twists. He struck up a conversation with Lenny between shows and ended up paying him to help with some of the humor in the book. As Brad recalled, he told Lenny to look him up if he ever got back into town.

"Where are you?" Brad inquired.

"I'm in town for a couple of shows and thought I'd look up my old pal. You still writing?"

Brad dropped a tea bag into his cup then filled it with water. "Ya, I'm still writing. Guess it's the only thing I know how to do."

Lenny laughed a little as he always did when he spoke. "How about catching the show one night? I'll send you over some passes. That way I can use you and your lady friend in my act"

"Hold on a minute. There is no lady friend Lenny." Brad confessed.

"What the hell are you waiting for?" Lenny snapped. "You're not getting any younger, and you're certainly not getting any better looking. Now, I'm not saying you're ugly, but if my dog had a face like yours, I'd shave his ass and make him walk backwards!"

Brad began to laugh. He knew Lenny was about to be on a roll and there was no stopping him.

"And I'm not saying you're old" Lenny continued, "but isn't your birth certificate carved on a stone tablet? And that nose. It's not the biggest one I've seen, but when you lean your head back, it looks like a two car garage!"

"Enough!" Brad conceded. "I'll go, I'll go. I'll even bring a date if you promise not to embarrass her too badly." Once again, that annoying but familiar clicking was heard on Brad's phone signaling that another call was holding.

"I've got another call. I'll see you tomorrow." Brad hit the button switching the phone to the other line.

"Hello..." There was a pause. Brad thought perhaps the caller had hung up.

"I've told both of your friends, now I'm telling you."

"Who is this?" Brad asked, his voice sounding serious.

"I know what you did last night, the three of you. Do you understand what I'm saying? I know what you did."

"I don't know what you are talking about." Brad nervously responded.

"We'll talk again soon." The voice on the phone seemed unaffected by Brad's denial. There was a click and he was gone.

Brad slammed the phone down. His clenched fingers remained wrapped around it as he stared intently off into space, his body trembling with shock and panic. Before he could unclench his fingers from the receiver the phone rang again. Brad pulled it back to his ear.

"Look, I don't know what the hell you're talking about!" he shouted.

A very surprised Arthur was on the other end of the phone.

"I take it he called you too."

"Hell yes he called me. I just hung up from the son of a bitch." By this time Brad's fear had turned, as it always would, to anger. "It looks like we're about to get busted!"

Arthur spoke to Brad in a calm reassuring voice. "Brad if we were going to get busted, we'd have been busted by now. This guy is not a cop. And I don't think he's trying to black-mail us."

"Then what the hell does he want?" Brad asked, regaining his composure a little.

"I don't have any idea, but I'm sure he'll tell us when he's ready."

Brad was still shaken, but the fact that Arthur was not overly concerned at this point, gave him a little comfort.

"Why don't you meet Evan and me for lunch today and we'll try to figure this thing out."

Brad agreed then hung up the phone.

CHAPTER FOUR

A blanket of cigarette smoke hovered over the diners in the crowded restaurant. At a small table in the corner, Brad, Evan and Arthur sat picking at their lunch and discussing the events of the morning. Everything seemed to have gone perfectly until the phone calls began. None of them had any idea who the voice on the phone could possibly belong to. No one recognized it, and no one knew what the man was going to ask for. It was obvious though, that he was going to ask for something.

"Why do you suppose he called me first?" Evan asked. "I have an unlisted number."

Arthur thought for a moment. "Maybe he wanted to make a point."

"What point?" Brad snapped.

"That he has access to information that the rest of us don't for one thing." Arthur answered, taking a bite of his sandwich.

"So what do we do now?" Brad sneered. "None of us expected this. We had everything worked out, remember?" Brad's sarcasm was aimed at Arthur.

Arthur leaned closer to the table. "Did either of you mention this to anyone?"

"Are you kidding?" Brad snapped.

"Who would we tell?" Evan asked.

"As I see it, there's only one thing we can do." Arthur seemed somewhat at a loss. "Wait for him to call back." The three men looked at each other.

"I wonder who he'll call first this time." Evan hoped it wouldn't be him.

"That will tell us a lot." Arthur stated.

"How so?" Brad questioned, his voice just a touch calmer.

"I reacted differently than the two of you. If he wants to shake us down or blackmail us, he'll call one of you two first. But I have a feeling he will be calling me first next time."

"What makes you say that?" Evan asked, sliding a thin slice of pickle from his sandwich and popping it in his mouth.

"Just a hunch" Arthur replied as he watched Evan eat the pickle and leave the rest of the sandwich untouched.

The noon rush had cleared out of the restaurant before the three men noticed how long they had been talking. Arthur and Evan had managed to calm Brad down, at least for the time being. Brad felt more threatened than did Arthur or Evan. Arthur seemed in complete control despite the recent developments, and Evan honestly believed that there was no problem that his father's money could not buy him out of. Before they left, Arthur reminded them to be themselves tomorrow at the treatment center. Derek must know nothing of what was going on.

The morning sun filtered through the mini blinds in Derek's kitchen making tiny lines of light across the day old newspaper lying on the table. Katie brought a newspaper home with her each night. The news was a day old by the time Derek got to read it, but that was okay, it was free. Derek sat his cup of coffee down on the table and picked up the newspaper. A story in the second section caught his eye and he began to read. Slowly he sipped his coffee as he became more and more absorbed in the article. His eyes widened when he read the name of the criminal who had fallen victim to a crime himself. He lowered the paper and starred intently at the wall for a moment.

"No" he said aloud to himself, "it couldn't be."

"What couldn't be?" Katie asked as she passed by the table on her way to the coffee pot.

"Oh nothing, I was just thinking out loud." Derek folded up the paper and tucked it under his arm. "I'm off!" he said, kissing his wife good bye. Katie smiled at him.

"See you tonight."

Derek smiled back and winked at her as he walked out the door. But the smile soon turned to a scowl. He slammed the car door and began thinking out loud again. "Surely not." he said to himself. "They wouldn't be that stupid!"

That afternoon Brad and Arthur were sitting, as they usually were, in the lounge when Derek walked through the doors.

"Afternoon" Brad said as Derek approached.

"Either of you guys read the paper yesterday morning?" Derek asked sarcastically, almost angrily.

"Read it every morning." Arthur answered without looking up from what he was reading.

"Well did you read this?" Derek tossed the paper into Arthur's lap. Arthur looked at Derek over the top of his glasses as he picked up the paper. He looked at it a moment then put it down.

"Yes I have." He answered calmly.

"Did you read it or do you know about it first hand?" Derek's anger was beginning to show.

"What's that supposed to mean?" Brad snapped.

"I think you know damned well what it means!"

"Alright, that's enough." Arthur raised his hands in the air.

"You want the truth? Okay, we did it; Brad, Evan and myself. We took the guy and dumped him out on the lower east side. It has nothing to do with you. We made sure you had an air tight alibi. So don't get you're knickers in such a twist." Arthur leaned back in his chair.

"Besides" Brad confessed, "we're already in deep shit over it."

"What's that supposed to mean?" Derek asked as he sat down on the couch.

"It means somebody knows it was us!" Everyone's head turned towards the doors. Evan was making his way through maze of chairs and couches.

"You told him I see." he concluded as he took his place with the others.

"He already knew." Arthur replied.

"Now it all makes sense." Derek stood up and walked over to the window. "I got a phone call last night. He sounded like an older man. He didn't say that much but what he did say, he said very well." Brad looked over at Arthur who was already looking back at him.

"He told me that I wasn't in on this one, but I would be on the next one." Derek turned and faced the three men. There were a few moments of silence before Evan spoke up. "Well, I guess we're all in deep shit now."

They all remained speechless for a moment. The silence was interrupted by the technician's footsteps and the ensuing treatments.

Two and a half hours later as they walked down the long corridor towards the exit, everyone was unusually silent. The cold February air greeted them as they approached the door. The wind was holding it slightly open. Derek spoke up as he buttoned his coat.

"Listen, I'm sorry I acted the way I did back there. It's just that this all kind of took me by surprise. It's the last thing in the world I would have expected you guys to do. But I think I understand why you did it, and I'm flattered that you felt that Katie and I were worth the risk."

Arthur looked at Derek and smiled. "We were just looking out for you."

Arthur extended his hand to Derek. He looked back at Arthur, and then down to the floor. "Ah shit. I guess we can't stay mad at each other can we?" Derek said as he shook Arthur's hand.

"You know what we need?" Brad asked in a more cheery tone as they began once again to walk towards the door.

"To get laid?" Evan replied.

"No Evan." Brad mocked. "Shift your mind into a different gear. We all need a good laugh, and I know just the place." He reached into his coat pocket and pulled out an envelope with eight passes to Lenny's performance at the comedy club. "Tonight at seven thirty, I'll reserve us a table." Everyone agreed. So, after putting it off for as long as possible, the four men pushed open the door and braved the cold as they made their way through the parking garage.

By seven the club was almost full. Lenny had saved a table up front for Brad and his guests on the condition that he would not pick on any of them in his act. But as usually happened Lenny's fingers were crossed behind his back when he made that promise.

Brad sat next to a young lady from his agent's office. They'd been to dinner several times before, but it was always business. This was the closest thing to an actual date that they had ever had. Arthur and his wife were to Brad's left and to his right were Derek and Katie. Evan and a young lady in an extremely snug, low cut dress were sitting across the table from Brad.

When Lenny came on stage, it didn't take long before he began to include Brad in his comedy.

"I want you all to say hi to a friend of mine." Brad raised his hand to his forehead. He knew what was coming.

"Brad, stand up." Lenny instructed. Brad tried to hide his head. "Come on Brad. Do you want me to tell all these people about that incident in Cleveland?" Lenny prompted.

Of course there never was any incident in Cleveland, but Brad knew if he didn't stand up, Lenny would make something up that would be far worse that standing up, so up he stood.

"There he is ladies and gentlemen, my friend Brad. The only man I know that can brag about being the best breakfast waiter in a nudist camp. He would deliver coffee in one hand, tea in the other and carry half dozen donuts at the same time!" Lenny thrust his groin forward to indicate exactly what Brad carried the donuts on. "I think his record was eight, but of course, he was younger then, and it wasn't quite so cold." Brad sat back down and put his face in his hands as his friends laughed at Lenny's relentless references to him. Brad's date leaned towards him and winked, "I had no idea, big boy!" Brad looked up at her momentarily then returned his face to his hands.

About mid way through the performance, a waiter approached Arthur and whispered in his ear that he had a phone call. *It's probably the kids,* he thought, *they can't stand to see me have a good time.* He made his way to the bar where a telephone receiver lay on a napkin. He picked it up.

"This is Arthur."

"Good evening, Arthur. I apologize for the interruption, but we need to talk." Arthur recognized the voice immediately. It was the same man who had contacted all of them earlier.

"What do you want?" Arthur asked.

"I will call you tomorrow morning at your office, at ten o'clock. I will answer all of your questions at that time. Ten o'clock tomorrow morning." The phone went dead. The man had hung up. Arthur stood with the phone in his hand for a few moments. The bar tender, noticing that his conversation had ended, was standing with his hand out waiting for the phone. Several seconds passed before Arthur realized his presence and with some degree of embarrassment, returned the phone to him.

Arthur walked back to the table, regaining his composure as best he could on the way, all the while trying to come up with something to tell his friends. As he sat down his wife leaned over to him. "Are the kids okay? Was it Angie?"

"No, it was business." he replied. By this time, Brad was looking in his direction. He could tell by the look on Arthur's face that something was wrong.

"Everything alright?" he asked, talking over the noise of the club.

"Ya, everything's fine." Arthur answered. "It was about that group venture we've been talking about lately." Brad knew immediately what he was referring to. His eyes widened.

"He called you here? How did he know?" Brad was trying not to be conspicuous. Now Evan's eyes had caught the activity. He leaned towards Arthur and raised his eyebrows as if to ask a question.

"It was our mutual friend." he told Evan.

Evan looked down at the table for a moment trying to figure out who he was talking about. Then it hit him. He looked back up at Arthur. His look in and of itself was a question. Arthur nodded slowly, confirming Evan's suspicion. Evan sat back in his chair in disbelief. "Son of a bitch" he mumbled to himself.

After the show, as they made their way back to their cars, Arthur let Derek in on what was going on. He was not even aware that Arthur had received a phone call. He slipped Derek a piece of paper with the number to his direct office line, so he would not have to go through the switchboard. Arthur assured him that there was really nothing to worry about. He was beginning to get an idea of what his conversations with this mystery man were leading up to. The four couples left and went home for what was sure to be a long and sleepless night.

The morning was going like most others did in Arthur's office. The phones were ringing, people were hurrying frantically to buy and sell stocks, and printers were churning out endless pages of reports. Arthur sat in his office reviewing some over-seas stock prices, adding numbers on a calculator with one hand and aligning columns with the other. About mid way through the second column, his private line rang. He put down the papers he was holding and stared momentarily at the flashing button on the phone. After taking a deep breath, he picked it up.

"This is Arthur." he stated in his most business like voice.

"Good morning Arthur." the voice replied. Arthur recognized the voice immediately. "I hope I didn't alarm you last night by calling you at that club, but it is necessary that we have a complete knowledge of each other's capabilities. I have seen, and am impressed with yours. Now perhaps you have some idea of mine." The man paused, giving Arthur a chance to speak.

"Fine." he replied. "Now that we have successfully impressed one another, why don't you tell me where all of this is going."

"That is the purpose of my call." The man stopped to clear his throat then continued. "As I told you in an earlier conversation, I know what you did. I have only an idea as to how, but I do know why. Shall I tell you why?' the man asked.

"Please do." Arthur prompted, as he leaned back in his chair and removed his reading glasses.

"A very strong bond exists between you and your friends. One of the obligations to that bond is to ensure a balance among all of you. That man, who you so aptly punished, upset that balance and the courts did not tip the scales sufficiently to compensate for his actions. So you, Brad, and Evan counter balanced the scale by doing something that our criminal justice could never do. You punished him, not by sending him to a glorified detention hall, but by making him pay in a commensurate fashion for what he did. And you did so, I might add, quite brilliantly."

Once again the man paused, giving Arthur a chance to speak.

"Look" Arthur said as he sat forward in his chair, "I'll do you the courtesy of being blunt. Your understanding of what we did is correct. It was wrong that he not be punished at all, and since the courts disagreed with us on that, we felt compelled to do something to ensure that he would never pay another visit to Derek's wife or anyone else. Derek had nothing to do with it. In fact he found out about what we did by reading about it in the newspaper. Now, I've been honest with you, so why don't you tell me just what it is that you want." There were a few moments of silence before the man spoke.

"Fair enough." he agreed, "I suppose you are due an explanation. You and your friends accomplished in one night what our legal system hasn't been able to do since its inception. You imposed swift justice, a rare commodity in this day and time. And you did it flawlessly. Your only mistake, if indeed it can be considered a mistake, was my finding out about it. That fact however, was unavoidable. I believe no talents should be wasted. The Bible tells us it's a sin. Therefore, it is my intention to use your talents and those of your friends to affect justice upon those who have somehow managed to evade it."

Arthur sat for a moment, trying to absorb all that the man had said.

"Look, you don't understand. We are not vigilantes. We just settled the score for our buddy, that's it."

The man's voice became more determined. "No my friend, you don't understand. You and your friends will assist me in this endeavor, or you will all suffer the consequences. This is not a request I'm extending. You should look on it as an opportunity. Don't be foolish in your decision. Our relationship can be a positive one, for both of us." The man's voice changed slightly, becoming less intent.

"Let me ask you a question." Arthur responded. "Can you give me one good reason why we should go along with all of this?"

"Yes I can." the man answered. "All four of you have an illness that can and probably will significantly shorten your life. In exchange for your cooperation, I and the group that I represent will see to it that your families are taken care of financially, in every respect, after your passing. I'm sure this will most beneficial to Derek's family. I understand his place of employment offers no retirement or disability benefits. Please, think of your families and the families of the victims who will feel some sense of justice because of you and your friends."

Arthur sat silent as he struggled within himself. Finally he spoke.

"I can't give you an answer until I talk to the others."

"I understand." the man said. "I'll give you a few days to speak with them about this. I'm sure you will be able to convince them."

"Just out of my own curiosity, if we agree to this how will it work?"

"It's very simple. I will provide you with a target, and all pertinent information about that target. The criminals you will be punishing are those who have successfully and completely evaded justice. You will review the information and determine an appropriate course of action to exact a just punishment. I will provide any funds and equipment that you deem necessary to successfully carry out the task. In other words, I will provide everything. All I need from you is a plan and the ability to carry it out."

"Okay, I'll talk to my friends. But the choice will be theirs. I can't make them do this if they don't want to."

"I'm sure you will be persuasive." the man replied. "I will be contacting you in a few days." With that the line went dead. Arthur slowly returned the receiver to the phone.

What had they gotten themselves into? Before the end of the day, Arthur had called the other three and arranged a meeting at Evan's house, the same place that this all began.

CHAPTER FIVE

Brad stepped briskly up the flight of steps to his apartment. Fumbling for his keys, he did his best to withstand the frigid north wind. He unlocked the door and hurried inside. The warmth of his apartment embraced him. Quickly closing it, he leaned back against the door, catching his breath before removing his coat. He threw the mail he had been clutching in his hand onto the table. As the envelopes scattered, one caught his eye. It was from Carol, the young lady who had accompanied him to the comedy club. He picked it up, noticing a small heart that she had drawn on the back flap. As he tore it open, he wondered what it was she could be sending him. He removed a card; a no occasion card. It said, 'thanks for a lovely time...hope we can do it again sometime.'

He closed the card, resting it on his chin for a moment as his thoughts drifted back to the evening spent with Carol. He was having a wonderful time until Arthur got that phone call. *Just my damned luck*, he thought to himself. He seemed to be having that thought a lot lately.

Thirty minutes had passed before Brad found himself stepping out of the shower to the sound of the ringing telephone. He ran out of the bathroom, leaving a trail of water behind him. As he reached for the phone, a hundred names of who it might be were going through his mind. He picked it up. It was Derek.

"Brad, I was wondering if I could catch a ride with you tomorrow night to Evan's house."

"Of course you can. We probably need some time to talk anyway." Brad was feeling guilty for Derek having to be involved in this whole mess.

"Great, thanks." Derek seemed relieved. "Katie is going to a baby shower for a friend of hers so she needs the car."

"Pick you up about seven then."

"See you then." Derek replied and hung up the phone. Katie walked into the room as he was hanging up.

"Who was that?" she inquired.

"It was Brad. Since you're going to the shower tomorrow, and your parents have been bugging us to let them baby sit their grandson, Brad, Arthur and I are meeting Evan at his house to watch the game on his plasma TV." Derek could honestly say that he had never lied to Katie before, but the truth in this instance was out of the question, at least for now.

"That sounds like a good idea!" she replied. "Can you drop me off on your way to Evan's?"

"Brad's picking me up, so you can have the car." Derek walked over and hugged Katie.

"What's that for?" she asked.

"Do I have to have a reason?" He looked into her eyes and smiled. She smiled back at him with that same smile that melted his heart the day they met. Her smile, for the moment, made all of his other problems seem to fade away.

"Son of a bitch" Evan shouted as he burned himself for the fifth time with his soldering gun. The board he was working on was very small, and the work very critical. A seemingly endless array of test equipment bordered the table upon which he was working. Periodically, he would place his soldering gun in its holder and grab a pair of wires attached to one of the testing devices. And after the correct response of lights and beeps, he would return to the plan and make his notes. He came up for air after several hours only to stretch, and take a sip of what was now warm, flat ginger ale. He glanced down at his watch to check the time. As he strained to focus his eyes, his concentration was broken by the sound of the door bell. Walking towards the front door, he rubbed his eyes in an attempt to get them accustomed to the darkened hallway. When he reached the door he unlocked the deadbolt and opened it.

"Hi! Remember me?" Standing in front of him was one of the most beautiful women he had ever seen.

"Yes, I do." Evan answered. "It was three, no, four months ago. We sat next to each other on a flight from L. A. I was 3A, you were 3B. Am I right so far?"

"You have an amazing memory." she observed.

Evan smiled, "And that's only one of my attributes. Come on in and we'll discuss the rest of them." She stepped through the door. Evan closed it behind her.

"Can I take your coat?" Evan asked as he slipped the coat over her shoulders, revealing a low cut, tight fitting sweater. He hung the coat on a hanger in a hall closet and the two walked down the hall and into the den.

"So, how did you find me?" Evan asked.

"It was easy" she replied, "you gave me your business card on the plane, remember?"

Evan paused for a moment. "That's right" he answered, "I'd forgotten." He stood up and walked over to the wet bar in the den. "Something to drink?" he asked.

"Gin and tonic"

While Evan mixed her a drink, the young lady's eyes wandered throughout the room, stopping at a family portrait hanging on the wall. After studying it for a few moments, her attentions shifted one by one, to the many sculptures decorating the den.

"What brings you here?" Evan asked.

"Business, I work for a market research firm. We're setting up a survey of local grocers to determine produce buying habits. Not very exciting work, but it pays the bills."

"That's interesting" Evan remarked, "I have a friend who works for a market research firm in L. A. He works for Whitmann, Anderson and Associates. His name is Stewart Reynolds. Do you know him?"

"Well" she paused, "I know a few people at Whitmann, but I can't say as I've ever met him."

Evan returned to the couch with her drink, handing her the gin and tonic before sitting down.

"That's too bad. Stewart is a great guy. You'd like him." Evan watched carefully her responses to his questions. "Are you going to be in town long?"

"No, just a couple of days"

Evan sat his glass on the coffee table. "Unfortunately, I have a meeting to attend tonight, but maybe we could get together before you leave, say for dinner."

"I'd like that." she replied, smiling at him over the top of her glass.

The conversation continued for a short time longer, but seemed to become more strained as time went on. Sensing this, she excused herself, but not before confirming plans to have dinner with Evan before she left town.

It was dusk as Arthur navigated through the express way traffic. The radio was playing inconspicuously in the background while he collected his thoughts. He honestly wasn't sure if he would be able to talk his friends into the proposition offered by their mystery phone caller. He was putting together a list in his mind of pro's and con's. About mid way through the list, his cell phone rang. He reached for it, expecting to see his wife's number on the screen. The call came through as 'Private'. Arthur answered it.

"Good evening, Arthur." It was him.

"Good evening." Arthur replied

"I just wanted to call and wish you luck with your meeting tonight. I have a great deal of confidence in your abilities. I'm sure you will be successful." The man paused, allowing Arthur to respond.

"I wish I shared your optimism, but I know my friends better than you do."

"You would be surprised what I know." the man replied, his tone more serious.

"How did you know I was meeting with them tonight?" Arthur asked.

"That is not something I am prepared to discuss at this time." Once again, the man's voice showed some emotion. He seemed slightly agitated at Arthur's question.

"Fair enough" Arthur conceded.

"I will be in touch with you after the meeting. I'm sure you will have good news for me." With that, the line went dead. Arthur never seemed to get as much information out of him as he wanted. Now he was feeling more pressure than ever.

By seven twenty, everyone had assembled at Evan's place. Evan was busy mixing drinks.

"I get the feeling we're all going to need these!" he said as he passed them around. Arthur took a sip of his drink then stood up, as the others sat on the couch and Evan in a large antique chair.

"I'm going to be straight and to the point." Arthur began slowly pacing. "Our friend contacted me at my office yesterday. He knows the number to my private line and my cell phone. He obviously has access to a great deal of information about us. During the course of the conversation, he told me why he has been calling. He knows what we did to the guy that assaulted Katie. I don't know how, but he knows. So, this is what he wants." Arthur paused and took another sip of his drink. "Basically, he wants us to do it again, probably a number of times, or at least as many times as he sees fit to ask."

"You've got to be kidding." Brad shouted.

"I'm afraid not. He'll provide us with information about certain individuals that he feels have evaded justice. He will provide any support and funds needed to punish the person in a manner befitting his crime. In exchange for this *service* as he calls it, he and his associates will establish trust funds for our families which will be disbursed to them when we're gone." Arthur paused to let his friends ask questions.

Brad was the first to speak up. "What happens if we tell him no?"

"The obvious" Arthur replied. "He goes to the police with what he knows and we will probably wind up in prison."

"So, what you're saying," Evan clarified, "is that he has us by the balls."

"In a manner of speaking, yes. I did tell him that this would have to be agreed to by all of us, or none of us would participate.

"How do we know any of what he says is true? Derek asked. "Even if we agree to do this, how do we know he won't try to black mail us?"

"He's black mailing us now." Brad snapped.

"Then why offer to pay us?" Evan questioned.

Arthur ran his fingers through his hair. "None of it makes any sense. What we need to decide here tonight is whether we're doing this or not? The only proper way to determine that is to vote on it. It's only fair that we vote secretly though, so nobody feels pressured. Evan, would you get us four pieces of paper?" Evan walked over to the bar and picked up four cocktail napkins. He passed one out to each man along with a pen. In the mean time, Arthur walked behind the bar and picked up a large glass pitcher.

"Think about your answer." he cautioned. "Write yes if you think we should, and no if you think we shouldn't. I'll collect your votes in this pitcher."

Everyone sat silently for several minutes. Evan was the first to write on his napkin. After doing so he folded it into a small square and laid down his pen. Shortly after, Derek and Arthur wrote their answers. When Arthur finished folding his napkin, he looked over at Brad, who sat with his eyes intently focused on the floor. He tapped his pen nervously on his knee displaying his discomfort. Periodically he would uncross then re-cross his legs. It was apparent he was struggling. Finally, he moved the pen toward the napkin and scribbled his answer. Hurriedly, he folded the napkin then looked up, not realizing that everyone else was finished and waiting for him.

"Let's get this over with." he said as he tossed the napkin in Arthur's direction.

Arthur picked up Brad's napkin and dropped it into the pitcher then passed the pitcher to each man, allowing each of them to drop their vote in. After he had collected them, he shook the pitcher to mix them up. Then, one by one, he removed and read each one aloud. The first was a yes. He removed the second, again a yes. As he unfolded the third one he paused, then announced, yes. He removed the fourth and last from the pitcher. He unfolded and read it to himself. Then he raised his eyes to his friends. "Yes" he announced.

"Are you all sure? Remember, we do this as a group or we don't do it at all."

Brad spoke up. "This really scares the hell out of me, but I don't see that we have a choice."

"Neither do I" Derek added, "but it's worth it to me to know that Katie and Derek Jr. will be taken care of after I'm gone." He took the last sip from his glass and sat it on the table as Brad again spoke.

"Now that we've all agreed to become career criminals, I need another drink."

Evan got up and collected everyone's glass. As he was mixing the drinks, his thoughts went back to the young lady who paid him a visit earlier that afternoon. "You know, a strange thing happened to me this afternoon, and I wonder if it has anything to do with this." Arthur turned toward the bar.

"What's that?" he asked.

"Well, a woman came to visit me today. I met her on a flight several months ago."

Derek looked at him and smiled. "What's so strange about that? I hear you have women here all the time.'

"I wouldn't be surprised if there was one upstairs right now!" Brad scoffed.

"No, this is different." Evan argued. "She told me she looked me up from a business card that I gave her on the plane."

Arthur walked over to the bar to pick up his drink. "I didn't know you had business cards."

"I don't." Evan admitted. Everyone looked somewhat puzzled.

"Not only that, I told her I had a friend in the market research business. That's what she told me she did for a living. I gave her his name and the company he worked for. She said she knew several people at that company, but had never met him."

"Should she have met him?" Brad asked.

"Not likely. I don't have any friend in the market research business, and there is no such company. I made it all up after she told me I gave her a business card." Brad looked at Arthur, and Arthur at Brad.

"Well now." Arthur remarked, "Maybe we know how he comes by some of his information."

As they were pondering the motives of the young lady, Evan's telephone rang. He picked it up. The voice on the other end was a familiar one.

"Might I speak with Arthur please?" the voice requested. Evan handed the phone to Arthur. Arthur asked who it was with his eyes.

"It's our friend!" Evan answered. Arthur took the phone. Derek and Brad got up and walked over to the bar.

"This is Arthur."

"Well, do you have good news for me?" the man asked.

"I suppose I do. We have all agreed to go along with this for the time being." Arthur replied, "But whether that can be considered 'good' remains to be seen."

"I assure you it can." the voice answered confidently.

"Since we're going to be working together" Arthur added, "would it be unreasonable to ask your name?"

"Indeed it would." the man answered, "But for purposes of our relationship, why don't you call me.....Sam. And, as a gesture of good faith, I have set up a numbered Swiss bank account for each of you. The account books are in a safe deposit box at the downtown branch of the First Federal Bank. A key to that box has been mailed to you, Arthur. You should receive it within three days."

"I thought you had to provide the bank with a signature in order to rent a safe deposit box." Arthur questioned. "How will I be able to access it?"

"The bank has been provided with your signature. You won't have any problems." Sam's voice was confident.

Arthur had put the man on speaker so the others could hear the conversation. The man continued. "By the way, I have prepared your first assignment. I will call you tomorrow at your office with the details. And again, thanks for the wonderful news. I promise you won't regret your decisions." With that, the man hung up. Arthur stood holding the phone for a moment before putting it down.

"Boy, he doesn't waste any time does he?" Derek said nervously.

"I know I've said it before" Brad jeered, "but I can't believe we're doing this shit!" He took his drink from the bar and returned to the couch.

"Come on, Brad." Evan prodded, trying to console him, "Relax. We did it once, we can do it again. Besides, if anything happens to us, we'll have the best legal representation my father's money can buy." Brad looked at him with a scowl.

"Oh that makes me feel much better." Brad said sarcastically. He was even more uncomfortable this time than he was the last.

Arthur lifted his drink from the bar and took a sip. He turned towards Evan. "Tell me more about this visitor you had this afternoon."

Evan finished stirring his drink then tossed the plastic stick into the trash. "Well" he pondered momentarily, "she didn't stay very long. We had one drink and some small talk. She said she'd be in town for a couple of days. I told her I'd like to take her to dinner, and that's about it."

Arthur thought for a moment. Then he walked over to the bar and began to write on a napkin. Evan looked curiously at him until he slid the napkin over to him. He picked it up and read it. Arthur had asked what room the two had used that afternoon. Evan motioned with his finger indicating the room they were currently in. Arthur grabbed another napkin and began writing again. By this time Brad and Derek had become curious. They both stood up and walked towards the bar. Arthur met them, holding the note in front of each of them. The note instructed each of them to carry on a conversation as normally as possible.

"I need to hit the john. I'll be back in a minute." Arthur announced. He looked at Evan and pointed to the sink.

Evan nodded, "Give me you're glass. I'll rinse it out." He then walked over to the sink and turned the water on. Then he turned to Arthur and mouthed, "What the hell are you doing?"

Arthur turned to Brad and Derek signaling them to begin the conversation. He then motioned for Evan to walk towards the couch. He whispered, "Where was she sitting?"

Evan pointed to the left side of the couch. Arthur walked over to that side of the couch and got down on one knee. He began searching the couch and then the end table and lamp.

Evan nudged him on the shoulder. "What are you looking for?" he whispered.

Arthur continued searching for another moment, then whispered, "This!"

He had lifted a brass likeness of an elephant from the end table to expose a small round, silver colored device attached to the bottom of it. Arthur turned and looked at Evan. Evan looked down at the bottom of the elephant. His eyes widened.

"Is that a bug?" he whispered.

"I've never seen one before, but I bet that's what it is." Arthur whispered in turn. Arthur put the figure back on the table and walked over to the door, opening and closing it as if to re-enter the room. All the while, Derek and Brad had been carrying on a meaningless conversation about the consequences of an inaccurate Rockwell test on imported steel. The conversation came to a stop as Arthur walked back from the door.

"Well, I guess the ball is in his court now. All we can do is wait. I'm going home."

The others followed Arthur's lead and excused themselves for the night. Once they were out in Evan's drive way Arthur explained to Brad and Derek what was going on.

"What am I supposed to do now?" Evan asked. "She's expecting me to take her to dinner."

"Take her!" Arthur replied. "Just let me know when and where and I'll follow her. Maybe she'll lead me to our mysterious friend 'Sam'."

Brad shook his head. "Man, this shit's getting deep!" Derek looked at him and nodded in agreement.

"Come on." Derek said as he slapped Brad on the shoulder. "Take me home."

The three men left and Evan walked back into the house. He finished cleaning up the den, pulling the door closed to the room as he left.

On the other side of town, in a dimly lit room, a white envelope passes from the wrinkled and weathered hand of an older man to the smooth, dainty hand of a young woman. She opened the flap of the envelope glancing quickly at its contents.

"It's all there, you needn't count it." the man remarked. The voice belonged to 'Sam'.

"Will you require my services further?" the young lady questioned.

"Follow through on what you have already begun." the man answered.

With that, the young lady turned and walked towards the door. As she passed through the beam of light from a floor lamp, her face revealed the same smile that greeted Evan at his home earlier that afternoon. Assuredly, this type of work pays much better than market research.

CHAPTER SIX

"He's a nice guy daddy, really!" Arthur's daughter whined as she pleaded her case for tonight's date. "You just have to get to know him."

Arthur lowered his morning paper, looking at his daughter over the top of his reading glasses. "Angie, nice guys don't have pierced tongues!" he replied, raising the paper once again.

"Didn't you ever do anything a little crazy when you were in high-school?"

Arthur mumbled to himself behind his newspaper, "Nothing as crazy as drilling a hole in my tongue."

The conversation was temporarily diverted as Arthur's wife sat a plate of eggs and bacon in front of each of them.

"This is not over!" Angie said, picking up her fork.

Arthur laid his paper on the table and looked over at her with a smile. "Somehow, I knew you were going to say that." He gave her a wink and then focused his attentions on breakfast. But his attention was quickly diverted by Angie's relentless pleas for her latest crush.

"Dad, having a pierced tongue isn't a bad thing. It shows courage, conviction, the ability to stand out in a crowd. It shows he has backbone and character." Angie sat there smiling, strangely impressed with herself that she was able to come up with words sounding so profound.

"It shows he's a raving idiot." Arthur felt compelled to end this monologue of what he often referred to as 'verbal flatulence'.

"That's unfair. You haven't even met him."

"That's right, and with a little luck I'll be able to keep it that way."

But, as often happens, luck was not smiling on Arthur today.

"Arthur, maybe he's not such a bad kid." his wife said as she refilled his coffee cup. "It's just a more extreme form of self-expression, you know, that tongue piercing stuff. Remember the tight jeans I used to wear?"

Arthur smiled a little, recalling how his wife looked back then. He sure did like those jeans. The truth is her legs look as good to him now as they did back then. Arthur sat momentarily mesmerized by the thoughts of his wife in her twenties.

"So does this mean I can go?" Angie's persistent, pleading voice brought him back to reality.

"Well..."

Here it comes, Angie thought.

"Personally, I feel that anybody who derives pleasure from wearing an earring in his tongue needs a saliva test. But, if you feel you know him well enough..."

Angie sat up in her chair, smiling the smile that always reminded him of Christmas morning.

"Just make sure you're home by ten."

Yes, Angie thought as she took her first bite of what was now a plate of cold eggs.

Katie cradled her coffee cup in both hands as she scanned the front page of the morning paper. After reading a few lines, she began to shake her head.

"Have you been following this story about the guy that kidnapped the little girl?" she asked Derek.

Derek took a second to finish chewing, and then replied. "I've heard a little about it. Didn't they catch the guy?"

Katie sat her cup down and picked up the paper. "According to this, they're letting him go."

"Why?"

"Well, it says here that they can't find the girl's body and the man won't say where it is. Apparently, without it there isn't enough evidence for a trial."

They both sat silently for a moment, imagining how they would feel if someone kidnapped their child. Then Katie spoke up again.

"It seems like someone could do something. That little girl's parents need to lay their child to rest, and not be left wondering where her body is. Somebody should be able to do something."

Derek stopped chewing after hearing those last words. For a moment he became lost in his thoughts. Then, thinking for a second, he answered her. "Maybe somebody will."

What if it was this guy they would soon be told about? In a selfish sort of way he almost hoped it was. *Only a father could understand what that little girls parents must be going through,* he thought to himself. There was a long moment of silence as they were both thinking the same thoughts.

"I'm going to go check on Derek Jr." Katie said.

"I'll go with you."

The two got up and hurried back to the baby's room. He was, as they were sure he would be, still sleeping. They watched him for a few minutes, and then having convinced themselves no one was going to take him away from them, they returned to the kitchen.

The ringing phone awoke Evan from a sound sleep. He bolted up in his bed, starring momentarily at the phone before picking it up. It was his father.

"Dad, how are you?" He hadn't heard from his father in months.

"I'm fine son." his father replied. "I just wanted to let you know, I had to do a little financial maneuvering to manipulate a P & L, so I have temporarily deposited some capital in your personal savings account and your trust fund. Try not to spend it all. I'll need it back."

"How much this time?" Evan asked, rubbing his eyes as he tried to wake up.

"Somewhere in the neighborhood of eighteen million." his father replied casually.

"Nice neighborhood" Evan mumbled to himself. "No problem dad, whatever you need to do." His father quickly ended the conversation. Evan hung up the phone and staggered towards the shower. He would have gladly talked with his father longer, but there was a profit to be made and time is money. Sometimes it bothered Evan that he took a back seat to commerce, but it had been that way for so many years that Evan came to expect it. "I should be used to it by now." he said aloud to himself. But he wasn't, and he never would be.

"Eighteen million dollars" Evan said to himself. "Wouldn't dad be pissed if I spent it? Let's see, what would I buy?" He thought for a longer time than most people would when asked with a question like this. "Well, I'll be damned. Eighteen million in the bank and there's not a thing I need. What a life." He spoke aloud with no little degree of contempt. "Ya, what a life."

Brad made his way quickly through the lobby of the upscale hotel toward the dining room. He was clutching a small attaché case in his right hand. As he approached the dining room, his eyes scanned the crowd, stopping at a familiar face. He walked over to a table where a young lady was sipping a cup of coffee. It was the same young lady that Brad had accompanied to the comedy club that night.

"Good morning, Carol." he said as he sat down across from her. "I hope you haven't been waiting long."

"Not at all." she replied.

Brad opened his case and removed a manuscript with a CD copy clipped to the first page and laid it on the table. As he was closing the case to return it to the floor, she asked, "Now, is this meeting business, or personal?"

Brad looked up at her and smiled. "Is there any reason it can't be both?"

"I was hoping you would say that." she replied. "Now, let me look at our next best seller!" She reached over and picked up the manuscript, brushing deliberately against Brads hand.

Brad drew in a deep breath. He was beginning to experience feelings he hadn't felt for years. He ordered a cup of coffee as she read the first few pages. The more he looked at her, the more beautiful she became to him.

"So, what do you think?" he asked.

"Each book you write gets a little better and sells a few more copies. I'm sure this one will continue the trend."

"I wasn't talking about the book." Brad said as he took a sip of coffee. Carol looked up at him. That remark was a little out of character for Brad, but she was glad he made it.

"I was beginning to wonder if we were ever going to get past the business end of this relationship." Her smile was seductive.

"Well, consider that line crossed." Brad smiled back at her, feeling confident about the direction in which things were now moving.

"So where do we go from here?" she asked

"How about dinner, say sevenish? I'll pick you up."

"I'd love to."

Before the conversation could continue, a waitress, appearing from nowhere began refilling their coffee cups.

"Do you know what you'd like yet, or do you need a little more time?"

"Oh I know exactly what I'd like." Brad answered. He looked over at Carol and winked. Carol though, knew what he was thinking, probably because she was thinking the same thing.

"Two eggs over easy with sausage and toast, and you can refill this." Brad said, sliding his empty cup towards the waitress.

"What about you miss?"

"I'll have what he's having." Carol replied.

Brad looked up at her from the Day-Timer he was writing in. "Good choice."

"Okay, I'll have that right out for you." The waitress hurried back to the kitchen with the order.

"Take your time." Brad called to her. "Take all the time in the world."

The morning rush hour traffic was heavier than usual as Arthur sat mired in an endless stream of illuminated brake lights, all of them inching their way towards downtown. It seemed he was catching every traffic light red. He took the last sip from his coffee cup then returned it to the holder in his console. Fumbling with the radio, he tried to find a station with a traffic report. As he was scanning the stations, his phone rang. He turned down the volume as he slipped the phone out of his pocket.

"Good morning Arthur." It was 'Sam'.

"Good morning Sam."

"Traffic is unbearable this morning, isn't it?"

"That it is." Arthur replied curiously. *How did Sam know how bad the traffic was unless he was in it,* he thought to himself. "What can I do for you this morning?"

"You can lower your rear passenger side window." he asked.

"What?"

"Just do as I ask. At the next light, lower the window about three inches and keep your eyes facing forward."

"Okay." Arthur agreed. As he came to a stop at the next light, he reached down and pushed the button that lowered the rear passenger side window. He also hit the auto lock button, locking all four of the car's doors. He sat facing forward, not knowing what was to happen next. He heard the sound of paper rustling as an envelope was pushed through his open window. He did not turn around.

"Now" Sam continued, "roll up your window. This is a dangerous city." Arthur again pushed the button and raised the window. Sam continued.

"There is an envelope in your back seat. In it is a flash memory device. Once you get to your office, park on the top floor of the parking garage. Unwrap the device and plug it into your notebook computer. You do have it with you this morning, don't you?

"I have it with me every morning as I'm sure you well know."

The file on the memory device will outline the details of your first assignment. I will contact you after you have had an opportunity to review the information. I have taken the liberty of establishing a new e-mail address for you. It will set up automatically when you plug the flash drive into your computer. From now on this will be our primary means of communication. All further communication will be in the form of an e-mail unless I deem it necessary to call you. Be advised that my e-mails will delete automatically once they have been read. Do you have any questions?" Sam paused for a moment offering Arthur a chance to speak.

"Not yet." Arthur answered, after which the line went dead.

It took Arthur another fifteen minutes to get to his office. He entered the parking garage and went all the way up to the roof. Finding a remote spot, he parked and reached back to pick up his computer. He opened the envelope and removed the drive. Once his lap top was booted up he plugged it in and a few seconds later he was reading Sam's file.

As he began reading, he became angered, almost to the point of rage. After nine pages, he had reached the end. He felt sick inside.

Brad and Carol were still finishing breakfast long after the morning rush had passed. The business portion of the meeting had ended long ago and the two were engaged in a conversation about skiing. Brad was directing the conversation to a specific end and Carol was eagerly following.

"So you've never been skiing?" Brad asked again.

"No, never."

"Is there a particular reason why?"

"Yes there is. I've never had the opportunity."

Brad looked at her for a moment. "Suppose someone was to give you the opportunity, would you go?"

"That would depend." Carol said as she took one last sip of coffee.

"On what?"

"On who was asking"

Brad smiled and sat his cup back in its saucer. "Suppose it were me."

Carol looked up at him and smiled back, "You wouldn't let me break my leg, would you?"

"I would never let anything happen to you, I promise."

"In that case, I'd love to."

"Fantastic!" Brad exclaimed, "I have reservations for a three day weekend at the end of March. Can you work it into your schedule?"

"I'll make it a point to." she answered. "But for now, I have to get this back to the office." She picked up the manuscript and put it into her case. Brad paid the check and the two left the dining room together. As they passed through the lobby towards the doors leading to the street, Brad's cell phone rang. He looked down to see who was calling him. It was Arthur.

"I need to answer this." he said, flipping it open. "Hold on." he spoke, and then focused his attention back on Carol.

"Well, thanks for a wonderful breakfast." Carol leaned forward and kissed him on the cheek. Brad was pleasantly surprised and even blushed a little.

"The pleasure was all mine." he said as he tried to recover.

Carol smiled and then turned towards the door. Brad watched as she walked out the doors and disappeared into the cold February morning. After he could no longer see her, he raised the phone to his ear.

"What's going on Arthur?"

"It's Sam." Arthur replied. "We have our first assignment."

"Damn. Every time things start to go my way, that son of a bitch calls and screws it up for me."

"Sorry buddy, but we need to get together. You open for lunch today, say about one?"

"Ya, I can do that, where?"

"There's a sandwich shop here in the building. We won't be disturbed." Arthur waited for Brad's response.

"I'll be there at one." he reluctantly agreed, and the two hung up.

Arthur closed his phone and returned it to his pocket. Before he had time to get focused on the spread sheets that were in front of him, his office phone rang. He answered.

"This is Arthur."

"It made you sick didn't it?" It was Sam.

"Yes, it did." Arthur replied.

Sam continued, "The system has taken this man as far as it can. With the heavy back log of cases and the pressure from above to save tax dollars, unless a case is near one hundred percent winnable, the District Attorney is not willing to litigate. And that is only half the tragedy."

Arthur flipped his computer open and brought up the file. On the first page was the picture of a little girl and below, a newspaper clipping detailing how the child had been kidnapped. The latter pages contained clippings of court hearings. And on the final page, an article explaining why the man was set free, the same article Katie had read that morning. Sam's voice became more intense as he spoke.

"This man murdered that child. He knows it, the authorities know it, and I know it, but without the body, or some other hard evidence, he can't be held. Arthur, he knows where that child is buried. It's up to you and your associates to get him to admit to the kidnapping and the murder and, most importantly, to reveal where the child has been buried."

Arthur thought for a moment, and then spoke. "Do you have any idea how we are going to get him to admit to these things?"

"No" Sam replied, "and I don't want to. You will find a way."

"We'll do our best." Arthur assured him.

"I don't need your best" Sam quickly responded, "I need it done."

Arthur paused for a moment. "It will get done, trust me."

"Tomorrow" Sam continued, "I will e-mail all of the personal information I have on this man to you."

Before Arthur could acknowledge his statement, Sam had hung up.

He looked for a few more moments at the photographs and articles that Sam had given to him. The little girl looked so innocent. Her parents appeared devastated at their loss. The killer displayed no emotion. As he read further, he began to understand what it would take to make this man admit to what he did. He closed the file and slipped the flash drive out of the port and tucked it away into his pocket. The look of resolve on his face gave but a clue as to his determination. Arthur was glad that it made him angry. It made doing this that much easier.

Row upon row of bins containing electrical circuits, diodes and numerous other electronic gadgets made navigating the tiny shop difficult, but Evan didn't seem to mind. He had written a list on a scrap of paper, and just like a woman in a grocery store, he picked up and examined each item before deciding on which one to buy. The man behind the counter, seeing Evan's periodic indecision, approached him to offer assistance.

"Need some help?" the man asked.

"Ya" Evan replied, "what's the load capacity on this board?"

"It depends on what is driving it."

Evan thought for a moment. "Oh I guess it would."

The man reached into his pocked and pulled out a note pad. "Here's a simple formula to determine capacity. Take the input signal, multiply it by the difference between the high and low frequency range and that will give a frame of reference to fine tune."

All of this seemed to make sense to Evan. He picked up several more electrical components, some solder, a roll of electrical tape and a replacement antenna, the kind you would find on a portable radio. Having completed his selections, he walked to the front of the store to pay for his purchases. He paid cash as he always did, then grabbed the bag and left the store.

As he walked through the parking lot, he noticed someone leaning against his car. He was unable to make out who it was at first, but a few steps further revealed her identity.

"Didn't you say something about dinner?" It was Evan's visitor from the other morning.

"I believe I did." Evan replied. "How did you find me here?"

"I just happened to be passing by and saw your car. There's not that many midnight blue Porsches' with a license plate that reads, Born Rich."

"Guess you're right." Evan thought for a moment. "Are you free tonight?"

"It just so happens I am."

Evan paused, choosing his words carefully.

"Well, tell me where you're staying and I'll pick you up."

She stumbled with her words slightly then answered, "I'm checking out of my hotel this afternoon, so why don't I just meet you at a restaurant?" This was not the answer that he was looking for, but he had to make the best of it.

"Okay, there's a place on the south side of town that serves a great manicotti, it's called Romero's. It's on fifty second street, on the corner of Flagstaff. Think you can find it?"

"I'm sure I can. I found you, didn't I?"

Evan looked at her, his lust fighting with his common sense as to how to proceed. Part of him wanted to take her back to his place and spend the rest of the day in bed, but the more sensible part of him wanted to get as far away from her as possible. Sensibility usually took a back seat to lust, but not this time.

So, with the plans all made he began his journey home. As he pulled out of the parking lot, he called Arthur.

"Arthur, you asked me to let you know when the mystery lady and I were going to dinner. Well, its tonight."

"Where are you going?" Arthur asked.

"Romero's on the south side, about seven thirty."

"I'll be there." Arthur quickly answered.

The traffic in front of Romero's was light as it usually was in the middle of the week. A fuzzy image of the neon sign reflected dimly on the wet street. The reflection was temporarily distorted as Evan turned from the street into the parking lot.

The headlights disappeared into the body of his car as he opened the door. He checked his watch, and then walked around to the front of the restaurant. Across the street, a car slowly coasted to a stop. Evan looked twice at it before realizing it was Arthur. Arthur lowered the window slightly, making eye contact with Evan just as a taxi pulled up in front of the restaurant. The door opened and a pair of long legs slowly emerged from the back seat.

"I hope I didn't keep you waiting long." Rita asked as she buttoned her coat.

"No" Evan answered, "I just got here myself." Evan threw the cab driver a twenty dollar bill. He made a mental note of the mileage on the taxi's meter before closing the door.

"Where's your car?" Evan questioned.

"It was a rental" Rita quickly answered. "I returned it as I'll be leaving town tonight."

Evan extended his hand towards her. "Shall we?" he asked as he motioned toward the stairs leading to the restaurant. Rita gently wrapped her hand around Evan's arm and the two walked up the stairs and through the door.

Arthur watched as the brightness inside the restaurant faded to a narrow line of light then disappeared altogether as the doors closed. He settled back in his seat and pulled out a sandwich, looking at it for a moment with contempt. "They're in there eating veal, and I'm out here eating a bologna sandwich." he scoffed.

He took a bite from the sandwich and tuned in a basketball game on the car's radio. It was for sure going to be a long night.

Romero's was one of those cozy, warm 'mom and pop' restaurants. The food was home cooked and the service was informal but very good. Evan and Rita were led to a table in the corner as he had requested when he made the reservations. The table was small and in the center of it was a candle in a glass holder. As they both sat down, they each took a minute to glance around at the many pieces of Italian artwork hanging in the walls.

"This is very nice." Rita commented as she took a sip of water from a glass the waitress had just sat in front of her.

"Yes it is." Evan agreed. "It's a nice quiet place where people can visit without being disturbed." He too took a sip of his water, and then asked "What shall we talk about?"

In a dimly lit room on the other side of town, the lone figure of a man moved page by page through a large book. The book contained photos and case histories of criminals as well as those charged with crimes but never convicted. Occasionally the man stopped to make notes on a legal pad. After completing his notes, he turned his chair towards a computer to his left. He pushed several buttons after which a screen appeared requesting a password. He reached into his brief case and removed a small black notebook. In the notebook were pass codes to virtually every government agency's files. He flipped through the pages until the correct pass code was found. Upon entering it, a screen appeared reading 'NCIC', a national criminal database. He then proceeded to access and print the information he needed.

As the printer began to print the documents, a phone sitting on the left corner of his desk rang. He picked it up and had a brief conversation with the person on the other end.

"Yes, I've given them their first assignment." There was a pause as the other party spoke.

"They have all the information. I suspect they will attempt it within the next five days." Again a pause as the man listened.

"I'm confident they'll be successful, so confident in fact that I am preparing their next assignment." The man listened for a moment then agreed on a time to speak again and hung up. He spun his chair around and once again returned to his computer.

"I couldn't eat another bite." Rita admitted as she finished the last spoonful of desert. "Everything was delightful."

"Glad you liked it." Evan replied. "I'm sorry you have to leave so soon. We were just getting to know each other again."

"I'm sorry too" she confessed, "but I have to get back and prepare my report. It's due the day after tomorrow." Evan reached into his pocket and pulled out a small box.

"I got you a little something to remember me by." He handed the box across the table to her. She took it with a somewhat surprised look.

"You didn't have to do that." she told him as she opened the box. It was a shiny gold pin in the shape of an elephant. "It's beautiful!" she remarked.

"Put it on."

"Okay" she replied eagerly.

Evan reached over and helped her pin it on her blouse.

"I'll think of you every time I wear it."

Outside in his car, Arthur was checking his watch for the tenth time as Evan and Rita walked down the stairs in front of the restaurant. He watched as Evan gave her a kiss, and then waved down a taxi. Arthur started his car. As the taxi drove away, Arthur made a U turn and began following it at a distance. The cab was traveling very quickly. It made several turns as if to go downtown. "She sure isn't going to the airport", he spoke aloud to himself.

The cab made a hard right turn a block ahead of him. Arthur sped, up trying to close the gap. As he turned the corner, a car pulled out of a parking garage directly in front of him. Arthur slammed on his brakes and skidded to a stop, just inches from the car. Two men got out of the car and ran over to Arthur. Before he had a chance to say anything, the taller of the two men reached in the window and grabbed Arthur by the front of his shirt. Arthur was stunned by the man's actions.

"We know you made the girl" he said, "but Sam's identity must remain anonymous. It is in everyone's best interests, especially yours. Do you understand what I'm saying?"

Arthur sat speechless as he watched the taxi disappear into the darkness. The man released Arthur's shirt and the two returned to their car and sped away.

Arthur took a moment to regain his composure when a set of headlights came to a screeching halt behind him. The car's door opened and Arthur watched in his mirror as a lone figure ran to his window.

"Park your car!" It was Evan.

"What?"

"Shut up and park the damned car!" Evan demanded. Arthur pulled ahead about a half a block to a public parking lot. He drove in and parked. Evan pulled in behind him. Arthur got out of his car and locked it. He ran a few steps to where Evan had stopped and got into his car, and the two raced out of the parking lot.

"What the hell are we doing?" Arthur asked as he buckled his seat belt.

"Turn about."

"Turn about? Speak English." Arthur protested.

"Turn about. Remember the bug she planted in my den? Well, I planted one on her tonight. The problem is the range. It has a limited range because it's so small. It's the first one I've built so don't give me any shit about it."

Evan reached under his seat and pulled out a receiver. "Pull up the antenna and let me know if you hear anything." Arthur did as he was told, but the receiver was silent.

"Why did you stop in the middle of the street back there?" Evan asked as Arthur held the receiver to his ear.

"Sam's people stopped me. I tell you, that man has his bases covered like you wouldn't believe." He took the receiver from his ear and shook it a little. "Are you sure this thing is working?"

"Ya, it works" Evan admitted, "but I'm afraid she's too far away. She could be anywhere. Why don't we call it a night?"

"You won't get any argument from me." Arthur pushed the antenna down and handed the receiver back to Evan. Evan took it and tossed it behind his seat, then made a U turn and headed back to Arthur's car.

Arthur had driven only a couple of blocks before his phone rang. He knew it would be his wife wondering what time he would be home. He pushed the button. It was not his wife.

"I am willing to overlook tonight's little escapade, but I must have your word it will never happen again." It was Sam.

"You can't blame us for trying." Arthur spoke on his own behalf. "You have left us with a lot of questions and very few answers."

"You're going to have to trust me. If you were to learn my identity, all of you would be in a great deal of danger. I have gone to great lengths to insure my anonymity and I will not have it compromised. Do we understand each other?" Sam's voice revealed more than a trace of hostility.

"We do." Arthur acknowledged.

"Good. Now I suggest you focus your attentions on the matter at hand. You and your friends have a job to do. That poor girl's parents are agonizing while you and Evan are playing cops and robbers in the street. I will contact you in two days."

The phone went dead. Arthur felt as a boy who had just been scolded by his father. It seemed as if he was always a step behind, or perhaps Sam was always a step ahead.

"Alright, let's get this over with." Brad grumbled as the four men took their usual places once again in Evan's den.

"I guess we'd better get used to this, at least for the time being." Derek said as he stirred his drink.

Arthur, who had been silently reading some papers in a file folder, closed the folder and stood up. "Well, we've got our first assignment from Sam. You may have read about this in the papers, I know I did. Apparently a guy named Jerry Kinson kidnapped a young child and held her for ransom. When the ransom plans were not met to his satisfaction, he killed the child and buried her. To make a long story short, without the child's body, an airtight case cannot be made against the man and he will be released from custody the day after tomorrow. It is now our responsibility to convince this man to tell us where the child is buried so her parents can lay her to rest and he can be prosecuted."

"I read about that guy." Derek remembered.

Brad leaned forward in his chair. "Do you have this one worked out yet?" he asked Arthur in a mildly sarcastic tone.

"I think so." Arthur replied. "But this one is a lot more complicated and involved than the last one. Our jobs are going to be a lot tougher this time."

Evan spoke up. "Arthur and I have been working on this already, and I have come up with a couple of things that will make the job a little easier."

Evan lifted a wooden box, about a foot square, from the floor and sat it up on the bar.

"What the hell is that thing?" Brad asked.

"Come here and I'll show you."

For the next two hours, the four men laid out the plan and worked out the details. When every eventuality had been discussed and every scenario played out, the four went home. Arthur was right. This one was going to be a lot tougher.

It was the day before Jerry Kinson's release when Arthur's private line rang. He picked it up.

"Good morning, Arthur." It was Sam.

"Good morning Sam. I'm glad you called."

"Really, why?" Sam asked.

There is one additional piece of information we need. I could have used it yesterday, but I wasn't in front of my computer and had no way of getting in touch with you."

"What was it you needed?" Sam asked.

"I wanted a list of Jerry's prior convictions to determine exactly what he is capable of."

"I will e-mail that information to you immediately. Now, when will this all take place?"

"Tomorrow night." Arthur answered.

"The day of his release, how appropriate."

"Shall I e-mail you when we have completed the assignment?"

"No, that won't be necessary. I'll contact you."

"Okay." Arthur agreed.

"Please express my thanks to your friends. I'm sure you will be successful." With that the conversation was over. Arthur slipped the phone back into his pocket.

CHAPTER SEVEN

A trickle of vapor rose from a manhole cover in the dark street bordering the apartment house. It was a part of town that did not get prompt attention for such things as street light repair, something it was badly in need of. Parked inconspicuously among the cars on the street was an older model green sedan. In it were Arthur, Brad, Evan and Derek, each reviewing their responsibilities one final time. After going through the entire procedure twice, they put away their notes and waited.

"Whoever heard of a green car with a blue interior, anyway?" Brad scoffed, looking at the tattered upholstery.

"It's been painted." Derek answered.

Evan reached for the handle to roll the window down. After the second turn, it came off in his hand.

"Where did you get this beater?" he asked, dangling the handle in front of Arthur.

"Sam provided it."

"Is this the best he could do?" Brad complained. Arthur turned and looked at Brad in the back seat.

"We'd look a little conspicuous sitting in a Mercedes in this neighborhood, now wouldn't we?"

"I guess you're right." Brad admitted. Before the conversation went any further, a cell phone that had also been provided by Sam began to ring. Derek answered it.

"Franco's pizza, can I help you?"

"Ya you can." the voice on the other end of the phone replied. "I got one of your flyers in my mail box. I want to order a large pizza with everything for four bucks."

"One special, all the way, will there be anything else sir?" Derek asked.

"No, that's it."

"Can I have your address please?"

"Twenty six twenty two Sunset, apartment eighteen, back building, last door on the left. How soon will it be here?"

"About twenty minutes sir. Your total is four forty five. Thanks for your order." With that Derek hung up. "We're on in twenty minutes." he said nervously.

Fifteen minutes later the four men got out of the car. Arthur opened the trunk and removed a large empty pizza box. Derek put on a striped shirt and matching cap. The cap had a fake blond pony tail hanging from the back of it. It covered almost all of his hair. The blond moustache he applied completed his transformation. Evan removed a box from the trunk as well. It was the same box he had in his den the night the plans were made. Evan and Brad carried the box, each taking an end. They remained several steps back from Derek. Arthur followed close behind, making sure they were not seen.

Derek walked up to number eighteen. He took a deep breath, and then rang the bell. A voice from inside the apartment called out.

"Who is it?"

"Pizza delivery" Derek shouted. The man looked at Derek through the peep hole in the door. Derek couldn't actually see him looking at him, but he could feel his stare. Then he began unlocking the door. As the latches were being unlocked, Arthur, Evan and Brad pulled ski masks over their heads. Derek looked over at the other three as their faces disappeared under the masks. The door opened, only a couple of inches. The safety chain was still secured. A suspicious pair of eyes studied Derek for several long seconds, saying nothing.

"That will be four forty five sir." Derek politely repeated. The door closed once again. Derek could hear the chain being removed. Again the door began to open. Derek took a step back. The door slowly opened revealing a short but husky man in a dirty tee shirt. He had a half-smoked cigar in his mouth and two days growth of beard on his face which was fat with a seemingly permanent scowl. He stood only about five foot two or so. His bulging waistline gave evidence not only to the fact that he was a beer drinker, but that he rarely if ever exercised.

Once the door was fully opened, Arthur, Brad and Evan rushed through it, pushing him back inside. Arthur grabbed him, covering his mouth with his hand. Derek was the last one in. He closed and locked the door behind himself, then pulled off the hat and put on his ski mask. While Arthur restrained him, Brad taped his mouth closed with a long piece of duct tape. Then he and Arthur drug him to a wooden chair next to a table in the kitchen. Arthur secured his wrists to the arms of the chair and his ankles to its legs with nylon tie straps. At this point the struggling stopped. The man, Jerry Kinson, glared at the four with a look of both fear and rage.

Arthur stood in front of the man, tightening his gloves as he began to speak.

"Now that I have your attention, let me tell you why we're here." As he spoke, Evan was busy setting up the equipment that was in the wooden box.

"We're here to help you do the right thing." Arthur leaned toward the man, resting his fists on the arms of his chair.

"You kidnapped a little girl, and because that little girl's parents couldn't get the ransom money to you fast enough, you let that little girl die. Do you know why they didn't meet you with the money at exactly three o'clock that afternoon? It wasn't because they were trying to stiff you. They hadn't even gone to the police. They were in a traffic accident."

Jerry looked up, surprised at what Arthur had just told him. You're a stupid son of a bitch. You had it made, and you blew it. And now a little girl is dead, and you're going to tell us where she is buried."

Jerry looked in disbelief at Arthur. Then he looked over at Evan who had finished setting up the device, and was plugging it into an outlet in the wall. His eyes moved to Brad who had set up a tripod and video camera. Everything was in place. Arthur reached over to Evan's box and picked up a wire with a round metal disc on the end of it.

"In a moment I'm going to take the tape off of your mouth. But before I do that I need to show you something." Arthur grabbed the front of Jerry's shirt and tore it open. He then attached the disc to his chest with a piece of tape.

"This device regulates and delivers an electric shock based on the sound levels around it. In other words, the louder the sound, the higher the voltage. Let me show you." Arthur looked over at Derek and nodded. Derek walked over to the TV playing softly in the background. He began to raise the volume. As the volume was increased, a meter on the box began to move slowly upwards and a low, steady current of electricity was delivered through the disc on his chest. Jerry's body lunged forward in the chair. The nylon ties restricted his movement, but the muffled screams of the man and the violent tremors his body underwent proved Arthur's point. Arthur looked over at Derek, who immediately turned the television volume back down.

"Now, do you see what will happen to you if you yell when I take the tape off of your mouth?"

Jerry, who was by this time sweating profusely, nodded.

"Good." Arthur responded. He grabbed the tape and pulled it off of Jerry's face in one quick motion. Jerry winced briefly, and flexed his jaw.

"What makes you think I'm going to tell you anything?" Jerry asked sarcastically, staring past the ski mask into Arthur's eyes.

"Two things" Arthur replied, "fear and pain."

"Piss on you, all of you. The cops couldn't rattle me and neither can you, so why don't you just pack all this shit up get the hell out of here."

"You don't seem to understand." Arthur explained, taking a black padded case out of his coat pocket. "We're not the cops. We're not bound by the same rules that they are. In fact, we're not bound by any rules at all." Arthur slowly undid the zipper on a small black case to reveal a hypodermic needle and a small vile of clear liquid. "So, you're either going to tell us what we want to know or you're going to OD right here in this chair."

Jerry glared at him as he removed the syringe from the case.

"I know all about your bad habits Jerry." Arthur told him, smiling as he prepared the syringe.

"How much of this stuff do you use at a time?" he asked, drawing up the fluid. "This much" he filled the syringe to the first line, "or maybe this much?" The fluid now reached the second line. "This is a special occasion, what with you getting out of jail and all; maybe we should fill it to here." The fluid now neared the top. "Oh, what the hell, lets go all the way." Arthur drew the last few drops of the liquid, completely filling the syringe. Arthur's eyes moved from the needle to Jerry's arm, which was secured to the arm of the chair. He inched toward him, holding the needle conspicuously in the air in front of him. Looking Jerry firmly in the eyes, Arthur took the needle and jabbed it into his arm. Jerry looked down in horror and disbelief at what Arthur had done.

"Are you nuts?" he yelled. "That much will kill me!"

"I think I'm finally getting through to you." Arthur said sarcastically.

He let go of the needle, leaving it dangling from Jerry's arm, then grabbed the front of his torn shirt and pulled him upwards as much as the nylon ties on his wrists would allow.

"I'm through dicking around with you. You've got five seconds to tell us where that little girl is buried otherwise you'll be taking the trip of your life." Arthur pushed him back down in his chair with a force that was more than adequate to do the job. He glared at Jerry for what seemed an eternity, before looking over his shoulder at Brad, who immediately pushed a red button on the camera and began recording. The camera was positioned in such a way that only Jerry's head and shoulders were in view. This was to avoid anyone seeing that he was tied to the chair. Arthur began counting backwards from five with his fingers so that his voice would not be heard on the video. By the time he got to three, Jerry began screaming. As he did, the meter began to move on the device and Jerry was blasted with another surge of electricity. Brad stopped the disc and backed it up so that he could record over what had just happened.

Arthur leaned forward until he was almost nose to nose with Jerry. "You do that again" he warned, his teeth clenched in rage, "and I'll take that frying pan off of the stove and beat against the refrigerator door. Now where is the body?" Arthur walked over to the stove and took hold of the frying pan. Brad once again started recording.

"The landfill on the south side of town, she's buried in the far west corner, next to a big pile of tires. I marked the spot with an old car bumper." Arthur looked over at Brad once again. Brad immediately shut the camera off and began breaking it down. Evan and Derek began dismantling the other equipment and putting it back in the box. Brad picked up the pizza flyer they had put in Jerry's mailbox as well as the pizza box he had brought in. Then he picked up the phone and dialed a number. When the party answered, he hung up.

"There, I told you. Now get this damned thing out of my arm." Jerry demanded. Arthur leaned forward until he was again almost nose to nose with Jerry.

"You know, I've been thinking. Maybe you need a taste of what that little girl went through. The fear of knowing that death is just a heartbeat away. Maybe you've gotten off once too often. You know everybody's luck runs out sooner or later. I think yours just has, and now its time for you to pay!" With that, Arthur reached down and injected the entire contents of the syringe into Jerry's arm.

"You son of a bitch" Jerry yelled. Arthur pulled the needle out of his arm and put it back in the little black case. A small trickle of blood followed the needle. Jerry sat clutching the arms of the chair, waiting for the inevitable. Arthur looked down at him. "How does it feel Jerry, knowing that death is near?"

Jerry closed his eyes tightly and clenched his fists.

"Do you really think you're going to die?" Arthur asked. Jerry slowly relaxed his grip on the chair as his eyes reluctantly opened.

"If you do, you'll be the first person ever to die from a syringe full of saline solution!" Arthur turned and walked towards the door. With a bizarre combination of relief and panic Jerry began to realize what had just happened. Evan, Derek and Brad had already left and were loading the equipment back into the car. Arthur reached down and slipped Jerry's wallet from his pocket, then headed for the door. He paused and turned back to take one last look at Jerry. Jerry looked back at him.

"You prick!" he uttered in a deep, loathsome tone.

Arthur continued to look at him for a moment then left, locking the door behind him. Everyone else was already in the car waiting for Arthur as he rounded the corner of the building. Evan reached over and started the engine. Arthur slid in behind the wheel and threw the car into drive. A cloud of white smoke trailed them as the car disappeared into the darkness. The smoke soon dissipated, leaving only the muffled sounds of Jerry's cries for help, barely audible but nonetheless persistent.

"All things considered, I thought it went very well." Evan remarked as he wiped the sweat from his forehead.

"Ya, I've heard that shit before." Brad snapped. Everyone's eyes quickly turned towards him. Somehow feeling compelled to say something positive, he added, "Maybe we've gotten better since the last time."

Arthur threw Jerry's wallet up onto the dashboard of the car.

"What's that?" Evan asked.

"Jerry's wallet." Arthur answered.

"You took his wallet?" Brad screamed. "Did you feel the need to take a souvenir? Do you want us to get caught?"

I took his wallet to provide the police with a reason for Jerry to be tied to a chair." Arthur said calmly.

"Oh" Brad replied, feeling a little embarrassed for getting upset, "why didn't you say that in the first place?"

Arthur looked at Derek in the rear view mirror. "What about you? Are you alright?" Derek removed the false moustache.

"I was scared to death. I just hoped you guys knew what you were doing."

Evan collected the ski masks, Derek's hat and Jerry's wallet in a pillow case. As he closed the top of the bag, he looked over at Arthur. "You know, you can be one mean son of a bitch when you want to. You sure got your point across to Jerry." Evan stuffed the pillow case into a duffel bag on the floor by his feet. Then he mumbled to himself, "I hope you don't ever get pissed at me."

As Evan zipped up the bag, Arthur's cell phone rang. He reached for it and flipped it open.

"Well, how did it go?" It was Sam.

"We got you what you wanted, so I guess it went pretty good." Arthur replied.

"Excellent. I trust you didn't kill him."

"As much as he deserved it, we didn't kill him."

"Please express my gratitude to your friends." Sam added.

"Why don't you do that yourself?" Arthur put the phone on speaker so everyone could hear.

"Gentlemen thank you and congratulations on a job well done. Our gratitude will be reflected monetarily as well. By the way, Arthur did you get any proof other than his words regarding the child's whereabouts?"

"Yes we did." Arthur confirmed. "We got his confession on video. And since we have you on the phone, maybe you'll tell us what we're supposed to do with it."

Sam thought for a moment.

"Put it in a plain brown envelope and take it to the channel six studios. They have a mail drop at the front entrance. I only hope he will still be around when the police come for him."

"I'm sure he will. We left him tied to a chair."

Sam laughed aloud. "Once again, you have reinforced the wisdom of selecting you gentlemen to help us in our endeavor. I thank you."

"You said 'us'." Brad repeated, taking the phone from Arthur's hand. "Just how many of you are there?"

"Curiosity killed the cat, Brad, and it won't do you any good either." Sam cautioned. "Suffice it to say you are in league with a tremendously powerful group of people whose anonymity must not be compromised." Sam paused for a moment. "I will contact you again when your services are required. Now, go home and get some rest. You've certainly earned it." His words were followed by the all too familiar click, and he was gone. Arthur looked over his shoulder at Brad.

"Nice try."

Brad shrugged his shoulders as he handed Arthur the phone. "You never know if you don't ask."

Before the conversation went much further, they were pulling into the mall parking lot. Brad was the first to get out.

"Don't forget to go back to the mall and buy something." Arthur reminded him.

"I'm spending a small fortune on things I don't really need just to prove I was at the mall. I hope this doesn't go on much longer or I'll have to get a bigger place.

"I've got an idea." Evan announced. "Maybe we should park at a strip club. You'd still spend money, but you're apartment wouldn't get so cluttered. Brad looked over at him with his usual, 'I should have expected something like that from you', look.

"Wouldn't there be a greater chance of our cover being blown there?" Derek asked.

Before Evan could answer, Arthur spoke for him. "It's not your cover that gets blown at the places Evan has in mind." Derek suddenly snapped to what Evan was getting at. Brad opened the car door and got out, mumbling something about leaving the rest of them to their perversions. But perversion is merely a state of mind. And the state of Evan's mind allowed for most any type of unusual sexual behavior as simply a broadening of one's horizons.

Within another thirty minutes, they were all on their way back home, and back to a life they were struggling to keep separate from the one they had been thrust into.

At a cluttered desk in a noisy precinct station, a middle age and slightly overweight detective poured his third cup of coffee for the morning. The first of several chins bulged slightly as he tipped his head to take a sip. His unbuttoned suit jacket revealed a shoulder holster and a thirty-eight police special. His belt, which he'd obviously had for quite some time, was now buckled in the very first hole. The progression of worn spots back to near the last hole offered evidence of somewhat lighter days gone by.

As he walked back to his desk, he noticed the presence of a new file folder on the top of the pile. He loosened his tie, which was never very tight to begin with. As he picked it up, he noticed the name 'Jerry Kinson' on the flap. He opened the file, taking another sip of coffee then sitting the cup down next to the name plate on his desk, Detective Mo Harris. Mo was short for Morris, the name his mother gave him and one he'd hated all his life. As he scanned the file, a voice from the adjacent desk interrupted his concentration.

"Pretty weird, isn't it?" It was Mo's partner, Patrick Findley, a relatively new detective, recently promoted from the uniform division. He wore a new suit, about as new as he was to detective work. His face was young and void of the lines and emotional scars that are earned from being exposed to more violence and cruelty than anyone should be. But his innocence was not from inexperience. He knew what this city was like, and he knew he would have to deal with more of it as a detective than he had in uniform.

"Sounds like we have a self-appointed judge, jury and executioner out there." he suggested. As Mo continued to read the police report, his phone rang. He answered it, listening silently for a few moments before speaking. He thanked the person on the other end of the phone, telling them he would be right there.

"Well, whoever did this delivered a video confession to channel six. Jerry has apparently told where he buried the body." Mo said as he pulled on his jacket. Pat took a last sip from his cup as he and Mo headed towards the door.

"The son of a bitch must have been pretty rattled. I was there when they brought him in the first time. He wouldn't say anything to anybody. It was like he knew we couldn't make anything stick." Pat recalled.

"I guess whoever got him to confess was a bit more persuasive than we were." The glass shook in the door as it slammed shut behind them.

Several hours later, in a small, dark interrogation room, Jerry sat with his hands folded in front of him at a table. Mo paced back and forth behind him while Pat sat across from him. Mo lit a cigarette, and then spoke.

"So what you're telling us is four guys came to your apartment last night as a result of your ordering a pizza, and forced a confession out of you by threatening to inject you with a lethal dose of heroin."

"That's what I've been trying to tell you. They stuck a needle in my arm and injected me with saline solution." Jerry screamed.

"I thought you said they threatened you with heroin." Pat repeated.

"They told me it was heroin, but it turned out to be saline. Look, you can still see where they put the needle in my arm, look!" Jerry rolled up his sleeve. Mo and Pat both leaned over to look.

"That looks like a shotgun pattern. You've got so many needle marks in your arm, how are we supposed to know that one of them was from last night?" Mo asked.

Jerry looked up at him. "Because I'm telling you, that's why."

"Just like you told us you had nothing to do with that little girls kidnapping?" Mo shouted.

"I was lying then, but I'm telling the truth now. That's what really happened. These guys broke the law and violated my civil rights. That confession was, what do you call it.....?" Jerry thought for a moment before it came to him. "Coerced, that's it. I was coerced into saying those things. You can't use that against me. I wouldn't be surprised if they worked for you." Jerry scoffed. Pat leaned over the table towards him.

"You were lying then and you're lying now. There is absolutely no evidence to back up what you are saying. And if the guys that visited you were working for us, there wouldn't have been saline solution in that needle."

Jerry thought for a moment. "Yes there is. There is too evidence; the ad for the pizza place. It should still be at my apartment. And check the redial on my phone. It will dial that same number. Go check it out. That was the last call I made."

"Oh we will!" Mo growled. "But if this is just another load of crap, this whole thing is over, and you're going down for the count."

Having said that the two left the room, stationing an officer outside the door to make sure Jerry didn't try to leave.

It was about a fifteen minute drive to Jerry's apartment. The door was still protected with yellow crime scene tape. The two entered and began looking for the evidence that Jerry had described to them. There was no sign of the flyer advertising the pizza place. Mo found the phone and picked up the receiver. He pushed the redial button. Several seconds later, it rang. A voice answered.

"Good morning, Capital pizza. Can I take your order please?'

"This is detective Mo Harris, mid town police. Could you tell me your address please?"

"Certainly" the voice answered, "we are at thirty six hundred West Seventh Street. But we do deliver."

"No thank you." Mo replied, "I'm just following a lead." He hung up the phone and looked over at Pat.

"He's just jerking our chain." he grunted. "Let's get the hell out of here. We got him by the balls this time, thanks to whoever came to see him last night."

"Who do you suppose they were? The kid's parents maybe."

"Not likely." Mo figured. "The kid's parents are still out of state with family. They got no relatives here. Whoever it was deserves a prize. Too bad what they did makes them criminals. To tell you the truth, I just want to see Jerry Kinson in prison.

And personally, I don't give a rat's ass if these four guys he's talking about are ever found. I know I'm not going to lose any sleep over it."

"As far as I'm concerned, he made the whole thing up." Pat concluded and the two detectives left Jerry's apartment and headed back to the station house.

CHAPTER EIGHT

Things went on quite uneventfully for several weeks. It was beginning to look like they had all heard the last of Sam. Arthur and his daughter had come to terms on clothes and boyfriends. Brad's relationship with Carol was developing, and Evan spent more and more time working on electronic gadgetry that no one understood but him. Derek, much against everyone's better judgment, attended the funeral of the little girl whose body had been recovered from the landfill. Jerry, the man who kidnapped her, had a new trial pending. It was rumored that the prosecutors were seeking the death penalty. Everything was going well, perhaps too well.

Arthur had been carrying the flash drive Sam had given him in the bag with his computer now for weeks, if for no other reason than to keep anyone from finding it. On his way to work this particular day, he had decided that he would erase the contents of the memory stick before someone got a hold of it that shouldn't. But that was not to be. Two blocks from his office, his cell phone rang. It was Sam.

"Arthur, when you get to your office, plug the flash device into your computer, and then access your email. The message I sent will automatically load onto the device, then the email will be deleted. I will call you when you have done this." Sam hung up.

Arthur did as he was instructed. The light on the end of the memory device flashed briefly, and then the email disappeared. Arthur opened the file he had just loaded and began reading. It was an investment contract, and a very poor one at that.

He made some notes as he read. This contract was barely legal by even the broadest standards. Despite its flowery language, it stipulated that the risk, as calculated, was no greater than twenty per cent. The asterisk directed Arthur's attention to a formula in small print on the second to last page. The formula, when applied, worked out to an amount closer to eighty per cent. It was without a doubt a deliberately deceptive instrument.

Arthur closed his laptop and took a sip of coffee. He knew that at any moment his private line would ring, and it would be Sam. He was correct. Moments later his private line did ring, and it was indeed Sam.

"Good morning Arthur. How are you this morning?"

"Well, that depends. Are you expecting me to sign this contract that you emailed to me?"

"Of course not, I just wanted you to read it. Have you had an opportunity to do so?"

"As a matter of fact, I have." Arthur answered. "Where did you get this piece of garbage? I doubt that anyone who actually read this thing would invest any money in it."

"Unfortunately Arthur, quite a few people have. This investment scam was cooked up by one Theodore Messina, Ted as he is known to his friends. He sold this product mostly to senior citizens and retirees. He is a slick talker, the kind of guy that makes it all sound so safe. He became their friend first, making multiple visits to each prospective investor. In some cases he even advised them not to invest, but because of the relationship he had developed with these people, most of them did invest. And all of them lost almost everything. The best information we have indicates he has swindled his clients out of three point two million dollars."

"With this?" Arthur asked in disbelief. "I wouldn't invest ten cents in this. It's a dog with fleas."

"But you're trained to spot these 'dogs with fleas'. You know what to look for but most people don't. They relied on the only thing they had; trust. They trusted him, and he took their money."

"But what he did is illegal. Can't the state bring an action against him?"

"The state did, but there was no direct evidence linking him to any illegal activity."

"But what about cancelled checks or bank records, isn't that evidence?" Arthur asked.

"There were no cancelled checks. He used a lap top computer to electronically transfer funds. It was all part of his sensitivity towards his investors. They didn't have to leave their homes, or even sign a check. All he needed was the account number, and he took care of the rest. He covered himself extraordinarily well. So well, in fact, that he was just acquitted three days ago."

"How could this happen?"

"Our legal system; lawyers, they're all a bunch of snakes. Nonetheless, we must play the cards we are dealt. I will be emailing you all the information I have on this man, so if you had any thoughts about dropping the flash device in the ash tray of your car, you can forget them." There was a click and Sam was gone.

By noon the next day, Arthur had all of Ted's personal information, his name, address, where he went to school, and his hobbies. Then came what this was all about; the names and account numbers of those people he had swindled out of their savings. Each name had a dollar figure next to it, no doubt how much money that person had lost. There were several pages of court transcripts from his recent trial. At the end of the document was a note from Sam. It read, 'We must move quickly on this. Ted has purchased an airline ticket, one way, to New Zealand. His flight leaves two weeks from tomorrow. Please meet with your friends as soon as possible, and then let me know what you need to carry out this assignment. Good luck.' It was signed, Sam.

Arthur sat the papers down. He tapped his fingers on the desk, starring intently at a picture on the wall. All at once his fingers stopped. A look of satisfaction appeared on his face as he reached for the phone. He pushed the buttons, leaning back in his chair.

"Evan, its me." he began. "We've got another assignment."

"We do?"

"Yes, but this one won't be as risky as the last one. Our guy is not violent this time. I've got an idea already, but I need some of your electronic know how. Can you rally the troops at your house tomorrow night?"

"Sure, I'll call everybody. I don't know how happy they will be, but I'll call them.

"Thanks Evan." Arthur hung up. He leaned back in his chair once again, and rested his hands behind his head and looked up at the ceiling. He had something worked out alright.

A small cloud of frost floated into the air as Brad closed the freezer door. He had invited Carol over for dinner and was thawing out the meat for the only dish he knew how to cook; spaghetti. He carried the ground pork over to the sink where it would thaw while he was working. Before he had a chance to dry his hands, the phone rang. He answered it.

"Brad, this is Evan. How are you doing?"

"Are you going to screw up my day?" Brad asked. He had a sixth sense about it now.

"I'm afraid I am my friend. We've got another job. We've got to move on it pretty quick. Can you make it tomorrow night, my place?"

"Same time as usual?"

"Same time" Evan responded. The two agreed and the conversation ended. Brad walked out of the kitchen and over to his computer. "One of these days I'm going to have to write about this shit." He thought for a minute before reconsidering. "No one would believe it. This stuff's too strange even for fiction."

Immediately after the call to Brad, Evan placed one to Derek. No one was home so he left a message on Derek's answering machine.

"Derek, this is Evan. There's a great boxing match tomorrow night on pay-per-view. Arthur and Brad are coming over and I thought you'd like to as well, that is if Katie doesn't mind. Please give me a call when you get in. Thanks."

As the four sat around Evan's bar the next night, Arthur explained the situation and the urgency. No one seemed to be as nervous as the last time, or the time before. Arthur had the ability to plan things down to the last detail. Evan had a gadget for every need. Brad was the cool head when the plan occasionally veered off course, and Derek was able to do anything that was asked of him. By the end of the evening, the plan was worked out, and Arthur was on his way home to leave an e-mail for Sam.

CHAPTER NINE

Ted Messina was the nicest guy in the world, or at least that's what he would have you believe. He had an uncanny ability to adapt his personality, his mannerisms, even the way he spoke, to identify with whomever he was dealing with at the time. But Ted was also an extremely cautious individual. He executed his plans precisely and covered his tracks flawlessly. This was evidenced by the fact that he was not in jail.

For all his abilities, Ted was not a powerful or intimidating looking man. In fact, he was rather average. He stood all of five foot six and weighed no more than one hundred thirty pounds. He had the textbook baby face; sincere, trustworthy, a face belonging to a person that could never lie to you. And although many men in their late thirties had thinning hair, Ted's was as thick and black as it was in his teens.

Ted's knowledge and use of his craft was far above average. His methods were precise and their results predictable. But all of his successes contributed to the one thing that would eventually be his downfall; over-confidence. Ted had made so much money with so little effort that he believed most of the world to be of lesser intelligence than he. Each person he conned bolstered his opinion of himself and reinforced his feeling of invincibility. Both his self image and his bank account were at an unjustly distended level.

But Ted was not stupid; greedy, but not stupid. His close encounter with the law had bruised his ego, and sent him a message in no uncertain terms. It was time to move on. He had harvested all there was to be had and greener pastures awaited him elsewhere. After all, there is a whole world full of people to call on. And with a one way ticket to New Zealand, it was quite clear he intended to continue what he perceived to be his calling. His plans though, were destined to be altered.

Evan stood, clad in blue coveralls, at Ted's door. The patch on his pocket read "Security Services Inc'. He could see Ted looking at him through the peep hole. Moments later, the door opened. Evan raised a clipboard and read from it.

"Mr. Messina?"

"Yes, that's me. What do you want?"

"My name is Al. I'm with SSI, the company that maintains the security systems for this apartment complex. I need to look at your panel, the one in the master bedroom closet. May I come in?" Evan took a step forward, but Ted took a step as well blocking Evan's path.

"Just what is wrong with the system? It seems to be working fine."

"We had a down line power surge. Some guy got drunk and hit a light pole. When it fell, there was a short, and some of the units in this building have had damaged transistors on the main board. It will only take me a second to check it, and if it needs to be replaced, I have a new one with me. I'll be out of your hair in five minutes."

Ted studied at him for a few seconds, looking back and forth between the badge on Evan's coveralls and his face, taking ample time to reconcile one with the other. Having satisfied himself that he was legitimate, Ted let him in.

He walked through the door. Ted closed it behind him. Evan had a vision of what Ted's place should look like, but this wasn't it. It was a modestly decorated place with some rather cheesy furniture, a TV that looked like it had been bought back from the seventies, and a table and chairs that wouldn't fetch much at a garage sale. It looked as if this was only a stopping-off point for Ted on his way to bigger and better things.

The only thing in the entire apartment that appeared to be of any real value was a computer (which probably cost more than the entire contents of the apartment combined). As he passed through the room, Evan studied it for a split second, quickly realizing that it was one of the best, and most expensive ones on the market. It looked as conspicuous as a Rolls Royce at a flea market. He wondered as he walked how he was going to accomplish his task since he was making most of it up as he went along.

Evan followed Ted back to the bedroom closet where the security system was located. Once inside the closet, Evan took a screwdriver from his tool belt and removed the cover from the box. Ted stood behind him looking over his shoulder. Evan removed the cover and sat it on the floor. Then he took a tester from his tool belt and began placing it at various points on the main circuit board. After testing five or six locations, Evan announced that the board was indeed bad. Ted took a step closer.

"How could you tell that?"

"There are seven points most likely to be damaged by a power surge. The bad boy was number six. I'll just replace the whole board, and repair this one back at the shop."

"You know how to fix these things?"

"Ya, I've been working with security systems and computers for twelve years now."

"What sort of work do you do with computers?" Ted asked, his demeanor changing.

"Well, I've built a number of them. But mostly, I install upgrades, you know, extra memory, larger hard drives, more powerful processors, video cards, that sort of stuff. It makes me a little money on the side and I enjoy doing it."

Ted thought for a moment. "Are upgrades very expensive to install?"

"What sort of upgrades?"

"Well, I bought some memory upgrades the other day. I was going to put them in myself, but if it won't cost too much, I'll let you do it." As they were talking, Evan had removed and was installing a new board in the box. He thought for a moment as he replaced the cover.

"What are they, just single in line memory modules?"

"Ya, that's what the package says, SIMMs. I have two of them, one gig each. What would you charge me to install them?"

"Those are easy, nothing to it really. Tell you what. Since this is my last stop in this complex, I'll put them in for a cup of coffee. I had to leave home early this morning, and I haven't had my first cup yet."

"You got a deal." Ted replied anxiously.

Evan tightened the last screw on the box and put the screw driver back in his pouch. "Now, let's take a look at that computer." They walked back through the living room to the dining area.

"It's on the table." Ted said, "I'll get the coffee going." Ted walked into the kitchen, leaving Evan to remove the cover from his computer.

Despite getting a lucky break, Evan was nervous. *Things don't normally go this easy,* he thought to himself.

There were two memory chips in a bag next to the printer. Evan picked them up, holding them briefly in his hand as he thought. He lifted the cover from the computer, and located the expansion slots for the modules. There was already a one gigabyte chip installed. He reached in and unsnapped it, leaving it sitting unconnected in the slot. He placed the two new chips in the empty slots but left them unconnected as well. This defeated the random access memory completely. Evan switched on the computer as Ted walked over to the table with two cups of coffee.

"Let's see how it works." Evan said, taking a sip of the coffee. Before the main screen came up, a default screen appeared indicating an error in the RAM.

"What's wrong?" Ted asked.

"Let me see the package these things came in." Ted handed him a package. Evan read it, and then shook his head.

"Where did you buy these?"

"At the computer store down on North Main, why?"

"Those idiots sold you the wrong ones." Evan shut the system down and removed the loose modules. He looked closely at the small writing on the back of them.

"I might have something out in the van that will make this work. If you've got a few minutes, I'll go check." Ted agreed and Evan went out to his van to get something he already had in his tool belt. But he had to make it look good and so far, Ted was buying it.

A few minutes later, Evan returned to the apartment. He held a small square circuit in his hand.

"This is your lucky day." he told Ted. "I replaced some parts on a mother board yesterday. I wound up with one of these left over. It will take me just a minute to put it in."

"What is that thing? Ted asked.

"It changes the path that the current follows to accommodate the different modules you have. A minor component, but the system won't work without it." Evan took the last swallow of coffee and began working.

"Can I get you another cup?"

"That would be great." Evan said as he plugged in his soldering iron. Ted returned to the kitchen. Evan began installing the circuit. It was not, however, the type of circuit he had just described to Ted. It was a tiny transmitter that would transmit the key strokes typed on this computer to a receiver in the trunk of a car parked a block away in a parking lot. From there the signal was amplified and re-broadcast to another receiver at Evan's house.

Once it was soldered into place, Evan correctly installed the memory modules and re-booted the system. Ted walked back to the table with a fresh cup of coffee just as the start-up screen appeared on the monitor.

"It works!" Ted exclaimed. "That was all it took, huh?"

"That's all." Evan answered.

"Well, how much do I owe you for the part you installed?"

"Forge about it. It was a used part from another board. I didn't have any money in it. Besides, I got two free cups of coffee. I'm a happy man."

Evan drank half of the second cup, and then left the apartment. He could see how Ted's nature could make people trust him. Evan was beginning to like him himself, and he knew what an asshole he was.

"Worst damned coffee I've ever had in my life."

Evan walked down the stairs and back to his van. The first step had been completed.

That same night after dinner, Arthur retired to his study and locked the door. He switched on his computer and sent Sam an e-mail. He left the message as to the things they'd need to complete the assignment. Sam emailed back telling Arthur he would leave them at the safe deposit box which had become a pick-up point. Arthur deleted the email then shut his computer down and went to bed.

Brad and Derek's role in this assignment began Saturday morning. It began with a phone call to Ted. Brad, posing as an art dealer, placed the call. The information given them by Sam revealed Ted's passion for rare sculptures, particularly those of Central American origin, dating back to the fifteenth century. These were extremely rare and most certainly valuable, usually selling for many hundreds of thousands of dollars. It was rumored, although never proven, that Ted had a collection of these sculptures hidden somewhere.

Derek looked curiously at the strange looking sculpture he held in his hands. It was a statue of a bird, and a rather ugly one at that. It stood about twelve inches tall and no more than five inches across at the broadest point. It had been carved out of solid granite which made it extremely heavy. But its age and the strange markings on its base made it worth a fortune to those who collect this type of antiquity. Brad sat across the table from him, the phone in his hand, waiting for Ted to answer.

"This thing is worth how much?" Derek asked, for the third time.

"Three hundred and fifty thousand dollars; its value has not increased since the last time you asked me." Brad smiled at him, amused by the sheer amazement Derek had for the value of this piece. The phone rang seven times before Ted answered it.

"Yes, is this Ted Messina?" Brad asked.

"It is. Who is this?" Ted's voice was cold and distrusting.

"My name is Louis Roth. I deal in rare and unusual antiquities. Your name was given to me by an associate of mine as someone who might be interested in purchasing a piece of Central American sculpture that will soon be on the market."

"Your associate was wrong. I don't buy antiques."

"That's too bad." Brad continued, "This is the much coveted 'Bird of Prey' piece."

Ted interrupted. "The 'Bird of Prey' is part of a collection owned by some guy in Indiana. There was only one found. It's worth a fortune."

"You are quite correct. The owner of this and many other pieces finds himself in a rather compromising position with the Internal Revenue Service. It has become necessary for him to liquidate certain of these pieces to fund his legal defense. The 'Bird of Prey' is one of those pieces. But, if you are not a collector, then I suppose I have called you in vain."

"No, no wait. I might be interested in the piece. How much is your client asking."

"In an effort to raise a rather large amount of cash in a short period of time, my client is willing to sell the piece at a greatly reduced cost. He will accept two hundred thousand dollars, with the stipulation that the payment be made in cash. My client will not accept checks, drafts or any other form of currency transfer. Is this something you might be interested in?"

"I need to see it first." Ted answered.

"As well you should. I will make the necessary arrangements and contact you when the piece may be viewed." With that, Brad hung up. Derek had been snickering under his breath throughout the conversation at the way Brad was speaking.

"Do art dealers really talk like that?" he asked.

"How the hell should I know? I've never bought any art before. I just didn't want to sound like myself."

"Well you didn't. As a matter of fact, you sounded like a real tight ass."

"Good." Brad exclaimed. "Now, if it's okay with you, I'll take my tight ass into the kitchen and fix us some lunch." Brad left Derek sitting at the table and began fixing lunch for the two of them.

"Is Katie working today, or did you have to make something up?"

"No. Even though it's Saturday, she's working, but you're not going to believe what she's working on."

Brad stopped what he was doing and turned around. "What is she working on?"

"She is researching what were supposed to be two unrelated incidents." Brad took a couple of steps closer to the dining room.

"What are you talking about?" There was a trace of concern in his voice.

"The paper is doing a story on the guy that beat up Katie and the guy that we got the confession out of to see if there is a link between them." Brad walked back into the dining room.

"You've got to be kidding. You are kidding, aren't you?"

"No, I'm serious as a heart attack. She hasn't told me yet, but I'm sure she will. She's been asked to help on the project but she's expecting to be assigned to it full time. When that happens, she'll probably tell me."

"Well how much have they found out so far? Are they getting close?"

"I don't think they've found anything out yet. They've just started."

"Well how good are they at finding things out? I mean, most of the stuff you read in the newspaper is a bunch of crap anyway. Do you think they will actually look into these incidents or just screw around then make something up?"

"Oh they'll look into them alright. But I honestly don't see how they could ever connect them to us." Derek enjoyed a confidence that Brad did not.

"Well if somebody has to do it, I guess it's best that it's someone that we can keep an eye on. Just our damn luck though." Brad felt as if he were saying that all the time now.

Evan grabbed a beer as he put the mustard back in the refrigerator. He popped the top and took a sip before picking up his sandwich. Walking back into the den, he noticed things to be pretty much as they were before he left. A television monitor was illuminated in a bright blue color. Next to it, a video tape recorder was on and ready to record. Above the VCR sat a small box with a signal strength meter and a red light indicating 'signal lock'. Beside that was another small box with a series of lights which read 'signal transfer strength'. It all looked to be working although nothing seemed to be happening. Evan took a bite of his sandwich and continued to watch the screen.

About mid way through lunch his door bell rang. He walked over to the intercom behind the bar and pushed a button.

"Who is it?"

"It's me, Arthur." Evan pushed another button on the intercom.

"Come on in." A buzz sounded and the door unlocked. Arthur opened it and made his way down the main hallway, past a collection of life-size busts of men that he didn't recognize. They must have been important though, otherwise, what would they be doing in Evan's hallway? Although they were only statues, Arthur always felt they were watching him as he walked by. He made his way back to the den where Evan was watching the blue TV screen.

"Is it working?" Arthur asked.

"Of course it's working."

"How can you tell?"

"The screen is blue. When the computer is off, the chip transmits a blue screen. When he turns the computer on, the computer's signal over-rides the blue screen and his screen and key strokes are transmitted. Understand now?"

Arthur just shook his head. He never understood how Evan could figure all this stuff out.

"So tell me again what's going to happen when he turns on his computer." Arthur pulled a chair over next to Evan and sat down.

"When he turns his computer on, whatever keys he hits will be transmitted to us and will appear on this screen. So, when he accesses his numbered Swiss bank account, we will see his access code and account number. Then we will be able to do a little creative accounting of our own."

"But I thought when you entered a pass code the screen showed an asterisk instead of the number? At least that's the way it works on my computer at home."

"You're right, that's the way it is. That's why this chip transmits key strokes, and not just what shows up on the screen.

"I should have known better than to ask." Arthur admitted.

The two sat silently for a few minutes before Evan got up to take his empty plate back into the kitchen.

"You want a beer?"

"Sure, I'll take one."

Evan left the room and went to the kitchen. Before he could make it back to the den, the screen went black. Arthur sat up in his chair, not knowing exactly what was going on or what to do about it.

"Evan, get in here. Something's happening." he barked. Evan ran back into the room. He looked at the screen and smiled. Ted had turned on his computer and was accessing the bank.

"Push the record button on the VCR Arthur, quick." Arthur reached over and pressed a button with a red stripe across the front of it. A red light illuminated and the counter began to advance. Evan grabbed a legal pad he and began writing numbers as they appeared on the screen. Arthur watched as screen after screen of numbers and letters appeared on the screen. They appeared then disappeared quickly. He understood now why Evan wanted to record this.

There was a pause after which a spread sheet of sorts came up. There were numerous entries visible, the latest one a credit dated yesterday. That entry was then highlighted and a confirmation screen came up. It confirmed that a transfer was made from this account to a second one.

"Ted must have two accounts." Arthur observed.

"Looks that way"

"He must keep one account for disbursements and the other for initial deposits. This guy covers his tracks very well."

After the verification, each screen exited to the previous one until the process had completed and the screen was once again blue. Evan rewound the tape and checked it against the numbers he had written down.

"Ted has a lot of money." Arthur said as he reached for the stop button on the VCR.

"Not for much longer." Evan smirked, finishing his notes.

They now had everything they needed to pull off the job. The rest would be up to Brad and Derek.

The shiny blue panel van looked a little out of place parked in a remote corner of the mall parking lot. A steady trail of vapor from the tail pipe dissipated quickly in the cold March air. Inside the van, Brad and Derek, their appearance altered to avoid being recognized, sat trying to keep warm.

"Are you sure this stuff will come out?" Brad asked as he ran his fingers through his formerly brown, but now blond hair.

"Sure it will. The next time you wash your hair, you'll be back to your old self again." Derek assured him, resting his hands on the top of the steering wheel.

Brad looked at himself in the mirror on the back of the sun visor. "You know, I don't look half bad with a beard either." he stated as he stroked the fake hair that had been applied to his face. Maybe I should grow one."

Derek looked over at him from the driver's seat.

"And cover up those natural good looks?"

"You're right." Brad agreed, "It would be selfish to deprive the world of this face." He looked over at Derek and smiled.

Derek just shook his head. His hair had been dyed black, with some amount of gray added to make him look older. He wore dark glasses which covered a large portion of his face, and the cap he wore shaded what part of his face was visible. The two waited some twenty minutes before a late model conservative looking sedan pulled up along side the van. A lone figure got out and looked around nervously.

"This must be him." Brad concluded as he slid into the back of the van. He opened the large sliding door about halfway.

"Mr. Messina?" he called, in perfect 'tight ass' dialect.

"Ya, I'm Ted Messina"

"I am Mr. Roth." Brad continued. "Please step into the van." Ted took one last look around, and then entered the van. He climbed up and sat at one of the seats that surrounded a small table. Brad pulled the door closed and sat down across from him.

"Who's this?" he asked, pointing to Derek.

"This is my driver, Mr. Cunningham." Derek looked at Ted in the mirror without turning around then returned his eyes forward as if to be watching for something.

"Before we go any further" Brad began, "I must remind you of the conditions of the sale. My client will accept only cash. The denomination is unimportant. There will be no receipts or bills of sale. I would also add there is nothing illegal about the transaction. These are merely the wishes of my client and the demands his current fiscal inconvenience."

Derek fought back a smile from the front seat at the way Brad was speaking. It was very eloquent, although quite uncharacteristic.

"Ya, ya, I understand." Ted answered impatiently. "The cash is not a problem, if the piece checks out. There are a lot of fakes out there you know."

Brad reached under his seat and removed a rather impressive looking wooden box. From the box he removed an object wrapped in a purple velvet cloth.

"I assure you" he said, holding the piece up until it reflected the sunlight coming through the van's windshield, "this is not a fake."

He handed the piece to Ted. Ted reverently lifted the piece from Brad's hands and gently cradled it in his own. After gazing at it for a few moments with a look that embodied both lust and worship, he began examining it. He studied numerous specific areas which would indicate its authenticity. Slowly and carefully he turned it over revealing the strange markings on the bottom of the base.

A smile crept slowly across Ted's face. He looked over at Brad.

"I can have the money to you by the day after tomorrow." He handed the piece back to Brad who immediately returned it to the box and placed it back under the seat. Then Ted looked as if he were having second thoughts. "How do I know that you guys aren't cops, or just trying to set me up?"

Brad stared back at him intently. You were not the first collector I contacted. There are several people that have expressed interest in acquiring this piece. If you have apprehensions, my advice would be to purchase your pieces through more conventional means. I do not want to do business with you if you are uncomfortable with the circumstances."

"No, I'm comfortable. I was just being careful." Ted was now defending his position.

"Good, then shall we meet in this same place when you have the money?" Brad asked.

"Ya, this is fine."

"I will call you tomorrow to confirm our arrangements."

With that, Brad got up and opened the door. Ted stepped out of the van and got into his car. Brad closed the van door as Ted started his car and left the parking space heading out towards the street.

"Well I thought that went rather well, didn't you?" Derek asked, shifting the van into drive.

"We'll find out the day after tomorrow."

Derek released the parking break then, mimicking the way Brad spoke to Ted, added, "Since our transactions have been realized, I suppose we should vacate the area before we are assailed upon by the authorities!"

Brad responded immediately.

"Oh, quite, let us make haste." He pointed towards the exit and the two left the parking lot. The next step was up to Evan.

Ted wasted no time returning to his apartment. He had wanted that piece for years, but until now it had not been for sale. Ted had more than enough money to pay for it, and the fact that it had to be a cash transaction was just fine with him.

When Ted reached his apartment he closed and locked the door, then went straight for his computer. He switched it on. While it was coming up, he flipped through the pages of a ledger he kept on the top shelf of his pantry. Once up, he accessed the bank. From there, he entered his account number and access code. Seconds later his account information appeared on the screen. He typed in his request for 'account balance'. Upon doing so, the sum of six hundred and eighty four dollars appeared in the box on his screen. "What the hell" he said out loud. He retried the command three times and came up with the same response each time.

Angrily, he grabbed the phone and placed a long distance call to the bank. The line rang four times before someone answered and directed him to an officer of the bank.

"This is Ted Messina, account number four six four seven nine eighty three hundred. I just tried to access my account balance and it shows a balance of six hundred and eighty four dollars. I have over six million in that account. What the hell is going on?"

From a van with phone company markings parked outside Ted's apartment complex, a voice answered that Ted should have recognized. "I'm sorry for the inconvenience sir." Evan explained, sitting on a stack of phone books in the back of the van. A line leading from the van to the to the main switch box of the complex swayed back and forth in the cold north wind as Evan spoke. "A virus has penetrated our system. It has moved all of the decimal points to the left by five places. Tell me, was the balance that appeared on your screen exactly one hundredth of one percent of your actual balance?" Evan's accent wasn't by any means perfect, but Ted's anger had overtaken his suspicions.

"Hell, I don't know. I don't have a calculator in front of me. So what are you going to do about it?"

"We are in the process of correcting the problem. Unfortunately, it will take several days. Until that time, the bank has frozen all accounts. We will neither accept deposits nor authorize withdrawals."

"That's a crock of shit!" Ted yelled. "I need my money and I need it now!"

"I quite understand." Evan continued, "The bank is prepared to cover any and all expenses incurred by this difficulty. We understand that many of our clients may not wish to borrow money through conventional means. Therefore, the bank will reimburse expenses to the limit of one percent of the account balance per day. This will allow for even the most extreme circumstances, if you know what I mean."

Ted certainly did. He had dealt with loan sharks in the past. But in this instance, at one percent of his balance, it was possible for him to actually make a few bucks at the banks expense by borrowing the money, so why not.

"Well when do you expect to have your system up again?"

"We will be back on line by midnight tomorrow our time, I assure you. And again, we regret any inconvenience this problem may have caused."

Before Evan had completed his apology, Ted hung up the phone. Evan quickly stepped out of the van and disconnected the wires from the box. He secured the cover, and then left the complex.

Later that afternoon, Ted contacted a man from whom he had borrowed money in the past. The sum he was asking for was extreme even for a loan shark. But Ted was convincing, and the deal was inevitable.

"Look" Ted pleaded, "I can show you my bank statement. Their computer screwed up. I have the money. The bank just won't release it until their computers are fixed. They have even agreed to pay the interest on the loan. I'll only need the money for two days, and then I can pay you back." The voice on the other end of the phone was cold and indifferent.

"The rate is three percent per week."

"That's no problem." Ted quickly replied. "Like I said, I only need the money for two days. It's the fastest profit you could ever hope to make. So where do you want to meet?"

"Don't worry about it. With this much money, we'll come to you. I don't want anybody ripping you off before you get to wherever it is you're going with it. You do remember what happens when you're late with their payments, don't you?"

Ted swallowed. His mouth always got uncomfortably dry at the mention of this. "Ya, I remember. But you guys need to wake up and smell the millennium. Surely there is a better way of collecting past due debts than that?" Ted laughed nervously.

The voice on the phone was not amused.

"There is no greater motivation to repay a debt than the threat of having your legs broken. It's a time proven remedy, so why change it? Besides, I don't tell you how to spend your money, so don't tell me how to loan it." The man's voice became even harsher. Ted realized he'd said enough, maybe too much. The two agreed on a time, and the conversation was over.

The next morning the money was delivered. Two extremely large men clad in cheap, shiny suits knocked on Ted's door around ten o'clock. They both had very conspicuous bulges in their suit jackets. The fact that they were delivering two hundred thousand dollars in cash could have been the reason, but it wasn't. Ted knew who they were before he opened the door. Their appearance was about what he had expected. One thing he noticed about these 'goon' types was that their IQ was usually exceeded by their waistline. They were all strong but most were dumb. These two were no exception.

"There is two hundred grand in this bag. Wanna count it? The boss thought maybe you should."

"Yes, I suppose I'd better." Ted replied. He spent the next five minutes counting the money. It was all there.

"You know the terms and conditions of the loan?" the larger of the two asked in a well rehearsed voice.

Ted looked at him for a second too long before thinking of his response.

"The first payment is due in two days. If you don't got the money for the payment, you at least gotta pay the interest. If you don't got enough money to pay the interest, then me and Abe, well, we gotta break one of your legs."

"I'll have the money, don't worry." Ted was sorry he had hesitated with his response. He really didn't need to hear what happens if the payments are not made in a timely manner. He already knew.

So, having said their piece and delivered the money, the two thugs left Ted's apartment. Within an hour, Brad called to confirm the meeting for the next day. Everything was set.

The following day, in the same place as they had originally met the transaction took place. Evan and Arthur watched from across the parking lot to make sure Ted didn't try anything foolish with the money. Inside the van, Ted once again examined the piece and to make sure it was the same one he had seen two days earlier. He looked up at Brad, whose hair seemed to be a shade lighter today, and nodded. Ted slid a brief case over to Brad. Brad opened it and tried to conceal his amazement at what two hundred thousand dollars in cash looked like.

He picked up selected bundles of bills and flipped through them. He'd seen that done in the movies, so it seemed like the thing to do. Besides, he wanted to make sure there were bills all the way through the stacks and not just on top. Everything looked to be in order. He looked back over at Ted and nodded. The transaction was complete. Ted placed the piece back in its wooden box and secured the lid. He looked over at Brad and Derek and smiled.

"It's been a pleasure doing business with you."

"The pleasure was all ours." Brad said. As Ted reached for the handle to the van's sliding door, Brad asked, "Might I inquire about your collection? Ted stopped and turned back to Brad, glaring at him for a moment. "That is, should you ever decide to sell any of the pieces, I may be able to be of service to you."

Ted glared a few seconds more. "This is the only piece I have and I have no intentions of selling it." With that, Ted exited the van and walked cautiously to his car. The scowl remained on his face as he started his car and drove away.

"You poor bastard" Brad muttered under his breath.

Arthur called Brad on his cell phone as he and Derek were making their way out of the parking lot.

"Did you check the money?" Arthur asked.

"Of course I checked it. Do you think I would trust a guy like him?"

Derek spoke up loudly enough for Arthur to hear him. Hey, do we get to keep this money or do we have to turn it over to Sam?" He laughed a little, knowing full well the answer to the question he had just asked.

"I think it would be in our best interests if we gave it to him. I'm sure he had to pay somebody for that statue you just sold. Besides, I would certainly not want to get on the wrong side of someone like him, would you?"

"So where do you want to meet so we can get rid of the money?" Brad asked.

"There's a restaurant about a mile ahead on the right. Pull into the parking lot and I'll take it from you."

It took only a couple of minutes to get to the restaurant parking lot. Brad walked the brief case over to Arthur's car. He was relieved to be rid of it. Arthur took it to the airport and placed it in a locker. Then he took the key and put it in the bank safe deposit box that he and Sam used.

When he got home that night, he contacted Sam by e-mail and updated him as to their progress.

It was two days later when Ted switched on his computer and accessed his off shore account. As the screens appeared, he entered the appropriate codes, hoping all the time that the problem had been corrected. When his account was finally accessed, he was stunned to see that the balance was the same as before, six hundred dollars and change. He was enraged.

He grabbed the phone and began dialing the bank in Switzerland again. "Those idiots promised me they'd have it fixed by now." he muttered to himself.

A pleasant sounding young lady's voice answered the phone. "Good afternoon, Royal Trust Bank, can I help you? Her accent was thick but her speech was comprehensible"

"I need to talk to someone about my account, right now!" he demanded. Momentarily, a man's voice greeted him.

"This is Claude. How can I help you?" Again, the accent sounded different to him than it did two days ago.

"I'll tell you how you can help me. You can fix your damned computers so I can have access to my money. When the hell do you think that might happen? There was a pause.

"Excuse me?" the man responded quite curiously.

"Don't play dumb with me. The guy I talked to two days ago told me all about the computer virus and assured me that it would be corrected by today. So what's going on?"

"I'm sorry sir, but I have no idea what you are talking about. There is nothing wrong with our computers, nor has there been." Ted began to feel flushed.

"Look" he replied angrily, "I had, up until two days ago, over six million dollars in my account. Then all of a sudden, my account showed a balance of only six hundred. I called your bank and the man I spoke with said there was a computer problem that shifted the decimal over five places. He told me the bank would cover any expenses incurred as a result of the problem, and that the problem would be corrected within a day and a half. But my account still reads six hundred and not six million, and I have incurred some expenses because of it."

Ted heard the sound of computer keys as Claude began to access the account.

"What is your account number?"

Ted gave him the numbers and his balance was called up.

"I show a balance as you have indicated, but I am not aware of any computer malfunctions. Let me check your recent transactions."

Several seconds passed before the man spoke again.

"I think I have found it."

"Thank goodness." Ted replied.

"You made a transfer of six million five hundred and seventy thousand dollars from your regular account to your disbursements account three days ago. From there, you transferred the money to a bank in the United States. I can give you the name of the bank, but I do not have documentation regarding the account number at this time. Shall I fax you a copy of the transaction?" Ted was horrified.

"I never transferred any money three days ago. There must be a mistake. Check it again!"

"There's no mistake sir. Your account is pass-coded. Have you given the code number to anyone, or could someone have taken it from you?"

"No." Ted shouted. "No one even knows I have an account in your bank. You guys screwed up. Let me talk to the bank manager."

"I assure you there is no mistake, but I will give your message to the bank manager. He is out of the office today, but I will see to it that he returns your call first thing in the morning, which, considering the time difference would be..."

"I know what the time difference is." Ted interrupted, "Just have him call me as soon as possible."

He slammed the phone down, and sat tapping his fingers nervously on the table. His thoughts were soon diverted by someone knocking on his door. He got up and opened it. Standing there were two very large men in suits, the same men that had delivered the money, and the warning, two days earlier. Ted knew immediately who they were. They had a different look about them today. Last time they were merely delivery boys. Today they were collection agents.

"We were sent here by Mr. Damien to collect the money you told him you'd have by today." Ted's face turned white.

"I'm afraid there's been a little mix up with the money." he said, trying to conceal his nervousness.

"Do you got it or not?"

"Well" Ted hesitated, "not exactly."

"Do you got the interest on the money?"

"No, but I could probably..." The two men pushed their way into Ted's apartment, slamming the door behind them. From the outside, few words could be heard. But the sound of Ted's persistent screams were unmistakable.

Later that afternoon, just as Arthur was firing up his barbecue to grill some hamburgers, his phone rang. He picked it up. It was Sam.

"I know I'm taking a chance calling you on your home phone, but I wanted to talk to you."

"I figured you might." Arthur replied.

"I want to congratulate you and your friends on a job well done. But I do have one question. What happened to Ted's money?"

"Evan transferred it through several banks until he felt it was untraceable. We have set up a series of accounts in three different banks in Reno, Nevada. The account numbers are in a brief case along with the two hundred thousand he paid for the sculpture. The brief case is in a locker at the airport. The key is in the safe deposit box. We thought maybe you could find a way to reimburse some of the people Ted ripped off with the money in that account."

There was a brief moment of silence.

"You know" Sam said in a more personal tone, "you could well have kept that money for yourselves. As you said, it is untraceable. What made you want to do with it what you did?"

"The same thing that makes you do what you do I suppose." Arthur said. "Keeping it wouldn't be right. Besides, you're paying us, in a round about way. The people who lost that money need it a whole lot worse that we do."

"Once again, you have proven to me that I have selected the right men for the job. Please express my gratitude to your friends." With those words, Sam was gone. Arthur held the phone in his hand for a moment before hanging it up. No sooner had he done so, than his wife entered the kitchen.

"Was that for me?" she asked.

"No." Arthur replied, "Just business." He smiled, feeling a greater sense of accomplishment than he had on either of the last jobs.

CHAPTER TEN

In a dimly lit room in the heart of down town, a small group of solemn looking men most appearing to be in their sixties, were gathered around a large oak table. The odor of cigar smoke weighed heavy in the air. On the table was a stack of file folders. Each folder was being reviewed and evaluated. Small directional lamps on the table provided less than adequate light for anything but reading. Each man was little more than a silhouette against the light and cigar smoke. And although the faces were unrecognizable, one voice was unmistakably familiar. It is that of Sam.

"I'm not so sure we're doing the right thing here." one of the men cautioned.

"There are other avenues that could be pursued." added another.

"It's risky." Sam argued. "I am uncomfortable operating outside of our established parameters."

"It all boils down to qualifications and abilities." yet another offered. "Are both of those elements present in any one contingent?"

"I feel they are." Sam answered.

"Let's look at this judiciously. It's the only way we're going to resolve the matter." suggested a man who, to this point, had been silent. "Let's make a list of pros and cons based on the premise, should we bring in outside help."

"I say yes. This job requires experience that I feel is missing from any of our people." came a reply from the other side of the table.

"We will most certainly be compromising our security." Sam argued. "Bringing in outside help without the proper screening and under these conditions could breech our anonymity. And we all know what the consequences of that would be."

"There is not sufficient time to afford the kind of scrutiny to any new personnel that would preclude a breech from taking place." another man agreed.

"Therefore" Sam concluded, "can we assume that the risks far outweigh the benefits here?" There was a momentary silence.

"As much as I hate to admit it, you're correct." the man sitting near the head of the table replied. "I must confess though, I have serious reservations about this entire affair. But due to the personal nature and circumstances under which this has been thrust upon us, we have no choice." His voice was heavy with concern.

"Let's take a vote." Sam suggested. "All in favor of employing existing resources signify by raising your hand." It took a few moments but each of the men, though some reluctantly, raised their hands.

"Then its settled." decreed the man sitting at the head of the table. He looked toward Sam. "I trust you will make the arrangements."

Sam nodded in agreement. The man slid a file folder down the length of the table. Sam stopped it abruptly with his hand. The label on the file read 'Jensen, Martin, Williams & Marshall'. A small driver's license type photo of Arthur was paper clipped to the cover. Sam picked up the file and placed it in his brief case. As he was snapping the clasps shut, a voice spoke up that had been silent until now.

"This whole situation could be eliminated very easily and quickly, and without going to the lengths we are about to embark on."

Sam's hands went momentarily still. He looked through the haze of smoke at the man.

"And just how do you propose to accomplish this?"

"Very simply." the voice answered. "If the problem cannot be resolved through conventional methods, which it has not thus far, the problem should be eliminated at the source."

The voice of the man at the head of the table spoke up. "If you are using the word 'eliminated' as a euphemism for murder, then perhaps you should look more closely at what it is you do for a living."

There was a moment of stark silence in the room before the man spoke again. "That is not an option, and I am compelled to seriously question your intentions for making such a proposal."

"My intentions are, as they have always been, in the best interests of this organization. I was merely making a suggestion commensurate with the potential consequences that exist here."

"So noted" Sam said as he snapped the last clasp on his brief case. "I trust we are through here?"

"We are." the voice at the head of the table agreed. Then one by one, the men turned out their reading lamps and left the room.

A crowd of people made their way through the doors of the movie theater and into the parking lot. Midway through the crowd, Angie, Arthur's oldest daughter, and her date for the evening, inched their way out of the crowded lobby. Barry, the young man that had taken her to the movies that night, was a relatively clean cut, normal looking boy unlike Angie's more recent dates. That was the main reason that Arthur allowed her to go out on a school night. As they made their way to the car, Barry crossed in front of her to unlock the passenger side door. Angie was unaccustomed to this type of treatment, but she was beginning to like it. And although it was their first date, she was beginning to like Barry, too.

After closing her door, Barry made his way around the car and slid in behind the wheel.

"I had a great time." Angie told him. "But, it's getting late, and tomorrow's a school day, so I guess you'd better get me home."

"It's not that late." Barry argued. "Let's go for a drive."

"No. You'd better take me home. My father never lets me go out on a school night. If I come home when I'm supposed to, maybe he'll let me go out again during the week."

Angie looked down again at her watch. Without saying anything, Barry left the parking lot and headed down the street. Angie watched the street signs pass, noticing one in particular.

"You missed the turn." she told him. Barry ignored her, and continued on down the street driving faster than the speed limit.

"Barry" she repeated, "you missed the turn." Barry looked over at her.

"I didn't miss anything." The tone of his voice changed as he spoke. Then he began to slow down. He made a right turn into the parking lot of a grocery store and pulled into a space at the far edge of the parking lot away from the lights. He turned off the engine.

"Now" he said with a smirk, "let's have a little fun before we take you home." He reached for the buttons on her blouse and began to undo them. She slapped his hands away, shocked that he would try such a thing.

"Barry, what's the matter with you?"

"Relax." Barry answered casually, "You'll get used to it."

"The hell I will!" Angie shouted. "Take me home."

"Look bitch, either you give me what I want or you can walk home."

Barry once again reached for the buttons and once again Angie pushed his hands away. Barry glared at her for a brief second, then reached past her and opened her door. With his other hand, he pushed her backwards out of the car and onto the empty parking lot. Unable to break her fall, her head struck the pavement.

"Have it your way." Barry shouted as he pulled the door closed and started the car. Angie tried to get up, but her wrist was throbbing from the fall. By the time she made it to her feet, Barry was out of the parking lot and his tail lights had merged with the all of the others on the street.

She stood alone in the parking lot. Behind her, the lights inside the grocery store were going out, one by one. Angie wiped a tear from her eye and began walking toward the street.

It was unusual for Arthur to be up this late, but he was preparing a presentation for a stock holder's meeting. He had been working for almost three hours when he heard the back door open, then close quite loudly. He looked down at his watch. He was surprised at the length of time he had been working. He also wondered who it was that had just come in his back door. He got up and opened the door to his den just in time to see Angie quietly making her way up the stairs.

"Isn't this a little late for a school night?" Angie stopped, one foot above the other on the steps.

"Sorry dad." Something about her voice was different.

"Is everything okay?"

Upon hearing this, Angie clutched the handrail with her left hand and dropped her shoulders. She began to cry. Arthur walked up to her and gently turned her around by her arms. It always broke his heart to see his children cry.

"What's the matter?"

"I went to the movies with Barry. You met him when he picked me up tonight, remember?"

Arthur nodded.

"Well, after the movie I told him it was getting late and that I needed to get home. But when we left the theater, he was going the wrong way. I tried to tell him, but he kept telling me not to worry about it. Then he pulled into a parking lot. I asked him what we were doing here and he just looked at me. Then he tried to unbutton my shirt."

Arthur's look quickly turned from one of concern to one of rage. His clenched jaws created ripples in the skin on the sides of his face as he listened. Angie could see the anger in his eyes.

"I pushed his hand away and told him to take me home. He just looked at me and laughed. Then he told me I'd better get used to it. He reached for my shirt again and I pushed him away again. That's when he got mad and pushed me out of the car. Before I could get up off the ground, he took off." A tear trickled down Angie's cheek. "I wanted to call you but I was afraid of what you might think." she said, fighting back her tears. "So I walked home. That's why I'm so late. I'm sorry daddy."

Arthur held her close and promised her that everything would be alright. He wiped her tears away with his thumbs. Cupping her face in his hands he smiled at her as only a parent can. It's sort of an unspoken language between a parent and a child. It lasts mere seconds, but it speaks volumes.

"It's not your fault." Arthur told her. "You did the right thing. The best thing you can do now is to put it all behind you."

"I guess you're right, daddy."

Arthur watched as she made her way up the stairs and into her room. Once her door was closed, Arthur returned to the study. He was consumed with rage. He sat back down in his chair, tapping his fingers nervously on the desk. He starred at the phone for several minutes before picking it up.

Brad held the champagne bottle upside down over Carol's glass, allowing the last few drops to slowly trickle out.

"I can't believe we drank a whole bottle of champagne, and on a work night." Carol exclaimed.

"It's okay." Brad told her. "We're both past the age of consent. Besides, I've always wanted to get you drunk and take advantage of you." He leaned over and kissed her on the cheek.

"You don't need to get me drunk for that." Carol teased, as she returned the kiss. Brad sat the empty bottle on the coffee table then took Carol in his arms. He gently kissed her on the tip of her nose.

"Now, where were we?" he asked.

Before she had a chance to answer, the telephone rang. Brad pulled away, sighing deliberately before reaching for the phone.

"Hello" he said with more than a hint of exasperation.

"I know I'm disturbing you" Arthur admitted, "but I need to talk." Brad leaned back on the couch. He could tell by Arthur's voice that something was wrong.

"What's going on? You sound upset."

"You're damned right I'm upset. I'm upset to the point that I'm ready to go out and kick somebody's ass, but I can't."

"What are you talking about?"

"I'm talking about Angie."

"Is she okay?"

"Ya she's okay, no thanks to the son of a bitch she went out with tonight."

"What happened?"

"She refused to give this guy what he wanted, so he pushed her out of his car in a parking lot and drove off. She walked twelve blocks in the dark to get home."

"It sounds to me like the little bastard needs to learn some manners." Brad sneered.

"Look, I called you because I momentarily lost my temper. You're always so even headed, so I figured if I talked to you for a few minutes, you could give me one good reason why I shouldn't go to this kid's house and beat the shit out of him."

Brad thought for a moment.

"You definitely need to stay away from him. He's probably a minor, right?"

"Yes he is the little prick."

"Then leave him alone. There's a better way of dealing with him than that. We both know it, so what you need to do is forget about it for now. I'm sure you of all people should be able to come up with a better way to modify this boy's behavior."

"I doubt I can forget about it, but I think I have calmed down some." Arthur paused for a moment. "I'm sorry for disturbing you, but I felt a rage that I haven't felt for years. I didn't want to do anything I'd regret. Thanks for letting me bend your ear. I owe you one."

"Arthur, go upstairs and check on Angie, then go to bed and make mad, passionate, unbridled love to your wife. It'll make you feel better."

Arthur jokingly agreed and hung up the phone.

Brad then directed his attentions back to Carol.

"Problem?" she asked.

"Not yet, but I'm sure it will be before it's over." He leaned over towards her and took her in his arms once again. "But for now, the night is young, the champagne is empty and I have been undressing you with my eyes all evening."

Carol leaned back away from him, crossing her legs to expose even more of her near perfect thighs.

"I hate to be the one to tell you", she spoke in a low seductive voice, "but it's going to take more than just your eyes to get me undressed." She winked at him, and he smiled back at her and before long, the two had retired to the bedroom.

The coffee maker was only half through making its morning pot of coffee when Derek, unable to wait, pulled out the pot and quickly stuck his cup under the stream. When the cup was full, he pulled it out and replaced it with the pot, but not before a sufficient amount of coffee had dripped onto the burner and the tell tale sizzling sound alerted Katie to his impatience.

"Are you frying bacon or just stealing a cup of coffee?" she asked from the bedroom.

Derek shook his head. He could never hide anything from her, and with one exception, was quite happy to keep it that way. He took his ill-gotten cup of coffee and sat down at the table where the morning paper was waiting for him. Mid-way through an article in the metropolitan section, Katie walked into the kitchen. She stopped at the refrigerator for the eggs and the orange juice.

"Fried, scrambled or raw?" she asked Derek, who was absorbed in the article he was reading. Without actually hearing what she had asked him or even looking up, he answered her.

"However you want to make them is fine."

Hearing this, Katie knew that he was not listening to her and decided to have a little fun with him until he noticed.

"Raw it is." she said. "Oh, and honey" she continued.

"I'm listening" Derek answered as he searched through the paper for page eighteen and the rest of the article.

"The paper wants me to go undercover in a strip club. I'll have to dance naked in front of hundreds of vile, disgusting men who will lust after me." She looked over at Derek who, by this time had found the rest of the story he was reading.

"Really?" he commented, having no idea of what she had just said.

"Oh, and honey" she continued, "My boss said if I'd sleep with him, I would get a promotion. I think it's a good idea, don't you?"

Without missing a word of the article, Derek responded, "Whatever you want to do, honey."

Katie smiled and shook her head as she broke the eggs into the frying pan. Before she had a chance to throw the empty egg shells into the trash, the phone rang. This did get Derek's attention. Katie answered it. Derek watched and listened as Katie's face lit up. She agreed with whatever had been said, then thanked the person and hung up the phone.

"I just got permanently assigned to a great story." she said with excitement.

Derek knew what she was talking about. He had seen some of the research she had done and had even told Brad about it.

"What is it?" he asked.

"The paper is doing a story on a possible connection between what happened to the man that kidnapped that little girl, remember, you read about it in the paper?"

Derek nodded. "And what happened to the man that broke into our house. They were afraid that I might not want to work on the story because of what happened to me, but I told them that as long as I don't have to talk to that man, I'd love to."

Derek thought for a moment. "Are you sure you'll be okay with it?" he asked.

"Sure I will. Besides, it's a great opportunity for me."

Katie seemed to be quite excited about the prospect of doing research for the story.

If she only knew, Derek thought to himself. But he smiled and assured her that she would do a great job.

"I'm kind of interested in that myself." he commented as he picked the paper up again. "Can you let me know what you find out?"

"Sure. It'll be nice to have another opinion. You can be my sounding board."

Derek began reading the paper once again, glancing at Katie over the top of it from time to time. He was somewhat relieved that he would be able to keep an eye on what was being discovered, but he was also nervous that she might discover what they had all worked so hard to keep secret.

Before long, breakfast was ready and Derek folded the paper and laid it down on the chair next to him. Visible was the headline, which would escape his attention, 'Long Time Senator Linked to Multi-Million Dollar Bribery Scandal'.

Breakfast was also being served at Arthur's house. Arthur sat at the table, sipping a cup of coffee as he reviewed the material for his presentation that morning. His son Todd sat next to him eating a bowl of cereal. Sandy was busy making pancakes at the stove when Angie came downstairs and took her place at the table. Arthur looked at her and smiled a little smile.

"How are you this morning?"

Angie smiled back at him. "I'm okay." Although nothing was said, they both knew what each other meant.

"I didn't hear you come in last night. You did make it home before ten thirty, didn't you?" Sandy asked.

Before Angie had a chance to reply, Arthur answered. "She was home on time. I was working in the study and I heard her come in."

Angie glanced at him with a look of relief on her face. She didn't want to lie to her mother, but she didn't want to tell her the truth either. Then Todd spoke up.

"Well, I heard her walk up the stairs and it was more like eleven....."

Arthur looked over at his son with that 'if you continue, you're in trouble' look.

"It was me you heard coming up the stairs at eleven thirty." Arthur told him.

"No it wasn't." Todd continued. "It was Angie."

Todd's skills at lying had not yet fully developed, apparently a common trait among children his age. Before he could say any more, Arthur interrupted.

"If you were still awake at eleven o'clock, then perhaps you need to go to bed earlier."

He looked Todd straight in the eye. Todd knew the battle was over and conceded.

"I guess it was you, not Angie." He was learning.

After hearing that, Arthur focused his attention back to his reports. He looked up again momentarily at Angie, who looked back at him with gratitude. Arthur was doing his best to put the incident behind him as Brad suggested, but it wasn't easy.

"Who's ready for pancakes?" Sandy asked as she made her way to the table. Arthur put down the papers he had been reading and reached for the syrup. Last night's episode was over and forgotten. The only real casualty was Arthur.

"So, how was your date last night?" Angie's mother asked as she sat down to her own breakfast.

"Oh, it was fine." Angie said, offering little emotion. Arthur stopped chewing and looked over at his wife.

"Did you enjoy the movie?"

"Ya, it was great. You'd have liked it. Maybe we should rent it when it comes out on video."

Arthur resumed chewing, hoping the topic would soon change.

"So tell me about your date, what was his name, Barry?" Angie's mother continued.

Arthur's fork stopped mid way to his mouth at his wife's question.

"Yes, his name was Barry. But I don't think I'll be seeing him anymore. We just don't have that much in common."

Arthur heaved a noticeable sigh of relief and continued with his breakfast.

"Did something happen?" Sandy asked. Arthur dropped his fork into his plate which splattered syrup all over his white shirt.

"Oh crap." he yelled. Sandy immediately got up and headed for the sink. She ran a dish rag under hot water and proceeded to try and get the stains out of Arthur's shirt. He glanced over at Angie who was quickly finishing up her breakfast. Arthur knew she would be done momentarily and the conversation which a moment ago seemed inevitable would be avoided. By the time Sandy had finished, Angie had left the table and was gathering her books for school.

CHAPTER ELEVEN

Winter seems to be lasting an unusually long time this year, Brad thought to himself as he made the trip from the parking garage into the lounge of the treatment center. The familiar silence of the lounge was interrupted by the sound of rustling papers. Brad made his way through the maze of chairs and couches looking for the source of the noise. As he rounded the corner, there was Arthur, holding some papers in his hands and pacing back and forth in front of the empty seats.

"This is not good." Brad spoke, interrupting the silence. "Every time you get here early, something's wrong."

"No, nothing is wrong." Arthur said, taking a seat in his usual spot.

"Then why are you here so early?"

"I got a phone call from Sam. He said he had something for me so I figured he'd get it to me like he usually does."

"Well, did he? Brad asked.

"No." Arthur responded. "He either sends me an email or has someone slip an envelope through my back seat window while I'm stopped at a red light."

"Are you telling me Sam can control the traffic signals in order to slip an envelope through your window? Brad asked mockingly.

"Would it surprise you if he could?" Arthur asked quite seriously.

Brad laughed a little. "Now that you mention it, no it wouldn't."

As their two minds momentarily drifted, the lounge doors opened, then closed again. Two sets of foot steps grew closer.

As they turned the corner, Brad and Arthur, who had been expecting to see Derek and Evan, were somewhat surprised to see instead two men dressed in suits and white trench coats.

"Excuse me" the taller of the two interrupted, "do either of you gentlemen drive a blue Volvo, license number KLA-412?"

"I do." Arthur replied, "What's the problem?"

"Oh, no problem buddy, you just left your lights on." With that, the two men turned and walked back toward the doors.

Arthur sat thinking for a moment. *It's daytime. Why would my headlights even be on? Besides, I didn't hear the buzzer when I opened the door.*

"Oh well" he said as he pulled his coat on, "I'd better go and check it out."

Arthur walked through the doors into the parking garage. The air was cold. He headed down the row where he had parked. A pair of glowing tail lights led him right to his car.

He unlocked and opened the door just enough to reach the light switch. Having turned off the lights he started to close the door when something caught his eye. He stopped and opened the door again. A note was taped to his steering wheel. He got in and sat down behind the wheel to read it.

'The information regarding your next assignment cannot be emailed. You will find it at the airport in a locker on the east end of the terminal. The locker number and the key have been placed in the bank safe deposit box. Please review the material, after which you will contact me by e-mail immediately.' There was no signature, though Arthur knew who it was from.

Brad was looking down at his watch when he heard the door open. Moments later, Arthur appeared around the corner. He was still holding the note that was taped to his steering wheel.

"Bet you can't guess what this is." he said to Brad, holding the note in the air.

"What?" Brad asked.

"Our next job"

"Son of a bitch" Brad grumbled. "If I'd known we were going to be doing so much of this I don't know as I would have accepted Sam's invitation to this party." Arthur sat back down. As he settled back in the chair he smiled a little.

"You know Brad" he said, still smiling, "I kind of like this stuff."

"I don't think I'm cut out for it on any sort of regular basis myself." Brad confessed.

Arthur thought for a moment. "Have you given any thought to writing about it?"

Brad sat uncomfortably silent, not knowing quite how to respond. "You know, I never thought of that." Brad was lying. Although he had originally decided against it, he had kept a detailed log of every minute of each assignment. It was on a CD, protected by a pass code.

"You'd have to be very careful." Arthur cautioned, "You don't want to write anything that would get us caught."

"I'll give it some thought." Brad said. "Maybe it would be worth writing about. I'll have to see."

The conversation was interrupted, much to Brad's relief, by the sound of the doors opening once again. This time it was Derek and Evan. Their voices could be heard, growing louder as they approached.

"How can you do something like that with two women at the same time?" Derek was asking Evan, their voices growing ever louder.

"It's easy! You just have to be sure to pay an equal amount of attention to both of them so neither gets bored or feels left out." Derek was shaking his head as they rounded the corner.

"I'd be so nervous with two women I'd probably never be able to get it up." Arthur, hearing only the last part of the conversation, spoke up.

"Don't let any of Evan's bad habits rub off on you Derek." he warned. "You know he wrote the book on deviant sexual behavior. I'm sure there's a chapter in there somewhere named after him."

Evan finally spoke in his own defense.

"You guys are just jealous because you don't have the same sexual appetite as I do."

Brad, hearing this, decided to add his two cents worth.

"You know, Evan is what I call 'sexually obese'. He gets more than anyone, but it never seems to curb his appetite!"

Before the conversation could degenerate any further, the doctor entered the lounge, and shortly thereafter the treatments began.

After the treatments, the four men walked down the corridor towards the door. Derek was still in awe of Evan for having enjoyed the pleasures of two women at the same time last night. Arthur, hearing enough of this conversation, took it upon himself to end it.

"I can settle this real quick." he announced. "Evan, do you have two dicks?"

"Of course not." Evan replied.

"Then you don't need two women." Everyone laughed, which was unusual for them to do so immediately after a treatment.

"You can't argue with that logic." Brad admitted. Before the four went their separate ways, Arthur broke the news about the next assignment. They agreed, as they usually did, to meet at Evan's house after Arthur had obtained the details of the job from the locker at the airport.

The sound of the laughter and applause faded to a dull roar as Lenny made his way down the hallway from the stage to his dressing room. The show had gone very well as most of them do. People standing in the hall slapped him on the back as he walked past, commenting on how much they enjoyed his performance. He opened the door to his dressing room and was greeted by his manager and several of his traveling companions. A small buffet of cold cuts and snacks had been delivered and for a short time, everyone ate and laughed at Lenny's seemingly endless reserve of jokes and one-liners. Within an hour, he was saying good night to the last of his guests. He closed the door and locked it behind him.

Lenny walked to an adjoining room and he opened a large suitcase that was lying on a couch. From it he removed a notebook computer. Sitting at a small table, he plugged the computer in and connected a wireless card. In a moment the screen was illuminated and Lenny was busily typing. Within seconds he was on line. He quickly typed in a short message. The e-mail address it went to was that belonging to Sam.

Arthur had not been to the airport since the end of the Ted Messina business. He really hated the trip. The closest parking place was a brisk ten minute walk from the terminal. As badly as Arthur needed the exercise, he complained under his breath the whole way.

As he entered the building, he looked up at the signs. Following the arrows, he headed to the east wing where the lockers were. He removed a key from his pocket. It was the key he had gotten from the bank safe deposit box. His eyes scanned the lockers. It didn't take long to find the one with the matching number. Opening the door he found a small gym bag. He took the bag and promptly left the airport.

The freeway traffic leading away from the airport was very heavy. As curious as Arthur was as to the contents of the bag, he left it closed and kept both hands on the wheel.

The trip home took over an hour. When he arrived, he locked the bag in the trunk of his car for safe keeping, and to avoid questions about its contents by his wife. It was almost dinner time as he walked into the house from the garage, and although his curiosity had been peaked since he picked the bag up, it would have to wait a little longer.

Derek was putting the finishing touches to dinner as Katie came home. She had called him earlier to tell him she would be late. She sounded very excited, mentioning something about the new assignment in the research department that she spoke of that morning at breakfast.

"I'm home" she announced, closing the front door behind her.

"In the kitchen" Derek hollered.

Katie walked up behind him and hugged him.

"We're finally beginning to make some progress." she told him.

"Well, tell me about it." Derek continued to stir the largest of three pots that were steaming on the stove.

"You know the paper is doing a follow up story on the man that attacked me and what happened to him, and the guy that kidnapped and murdered that little girl."

Derek's eyes widened and he stopped stirring momentarily. He looked up, starring intently at the steam as it rose into the air. He knew she was working on the story, but his heart reacted the same way each time the subject was brought up. Katie, who was still behind him with her arms around him, began to explain.

"One of our reporters has come up with some photographs taken by a security camera that might be the people we are writing about. Isn't that great?"

Derek's hands were trembling slightly as he responded.

"Yes, yes of course it is. Have you seen them yet?" he asked, trying to maintain his composure.

"Not yet." Katie answered. "They are being printed from the video tape. They'll be ready in a couple of days."

"Well, it sounds quite interesting. Will you let me know how it turns out? I'm kind of curious about this myself." Katie leaned around him and kissed him on his cheek.

"Of course I will. We have no secrets from each other, remember?"

Without answering, Derek turned the burners off and announced dinner was ready. It was going to be difficult to eat as he had suddenly lost his appetite.

Pictures, he thought to himself. *Where the hell was the security camera?*

Katie, who had momentarily disappeared, walked back into the kitchen with Derek Jr.

"Look who's awake."

The baby smiled as his mother held him. The temptation had never been greater to tell Katie what had been going on, but he knew that would cause more problems than it would solve. So for now it would have to remain a secret, but deep down inside Derek wondered how much longer he would be able to keep up this charade, and more importantly, what would happen when Katie found out the truth. These thoughts haunted him constantly.

Arthur helped his wife clear the table after dinner. His kids, much to his surprise, were too busy with homework to help. But that was okay as his schedule had kept him away from home more than usual lately and he was feeling a little guilty about that. The phone rang as he was about to finish. The call was for Sandy. Arthur finished up in the kitchen, and then whispered to her that he had work to do and pointed to the study. She nodded, as her conversation continued.

Arthur closed and locked the door, the last cup of coffee from the pot balancing delicately in his hand. He sat down at his desk after taking a sip, and then reached for the bag that had been hidden in his trunk. He unzipped it and removed a large brown pouch with a rubber band around it. The rubber band broke as he tried to slide it off. He tipped the pouch up slightly to allow the contents to slide out into his hand. They too, were contained by a rubber band. The top page was stamped 'Confidential'.

Beyond the cover sheet was a placard with a man's picture on it. The man was obviously running for public office. He was obviously already in office and looking to be re-elected to another term. It read, 'Re-elect Senator Ryan Edloe.' Beneath those words was a picture of Mr. Edloe. Beneath that were the words 'Strong, Honest Leadership'.

The pages that followed compiled a list of corporations which were substantial contributors to Mr. Edloe's past campaigns. The list was quite impressive. There were several oil companies, a stock brokerage corporation, three insurance companies and five hospital chains.

Arthur was not naive enough to believe that campaign contributions are made simply because a corporation likes a particular candidate. A campaign contribution is an investment, and as with any investment, there is expected a return. If there is no return, then there is no reason to invest. Arthur understood this better than most.

The following twenty six pages were a chronological listing of legislation that Mr. Edloe voted on, how he voted, and pieces of legislation he authored and how they were voted upon. The particular pieces of legislation that Mr. Edloe had authored had been high-lighted in yellow. Arthur counted seventeen highlighted portions in the twenty six pages. As he read, he began to see a connection, a common thread which inter-laced all of Mr. Edloe's bills. All of them, either directly or indirectly, contained language that affected the way government run hospitals were funded. Each piece of legislation cut a little further into the budget of the hospitals by reducing the funding provided by the government. The cuts were in many forms, from a reduction in the percentage of reimbursement for medical supplies to an increase of the mandatory quota of non-payment care that was provided to patients who had no money to pay for it.

The next pages contained photo copies of newspaper articles. All of the articles dealt with the closing of government run hospitals, and their replacement with private hospitals owned and operated by managed care corporations. It was becoming abundantly clear what was going on here. Another article revealed a piece of legislation that had been passed in the middle of the night that significantly reduced the number of 'non-compensatory patients' (that is those who cannot pay) each managed care facility was required to treat in order to comply with and still receive government subsidies.

Another article applauded him as being 'A General in the war against waste in our hospital system.' Still another labeled him as 'the taxpayer's best friend.'

The final article was a very recent one, from just a day or two ago. It alleged Senator Edloe to be involved in a multi-million dollar kick back scheme with several managed care corporations.

The final page was a hand-written note. It began, 'The decision to involve you four men in this assignment did not come without great forethought and no little degree of agonizing and indecision. Before I proceed, let me tell you that a successful completion to this task will relieve all of you of any further obligation to this organization. The nature of this assignment is extremely delicate. Our very existence is at stake, and more importantly, our anonymity. The man you have been reading about has accepted millions of dollars illegally from companies that have benefited from his legislation.

There is enough evidence against this man to convict him tomorrow but he is, through an unfortunate twist of misplaced trust, aware of our endeavor and more importantly, our identities. We are concerned that once these investigations begin, he will panic and attempt to use his former relationship with us as leverage to help himself out of his situation. We are in a position to forestall these investigations into ambiguity, but we do not believe this to be the prudent course to follow at this time.

He realizes the political value of the information he has, and he won't hesitate to use it. What you and your associates must do is to discredit him to the point that his credibility is virtually non-existent. I need not remind you that if he is successful in exposing us, he will be exposing all of us, you included. He has not approached us yet, but I am quite confident that he will, and soon. Therefore it behooves us all to accomplish this task as swiftly and expeditiously as possible. I await your response as eagerly as I anticipate your success.' It was signed, 'Sam'.

There was a PS. 'Due to the delicate nature of this assignment, I will be providing you with the services of a long-time member of our team. He will contact you at the appropriate time. Good luck and God be with you.

Arthur sat back in his chair. His coffee was cold. He was stunned at what he had just read. He had no idea how to approach this task. All of the previous assignments were successful because of manipulation and timing. This one was altogether different. And who was this person who was going to help them? This was all becoming very bizarre.

Arthur looked down at his watch. He had been in the study for over an hour. Quickly, he placed all of the documents back into the bag and locked it in his bottom desk drawer. As he opened the door to the study, he was relieved to hear Sandy still talking on the phone.

CHAPTER TWELVE

The Sunday morning sun filtered through the curtains in Brad's bedroom making a familiar pattern of lines and shadows on the wall next to the dresser. Brad's eyes slowly opened, then closed again trying to adjust to the daylight. When he was finally able, his eyes focused on the patterns of light on the wall. He looked at it for a moment, then smiled and rolled over. Carol, who was lying next to him under the covers, responded to his touch and moved closer to him before opening her eyes. Brad leaned over and softly kissed her. She looked up at him and snuggled closer.

"So the weather was pretty bad last night, huh?" she asked in her best patronizing voice.

"Oh yes" Brad answered, "the rain was blinding. There must have been at least a tenth of an inch, much too dangerous for driving, especially for someone as special as you." He kissed her again on the forehead, and then got out of bed.

"Leaving so soon?"

"Oh no, just going to get the newspaper off the steps."

He returned moments later with the Sunday paper still wrapped in plastic. He jumped back into bed then slid the paper out of the wrapper offering Carol first choice. She went straight for the comics. Brad smiled, picking up the entertainment section, as he did every Sunday, to see whose books had made the top ten. He was less than half way through the list when his phone rang. He considered not answering it, but with great hesitation, picked it up. It was Arthur.

"Good morning, Brad. I didn't wake you, did I?"

"No" Brad said emphatically, "but you are disturbing me!"

"Did Carol spend the night with you?" Brad's silence indicated consent. "Then I'll be brief. We need to get together. Remember, we have another assignment."

"Damn." Brad mumbled under his breath, being careful not create any suspicion on Carol's part. "When?"

"Sometime this week, I'll check with the others and let you know."

"Alright." he begrudgingly agreed, then hung up the phone.

"Problems?" Carol asked.

"No, it was Arthur." he said, picking up the paper again. "I bought some stock that's losing money and we need to dump it. I'm meeting with him next week."

His answer seemed to pacify Carol, so he left it at that. He glanced over at her as she re-focused her attention on the comics. He hated having so many secrets so early in the relationship, but it was in everyone's best interests at this point for things to stay just as they were.

The following day saw another typical Monday morning at Arthur's office. Monday's seemed to be the worst day of the week. Everyone that invested with the company had the weekend to ponder the rational of their stock choices and many, come Monday, were changing their minds. Arthur was less than half way through his Monday morning routine when his secretary buzzed him, laughing hysterically.

"I'm sorry to interrupt you" she said, trying to regain her composure, "but there's someone here to see you."

"Are you having an attack or something?" Arthur asked. "And who is it that wants to see me?"

"Oh, I'm sorry" she laughed, "but this man..."

"Who is he?" Arthur asked impatiently. Through the laughter, he could hear a man's voice speaking very quickly. He could hear others, besides his secretary, laughing as well. Regaining her composure once again she attempted to announce the visitor.

"His name is Lenny. He says he is a friend of Brads'." Arthur knew right away who he was and why his secretary was laughing. He leaned toward his phone and spoke.

"Send him in, then go to the ladies room and splash some cold water in your face."

Arthur pushed the button to hang up the phone. Within a few seconds, Lenny walked into his office.

"Lenny" Arthur greeted him with a handshake. "This is a surprise. To what do I owe the pleasure?"

The two sat down, Arthur behind his desk, and Lenny in a chair in front and to the left of it.

"I need to talk to you about something." Lenny began in an uncharacteristically serious tone. Arthur leaned forward in his chair.

"You want to invest some of that wealth you're gathering?"

"No, nothing like that" Lenny answered. "I'll explain it all to you as soon as you get off the phone." Arthur sat for a moment and looked at him, not understanding what Lenny meant.

"But.... I'm not on the phone." he said, looking bewildered. At that moment, Arthur's private line rang. He looked down at the phone, then back up at Lenny.

"You'd better get that." Lenny advised.

Arthur, still amazed at the coincidence, picked up the phone. It was Sam.

"Arthur good morning, how are you this morning?"

"Quite confused" Arthur confessed.

"Well that's why I called. I'm sure you have a lot of questions, and I'll do my best to clarify things for you."

Arthur leaned back in his chair, as Sam continued.

"You will recall in my memo, the one I included in the package you picked up from the airport, I informed you that I would be providing you with some help. Well, say hello to Lenny. He has been with our organization for seven years now, and will be an integral part of this assignment."

At this point, Arthur interrupted.

"With all due respect, how can Lenny help us? His greatest attribute is making people laugh."

"I must disagree with you, Arthur. That would be his second greatest attribute. Lenny holds instructor grade certifications in five different forms of martial arts. He spent six years with 'special forces' performing search and rescue." Arthur looked at Lenny in disbelief. Sam continued.

"Put the phone on speaker if you would you please."

Arthur obliged by pushing the button on the phone, then hanging it up.

"Lenny, show Arthur your tattoo."

Sam paused to allow Lenny the time to roll up his sleeve, which he did, revealing a Special Forces tattoo. Arthur leaned forward, recognizing it immediately. Then he leaned toward the phone and spoke.

"You know Sam I don't understand why we were selected for this assignment. I'm sure you have more experienced people at your disposal. We've only done a couple of jobs, so why us?"

"Arthur, you have demonstrated an above average ability to get the job done with a remarkable degree of anonymity. And since the very existence of our organization depends on both of these things, you were the logical candidates. Now, having said that, do you have any ideas on how to remedy this situation?"

Arthur responded immediately. "No, I don't. And that's what scares me. The other ones were relatively simple. The ideas came to me right away, but this one is different. I have nothing worked out to this point. That's why I hadn't contacted you yet."

Sam responded to Arthur's concerns with confidence and understanding. "Have you scheduled a meeting with your friends as yet?"

"I have; Thursday night at Evan's place."

"Excellent." Sam exclaimed, "I want you to take Lenny with you and explain to them his role in this, and between the five of you, I'm confident you will come up with a plan. I will keep you updated as to the status of Mr. Edloe. But you must understand time is of the essence. And as I indicated previously, we all have a personal interest in this." Arthur thought for a moment then asked a question of Sam.

"How did Senator Edloe learn your identity? Did he work for your organization at one time?"

Lenny slowly shook his head, indicating to Arthur that his question should not have been asked.

"Unless you thrive on disappointment that is a question you must not ask."

Arthur looked over at Lenny, who had an 'I told you so' look on his face as Sam continued.

"Please keep me updated as to your progress. We all have a great personal stake in this and we must be successful at all costs. I will contact you after your meeting Thursday. Till then I bid you good luck and God's speed." Sam hung up.

Arthur reached over and pushed the button, silencing the dial tone. He looked over at Lenny, who was rolling down his sleeve.

"This just keeps getting better and better."

"Get used to it." Lenny advised, as he stood up. "Can you pick me up Thursday night? I have no idea where Evan lives."

"Sure."

Lenny walked over to the door. "I'll call you when I get checked into a hotel."

Arthur nodded, still somewhat bewildered, as Lenny let himself out. The door closed and Arthur sat in the silence, his bewilderment rapidly turning to concern.

At a small desk in an office across town, Katie began another day of work on a new project. In front of her were files on the two incidents she had been researching. The newspaper had taken it upon itself to try and establish a link between them. The logical place to begin is by interviewing the two men affected by the actions of these mystery men. Talking to the man imprisoned for the murder of the child was nothing out of the ordinary, but talking to the man that assaulted her was another matter all together. For that, she solicited the help of one of the reporters.

The trip to the prison took less than an hour. Katie had called ahead to make sure that Jerry would agree to talk to her. She asked the questions to herself over and over in her mind that she would ask Jerry. By the time she reached the prison, she had narrowed them down to the ones that would best serve the twenty minutes she was allowed to spend with him.

As she entered the main entrance to the facility, she was stopped and her purse searched. The batteries and tape were removed from her recorder to ensure nothing was being smuggled in. These procedures came as somewhat of a surprise to her, but if she wanted the interview, they were necessary. Before she was allowed into the visiting area she was patted down by a female guard. Finally, having accommodated all of the prison's precautions she was led to a room. In the room was a row of small glass booths. In each booth was a telephone with no buttons. Katie was instructed to go to booth number six and wait. Within a few minutes, Jerry was led into the room and sat down opposite her. They both picked up the phone. Katie spoke first.

"If you don't mind, I'd like to record this conversation for the sake of accuracy."

Jerry shrugged his shoulders. "It don't make a shit to me." he said. "Did you bring the cigarettes?"

"I gave them to the guard at the front desk." Katie attached a microphone to the receiver and began the questions. "I want to ask you a few questions about the incident you related to the police that took place February twenty first of this year. How many men was there that came to see you that night?"

"Four." he replied.

"And did you get a look at any of them?"

"Only the guy that rang my door bell"

"What did he look like?" Katie asked.

"Oh, maybe five foot eight, hundred and fifty pounds, long blond hair and a blond moustache."

"So he was white?"

"Ya, he was a white guy."

"Was there anything out of the ordinary that you remember about him, a scar, a mole or something like that?"

"Ya, he had a scar on his forehead, kinda like what you get when you're a kid and you got the chicken pox and you scratch one you know, it leaves a little dent."

"That's not really out of the ordinary." Katie responded, "Lots of people have a chicken pox scar. My husband has one."

Jerry straightened up in his chair, his demeanor suddenly changing. "Well maybe it was your husband at my door that night."

Katie, sensing his frustration, moved on to the next question.

"What about the others?"

"They all wore ski masks. The biggest one seemed to be in charge. He did all the talking, that son of a bitch. One of the other guys hooked up a box that shocked the shit out of me and the other guy set up a video camera. Those two didn't say too much."

"Is there anything special you remember about the man who seemed to be the leader? What color were his eyes? Could you see a moustache or a beard through the ski mask, anything like that?"

"His eyes were brown, I remember that. The rest, well, I was not paying much attention to how he looked because I thought the guy was going to kill me!" Jerry's voice grew angered again as he recalled the episode, but Katie persisted, trying to get as many details as possible.

"What about the guy with the camera, do you recall anything special about him?"

"Naw, I didn't pay much attention to him. He really didn't say anything, except for when he was folding up the tripod."

"What did he say?"

"One of the legs got stuck. It wouldn't go up or something."

"So what did he say?" Katie repeated.

"Something like, 'it's my damn luck', or something"

"That's all he said the whole time?"

"That's all I remember lady. You try being tied up and almost killed and see how much you remember."

Katie knew exactly what he was talking about. And although her eyes may have given it away, she never let on to him that she knew.

"Let's talk about the guy who set up the device that shocked you. Is there anything out of the ordinary about him?"

"Nothin' special. He must have known a little about electricity though."

"Why do you say that?" Katie asked.

"Before he plugged the thing in, he stuck some kind of tester or something into the outlet. He tested a couple of them before he found one he liked."

"Did the box that shocked you look like something you could buy in a store?"

"No, it was definitely homemade."

"How could you tell?"

"The labels"

"What do you mean the labels?" Katie questioned.

"The labels under the knobs were made with a label maker, you know, the kind you can buy anywhere. You know what I'm talking about."

"Yes, I think I do." Katie checked her watch to see how much time remained. "Who do you think did this?" she asked.

"Beats the hell out of me. Whoever they were, they were damned smart."

"Why do you say that?"

"Cause they're the ones that screwed me over, but I'm the one in jail!" Jerry's eyes drifted down Katie's blouse as she leaned towards the glass.

"Is there anything else that stands out in your mind?"

"Something's standing out all right, but it's not in my mind. If you were on the other side of this glass I'd show you what it is!"

Sensing that she had gotten all the information was going to get, Katie thanked him and left.

"Come back anytime sweetheart." he called to her as she made her way out of the room and down the corridor.

The waitress refilled the tall ice tea glasses as she picked up the empty plates from the table.

"Can I get you gentlemen anything else?" she asked, tearing the ticket from her pad.

"No thanks, we're fine." Nathan Harwin, a reporter for the paper answered. He took the ticket and laid it down on the table next to his note pad.

"Now" he began, "let's talk about your little adventure in race relations."

"Very funny" Vince sneered. His full name was Vincent Elias Dugay. He was the man convicted of assaulting Katie and the man whose official punishment was probation and community service.

"When the police recovered your car, according to their report, it had a flat tire."

"That's right. That's why I pulled off the road that night."

"But the report also states that there was no leak in the tire. The air had simply been let out of it."

"Ya, that's what they say, but I was there. I know what happened, and I'm telling you, it went flat and I had to pull off the road."

"Okay, so you pulled off the road. Then what happened?"

"I got out and walked around the car to the flat tire, on the rear passenger side. I knelt down. It was dark and I didn't have a flash light, but I could see that the tire was flat. While I was still looking at it, a car pulls off the road in front of me and these three guys get out."

"You're sure there were three."

"Ya, I'm sure there were three. The bigger one walked in front of the other two. He's the one that asked me if I needed any help. I told him no and that I could take care of it, and then the three of them jumped me. They put a rag over my nose. It had something on it that stunk something awful. I must have passed out or something, 'cause that's all I remember until I woke up in the back seat of that car with the sheets on."

"You mean the Klan outfit?"

"Ya, the Klan outfit. The next thing I know these big black dudes are dragging me out of the car. They drug me off into an alley and worked me over real good. What chance did I have against them? There was three of them and only one of me. The next thing I remember after that was waking up in the hospital. I was in there for three and a half weeks."

"Your story is dramatically different from the story told by the three guys that beat you up." Nathan remarked. "They claim that you came up to them and threatened them, and that they merely defended themselves."

"That's a crock of shit."

"Maybe so, but the cops bought it."

"Ya, but it's only cause I got a record. They never believe you once you got a record. Besides, I got proof. I'm missing a valve stem cap."

"A what?"

"A valve stem cap. You know the little thing that screws on the valve stem on your tires. I got chrome ones and that one was missing. Someone took it off."

"Did you tell this to the police?"

"Sure I did, but they didn't believe that either." Vince picked up his glass and took a sip of his ice tea, then sat the glass back down in the very same spot from which he picked it up, resting it gently on top of the thin ring of water left on the table.

"Do you always do that?"

"Do what?" Vince asked.

"Set your glass down in the same place that you picked it up from?"

"It's a habit I guess. I used to be an accountant. I do everything the same way every time. It's just something I got used to."

"Why aren't you an accountant any more?"

"I got caught with my fingers in the cookie jar, so to speak."

"Embezzlement?"

"Embezzlement is such a harsh word." Vince said, picking his glass up for another sip. "I prefer to call it a temporary lapse of judgment resulting in a misappropriation of funds."

"What have you been doing since?"

"What ever it takes to survive." He returned the glass once again to the same spot.

"Let's talk for a little bit about the larger of the three men, the one that spoke to you. Can you tell me anything specific about him?"

"No. It was dark, and they didn't park behind me like they should have if they really wanted to help me change my tire. All I know is what I told you." Nathan finished writing and laid his pen down on the table.

"Personally, I believe you. I don't think you could make up a story like this. But whoever did this to you didn't leave any tracks, and we're all left asking ourselves, why? Why did this happen to you? Did you piss somebody off? Could this have been some sort of retribution for what you did to that woman?"

"I didn't think anybody was home at that house. She got in my way, that's all."

"Do you think it could have been her husband, or father that did this to you?"

"Naw, her old man's got some kind of disease. I saw him in court. It wasn't him."

"Then who?"

"Like I told you, it beats the hell out of me." Although Nathan had no more questions to ask, he knew there was much more to this than anyone realized.

"You really lucked out getting probation again. I'm surprised they didn't put you back in prison."

"Me too, I thought I was done for. This is not exactly my first offense you know. I guess something changed the judge's mind. It doesn't matter to me though. I'm just glad I didn't get locked up again."

Vince finished his tea, and then stood up as if to leave. He hesitated a moment as Nathan gave him a twenty for meeting with him. He tucked the bill away in his shirt pocket and disappeared out of the diner.

As Arthur turned into Evan's drive and stopped to enter the security code at the gate, he noticed most of the snow on the grounds had melted, exposing the brown dormant grass that had been blanketed for so many months. Lenny leaned forward and looked out through the windshield at the house.

"Damn, is this Evan's house?"

"It's one of several that his father owns." Arthur said, entering an access code on the key pad outside the gate.

"What does his father do for a living?"

Arthur turned to Lenny and answered, "He makes money."

Moments later Arthur and Lenny were ringing the bell at Evan's front door. A small red light on the intercom next to the door lit up as Evan buzzed them in.

The two entered the house, Lenny following Arthur through the main hallway to the den. Lenny couldn't ever remember being in a house of this magnitude before in his life. His eyes scanned both sides of the vast hallway. Each was lined with artwork and sculptures, and busts on intricately detailed pedestals. The ceiling in the hall was twelve feet high and arched, with hand carved trim boarding its perimeter. Lenny was so preoccupied he stumbled into Arthur who had stopped outside the door to the den. Arthur turned to Lenny and asked if he was ready. He nodded, and Arthur opened the door.

Brad and Derek were stirring their drinks at the bar when the door opened. Evan was the first to catch sight of Lenny. He looked at Arthur as if he were out of his mind.

"You brought a friend I see".

Upon hearing that, Brad and Derek both turned to see what Evan was talking about.

"Lenny" Brad exclaimed, "what are you doing here?"

Arthur closed the door behind them.

Lenny stood conspicuously out of place in this group. There was a look of shock and curiosity on everyone's face. It was as if they had all been caught doing something they weren't supposed to be doing.

"Lenny has something he wants to talk to us about." Arthur said, taking a seat at the bar.

Lenny looked down at the floor a moment before speaking. "I'm sure you're all a little surprised to see me here, especially you Brad. Let me start by saying I have been a member of Sam's organization for seven years now. He recruited me in much the same way as he did you. I settled a score, and somehow he found out about it."

"You, you're involved in this? What did you do?" Brad asked.

"Well, at the time my sister's oldest son was in high school. He was a good kid. He studied hard, and had the grades to get into any college he wanted. His dad had been killed in a car accident when he was little, so my sister had pretty much raised him herself. Anyway, not long after he got into high school, he was approached by a local gang member to join. He told him thanks, but no thanks. Unfortunately guys like that don't take no for an answer. They harassed him constantly, at school and at home. It got so he couldn't walk out the door without a car following him or someone threatening him. One Saturday afternoon it got violent. He was riding his bicycle home from the store when six of them confronted him. They told him that unless he joined, they were going to kick his ass. Well, that was putting it mildly.

A patrol officer found him barely alive. After several weeks in the hospital, and over a year of physical therapy, he was almost back to normal. There was a witness to the beating, a woman who saw the whole thing from her upstairs window. She gave a statement to the police, but the day the trial began, I could tell by the look on her face that they had gotten to her. Her testimony was deliberately ambiguous, despite her earlier statement. So, the boys walked."

"How did you react when you heard that verdict?" Arthur asked.

"Let me put it this way. I was almost charged with contempt of court. I made my feelings known to the judge in no uncertain terms. Were it not for the fact that I was a member of the immediate family, I would have been arrested."

"That's what would have happened with us if I hadn't grabbed Arthur and pulled him back into his seat. He was ready to do the same thing." Brad looked over at Arthur who sat shaking his head.

"Ya, that judge looked me square in the eye. I thought for sure I was going to jail." Lenny continued. "I was lucky that day I guess. But I just couldn't let it go. So, I decided to do what I had to do to get past it."

Evan handed Lenny a gin and tonic. "So what did you do about it?" he asked.

"One by one, I lured them into a secluded location and returned the favor. When they attacked my nephew, three of them held him and the other three beat him. The three that beat him received wounds similar to those they inflicted. Each got a broken collar bone, broken ribs, a broken nose and a dislocated shoulder. I did exactly the same things to all three so there would be no mystery as to who did it and why."

"What did you do to the three guys that held your nephew?" Derek asked.

"Well, it was probably more than they deserved, but I lured each of them to an equally secluded place and tied them up to a fence. Then I called a rival gang member anonymously, and told him there was a present for him at that location. He accepted with the understanding that if the boy was killed, the same thing would happen to him. Ya, that was probably worse than what I did to the other three."

"So, how long was it before Sam caught up with you?" Brad questioned.

"Just a couple of days. He called and told me he knew who I was and what I had done. Then he told me, as I'm sure he did you, that if I didn't cooperate with him, he would turn me in to the police. I've been working for him ever since."

"How many jobs have you done for him?" Arthur asked.

"Oh, I don't know. Probably close to twenty I would imagine."

Derek smiled in amazement. "I bet you have a small fortune in your account."

"Sam does pay well." Lenny admitted. "But enough about me, we have a job to do. This one is going to be different from the other ones you've done. I have read through the file and I have some ideas I'd like to talk about."

For the next three hours, the discussion continued. Although three hours barely began the planning for this assignment, it was all they could spend at a time without drawing suspicion. So for the next two weeks, three nights a week, the plan took shape and eventually became substantive.

The military background that Arthur and Lenny shared dictated that the gathering of information was crucial to the success of the operation. Through a contact that Sam had at the phone company, an arrangement was made to create a malfunction in the phone system at the offices of the Senator. The problem was created, and would eventually be fixed, from the offices of the telephone company. However, it would give Evan the opportunity to enter and install electronic eavesdropping devices on the phone system.

So, with the plan created and well rehearsed Evan stood, wearing a telephone company uniform, at the main reception desk in the Senator's office. He was greeted by a very attractive receptionist who seemed to be expecting him.

"Hi. I'm with the phone company. I understand you have a problem with your telephones." Evan gave her that smile that had worked so well for him in the past.

"Yes, we certainly do. I'm so glad you're here. Nothing works. We can't even use the intercom."

"Well, don't worry." Evan said reassuringly. "I'll take care of everything." He smiled at her again then asked, "Where's the main panel?"

The young lady came out from behind her desk and led Evan down the hallway to a supply room closet. Evan pulled up his tool belt, which he had put on too loosely, and knelt down in front of a large panel mounted on the back wall of the room.

"This is it." she said, then turned and headed back to her desk.

She made it only as far as the door before she turned back towards Evan. "If there's anything you need, anything at all, I'll be up front." Then she gave him her version of that same smile he had given her, and left the room.

"This assignment might not be that bad after all." Evan whispered to himself.

He removed the cover plate from the panel with a screw driver and sat it down next to the door. As he studied the maze of wires, he referred to a small, heavily worn manual he had brought with him. After running tests on several lines, he attached a small electronic device inside the panel box. There were three wires coming from the device that Evan connected to three terminals inside the box. Once the connection had been completed, he made a call from his cell phone to a number at the phone company, a number that Sam had given him. With in a few moments, the phone service was restored. He used one of those phone company test phones, the ones with the dial on the bottom, to make sure everything was working.

After he fastened the cover back onto the panel, he walked back up front to the reception desk. The receptionist, who had been checking her hair and make-up since Evan's arrival, was anxiously awaiting his return. He walked up to her desk and sat down in one of two chairs facing it.

"Everything's fixed."

"Wow. That was fast. I was hoping you'd be around at least 'til lunch time."

"Unfortunately, I have a lot of stops to make today. But I do manage to eat lunch almost every day, and sometimes in a restaurant on this very street. Frank's Deli. Ever heard of it?"

"Oh yes. I eat there myself sometimes." the young lady replied.

"Well, maybe if I knew which days those were, I might be at Frank's Deli at the same time that you are. Wouldn't that be something?" Evan was not used to beating around the bush this much. But this girl was young, and built. Boy was she ever built. So, after a split second's indecision, he decided to continue the game.

"You know what? I bet if you were at that restaurant tomorrow, a handsome and unattached employee of the phone company would buy you lunch."

"Really?"

"Absolutely" Evan smiled and got up from the chair. He leaned forward and whispered, "Be there around eleven thirty so we can get a good table." He winked at her and left the office.

She watched him as he walked out through the doors and down the hall, leaning forward in her chair to prolong the view. Her fantasy was interrupted by a very arrogant and untimely beckoning from her employer, Senator Edloe. The receptionist quickly sprang to her feet and made her way back to his office.

"Who was just in here?" the Senator asked without looking up from the papers he was reviewing on his desk.

"It was the telephone repair man."

"Really? Did you ask him for any identification?"

"No, he was wearing a phone company uniform and a phone company ID badge and he drove up in a phone company truck."

"So you're not really sure if he was indeed with the phone company, is that what you are telling me?"

"Yes sir, I am sure he was with the phone company."

"And what makes you so sure he was?"

"He fixed the phones."

The Senator looked up over the top of his reading glasses at his receptionist. "Lisa, if I wanted a smart ass to occupy your position, I'd have hired my ex-wife. Next time, ask to see identification. I don't care who it is. No one comes in here unless we are sure of their authenticity. Do I make myself clear?"

"Crystal clear sir." She placed special emphasis on the word 'crystal'.

Again the Senator looked up at her (Crystal was his ex-wife's name). Before he had the opportunity to reply, she had left his office.

"What an asshole." she muttered to herself as she sat down behind her desk. But soon her thoughts returned to Evan, and tomorrow's tryst.

Evan pulled the door to the van closed and started the engine. He reached over and flipped the heater control up all the way. Reaching behind his seat, he pulled out a large metallic brief case and placed it down on the passenger seat. He unsnapped the clasps and raised the lid. The inside of the case was a control panel. On it were rows of switches with a corresponding light for each switch.

There were three meters in the center of the panel. The first read 'signal strength'. The needle flipped all the way to the right once Evan activated the first row of switches. The second meter read 'relay level'. This one still read zero. The third was labeled 'battery remaining'. That meter read '96 hours'. It was reading the maximum level. The numbers decreased from 96 in twelve hour increments.

Evan closed and latched the case. Slipping the van into gear, he eased away from the curb and went around the corner to the entrance of the building's parking garage. He entered the parking garage and drove to the third and upper most level. Evan parked as close to the stairwell doors as he could, then turned the engine off and braved the cold one more time.

He entered the building's stairwell and climbed the six flights of stairs to the roof. After a brief tug of war with the wind, he opened the door and stepped through it. It was much colder there. He walked across the roof to a small structure that housed the main electrical breakers and switch panels. The doors to the structure were locked. Evan removed a thin black pouch from his coat pocket and produced two small surgical-type instruments. Within seconds the lock was picked. He opened the doors and sat the metallic brief case he had brought with him down and opened it. Flipping the last row of switches, he activated the third meter, sending the needle all the way to the right.

Evan raised an antenna on the outside of the case then closed it and slid it in behind a large breaker panel. He closed and locked the doors then headed back down to the parking garage. After spending a few seconds rubbing his hands together for warmth, he left the parking garage, driving back towards downtown. The first of many steps had been completed.

Arthur was right. This job would be very different than the previous ones.

CHAPTER THIRTEEN

Derek came home to an empty house as he had been ever since Katie became permanently assigned to her current project. As he walked through the house, he noticed her files and several legal pads full of notes strewn across the dining room table. He continued on into the kitchen and found a note taped to the refrigerator that said Katie had gone down the street to the market and would be back shortly.

He went to the refrigerator for a beer, then walked back into the dining room, but not before looking out the window to make sure Katie was not on her way down the sidewalk. Seeing no sign of her, he returned to the table and began reading. He read briefly through the two transcripts of the interviews that Katie and Nathan conducted earlier in the week. Nothing he read gave any clue as to who may have been responsible.

He picked up a large pile of papers and began to leaf through them. Nothing much caught his eye until he came across a photograph. It was in black and white and poorly focused, but Derek knew exactly what it was. It was them, three of them anyway. It was taken while they were standing behind the car outside of Jerry Kinson's apartment by a security camera at a dry cleaner across the street. On the top of the photograph were the words, 'Home Security, Inc.' Another photograph, underneath the one he had just looked at, showed Evan and Brad getting their gear out of the trunk. Arthur had gone on ahead and was in none of the photos. And still another showed three of them walking across the street back to the car. Paper clipped to the last photo was a note that read, 'send to Digital Enhancement Systems for computer imaging.'

At that moment, Derek heard the front door open. Katie, seeing the car in the driveway, called out his name. He quickly returned the papers and photos to their place on the table, and then took a few steps towards the kitchen.

"We're home." she announced.

"In the kitchen" Derek hollered. His heart was still pounding from what he had just seen.

Katie lifted Derek Jr. out of his stroller then walked into the kitchen and gave Derek a hug. He wrapped his arms around her and squeezed her tightly. He knew there would come a day when he would have to tell her everything. He did not want her to find out on her own.

"How's the research going?" he asked nervously.

"Pretty good." she replied with a sparkle in her eye. "We're beginning to make some real progress. We think we have a photo of what might be them and the car they used."

"Really" Derek remarked, "can I see it?"

"Sure." Katie shuffled through the pile until she came to the pictures that Derek had just looked at. She handed them to him. While he looked at them again, she dug deeper into the pile to find one additional photograph. He watched as she searched for it, wondering how bad that one would be. She found it and handed it to him. He knew immediately what it was. The photo lab at the paper was able to blow up one of the pictures to reveal very clearly, a most unique wrist watch. It belonged to Evan. He had been wearing it ever since Derek had met him almost two years ago.

"There can't be many watches like that around." she said.

Derek handed the photographs back to her. "So what's your gut feeling? Who do you think these guys are?"

"I don't know. We spoke with as many of Jerry's enemies as we could locate, and none of them knew of anyone that had it in for him bad enough to do what happened to him. We also checked out the dead girl's parents. They weren't even in town when this happened." Katie began to look a little discouraged as she spoke. "So at this point, pretty much all we have are these photographs."

"But they're so fuzzy and out of focus. How can you tell anything from them?"

"We're sending them off to a company that uses computers to digitally enhance them. They can sharpen and clarify them, hopefully to the point that the figures will be identifiable. We've used them before. They do a remarkable job."

That wasn't what Derek wanted to hear. If those photos were enhanced, they could all be identified.

"How long does something like that take?"

"It depends" Katie replied, "on how backed up they are. They do work for the police too. Last time it took about three weeks to get our pictures back."

Derek heaved a slight sigh of relief. Three weeks should buy them a little time. He had no idea what to do about this, or how he was going to tell the others.

"Soup's on" Evan announced as he walked into the den carrying a large pizza box.

"Great, I'm starved." Lenny replied. He and Evan had been working together that morning. What he had done was not unlike what they had done when working with Ted Messina. Evan installed a small, low powered transmitter in the phone panel at the Senator's office. That transmitter sent a signal to the larger, more powerful transmitter in the brief case that Evan hid behind the breaker panel on the roof of the office building. That transmitter sent a signal to the equipment in Evan's den. Here, the signal was amplified, processed and recorded. There was also a device which converted the tones produced when the buttons on the phone are pushed to numerical equivalents so they could tell what number the Senator was calling.

Evan sat the pizza box down on the bar. He reached down to a refrigerator under the bar and took out two beers. He handed one to Lenny. After a few moments of careful thought, he asked Lenny a question.

"Did you ever imagine your life would turn out this way? I mean, you're a comedian, but part of your life is spent doing all this black bag stuff." Lenny took a few seconds to finish chewing his first bite.

"No, this is not what I had in mind for myself when I got out of the service. I figured to use my ability to make people laugh as a living. But then I had that run in with those kids in that gang, and before I knew it everything changed. Sure, I still work the clubs. But most of my engagements are tied to my assignments. How do you think Sam knew to call Arthur at the club that night?"

Evan stopped chewing and sat stunned as if struck by lightning. "Son of a bitch, I never thought of that." Evan almost felt foolish for not figuring it out before. "But Sam always seems to know where we are and what we're doing."

Lenny took a sip of beer. "Correction; Sam knows someone who knows where you are and what you're doing."

"I guess you're right." The two ate in silence for a few minutes until Lenny spoke up again.

"What line of work is your dad in?"

"Investments mostly, but not what you're thinking though. He doesn't buy stocks, he buys companies. Usually companies that are about to go under because of mismanagement or slumping sales. He buys them. Then he replaces the management with his own people and gets them back on their feet and showing a profit. When the time is right, he sells. The companies he doesn't sell, he goes public with and sells stock. Either way, he has made a shit load of money at it."

"Why aren't you in business with him?"

Evan's expression changed. He looked down toward the floor, searching for the right words.

"My father always put one hundred per cent of himself into whatever he was doing. And as long as I can remember, that was his philosophy. He practiced it religiously, most of the time to the exclusion of me and mom. You see, when he and his parents immigrated to this country, they had nothing. They lived in poverty much of their lives, but they always had a strong family. Despite the fact that they were poor, they never went without something to eat and a roof over their heads. Dad used to tell me about the old days during the depression, and how he told himself that when he grew up, his family would never have to live like he was living. He was right. I always had anything and everything I ever wanted when I was growing up. Of course there was a price."

"What was the price?" Lenny asked.

"The price was dad. I grew up virtually without him. He was always working, so he never made any school functions, or little league, or my high school graduation. He would come up to my room late at night when he got home and tell me to keep applying myself and some day I'd be just like him."

"What about your mother?"

"Well, mom got tired of being alone. She and dad split up when I was young. She died four years ago."

"Does it bother you to think about your parents?"

"Ya it does, and I'll tell you why. I look at the way my dad grew up, and the way that I did, and I honestly wonder which one of us had a better childhood."

"I guess you could wonder that about all of us." Lenny said as he put his empty can down on the coffee table in front of him. "Personally, I wonder why the hell I got myself into all of this. But, we have more pressing problems than those to deal with right now. Why don't you back that tape up and let's listen to it again."

The two listened to a tape of the phone conversations that the Senator made earlier that day. And again, at Lenny's request, it was stopped in the same place.

"Is there a way, with all of this electronic wizardry you have here, to make a second copy of this tape?"

"Sure. It'll take just a minute a minute." Evan got up and switched on several other devices. More lights lit up and more electronic hums filled the room. Within minutes, Evan presented Lenny with a cassette tape of the original. Lenny looked at it for a brief moment, and then tucked it away in a file folder.

"I've got some homework to do." Lenny said as he got up.

"I'll walk you to the door."

"Good. I'm liable to get lost in this place. How many rooms are there in this house, anyway?"

"I'm not sure." Evan said curiously as they left the room. "I haven't been in all of them yet."

"Hey, you know, you'd make a good comedian. Not as good as me, but a good comedian."

Their voices faded as they walked down the hall. The tape machine was still paused in the same spot. On the bar was a legal pad. A transcript of the conversations had been written as the tape was played. Several lines of the Senator's conversation were highlighted. They read as follows:

'Edloe' -"I am still connected. What I mean is I still have some influence that will most certainly be of value to your employers. I know the problems you've been having with the three guys in jail. Trust me, if we can work a deal, they won't be there for long. I know what it will take to get them off and I know how to get it done. So you go tell your boss. If he agrees to the arrangement, I'll get started right away."

'Caller' -"What assurances do we have that you can actually pull this off?"

'Edloe' -"Tell your boss to look into my past. Tell him to look where I've been and what I've done. He'll know. Besides, they quit doing me favors a long time ago, and after all I did for them, I figure they owe me."

'Caller' -"What do they owe you?"

'Edloe' -"That's my business. I figure I can kill two birds with one stone here. I can take care of your boss's problem and one of my own at the same time."

'Caller' -"I'll talk it over with the boss and let you know."

'Edloe' -"Don't take too long. I got a Senate Investigation Committee closing in on me. If we are going to do each other any good, we'll have to move quickly, like within the next day or two." The conversation ended with those words.

Brad's apartment was dark except for the light above his computer where he had been working without a break for the last hour and a half. He had begun, sometime ago, a new project.

This one was different from any other he had done. It was something he never intended to have published, or even read by anyone other than himself for that matter. He had begun a detailed diary of the activities that he and his friends had been involved in from that day in that court room with Derek and Katie until the present. The file in which he was writing was pass-coded so that only he could access it. The disc that it was stored on was removed and hidden after each use.

As a writer he could not resist the opportunity to document his experiences, though he understood what the consequences would be if this diary was discovered by anyone.

Brad's reasons for keeping a diary of their activities were quite simple and maybe a little selfish. He looked upon this as the number one best seller he had always dreamed of writing. This had all of the elements; intrigue, suspense and mystery. And best of all, he didn't have to make any of it up. He was living it. The methods that Arthur had come up with to punish these people were nothing less than flawless, except maybe the very first one (the one that got them involved with Sam). Were they to do it all again, there are only a couple of things about that first job they'd have done differently.

Maybe it was fate that caused their paths and Sam's to cross. Maybe it was just a case of being in the wrong place at the wrong time. Regardless, it was a hell of a way to get material for a book.

Brad finished the last few words then saved the file to the disc. After it was saved, he removed it from the computer and hid it, as he always did in the center of a large old hard cover edition of Webster's Dictionary. He always slipped the disc into the same two pages, between inexcusable and infinity.

In the heart of downtown many lights were lit in the offices of the Federal Building, but few people were still working. Among those was the group of men responsible for the strange turn of events in the lives of Arthur, Brad, Evan and Derek. The drapes were drawn in the office on the eighteenth floor. The lights were, as they always would be, dim, consisting of small, directional reading lamps and nothing more. The men, each sitting in the same place as the last time, appear more concerned, and somewhat morose. The man seated at the head of the table drew the attention of the others as he began to speak.

"Let's begin, gentlemen." A silence fell over the room. "It is my understanding there have been some developments in the little war Senator Edloe has elected to wage upon us. Sam, would you bring us up to date on the latest communication from the Senator?"

Sam opened a file folder that lay on the table in front of him. "I received a letter from Mr. Edloe yesterday. After I established its authenticity, I called for this meeting. As you all know, Senator Edloe was once a member of this organization. During his tenure here, he was a valuable asset, contributing significantly to what we are trying to accomplish. It was mutually agreed that he be released from our group when he made the decision to become involved in politics. We all felt at the time that he would be of value to us regardless of his capacity. Well gentlemen, we were wrong. Senator Edloe has fallen victim to the snares and trappings of the political environment. I regret to inform you that our former colleague now poses the greatest threat to the existence of this organization that we have thus far encountered."

The silence within the room was deafening. All of the men were shocked by what they were hearing. Sam continued.

"Without going into great detail, Senator Edloe has become indebted to one particular organized crime figure by accepting numerous sums of money from him. Now it seems the day has come for him to repay that debt, and he intends to use his knowledge of our organization to do so."

Sam slid the wrapper off a cigar and placed it between his teeth. Then he struck a match and raised it toward the end of the cigar. The glow from the match illuminated his face.

"I'm a Judge, for heaven's sake. And you," he said as he pointed to his left, "you're the CEO of a multi billion dollar corporation, and sitting next to you is one of the foremost defense attorneys in the country. There is also a retired Army

General and a former Cabinet Member sitting at this table. And we all have one thing in common. We're all about to be black-mailed." Sam was right on all counts. He was a judge. In fact, he was the judge that presided over Katie's assault trial. It was he who witnessed Arthur's reaction to his verdict (a deliberate and calculated verdict), and it was he who watched and waited for Arthur to take justice into his own hands. Arthur did, and the rest quickly became history. Each of the men in the organization had experienced in his past, an event against either he or his family which went unpunished. The outrage and frustration each of them felt is what drove them to where they were today.

Sam continued. "The crime family that has subsidized Mr. Edloe for some years now has decided it is time for a return on their investment. There are three members of their organization currently in custody awaiting trial. These men were ranking members of the family. Two were cousins and one was the son of the old man himself, the man who took over the operation over thirty years ago from his father. What Mr. Edloe is demanding of us is this. There is a critical piece of evidence upon which the prosecution's entire case will hinge. A ruling will be necessary to determine the admissibility of this evidence. Since I have the misfortune of being the judge who will hear this case, the good Senator is trying to black-mail me into disallowing the evidence. Without this piece of evidence the prosecution has no case." Sam drew a long puff on his cigar. As he did, one of his colleagues spoke.

"Exactly how does he intend to try and black-mail us?"

Sam thought for a moment, choosing his words carefully.

"Very simply he has threatened to expose us and our organization if I do not disallow the evidence."

"Do you suppose he has spoken to anyone about his knowledge of us?" the man at the head of the table asked.

"No, but I have no reason to doubt that he will."

"Perhaps you should agree, and then rule as the evidence dictates when the time comes. If nothing else it will give you more time to consider an alternative." a man, who had, to this point been silent suggested.

"I must say I thought of that very thing myself, but I was warned against it in the letter. It was made clear to me that doing such a thing would not be in the best interests of my family's health."

Another man spoke up.

"What about the F.B.I. Should we consider getting them involved?"

"Again, we are between a rock and a hard place. If we bring in any federal agency, we will certainly suffer worse consequences in the long run. I would venture to say we would be spending time with many of the people who have come through my courtroom."

There was a long moment of silence before Sam continued.

"I have given this a great deal of thought, and I have come to a decision. It will involve some considerable degree of risk, but I feel it is the only alternative we have. I have decided to reveal my identity to Arthur Jensen, a team leader who has proven himself to be of exceptional talent. He is the only member that I would trust with this information. I know, once he understands the nature of this situation, he will affect its solution. He is very good."

A low mummer of discontent pierced the silence of the room.

"Are you absolutely sure you can trust this man?" was the question asked by the man at the head of the table.

"The only things I am absolutely sure of are the facts that our organization will be dissolved and we will most likely be incarcerated if I do nothing, and my family will most certainly be harmed if I do the wrong thing. I do not see a great deal of choice here."

At this point, another man, who had been silent until now, spoke up.

"At the risk of sounding repetitious, the quickest solution is still the easiest. But no one has brought it to the floor yet."

"Just what is that?" Sam asked.

"Why not simply eliminate the problem at the source?"

"We've discussed this before." Sam replied, growing impatient with the man's inferences. "Killing him would only complicate matters. Besides, there are more people than just Senator Edloe who are involved now. No, it is out of the question."

The man at the head of the table spoke once again.

"Sam, if you are sure this is the most prudent course to follow then I urge you to proceed."

Sam looked at him through the smoke and nodded. With that, the decision was made, and Arthur's life was about to take yet another unexpected turn.

The recent turn of events involving Arthur's daughter had drawn them closer together, but not without cost to his son. The time Arthur got to spend with his son of late was considerably less than normal and the lad was beginning to think something was wrong. So in an effort to achieve a bit of balance, Arthur had chosen to sit on the couch and watch a movie this evening with Todd. It was a science fiction film of sorts; lots of space creatures and blood and guts. It was not really Arthur's cup of tea, but he was enjoying spending a little time, just he and his son.

The bowl of popcorn was only half gone when the phone rang. Arthur had brought the remote phone into the living room with him as Sandy and Angie had gone shopping. He picked it up and pushed the talk button. It was Sam.

"Arthur, I hope I'm not disturbing you."

"Not at all, just watching a movie with my son."

"That's great. How is Todd doing?"

"He's doing fine, but I don't ever recall telling you his name."

"Oh come now Arthur. You should know by now." Arthur smiled a little, knowing full well that Sam knew or had access to every bit of information there was to know about him and his family.

"You're right, I should. So, what can I do for you?"

There was an uncharacteristic pause as Sam collected his thoughts.

"Arthur, there has been a very serious turn for the worse in this business with Senator Ryan Edloe. There are many things that you and I must discuss in this regard, however it is not be safe to do so over the phone. Therefore, after many hours of thoughtful deliberation with my colleagues, I have decided to meet with you in person at a place of my choosing to discuss how we shall proceed."

Arthur's jaw dropped. He could not believe what he was hearing. Ever since the beginning he had been wondering who this man was, and every time he tried to find out, he hit a brick wall.

"I must say I am surprised and somewhat flattered at your decision."

"It was a decision that did not come easy. I realize that I am assuming a great deal of risk by divulging my identity, but the sheer magnitude of this situation calls for drastic measures. I will call you at your office and we will arrange a time and a place to meet."

"I'll be in my office for the rest of the week. And for what it's worth, I give you my word I will not reveal your identity to anyone."

"I know you won't, Arthur. That's why I have chosen to proceed as I have. Until tomorrow then" There was a click and he was gone.

Arthur pushed the button on the phone and silenced the dial tone. He sat dumbfounded for a moment, until Todd popped him back into reality.

"Dad, is everything okay?"

"Sure son, everything's fine"

"Good, 'cause the best part's coming up; watch this. This guy's head is going to get zapped right off, watch."

Arthur, who was only half paying attention to the movie before, found it impossible to pay any attention to it now. After all this time of wondering who Sam was, he was finally going to find out. Only now he wasn't sure if he really wanted to know.

In a police holding facility on the far west side of town, a lone figure in a suit carrying a black brief case walked up the stairs and through the doors. Within a few moments he entered a room designated for use by prisoners and their attorney's. He sat down at the head of the table and lit a cigarette. Several moments passed before a man clad in prison fatigues entered the room. He was accompanied by a guard who left once he was assured by the man in the suit that he did indeed want to be alone with the prisoner. Neither man spoke until after the door closed.

"So, what's the word? Is the fix in yet?"

"It's a done deal. The three of you should be free men the day after the trial starts."

"Are you sure? I mean this is my life we're talking about here, and I don't intend to spend the next twenty five years of it in this place. So what if we killed those guys, it was business, that's all."

"Take it easy. I'm telling you the judge is going to disallow the evidence that was taken from the trunk of your car. Without that, they got no case. They'll plea bargain down to probation, you watch."

"You better be right. I can't take much more of this place."

"Bide your time and don't give them a reason to keep you here. Do you understand?"

"Ya, ya, I'll take up needlepoint or something. Don't worry."

The attorney opened his briefcase and slid a carton of cigarettes across the table to Carlos, one of the three accused in a triple homicide several months ago. He and his two accomplices were being held in different prisons for fear of retaliation from the family.

"I'm going to see Sal and Ray tomorrow. Now remember, behave yourself. Once it becomes clear that their case is blown, they'll try everything in the book to keep you on the inside. Don't fall for it. I'll be back in a few days."

"Well I'll be here."

As the door closed behind the attorney, Carlos heaved a heavy sigh, not of relief, but of dismay at the thought of having to go back to the cell block.

The sidewalk leading up to the doors of the treatment center was wet from the melting snow. Winter was finally showing some signs of surrender and the onset of spring seemed to be at hand. After months of walking briskly toward the doors, Brad found himself rather enjoying the trip between his car and the building. As he passed through the doors, he heard what had become a familiar rustling sound of newspaper.

"This is getting to be a habit with you." he called out to Arthur as he rounded the corner.

"What's that?"

"You're getting here before me. So do we have a problem again or is your watch broken?"

"No, there's no problem. I just wanted a little time to talk to you. I got a phone call from Sam last night."

"What does he want now?" Brad's voice was thick with contempt.

"Well, it seems this little project we're working on has gotten much more serious than either one of us realize. I figure it must be since Sam wants to meet with me in person."

Brad wasn't sure whether to believe him or not. "He wants to what?"

"That's right, he's going to call me at some point this week to arrange a time and place to meet."

"Isn't he worried about letting the cat out of the bag, so to speak?

"I gave him my word that I wouldn't reveal his identity to anyone."

"Does that include me?" Brad asked, looking at Arthur from the corners of his eyes.

"I told him I wouldn't tell anyone, and yes, that includes you. I gave my word; I can't go back on it. Besides, I'd hate to pay the consequences if he ever found out that I told anyone who he was. So don't ask."

"Well, I guess it won't make any difference anyway, since this is our last job. Personally, I'll be glad enough to be rid of this whole business. I know I've said it before, but I'm just not cut out for this crap. It keeps me up at night."

Before the conversation could go on any further, the doors opened and Derek entered the lounge. Quickly, before he got within ear shot, Brad leaned towards Arthur. "Are you going to say anything to Derek and Evan about this?"

"No, and don't you either."

Derek had an unusually concerned look on his face. He looked distant, almost to the point of being preoccupied. Arthur sensed something was wrong.

"Sit down; take a load off your feet."

Derek sat in his usual place, still silent.

"You look like someone who has a lot on his mind. Anything you'd like to talk about?" Brad asked in his best fatherly voice.

"Ya, I'm afraid there is. And I'm also afraid of how it's going to affect all of us."

Arthur leaned forward in his chair. "What's the problem?"

"Well, I think I mentioned that Katie's paper was doing a story about two of the guys we did a job on. Remember Brad, we talked about it one day?"

Brad nodded.

"Well, remember when we were waiting out in front of that guy's apartment for him to call and order a pizza?"

Again, both Brad and Arthur nodded.

"There was a security camera in the parking lot of the building we were in front of."

Arthur put his hands over his face, knowing full well what Derek was about to say.

"So did it get a picture of the car?" Brad asked, not sensing the worst as Arthur had.

"It got a picture of us!"

Brad sat motionless for a moment, but soon spoke.

"You've got to be kidding me. This is a joke, isn't it? Arthur, this shit isn't funny. You know how I feel about this stuff. Don't do this."

"This is no joke, Brad. I wish it were." Arthur turned back towards Derek. "How clear is the picture? Can you tell who we are, or is it fuzzy or blurry or anything?"

"Ya it is. You can't tell who we are, but Katie said there is a lab they send pictures like this to. They digitally enhance them and that clarifies them. But one thing that everyone noticed right off is Evan's watch. You can see that real well, but not our faces, at least not yet."

The sound of the doors opening and closing again abruptly stopped the conversation. Evan soon made his way through the lounge and, sensing the silence, decided to take advantage of it.

"You were talking about me, weren't you? Come on, what were you saying?" Evan sat down in his usual place, looking at three mostly blank faces. "You three look like a bunch of scolded children."

Arthur broke their silence.

"How much do you know about digital enhancement?"

"Audio or video?"

"Video"

"Well, I'm no expert, but I know it's pretty damn good at making something much clearer than it originally was. There are several companies that do that sort of thing, but the best is a company called Digital Enhancement Systems."

"How do you know about that company?" Derek asked, quite surprised at Evan's choice.

"My father owns it."

Derek sat in amazement. Arthur looked over at him.

"Is that the company that the paper is using?"

Derek nodded. Arthur looked over at Brad and smiled. Then both he and Brad spoke the same words at the same time. "His father owns it!"

"Alright, what's this all about?" Evan asked. He had grown a little impatient not knowing where these questions were going.

Arthur spoke up. "A security camera in a parking lot near where we parked to deal with Mr. Kinson photographed us. Our faces are fuzzy, but the pictures along with the video tape they were taken from, have been sent off to your dad's company for enhancement. I don't suppose there is something you could do about this, is there?"

"Hell, yes there is." Evan shouted quite loudly. "I'll just take a little trip over there tonight." Evan turned to Derek. "I need some information about how the tape and photos have been labeled. Then you and I are going to go up there after hours and do a little enhancement of our own."

"Me? Why me?" Derek asked, not wanting to be involved in the solution to this degree.

"Because you've seen the photos, and you know what they look like. Besides, I need someone to help me." Evan wasn't letting him out of this one.

"What if they have already done it?" Brad asked.

"I don't think they've had time." Derek answered. "Katie called them yesterday and they hadn't started on it yet. I guess they're pretty busy, but the paper's beginning to put pressure on them."

"Then you better find out today what the file name is and we'll go up there tonight.

"Are you sure you can get in there after hours?" Brad questioned.

Evan looked at him and smiled. "I have access cards and pass codes to every company my dad owns. There has to be a perk in it for me somewhere."

"Then it's settled. Derek, you'll find out what Evan needs then the two of you will take a road trip tonight, and by morning, maybe this whole thing will be over."

Arthur sat back in his chair, cautiously optimistic that this situation would be taken care of before it did anyone any harm. As he sat there, he thought to himself, *how could I have overlooked the possibility of a security camera? Damn.*

CHAPTER FOURTEEN

Senator Edloe's offices were busy as they usually were. A number of strange but temporary faces were busily working in every room of his suite. They were all tabulating and processing numbers, the results of a survey that the Senator took (through a very generous government grant). The deadline for funding was approaching and the Senator had a team of people, many of whom were related to him, working on finishing the project. Although virtually every square inch of the offices were noisy and crowded, the Senator's office was quiet. The door was closed. He had closed and locked it prior to picking up the phone to place a call. It rang only twice before it was answered.

"Ya" A voice on the other end of the phone answered in a somewhat disinterested tone.

"This is Senator Ryan Edloe calling for Mr. Russo. Is he in?"

"Ya, he's here. Let me see if he wants to talk to you."

Whoever answered the phone covered part of the receiver with his hand, only partially muffling his voice and those of the others in the room.

"Hey boss, there's a Senator Edloe on the phone for you. Want me to tell him to get lost?"

The Senator could not hear the reply, but it must have been no since Mr. Russo soon came to the phone.

"Senator, how are you today?"

"I'm fine sir, just fine. I called to bring you up to date on my progress with the judge presiding over your son's trial."

"I trust you're making him see things your way."

"I believe I am. I have offered him an incentive and a consequence. He is not a foolish man. I'm sure he will realize his choices are clear and make the right decision."

"So what you're telling me is you haven't got a commitment out of him yet, is that it?" Mr. Russo's voice quickly grew impatient.

"I am getting very close to nailing this thing down. I'm sure I'll have a definitive answer soon, very soon." The Senator, at this point was trying to side-step the issue as all good politicians do. This did not go unnoticed.

"You talk just like a politician. I don't ever get a straight answer out of you. So let me give you some straight facts. You'd better talk that judge into throwing out that evidence. I bought and paid for you a long time ago and it's time for you to start paying me back. Now I'm going to offer you an incentive and a consequence. You talk that judge into turning my son loose and I'll single handedly finance your next campaign, or your retirement, which ever comes first. But if you screw up, you'll be learning first hand how the hospitals spend all that money you've gotten for them. Am I making myself clear?"

"Mr. Russo, have a little faith in me. Have I ever let you down before?"

"You've never had the opportunity to let me down. And you don't now. So don't call here again until you have some good news for me."

With that, Mr. Russo hung up.

At the same moment Mr. Russo hung up, a tape machine clicked off in Evan's den. This conversation, as every one made on the Senator's phone, had been recorded. Senator Edloe sat silently for a few moments. He had never seen Mr. Russo so angry before, and he most definitely had never been threatened by him either. Convincing Sam to disallow the evidence had never been as important as it was now. The source of his motivation had changed from greed to desperation. This made him somewhat more determined and a great deal more dangerous.

Evan got home from the treatment center a little later than usual. He stopped and picked up some things he thought he and Derek might need tonight. Nothing to this point had gotten to Evan. To say he had no fear of, nor had he felt threatened by any looming consequences of anything they had done thus far would be true. But he was a little rattled about the pictures. It wasn't the end of the world, but it was a situation that he felt required immediate attention.

He had arranged with Derek to pick him up at his house around seven in the evening. There were a number of things he needed to do before then. He had made a list of items that he would take with him. Like a kid on a scavenger hunt, he went from room to room gathering up different and seemingly unrelated items and loading them into a duffel bag. The last item to go in the bag was a framed photograph that he had in his den behind the bar on one of the glass shelves.

Then he zipped the bag and took it out to the garage and placed it in the trunk of his car.

Derek took his shoes off outside the garage door before entering the house. Katie was already home. He could tell by the aroma of dinner which could be savored even before he opened the door. As he pushed the door closed behind him, his eyes scanned the house for Katie. He caught sight of her in the kitchen. On his way, he passed through the dining room and noticed a pile of papers and notes on the table. An opportunity may have presented itself to get updated on how the story was going.

"Is that you?" she called out.

"No, it's just the man you have sex with occasionally." Katie turned and wrapped her arms around him.

"Well, maybe tonight will be one of those nights." she said, winking at him before turning back around to the stove.

"Been working at home a little this afternoon?" he asked.

"Ya, I have. Things are kind of at a stand-still until we get the pictures back from the lab."

"How's that going? When do you think you'll get them?"

"I called today and the man I talked to said they'd probably start on them tomorrow. I sure hope so. Without those it's going to be a lot tougher to tie this all together."

Derek could tell that Katie was really getting into this assignment. He was relieved though, that the lab was as busy as they were. Hopefully it wouldn't be a problem after tonight. He had no idea what he and Evan were going to do. He didn't know if they were going to try and steal the video and photos, or destroy them or what. And he really didn't care, just so long as they got the problem taken care of.

He felt a little guilty that his wife was working on a story that was causing him and his friends so much grief, but it wasn't his fault or hers for that matter. It was just a job she was given, and one she intended to do to the best of her ability.

It was ten thirty when Evan and Derek pulled into the parking garage at Digital Enhancement Systems. There were no other cars there except a security patrol. As Evan began to get out of the car, the security officer approached him.

"Can I help you gentlemen?"

"I wish you could." Evan answered. "Its hell when your dad owns the company and he makes you work harder than anyone else." Evan showed him his company ID.

"He's got you up here this time of night?"

"Well, we're not here because we want to be. Fortunately, it should only take us about thirty minutes to finish. I don't know why it couldn't wait 'til morning."

The security guard walked them to the door. Evan took out his pass card and scanned it through the scanner on the door, then entered a code and the door unlocked. If there was any doubt in the security guard's mind about Evan's authenticity, it was dispelled when he produced and used the pass card. Before closing the door, Evan looked back at the guard.

"If I don't get time and a half for this shit, I'm gonna quit." The guard laughed.

"If your dad's anything like my boss, you'd better pack up your stuff while you're up there." Evan smiled and nodded, then closed the door. It locked automatically.

They took the elevator up to the fifth floor. Derek followed Evan through a maze of cubicles and several large rooms filled with electronic devices the likes of which Derek had never seen. This place made the electronics in Evan's den look like a two dollar radio. The walls were lined with large computer banks. There were desks as far as the eye could see; each one of them with a computer, printer and various other components.

Passing through this room, they made their way down a short hallway. This led to the nerve center of the company. On their way they stopped in a room filled with large file cabinets. There were row upon row of them. Derek guessed there must have been over a hundred, maybe more.

"Did you get a file name for me?"

Derek reached into his pocked. "There was no name. But I got this number off the note pad with the rest of the info from this place."

Evan reached out and took the small piece of paper that the number was written on. He looked at it intently for a moment, then walked several rows over and began looking in the top file drawer.

"Derek, start with that drawer over there. Look for numbers in sequence with this one. It's got to be around here someplace."

The two searched for almost ten minutes before Evan announced he'd found it. It was a large brownish envelope with the newspaper's name across the front of it and the number Derek gave him in the top right corner.

He pulled it out of the drawer and took it to a smaller room several offices down, turning on the lights as they passed through the door. There was a large computer system, several monitors and other electronic gadgetry. Evan sat down at a console that looked like it belonged in the control room at NASA and began turning things on. As he did, lights illuminated and three monitors that were suspended from ceiling at eye level came up. He reached down to the large duffel bag he had been carrying and unzipped it. From it he removed even more electronic apparatus.

"What's that stuff?" Derek asked.

"Scanner"

"What's a scanner do?"

"Watch and I'll show you."

Evan plugged a patch cable into the back of the scanner, then into a port located on the left side of the console, close to the bottom. Then he plugged it into an extension cord which Derek plugged in an outlet across from where they were working. He then took the photo out of the file and placed it on that device that looked like a small copy machine (the scanner). He pushed a button, and line by line, the photo appeared on one of the monitors.

Once it was complete, Evan took the photo out of the scanner and placed it in his bag.

"Aren't they going to miss that?" Derek asked.

"No. I'm going to make them another one." Evan told him.

"I'm confused. I think I'll just shut-up and let you do what ever it is that you're doing."

"It's not that complicated." Evan explained. "First, I scanned the photo that Katie sent into the computer. Now, I'm going to enhance the photo."

Evan moved the mouse around the screen, clicking very quickly on many different commands. When his maneuvers were completed, the screen went black for a moment, and then returned, line by line. This time, the picture was not blurred and distorted, it was clear. In fact it was very clear. Clear enough to identify all of them without a doubt.

"That's definitely us." Derek admitted.

Without looking at him, Evan asked Derek to find a most curious item in the bag.

"In my bag there is a framed photograph. Get it for me, will you." Derek rummaged through the bag and finally produced the picture.

"Take it out of the frame."

"What the hell are you going to do with this, Evan? You can't substitute this for the picture Katie sent."

"You just watch me."

Evan took the picture out of the frame and carefully laid it on the scanner, clicking on the menus once again as they popped up. As with the other, line by line, the photo appeared on the second monitor. Derek looked at both screens, still confused.

"Great, you put two pictures on two computer screens, so now what do we do?"

"Be patient" Evan told him, "and watch."

Evan carefully outlined the heads of each of the three men in the photo he had brought with him. When he finished, he removed the heads from their respective bodies and drug them over to the photo of the three of them. He did the same to that photo, removing their heads from their bodies. He carefully replaced their heads with those from the other photo, sizing them so as to achieve an exact fit. Then, after entering one final command, the screen went blank, but quickly reappeared displaying the new altered photo.

"Check this out." Evan said as Derek looked at the screen.

"Now I'm no expert" Derek admitted, "but I can tell this picture has been doctored."

"Sure you can" Evan agreed, "but that's not the point. The point is that we have replaced a photo of us with a photo of someone else. This is now their original."

When he was finished, he reversed the process, thus blurring the image beyond the point of recognition. It now looked as it did when Derek first saw it.

At this point, he slid back down the console a few feet and began pushing buttons. Soon a high pitched hum began, and a photograph slowly began to slide out from a slot in a printer at the end of the console. Evan slid down to catch it before it fell to the floor. He held it out for Derek to see.

"See, just like the original." Evan smiled. "You did put the real original in my bag, didn't you?"

"It's in there." he answered.

"Get the video tape out of the file." Evan requested. Derek handed him the tape from the file he had been holding.

"I still don't understand. If there's a video tape of us, why do they only have one photo?"

Evan answered him as he loaded the tape into the console. "The video tape doesn't record constantly. It only tapes for a couple of seconds in one minute intervals. We got out of the car fast enough that it only caught us one time. The photo was printed from the video tape. So, we'll have to make the video tape look like the picture we just created."

Evan advanced the tape to the place where they were seen getting out of the car. Then he taped over the original tape of their images with the different heads. Having completed this, he handed the tape back to Derek, along with the blurry photo, and he put them back into the file.

"Now" Evan exclaimed as he furiously turned off the last of the switches, "let's get the hell out of here."

"You won't get any argument from me." Derek mumbled under his breath.

Evan put the scanner he had brought with him back into his bag then zipped it up. Derek had already put the file back into the cabinet and was impatiently waiting for Evan by the door.

"Come on. Let's get out of here before somebody catches us." Derek was becoming even more nervous.

The two made their way through the file room to the main doorway then into the hallway. Evan almost had his hand on the knob when he heard a key slip into the lock. Before they had a chance to do anything but look at each other, the door opened and the head of a mop came through the door resting on the shoulder of a janitor as he backed into the office pulling a bucket of water. He seemed as surprised to see them as they were to see him. Without missing a beat, Evan turned to Derek and shouted at him.

"Maybe next time you'll do it right so we don't have to stay here till all hours of the night." Derek looked at him as if he were nuts. Evan looked over at the janitor.

"My brother-in-law." he said, pointing at Derek. "I try to give the kid a break and what does he do? He jerks me around, screws up his work, and now I'm here 'til damned near midnight pulling his ass out of the fire." Derek was beginning to catch on to what Evan was doing.

"I'm sorry. I promise to do better next time."

Evan reached over and grabbed him by the shoulder and pushed him past the janitor and out the door into the hall. As he passed him, the janitor watched curiously as he shook his head.

"If it weren't for my sister and her six kids, I'd kick his ass right out of here."

The janitor laughed, still shaking his head, then began mopping the floors as Derek and Evan ran down the hall toward the elevators. As they ran, Derek looked over at Evan.

"Six kids?"

"Hey, I had to make it sound good, didn't I?"

They slowed down to a walk as they reached the doors. Evan pushed them open and the two walked briskly across the parking lot to Evan's car. The security guard was nowhere to be seen, which was just as well. One close encounter had been enough.

CHAPTER FIFTEEN

It was raining, and although rain did not promote the safest of driving conditions, it was a welcome change from the endless months of snow that had turned the city's streets into little more than rows of tire tracks. Brad's eyes squinted as the rain pounded against the windshield. He couldn't ever remember it raining this hard so early in spring. Brad was not to be deterred by the rain though. He was on his way to meet Carol for another of their combination business and pleasure meetings. Of course by this time anything he did with Carol was pleasurable. He was beginning to care more for her than he ever expected to, and he was happy about that. It felt good; it felt right.

The meeting place was a bar in a downtown hotel. As he turned into the parking garage and up a short ramp, the steady rhythm of the rain gave way to the persistent squeaking of the windshield wipers rubbing against the dry glass. Brad pulled into the first available parking place. He got out and was greeted by the damp April air. He wasted no time in getting to the hotel.

It was an upscale hotel, a bit more formal than Brad cared for, but nonetheless very comfortable. He walked through the lobby and into the bar. Only a handful of people were enjoying a drink on this rainy afternoon. The weather and the fact that it was the middle of the week probably contributed to that. He scanned the room and spotted Carol at a table near the corner. As he walked in her direction, a couple at the bar appeared to be having an argument. The drinks they'd consumed had made them oblivious to the spectacle they were making of themselves. Brad tried to ignore them as he approached the table. Carol was busy reading through some papers and didn't see him walk up.

"Hope I didn't keep you waiting long."

Carol looked up at him and smiled. "You're always worth the wait."

Brad sat down as the voices at the bar grew louder. He glanced over in their direction then looked back at Carol.

"Have they been at it long?"

"Ever since I got here. That woman needs to get up and leave. Her friend's been getting louder and more belligerent by the minute. I'm afraid he's going to hit her."

"Let's hope not." Brad said as he reached over and took Carol's hand.

By this time a waitress had come over to the table with a small dish of peanuts. She placed it between them, and then took out a pad and pencil.

"What can I get you folks to drink?" she asked, looking at Carol.

"I'll have a glass of Chablis."

"And you sir?"

"I'll have anything so long as it's not the same thing those two are drinking over there." He pointed over his shoulder to the couple at the bar.

"Oh, don't worry about them, the manager's on his way in here to ask them to leave."

"Well in that case, I'll have a scotch and soda."

The waitress wrote down the order and walked back to the bar. Brad's attention was again focused on Carol.

"So, what's this great news you've got to tell me?"

"Well" Carol began, "do you remember that screenplay that you and the publishing company talked about a couple of months ago? You know, the one based on your book about the man that hijacked the airliner."

Brad knew exactly what she was talking about. That was the meeting he had to cancel because of their first assignment. An incredible amount of water had passed under the bridge since then.

"Ya, I know which one you're talking about."

"Well, get ready to see your name on the silver screen, because there's a studio in L.A. prepared to make you an offer on it."

Brad's eyes lit up. So many thoughts were going through his mind at the same time that he was unable to speak. This was a first for him. Carol, sensing his state of utter surprise, tried to pop him back to reality.

"So, is this cause for celebration or what?"

"Absolutely" Brad said, clasping his hands together. "Are they going to write it or do they want me to?"

"If we can make a deal, they want you to act as the script consultant and work with the screen writers."

"What do you mean if we can make a deal? Of course we can make a deal."

"You haven't heard what they're offering yet."

"I don't care what they're offering. I'll take it. Do you know how long I've been waiting for this to happen? One of my books becoming a movie, I don't believe it."

At that moment, the waitress arrived at the table carrying a small tray with two glasses. She sat two napkins on the table in front of each of them, and then sat the drinks on the napkins. "That will be eight fifty."

Brad reached into his pocket and pulled out a twenty and handed it to the waitress.

"Here you go. Keep the change."

The woman looked down at the twenty, then back at Brad. Are you sure sir?"

Brad looked up at her and smiled.

"Special occasion"

"Thank you very much sir. If you need anything else, you just let me know."

Before Brad had a chance to respond, a loud slap broke the relative silence of the room. Everyone's head turned toward the direction of the sound. It was the couple at the bar. The man was standing now with one hand on the bar to balance himself. The woman was lying on the floor. Her long, brown hair was strewn around her head and partially covered her face. Her hand was cupped over her left cheek. As she tried to get up, the man took a step towards her and began shouting.

"You want another one? Then get up bitch."

He took another step toward the woman as if to kick her. Brad bolted up from the table and over to him. He got between the two and tried to diffuse the problem before it got any worse. The manager, who had been called sometime ago, came through the doors at this same moment. Brad, facing the man, tried to get him to step back from the woman.

"Come on buddy, its over. Back up and sit down. Let the lady get up."

"Mind your own damn business, before I give you what she just got."

Hearing this, Carol got up from the table and walked about half way to the bar. She was trying to get Brad's attention. She knew his experience in self defense was extremely limited. In fact, the last time he had to defend himself was in high school. Nonetheless, he had put himself in the middle of their dispute.

"Look pal" Brad softly spoke, "all this is going to do is get you arrested. Why don't you just finish your drink and get on out of here?"

The man stood motionless as if in thought for a moment, then his face reflected the anger that had never left his eyes. Without saying a word, he drew back and punched Brad directly in his face. Brad's head snapped to the right and a long spurt of bright red blood splashed through the air.

He stumbled backwards, knocking over a table and several chairs on his way to the floor. Carol rushed over to him, but was pushed off to the side by the enraged man as he headed for the spot where Brad had landed. The man reached down and picked him up by his shirt collar. The manager came up behind him and grabbed him by his right arm in an attempt to get him to release Brad. Without missing a beat, the man quickly broke free of the manager's hold and struck him soundly in the face with his elbow. The manager stumbled back against the bar, holding his hand over his eye, which had begun to bleed.

"Call the police!" he yelled to the bartender.

The man once again focused his rage on Brad. He grabbed him with both hands and spun him around. Carol attempted to run to his aid again but was stopped by the waitress. The man now had his back to the doors that led out of the bar. Brad struggled furiously to break free of the man's grip, but the guy was just too big and too strong. Brad wrapped his hands around the man's throat and began to squeeze as hard as he could. This served only to anger him even more. He drew his right arm back to hit Brad a second time. But just as he was about to swing, a look of amazement then confusion overtook his face. His arm didn't move. Brad stood, waiting for another blow, and not quite understanding why it was taking so long. Then the man's face showed a distinct look of pain. He let go of Brad who immediately fell to the floor, breaking his fall with his elbows.

The man bent over backwards as if something had a hold of his hand. His knees buckled slightly. Then he was spun around, and in an instant his feet left the floor and he was propelled backwards, crashing down on a table, which broke into what seemed a hundred pieces.

Brad lay there staring at him for a brief second, then his eyes returned to the place where the man was standing to try and figure out just what happened to him. In an instant, he knew. Standing there in the middle of the floor was Lenny.

"Boy am I glad to see you." Brad said as he started to get up.

Lenny motioned with his hands for Brad to stay on the floor. Unsure of why, he looked back in the direction of the broken table where the man had landed. But before his eyes made it that far, the man passed through his line of sight in a dead run towards Lenny. Lenny stood steadfast and confident, waiting for him. Brad tried to get up to block the man's way, but his throbbing head weakened his legs and he fell back to the floor.

Carol broke free from the waitress' grip and ran over to him. She reached him at the same moment that the man reached Lenny. He was yelling and running with his hands out in front of him as if to go for Lenny's throat.

At just the right moment, Lenny dipped slightly. As the man ran within reach, Lenny grabbed him by one leg and one arm and literally threw him over his back like a sack of potatoes. The man flew through the air and hit the glass doors leading into the lobby. By this time he was completely upside down. His feet were the first thing to hit the glass, smashing it into thousands of tiny pieces as safety glass does. At that same instant his back hit the wooden frame of the door and broke it loose from the hinges.

When the sound of breaking glass and wood subsided, the man lay motionless on the floor. Brad, still unable to get up, was resting his head in Carol's lap. The bartender had wrapped a handful of ice in a towel, and the waitress was pressing it against the manager's eye.

The whole ordeal took less than a minute. But in that remarkably short period of time, two tables had been destroyed, three chairs were broken, one entry door was unrecognizable and the manager had received a black eye that would last for at least a week. Brad had the worst headache he'd ever had and a gash across his cheek. The man, who was lying unconscious, had logged enough time flying back and forth across the bar that he may well be eligible for frequent flier miles.

Lenny walked over to Brad and Carol.

"Are you okay?"

"I'm not sure yet. What were you doing here, anyway?" Brad tried to lift himself up a little, but dropped back down to Carol's lap, surrendering to the pain in his head.

"Just happened to be passing by. What caused all this, anyway? It's not like you to get mixed up in bar room brawls."

"She did." Brad answered, pointing in the direction where the woman was laying. Lenny looked over in her direction, the looked back at Brad.

"She who, there's nobody over there."

Both Brad and Carol looked back to the spot where the woman had been.

"She's gone!" Carol remarked.

"But she was right there." Brad said in disbelief. "We both saw her. We both heard her get slapped."

"Ya," Carol added, "That guy slapped her and Brad went over to help." She pointed with her eyes at the man, or at least in his direction. Then a look of shock came over her face. "He's gone too!"

Everyone turned towards the doors. Carol was right. There was nothing but broken glass and pieces of wood. The man was gone.

While everyone was still staring at the absence of a body on the floor, two police officers walked through what was left of the doors.

"Alright, what's going on here?" one of them asked.

The manager lifted the ice pack only a few inches from his eye. "You're too late." he said. "They're gone." Saying this he returned the ice pack to his eye.

The police officers took their hands off of their guns and took out their notepads. One walked over to the bar and began questioning the bartender and manager and the other spoke with Brad and Carol. When the questioning was over, Brad, Carol and Lenny sat down in a booth to a complementary drink from the hotel.

"What were you really doing here?" Brad asked Lenny.

Brad's face was quite swollen. The hotel's medical staff had put a butterfly bandage on his cheek and given him something for his headache. The swelling though, made his speech a little slurred.

"To tell you the truth" Lenny admitted, "I'm staying at this hotel."

"But how do you explain what happened to that couple at the bar? Where did they go?"

"Don't ask me. This was your fight. I just helped." Lenny smiled at Brad and Carol. They seemed almost as if they were married.

"We're just glad you happened by when you did." Carol added. She paused for a moment, not sure if she should ask the question that was on her mind.

Lenny, sensing that there was another question, broke the ice for her.

202 MARK E. SHAVER

"You look like there is something else on your mind."

"Well, now that you brought it up, there is. Do all comedians know how to fight like you do?"

Lenny smiled, knowing that she was going to ask something like that.

"Sure they do. We perform in front of rough crowds sometimes."

He smiled then winked at Carol. She knew that she didn't get the truth, but she knew that she wasn't going to either. That was okay.

Lenny took the last swallow of his drink and got up.

"Well Brad, if you don't plan to pick anymore fights, I think I'll go up to my room."

Brad looked up at him, removing an ice pack from his cheek. "No, I think I've had enough for today."

Lenny told them both goodbye and left the bar. The hotel manager passed Lenny on his way to Brad and Carol's table.

"The hotel wants to extend an invitation for the two of you to spend the night, free of charge, of course. Brad gratefully accepted, thinking to himself, *it's a hell of a way to get a free night in a hotel.*

It was about ten thirty the next morning when Katie's concentration was interrupted by the relentless ringing of the phone on her desk. She finished jotting down the last of the notes she was working on before answering it.

"This is Katie. Can I help you?"

"Yes Katie, this is Alan from DES (Digital Enhancement Systems.). How are you today?"

"I'm fine. Do you have some good news for me?" There was a pause.

"Well, not exactly."

"What do you mean? Didn't the enhancement work?"

"Oh, it worked alright. But I don't think what we've got is what you're expecting."

"You're not making any sense."

"This whole thing doesn't make any sense. Maybe I'd better drop these off to you myself. If I leave now, I should be there in about twenty minutes."

"Well, I guess I'll see you when you get here." Katie hung up the phone, not knowing what the man was talking about. One thing she did know however, was that she probably wasn't going to like what she was about to see.

The twenty minutes seemed an eternity, but it did eventually pass. And as he said he would, Alan tapped lightly against the open door of Katie's office.

"Come in. Have a seat."

"Thank you." Alan said as he took a seat in front of Katie's desk. "As I told you over the phone, the enhancement did produce a clear image of the three faces in the picture."

"That's great!" Katie exclaimed, "So we'll be able to establish their identity?"

"Well, I have already done that."

Katie looked puzzled. She thought for a moment, and then asked, "You know who they are, how?

Alan drew in deep breath. "I grew up watching these guys. I'm a big fan of theirs."

"Who are they?" Katie asked.

"They are two brothers, Moses and Jerome Horwitz and their friend, Larry Finestein."

"Who in the world are they?"

You probably know them better as Curly, Larry and Moe, The Three Stooges."

The look on Katie's face was even more puzzled than it had been when she spoke with Alan on the phone.

"Is this some kind of joke? I thought you guys were a serious company."

"Oh I assure you, we are." Alan reached into his briefcase and removed an envelope. From the envelope he took a picture and handed it to Katie. She studied it for a moment before sitting it down on her desk. It was indeed, three men bearing the faces of the Three Stooges. It was also obvious that the photo had been tampered with.

"How could this have happened?" she asked.

"My guess is somebody got to the photo and the video tape before we did. And I'll tell you something else. Whoever did this knows his way around a computer pretty darn good. I assure you, this is not the work of an amateur."

Katie picked up the picture and starred at it with a far away look in her eyes.

"I really hoped this would be a big break for us."

"I'm sorry we couldn't do more for you. But please don't hesitate to call on us again."

Alan stood up and, after shaking Katie's hand, left her office. Katie sat back down and looked one final time at the picture.

"I can't believe it" she said to herself, "The Three Stooges."

Arthur found it almost impossible to concentrate in anticipation of Sam's phone call. He limited his work day activities to minor things that didn't take long to complete. Most of his time though, was spent starring at the phone, waiting for it to ring.

It was early afternoon before the phone call came.

"Arthur, would it be possible for you to get out of your office for an hour or so this afternoon?"

"Of course, I kind of left this day open for that very reason."

"Good. Let me give you some directions. This may sound a little strange, but you must bear with me."

Arthur took out a pad and pencil. *How much stranger can things get?*, he thought to himself.

Sam continued. "I want you to go to the Grand Park Hotel, on Seventh Street. Go up to the main desk and ask if there are any messages for Dexter Morgan. Have you got that?"

"I've got it." Arthur replied.

"Good. You will receive further instructions when you reach the hotel."

Having said that, Sam hung up. Arthur slipped the note pad into his brief case and snapped it shut. As he walked past his secretary, he told her that he'd be back in a couple of hours.

The trip to the hotel took about fifteen minutes. It was not far from his office. He was hoping he could ask what he was supposed to ask and still keep a straight face. *Dexter Morgan. Where did Sam come up with that name?*

Arthur found a parking space about a half block from the hotel. He got out of the car and dropped three quarters into the parking meter, then headed down the street.

The doors to the hotel were made of dark glass with shiny brass frames. Arthur reached to push the doors open, but a doorman on the inside opened them for him, nodding slightly to Arthur as he walked through.

The main reception desk was about thirty feet inside the front doors. The lobby was quite busy for the middle of the afternoon. There seemed to be people everywhere and that was fine with Arthur. The crowded lobby made him feel a little less conspicuous.

The man behind the reception desk looked quite formal and proper. Arthur approached him in his most professional voice.

"Excuse me, sir. Do you have any messages for Dexter Morgan?"

The man behind the desk looked at him briefly but intently for a moment, and then turned to a maze of mail slots, searching until he produced a small folded piece of paper. He turned back around and handed it to Arthur.

"Here you are Mr. Morgan. You have one message."

Arthur took the piece of paper, thanked the man and walked back towards the elevators, to appear as a patron of the hotel. When he was a safe distance from the desk, he unfolded the paper. It read, 'Go back outside and put another quarter in the parking meter, then flag down the first taxi you see. When it stops, tell the driver you are looking for a good time. He will know where to take you.'

Arthur had seen a movie once where a policeman was delivering a ransom to a kidnapper. The policeman was bounced all over town by the kidnapper to make sure no one was following him. Arthur was beginning to feel like that officer.

He turned and looked back at the man behind the desk. He was talking on the phone and had his back towards him. Arthur made his way past the desk, hoping the man wouldn't see him.

Once he was outside, Arthur headed for his car. He still had forty one minutes on the parking meter, but he put another quarter in it anyway. That gave him over an hour. He couldn't imagine it taking that long, but then how could he tell.

Arthur's eyes then scanned the street looking for a cab. It was less than a minute before one made its way down the street. Arthur stepped off the curb, walking between the cars into the street and flagged it down. When the cab stopped, Arthur opened the rear door and got in. He pulled the door closed and the cab sped off down the street.

"Where to, buddy?" the cab driver asked, looking at Arthur in the rear-view mirror.

"Oh, I don't know. Where can a guy find a good time around here?"

"I know a place" the cabbie responded. Arthur sat silently for the next ten minutes, as the cab weaved through the heavy city traffic before pulling to a stop in front of a large gray building. He looked out the window, searching for a clue as to where he was. The sign on the front of the building soon answered his question. He was at the library.

The cab driver put the car into park and turned around, resting his arm across the back of the seat.

"What you're looking for is in the science section. It's a book called, 'The Fundamentals of Thrust and Propulsion', page three hundred and eighty six." The cab driver turned around and put the car back in gear. Arthur figured that was his cue to get out.

"How much do I owe you?" he asked.

"It's been taken care of." the cabbie answered without turning around.

Arthur opened the door and got out. He barely had time to close the door before the cab screeched away from the curb and merged into the heavy traffic.

This is just too weird, Arthur thought to himself as he climbed the steps to the library. He passed through the main doors, then through a second set, and found himself in front of a counter. It had been a long time since he had been in a library. He had forgotten how quiet they were. He stood for a moment before catching the attention of one of the librarians.

"Can I help you?" she whispered.

"Yes" Arthur whispered in turn, "I'm looking for the science section."

"Four isles down, on your left"

The young lady pointed in the general direction. Arthur thanked her and walked in the direction she had indicated.

He had searched through three rows of books on jet propulsion before he found the book that the cab driver had told him to look for. He pulled it from the shelf, quickly turning to page three hundred eighty six. After looking at it for a few moments, he noticed that four words or parts of words were underlined lightly in pencil. The word 'airport', the word 'west', the word 'wing' and the last three letters of the word 'crossbar'. It took him a minute to put it all together, but it did finally make sense to him. He was on his way to a bar in the west wing of the airport. But how would he get there? His car was back at the hotel.

Arthur closed the book and slid it back on to the shelf. He knew where he was going next, although he was not sure where he would be going from there.

He walked past the main desk and out the doors. Stopping briefly at the top of the stairs, he buttoned his coat. A traffic cop was resting his foot on the front bumper of a car parked illegally in a handicapped zone. Something about it looked familiar. As he started down the steps his eyes became fixed on the car. The closer he got to it, the more familiar it became.

"That's my car." he said aloud. "What's it doing here?"

The officer noticed Arthur looking at the car. "Is this your car pal?"

"Yes, it is."

"Well you don't look very handicapped to me. Why are you parked in a handicapped space?"

"I'm sorry, officer. I didn't realize this was a handicapped spot. I guess I wasn't paying close enough attention. It won't happen again, I promise."

The cop looked at Arthur for a moment. Arthur wasn't sure if he was in trouble or if he had talked himself out of it.

"Don't ask me why, but I believe you. But if I ever catch you parked here again, I'll have your car towed and you'll have to donate a hundred and fifty bucks to the city to get it back. You got that?"

"Yes sir." Arthur said as he walked around him and unlocked his door.

This was getting stranger by the minute. How did his car get here? The driver's seat had not been moved. The radio was set at the same station. Everything was just as he had left it.

It took about thirty minutes to get from the library to the airport. Arthur had made more trips to the airport in the past four months than he had in the past five years. He thought about that as he pulled through the parking gate and headed for one of the few empty spaces. It was a long walk to the terminal, as it seemed to be every time he came here. He eventually did make his way through the terminal, then on to the bar.

There was no one in the bar this particular afternoon. Arthur stood in the doorway scanning the empty tables. He sat down at the bar.

"What can I get for you?" the bartender asked.

"Just a Coke if you have it."

"Sure do" the man replied, and reached down to a cooler below the bar.

He pulled out a frosted beer mug and filled it with coke.

"Your name wouldn't happen to be Jensen would it?" the bartender asked as he sat the coke on a coaster in front of Arthur.

"As a matter of fact, it would." Arthur answered.

"Well, I have an envelope here for you if you can show me some ID."

"How about my driver's license?" Arthur asked, reaching into his back pocket for his wallet.

"That should do it." He looked at the picture on Arthur's license, then up at Arthur.

"Here you go."

He handed over an envelope. It was a plain white envelope with nothing written on it. Arthur picked up his Coke and walked over to a table. He sat down and tore the envelope open. In it was a short note. It read, 'Walk down the concourse towards the baggage claim. There will be a row of phones between two rest rooms on your right. A man wearing a gray suit will be standing in front of the far left phone. Identify yourself to him.'

"Damn" he mumbled to himself. "I'm beginning to get tired of this bullshit." But he persevered and headed down the concourse, leaving a half full mug of Coke on the table.

The concourse was not very crowded. He looked as far ahead as he could, trying to see the man he was to identify himself to. As he approached the phones, there was indeed, a man in a gray suit leaning against the left phone. Arthur slowly approached him.

"Excuse me" he began. "My name's Jensen."

The man looked at Arthur for a moment.

"So what do you want from me?" he asked.

"I'm sorry" Arthur replied, "I thought you were somebody else."

Arthur turned and began to walk away.

"Arthur" the man called out.

Arthur turned around, quite surprised.

"Come with me."

The two men began walking down toward the baggage claim area. They passed through the security gates and into baggage claim. Neither man spoke as they made their way through the maze of carousals to a security door. The man took out a pass card and slid it through a scanner next to the door, then entered a code on the key pad. The door opened and the two passed through. They walked silently down a long corridor. At the end of the corridor was another door. They passed through it, and then outside onto the tarmac.

There were a number of smaller planes parked there and several preparing to taxi. The man led Arthur past them on their way to a somewhat larger one. It was a sleek, white jet with a blue stripe down its side. The man motioned with his hand for Arthur to climb the short set of steps into the plane. Its engines were already running. Arthur looked at him in disbelief, then climbed the steps and got on board. He looked back at the man as he entered the plane. The man motioned for him to sit down in the seat directly in front of the door and buckle up. He did so reluctantly, wondering what he was going to tell his wife when she asked him why he was late for dinner. His seat belt had not been buckled for more that a few seconds when he heard a faint electric hum and noticed that the stairs were being retracted into the belly of the plane. After they had disappeared, the door closed with a slightly higher pitched noise. The plane was much quieter now, but Arthur could still hear the whine of the engines and felt the vibration as the plane began to move.

The plane taxied out to a remote runway at the far end of the airport. Arthur watched as several planes took off and several others landed. He was beginning to believe that maybe they weren't going to fly anywhere. Maybe they just wanted him to think that he was. Maybe the plane would stop and Sam would get on and they could talk. But the plane made a sharp right turn as the pilot powered the engines up. It was obvious to Arthur that none of what he was hoping for would happen.

The plane being the small jet that it was, took only a fraction of the runway to become airborne. Arthur could tell by the position of the sun that the plane was heading south.

CHAPTER SIXTEEN

Senator Edloe stared loathingly at his lunch as it lay on the desk in front of him. Because of the controversy that was voraciously consuming his career he was constantly hounded by the press. To avoid them, he rarely appeared in public, even to eat, for fear they would descend upon him.

So there he sat, eating a once hot but now barely warm roast beef sandwich in his office. He was growing very dissatisfied with his life, or at least the way he had to live it lately. After all, he was a State Senator for heaven's sake, and here he was eating a cold sandwich alone in his office at two o'clock in the afternoon. No sir, this was not what he had envisioned for himself when he decided to enter politics.

Having waited as long as his empty stomach would allow, he raised the sandwich to his mouth and took a bite. The cold, bland taste served only to anger him further. And as always happened he directed his anger toward the one person whom he perceived to be responsible for his situation, or at least the one who could most easily remedy it. That person was Sam.

As his thoughts drifted to his predicament and how easily it could be solved by Sam, he became angered even further by Sam's steadfastness in his beliefs and his dedication to the laws he had been sworn to uphold.

That damned goody two-shoes, he thought to himself, *all I need is one little favor. It's not like I never did anything for him before. But no, he has to uphold the law, to the letter. Well, I'll show him the letter. I'll make his life so miserable that even my life will look good to him. He's messing around with the wrong person. I'm going to make it my life's mission to destroy his fat ass.*

He had become so consumed with his own rage that without realizing it, he had squeezed his sandwich so hard that it was oozing out between his fingers. When he realized what he was doing, he threw the sandwich down on his desk. "I'm going to fix his wagon!" he mumbled to himself. He reached for the phone with one hand and a small black book he kept in his briefcase with the other.

"Time to turn up the heat." he said aloud as he punched a number into the phone.

It took several rings for the party at the other end of the phone to answer. The conversation was short and to the point.

"Ya, it's me" the Senator began.

There was a short pause as the other party acknowledged him.

"Remember what we talked about last week?"

Again there was a pause as the other party spoke.

"No not that asshole, the job, the job."

There was a longer silence as the other person once again spoke.

"Well, the timetable has changed. I want you to do it tomorrow."

There was again a pause as the man spoke, or at least attempted to, at length to the Senator, whose impatience was wearing thin.

"I don't care about that." Edloe replied. "You're supposed to be the best in the city at this, so you figure it out." With that, Senator Edloe hung up the phone.

He sat in silence for a few moments. Then a slight but distinct smile that revealed more evil than joy crept across his face. For the moment, his life felt a little better, but that feeling would most certainly be short lived.

The whining of the engines had leveled off to a muffled roar as the plane reached its cruising altitude. By this time, Arthur had convinced himself that he was on his way to wherever to meet Sam. Settling back in his seat, he prepared for what could be a long flight. He looked around for a magazine or something, anything to read to help pass the time.

"Lose something?" a voice asked from behind him.

The voice was very distinct but at the same time, familiar.

Arthur turned around to see who it was. As he did, a man passed by him in the isle and sat down in the seat opposite him. He was an older man, probably in his mid sixties, though very distinguished looking. His hair was completely gray, almost to the point of being white. But his hairline had not receded nearly as much as Arthur's had. He wore a three piece suit. He was one of those people who looked like he belonged in a three piece suit. Arthur did well to wear a tie and jacket to work. He stared at him for a moment before answering.

"No, I was just looking for something to read."

"I don't think you'll have time for that." the man replied. "Allow me to introduce myself. My name is Sam." He extended his hand toward Arthur and smiled.

Arthur shook his hand, feeling a little dumbfounded.

"It's a pleasure to finally meet you."

Arthur stared at him again for a long second or two.

"I feel like I've seen you before."

"You have" Sam replied, "in my courtroom."

"But I haven't been to court for years."

"That's not quite true. You, Brad and Evan were in my courtroom during the sentencing phase of the trial for the man that assaulted Katie Williams."

The light finally went on in Arthur's head.

"You were the judge!"

Sam nodded in agreement.

"Why in the world did you ever let that guy off? He was dangerous and unremorseful. He probably would have done it again if we hadn't done what we did to him."

"Arthur, I've been dealing with people of all kinds and on all levels for most of my life. To be a judge, you not only have to judge the guilt or innocence of a person, but you have to judge the person themselves. I have spent many years doing this and I have become very accurate in my determinations of one's propensities and abilities. I could tell by your actions and your reactions that you were in my courtroom to see justice done. I saw the five of you talking outside in the corridor before court began that day. I knew by looking in your eyes that if that man walked, you'd do something about it. Had I not seen you, I was prepared to give him a five year sentence. His attorney would have pleaded that down to eighteen months and he would have been out in six with good behavior. You and your friends fortunately changed all that."

Arthur did remember someone passing by them in the corridor of the courthouse. He didn't remember what the man looked like, but he did remember the man staring at him rather intently for someone he didn't know.

"So you were that certain that I would take matters into my own hands if I felt dissatisfied with the verdict?"

"There was no doubt in my mind."

"And you let him go on the assumption that I would punish him?

"Arthur, there was no assumption. I knew that you would."

"But what if I didn't.?"

Sam sat back, getting as comfortable as one can get in an airplane seat.

"Our organization was formed some twenty three years ago. During that time, we have perfected our methods to the point of flawlessness. If for some reason, you had chosen not to try and punish that man, or if you tried and were unsuccessful, we had a back-up plan in place to deal with the situation. He would not have gone unpunished."

"You took a big chance on us though, didn't you?"

"Not really, I pride myself on my accuracy. As I said, I knew you would do exactly what you did."

There was a short pause as Arthur worked up the nerve to ask his next question. "There's something I've wondered about ever since this began. How did you get all of the information about us? You know, the unlisted phone numbers, the details about our families, stuff like that?"

"Arthur, the small group of us that formed this organization are among the most powerful and influential people in the country. We can gain access to virtually every data base in the world. We can listen in on telephone conversations, review credit histories, and if given enough time, can tell you the name of the last prescription that your wife had filled."

Arthur sat silent for a moment, trying to absorb all that he had just heard.

"Now, if you have no more questions, I'd like to talk to you about why you're here."

Arthur shook his head, feeling a little embarrassed that he had let his curiosity get the better of him.

"You are the only person, out of all of the teams we have recruited, that I have divulged my identity to. Although you may look on this as a privilege, it does not come without a price. Should you ever, willingly or unwillingly, reveal my identity, you will be doing so at the cost of your own freedom and possibly much more. I trust no more need be said on this subject?"

"I gave you my word" Arthur reminded him.

"You did indeed. Now, to the business at hand. As you know Senator Ryan Edloe, whom we have discussed previously, has become a problem for our organization. And the problem has turned out to be a much larger one than any of us anticipated. Let me fill you in."

Arthur loosened his tie and unbuckled his seat belt as Sam began.

"Senator Edloe was once a member of our organization. At the time, he was a District Attorney, highly dedicated, and he displayed a degree of integrity and direction that we all felt would be useful to us on a long term basis. He also had a close family member that had been murdered. The man that committed the murder went unpunished because of a loop hole in the law. We agreed to allow him to leave our organization and pursue a political career. We felt he would be useful to us in that capacity as well, since being in politics precluded him from belonging to our group. It was our hope that he could enact legislation to close such loop holes and prevent some of the injustices that we find it necessary to right.

Unfortunately, he became involved with the wrong people and began taking full advantage of all of the financial temptations that are present within the political arena. Among his contributors was the Russo family."

"The crime family, organized crime gave him money?" Arthur seemed surprised.

"Yes, and he accepted it. Vast sums of it, much of which went to cover his weakness for women and his gambling debts, two vices that were not present in his life until he entered politics. Now it's time for him to return the favor to Mr. Russo. His son and two nephews are currently in prison awaiting trial on murder charges. The District Attorneys case hinges on the admissibility of one piece of evidence. The judge presiding over the case must rule as to the admissibility of that evidence. And sadly, I am that judge."

"Is there any question about the admissibility of the evidence?" Arthur asked.

"Not so far as I am concerned. But the problem does not lay there. The problem is what the Senator has threatened to do if I do not disallow the evidence. You see, Mr. Russo has required this of him, knowing there was a relationship between the Senator and me in the past. Edloe does not want to face the consequences should I convict those three men, nor do I want to face what he has promised should that happen."

"Has he threatened you?"

"He has, in no uncertain terms. He has threatened myself and my family, and intends to expose our organization if I don't cooperate with him. He is fighting for his very life here and he is desperate. It has already begun to affect your group as well, although you're probably not even aware of it yet."

Arthur leaned forward in the seat. "How?"

"Brad was beaten up yesterday in the bar of a hotel downtown. Fortunately, I got wind of what was about to happen and had Lenny intervene, but not before Brad had sustained some injuries."

"Is he okay?"

"He's fine. But he will be getting a message on his answering machine that will require some explanation. I trust you can provide one?"

Arthur nodded.

"Good. So with that behind us, I'd like to share with you some ideas I have to resolve this situation."

As Sam began, the plane banked slightly, beginning a slow turn back to the airport. The trip would take forty five minutes, as would Sam's discussion with Arthur. By the time the plane touched down, Arthur had a general idea of what needed to be done, and Sam felt even more secure in his choice of operatives for this task.

The sun was nearing the horizon as Arthur made his way through the busy airport. The lights that illuminated the parking lot had begun to turn on. As he passed under them, the light reflected the concern in his face. This assignment was not like any of the others. There was more at stake here, much more.

The work bench was clean, or at least cleaner than most. The tools that were lying on it appeared to be very well kept. There were also a number of transistors, circuit boards and other electrical components scattered across the bench. This however, was not the work place of an electrician. It was the work place of Gus Eastman. Mr. Eastman made explosives.

Taped to the wall in front of the work bench was a diagram of a car, sort of a schematic, showing both what was inside of the car as well as what was on the outside. The car was a Mercedes Benz, identical to the car that Sam owned and drove to court each day.

Slowly, a hand reached toward the diagram, its skin wrinkled and scarred from years of dangerous work. He reached with his index finger and pointed to a place between the fuel tank and the back seat. With his other hand he cupped his chin, his eyes squinting as if in deep thought.

Gus Eastman was fifty nine years old, but looked much older. The ravages of the life he had led had taken their toll on him, leaving him looking old and tired. His mind however, remained sharp and acute. His hair was long for someone his age, but not long for the sake of style. It was long because he has neglected to have it cut for quite some time. As he leaned forward, several long strands of hair dropped down in front of his eyes. For a few seconds they go unnoticed. Then, as methodically as are all of his actions, he reached up and ran his fingers through the greasy strands, pushing them back over the top of his head. Some stay, but most fall right back where they were.

After a few moments of study, he leaned back on his stool, lacing his fingers behind his head. He looked casually to his left at a wall that displayed at least a dozen newspaper clippings of bombings throughout the country. This was Gus' *wall of fame* as it were, and the articles were his trophies.

All his life, Gus had been controlled. As a child, his mother dictated his every move. Throughout his school years, the other kids pushed him around because of his size. Even his wife, who had left him many years ago, controlled him. But now it was his turn. The authorities had no idea who was planting the bombs. Now he was in control and he liked it. He liked it a lot.

The pain had gone away, but the blue circle under Brad's right eye would remain for another few days. As he sat in front of his computer, waiting for it to boot up, he saw his reflection in the dark screen. *I can't wait to be done with this shit*, he thought to himself as a screen appeared asking for an access code. He entered it and accessed his diary of their activities. He knew the incident in the bar had something to do with Sam and his business but he couldn't prove it, at least not yet. But that would soon change.

About midway through his entry into the diary, his phone rang. It was Carol.

"Hey, I've got some good news for you. Are you ready?"

"I was born ready, remember?"

"I'm not talking about that" Carol laughed. "I'm talking about the screen play."

"Oh that, well give me the good news."

"I have a contract for you to sign and I think you're going to like it."

"How much?" Brad asked.

"They're offering eighty thousand up front, and a percentage of the gross."

"Where do I sign?" Brad said eagerly, if not a little playfully.

"Why don't I bring them by your place tonight and I'll show you."

"I can't wait. Boy, this is a dream come true for me. Don't tell them this, but I'd have been happy with eighty dollars just to get one of my books in the theater."

Just then, that annoying clicking sound indicated Brad had another call coming in.

"That sounds like your other line." Carol noticed. "I'm going to let you go. But I'll see you tonight."

Brad said goodbye, then pushed the button on the phone to engage the other call.

"Hello." There was a short pause. Brad assumed it to be a wrong number until a voice on the other end of the phone convinced him otherwise.

"You got lucky in that bar yesterday. Next time you won't be so lucky."

"Who the hell is this?" Brad demanded.

"Maybe it won't be you next time. Maybe it'll be your lady friend. What's her name, Carol?"

"Hey!" Brad shouted, "You leave her out of this. She has nothing to do with it."

"She does now." The voice replied.

"If anything happens to her, I'll..."

"If anything happens to her you'll be responsible. I know about your arrangement with Sam. He wants you and your friends to pull his fat ass out of the fire. If you value Carol's life, you'll let him fry. Do you get my drift?"

"Oh, I get your drift alright. Now you get mine. You leave Carol out of this, or so help me I'll track you down and put you out of my misery."

"You have no idea who you're dealing with here. So take my advice and call in sick on this one. I'd hate to see anything happen to such a pretty lady."

There was a click. The man, who ever he was, had hung up. Brad gripped the phone with near uncontrollable rage. He had waited years for someone like Carol to come along, and he wasn't going to give her up, not for this or anything else. He slammed the phone down, his hand still clenched around the receiver. He thought for a moment before looking down at his watch. Then he picked the phone back up.

Arthur had just dialed his private line number at the office from his cell phone to retrieve any messages left for him while he had been flying in circles with Sam. There were two from clients, one from his wife asking him to bring home some milk and one from a voice he did not recognize. His eyes widened as he listened to the message.

"If you value your life and the lives of your family, you'd better tell Sam he's on his own on this one. You are way out of your league so back off before something happens that you'll be sorry for. However, if you chose not to, it's only fair to tell you that we're all looking forward to the pleasure of your daughter's company."

That was the end of the call. Arthur threw his cell phone down onto the passenger seat and floored his accelerator, weaving in and out of traffic as he made his way anxiously home. His phone rang before he had driven a mile. It was Brad.

"I got a call just a few minutes ago...."

Arthur interrupted, "So did I. They threatened my family. We're going to have to do something about this. I want you to bring Carol over to my house tonight. I'll call Derek and get him and Katie to come over as well."

"What are we going to do then?" Brad asked.

"We're going to come clean with them about what's been going on, and then we're sending them away until this is over."

"Well I agree with you so far, but what do we do then?"

"Then we find out who's doing this and kick their ass. Nobody threatens my family. I spent two years in a war zone to keep this sort of thing in somebody else's back yard, so if they think I'm going to roll over on this one they're nuts. All bets are off Brad, so you need to decide what you're prepared to do."

"That decision has already been made." Brad replied confidently.

"Good, then I'll see you both tonight."

Arthur hung up the phone and once again focused his attentions on the road. He was traveling about eighty five down the expressway. At this point, he didn't even think about the police, or the ticket he would get if he got caught. All he could think about was his family. Nobody was going to take them away from him. And although Senator Edloe and his mob friends thought they were in control of the situation, they had opened a Pandora's Box that would not easily be closed.

Later that evening, four very reluctant men and three equally perplexed women sat in Arthur's living room. No one ever thought it would come to this, but there seemed to be a number of firsts associated with this assignment. Arthur found himself about to reveal a secret that he had worked so hard to protect. When everyone was comfortable, he began.

"What I'm about to tell you must never leave this room. And the only thing I ask is that you consider all of the facts before you jump to any conclusions."

Arthur stood up and began pacing as he always did when he was nervous.

"It all began this past winter, right after the trial of the man that attacked you, Katie. The fact that the man that did what he did to you and went virtually unpunished was more than my sense of justice could tolerate. So, without Derek knowing anything about it, Brad, Evan and I took it upon ourselves to punish him, and we did. Everything went fine. The man got what he deserved. And yes, we were responsible."

Arthur's wife looked at him in disbelief.

"You three were the ones who did that?" she asked.

"I read about it in the paper," Carol added.

Then Katie spoke up.

"The police questioned me and Derek about it."

"Yes it was us." Arthur continued. "We did it and I'm not sorry that we did. And for a few brief hours, we thought we had committed the perfect crime, if indeed it could be considered a crime."

"It most certainly could!" Arthur's wife snapped.

"Well, it's all elementary now. It seems our good deed did not go unpunished. The next day we all got phone calls from someone who claimed he knew what we did. He turned out to be a high ranking member of some organization that recruits people like us to do the kind of thing we did to others who have managed to slip through the cracks in the legal system. He told us that unless we cooperated with him and began working for him, he would turn us in to the police. So, over the past several months, we have done two jobs for him and we're now working on a third. This third job has taken an unexpected turn. Our identities have been revealed to certain people who have indicated that if we proceed with this assignment, it will be at the risk of our families."

"What do you mean, risk?" Katie asked.

"These people are serious." Brad warned, "They called me and told me that this black eye is just a preview of coming attractions if we don't turn our backs on this one."

"You mean that whole thing in the bar was a set-up? That couple and the fight they had?" Carol was stunned at what she was hearing.

"I'm afraid so." Brad admitted.

Katie sat looking in disbelief at Derek. "So how many of these little episodes have you been involved in?"

"Just two" he answered, "plus this one."

Evan, who had been silent to this point, spoke up.

"Since we're all feeling like Abraham Lincoln here, Katie I owe you an apology."

Derek, knowing what Evan was about to say, put his face in his hands.

"An apology for what?" she asked.

"For the Three Stooges"

"The Three Stooges?" It took her a few seconds to realize what he was talking about.

"You did that?"

"I'm sorry to say, yes. I did it to protect our identity. That security camera had us cold. So you were right. There was a connection between the two incidents you were investigating."

"I knew it." Katie exclaimed. "I just knew those two incidents were tied together somehow. I was right after all." But her smile quickly disappeared as she turned toward Derek. "You knew all the time too, didn't you? Did you enjoy watching me make a fool of myself while you had the answers I was looking for?"

Before Derek had a chance to answer, Arthur spoke.

"The only reason we did not tell you about what we were doing was to keep any harm from coming to you. It seems now you're all in danger anyway, so we're telling you the truth. You can form whatever opinions you like, but the reason we got into this in the first place was because we care about each other, and our families. And, I might add, we were damned good at what we did, too good, actually. That's why we were chosen for this assignment. The reason we accepted it was because they promised it would be our last. But now that our families have been threatened, the gloves are off and there are no rules. So for your own safety, you are all going to have to go away for a while until we take care of this problem. It's for your own good."

"Go away where?" Carol asked.

"Evan's dad owns an estate in northern California. We want you all to go down there and stay until we get this thing cleared up. The people we work for will provide security. You won't see them, but they'll be there."

"So we're supposed to take the kids out of school and drive off to sunny California because somebody is pissed at you and they want to take it out on us, is that it?" Arthur's wife seemed to be the most upset. She and Arthur had been together for many years and she thought she knew him better than she apparently did.

"No, you won't be driving. You'll be flying out there in a private jet. And yes honey, I'm afraid that is 'it'. Only it's a little more serious than that. These people are more than pissed. They're desperate, and they'll do anything to keep us from doing what we have to do."

"What do you mean anything? You mean they threatened to beat us up like they did Brad?" Katie's concern was more for their baby than herself.

"No, they're beyond that. That's why you have to leave."

"Well it'll take me a week to cover things in the office before I can even think about getting away." Carol announced nonchalantly.

Brad turned to her and took her hands in his. "You're leaving tonight."

"Tonight" Carol repeated.

"That's not possible." Sandy snapped. "We'd have to pack, make plans and provisions for things to be taken care of while we're gone. I'll have to write notes to the school for the kids, not to mention packing for them. And how long are we going to be gone anyway? I'm sorry, there is just no way we could be ready in time to leave tonight."

Arthur took Sandy by her shoulders and looked her square in her eyes. "Sandy, these people intend to kill us, all of us. Do you understand?"

Sandy looked at him in disbelief for a brief moment, and then she turned to Carol and Katie. "Go home, get packed and be back here in an hour."

Carol was the first to stand up. "Since you put it that way, Arthur, I guess I can make arrangements by phone to cover myself at the office."

"Me too" Katie added.

And as quickly as everyone arrived, they left. Soon it was just Arthur and Sandy in the living room.

"I feel just terrible about all of this. You know I would never do anything to hurt you or the kids, but we had no choice. We had to go along or face the consequences." Arthur began slowly pacing again. "After the first job, they got easier and more satisfying. I actually felt good about what we were doing. But there were always rules. There isn't this time. That's why you have to go someplace safe 'til this is over with."

"Are you sure you'll be able to handle this? I mean, it sounds dangerous." Sandy's voice was filled with concern.

"Oh we'll handle it alright. Once you're safely out of the picture, we'll be playing without rules too. They messed up when they threatened our families."

Sandy wrapped her arms around him. "I'll miss you."

Arthur smiled. "You won't be gone that long, I promise"

"What'll I tell the kids?"

"Tell them what any loving, responsible parent would tell them; a lie."

Sandy giggled a little as she rested her head on Arthur's shoulder. Arthur's look of reassurance soon turned back to one of concern.

"Do you hate me?" Derek asked as he checked the rear view mirror for the fifth time.

"Of course I don't hate you. I'm surprised and maybe a little hurt, but I don't hate you."

"We all just felt it would be safer for everyone if nobody knew."

"Was it?"

"I guess not" Derek admitted, "but I'm glad you know. It has been sheer hell watching you work on that project and knowing all along what it was you were looking for, but not being able to tell you. I haven't felt good about myself for quite sometime now. Ya, I'm glad you finally know."

"Since you're so remorseful, how did Evan doctor up those pictures?"

"You know the company you sent them to?" Derek asked reluctantly.

"Ya" Katie replied.

"His father owns it. He just fired up their computers one night and scanned the three stooges over our faces. He is a real genius when it comes to electronics."

"How do you know so much about this?"

"Well, I was kind of with him when he did it."

"You helped him?" Katie shouted.

"No I didn't help him. I was just there, you know, not helping him. Besides, if you had seen those pictures, you'd have recognized us right away. They came out perfectly clear. We had no choice. I know it was the big break you were looking for and I'm sorry, but we had no choice."

"When we get back, you four are going to sit down and tell us everything, and I mean everything. Understand?"

"Absolutely, as long as you'll still love me"

"I'll always love you, you know that."

"Ya, but I just need to hear it every now and then."

Katie reached her arm across the back of the seat and rubbed his shoulder. He turned to her and smiled. Although he was comforted by her love for him, he was concerned for her safety and that of his son.

"I hope you're not relying on your skills as a fighter to do whatever it is you have to do to correct this problem!" Carol joked as she and Brad rounded the corner of her apartment building.

"As angry as I am right now I'd probably do okay. But no, we have something else in mind. Like they say, 'pay-backs are hell'."

"I'll worry about you anyway. But I must admit, knowing that you have been involved in this sort of thing, makes you even more attractive, in a macho sort of way." She smiled at him, trying to reassure him that everything would be fine. "I'll miss you."

"I'll miss you too, but don't worry about me. My heart really wasn't in any of the others. I just went along for the sake of my friends. This one is different. It's personal." Brad pulled into the parking space in front of Carol's apartment. "Let's get your stuff and get out of here."

It took Carol only ten minutes to pack. Although she didn't want to admit it, she was as scared as Brad thought she was.

A few hours later, a van slowly coasted to a stop in front of a hanger at the east end of the airport. In front of the hanger sat a small jet, its engines running. It was the same one Arthur had flown on earlier that day. All of the van's doors opened simultaneously. Brad was the first to step out. He walked briskly to the rear of the van and opened the doors. One by one, he began to remove the suitcases. Arthur and Derek soon joined him to help carry the bags. Evan, who had driven the van, stepped out and took a long, searching look around as Arthur, Brad and Derek carried the bags to the plane.

The pilot met them at the bottom of the stairs and unlatched the cargo door. He carefully placed the bags inside, strapped them down securely.

"Are we really going to fly in this?" Todd asked.

"Yes you are" Arthur answered.

"Cool. When can we get on?"

"Why don't you two come with me and I'll get you buckled in?" The pilot motioned with his hand for Angie and Todd to get on board. Todd had no idea what was going on, but Angie had plenty of questions that her mother promised to answer once they were in the air. They hugged and kissed their dad, then walked over to the plane and climbed the short flight of steps.

Sandy turned to Arthur. His look seemed distant and his eyes showed the concern he had tried so hard to conceal.

"How long do you think this will take?"

"Not long. You'll be back before you know it."

"We'll miss you a lot."

"I'll miss you too."

She leaned forward and kissed him. He held her tightly for a long moment, trying to convince himself that everything would be okay.

Brad and Carol embraced one another. As she pulled away from him, he saw the beginnings of a tear drop trickling down her cheek. For the first time in his life, Brad was at a loss for words. So he tried something he had not done for many years. He spoke from his heart.

"Maybe when you get back, we should talk about making our relationship a little more permanent. What do you think?"

Carol looked up at him and smiled. She hugged him again, tighter than before.

"I'd like that." She said. "I'd like that a lot."

Derek kissed his son on the forehead three times and Katie six times before he could muster up the courage to tell them goodbye. He had never been separated from either of them before and was having a difficult time of it.

"You'll be fine, I promise. I'll call to check on you every day."

"I know we'll be fine. It's you I'm worried about. You be careful. Don't get yourself into anything that you can't get out of, understand? We need you."

"Nothing's going to happen to me, but I miss the two of you already."

He kissed them both one final time.

The pilot appeared at the top of the stairs and looked at his watch. Then he motioned for them to get on board. As they walked up the steps to the plane, the three men stood with their hands in their pockets, and watched as the most important part of their lives was being taken away from them. And although they felt some sense of relief knowing that their loved ones would be safe, they also felt a rage that would serve only to motivate them further to get on with the task at hand.

The engines began to speed up as the pilot prepared to taxi. The clearance lights began flashing and soon, the bright taxing lights came on and the plane began to move. All four men waved at the faces as they looked somberly through the small windows of the plane. Soon all that could be seen was a silhouette against the misty night air and the flashing lights as they faded into the darkness.

Arthur watched as it disappeared from sight. His face showed only a trace of the anger he was feeling.

"They're going to pay out the ass for this."

"Come on" Evan shouted. "The clock is ticking and we've got a lot to do."

The three went back to the van and climbed in. Evan turned the lights back on and headed for the airport exit. The battle was at hand. Although they knew it would be fierce, they had no idea to what degree the next eight days would change their lives.

CHAPTER SEVENTEEN

The first thunderstorm of the season was bearing down on the city.
The unusually warm spring air was suddenly cool again. Sheets of rain pounded against Senator Ryan Edloe's office window, its constant rhythm interrupted only by the occasional deafening clap of thunder. As the lightning flashed, it cast a shadow against the wall. Senator Edloe stared coldly at the figure sitting in the chair for a long moment before picking up the phone.

Being Thursday, there was no court until eleven o'clock in the morning. Sam used this time to prepare for the remainder of the week. His office was silent as he read through some testimony, or at least it was until the phone rang.

"Sam, this is Edloe."

"What do you want Edloe?"

"Look, I'm going to give you one last chance to change your mind. I can't understand why you're being so stubborn about this. It's not that big a deal. Sam, I want you to reconsider."

"Apparently I haven't made myself clear. I will not throw a case. Not for you or anyone else."

"We have history, damn it. You and I go way back." The Senator's voice was desperate. "I was loyal to you. I did everything that was asked of me. Now, it's my turn to ask, and you're turning a deaf ear. It's not right. We're the same, you and I. We should be working together, not against each other."

"We stopped being the same when you crossed the line. Our purpose is to punish those who could not be punished by conventional means. They deserve it, and we don't profit from it. You knowingly took money from those whose intention it was to ask for something in return. You knew this day would come Edloe, and now you're looking to me to get you out of it. Well, I'm sorry. There is nothing I am willing or able to do for you."

"I thought I made it clear what would happen to your family if you didn't help me."

"Oh you did in no uncertain terms. The problem is that you are much better at taking bribes than you are at blackmail. My family has been sent away until the trial is over. I might add, so have the other families that have been threatened. We do appreciate the warning, but next time, if you intend to realize any degree of success, you should rely much more heavily on the element of surprise. Now, is there anything else I can do for you?"

The Senator sat silent for a moment. He had expected to appeal to Sam's personal side. He had not counted on such a blatant and quick refusal.

"You're a dead man, you know that don't you?"

"Edloe, I've been sending criminals to prison for over thirty years. And for thirty years, they've been telling me I'm a dead man. Now, if I won't take a cold blooded killer's word for it, what makes you think I'll take yours?"

"Because I got the Russo family behind me, that's why."

"That's right, and after this trial, there will be three less of them behind you. Now, if there is nothing else, I really must get back to work." Sam hung up.

The Senator sat with the phone in his hand for a second or two before putting it down. The lightning flashed, casting the shadow once again on the wall.

"Well?" asked the man whose shadow had darkened the Senator's walls.

Senator Edloe looked at him with contempt. It was as if he resented him being there, but at the same time, was glad he was. After several moments of maniacal concentration, he barked out his answer.

"Alright do it, the sooner the better."

"That's all I wanted to hear." the man said, standing up and pulling his hair back away from his face only to have it fall back again. Gus Eastman's hair still needed cutting.

Edloe slid an envelope across his desk. Gus stopped it with his hand, feeling its thickness and satisfying himself that the entire ten thousand dollars was there.

The device was a simple one; a wad of C-4 about the size of your fist, a motion sensitive mercury detonator and a D-cell flashlight battery. The concept was simple too. The device would be attached to Sam's car at the base of the fuel tank with a magnet. Its installation would take only seconds. The mercury switch would allow Sam to get in the car and start it up. The bomb would not detonate until the car was backed up and the brakes applied. The backward momentum created by the application of the car's brakes would cause the mercury to shift, thus closing the switch and detonating the bomb. Simplicity was Gus' trademark.

The movies lately had glamorized assassins and their elaborate firing mechanisms. But those were nothing more than signatures to Gus. Few people are capable of such complex devices. That made the list of suspects extremely short. Anybody with a library card and twenty bucks could make a device like the one he was about to plant on Sam's car, provided he could lay his hands on some C4. 'Anonymity beats prison any day' were the words that Gus Eastman lived by. And that living had just made him ten thousand dollars richer.

The rain had subsided a little as the older model Dodge Polaris made its way up to the third level of the parking garage. It coasted virtually unnoticed into an empty space near the exit ramp. From this dull green car emerged a tall man wearing a building maintenance uniform. Gus was one of those kinds of fellows that looked like he belonged in an occupation such as this, or any other where appearance didn't matter.

He took a long and deliberate look around the parking garage. It was quiet. There was no one there but him. Once he determined he was alone, Gus removed a tool belt from his back seat. There were a number of tools hanging from the belt along with a pouch. Pliers, a hammer, screw drivers and a roll of electrical tape all seemed to move in sync with his footsteps. The bomb tucked away in the pouch remained completely still. The battery had been removed and was in Gus' pants pocket.

As he made his way through the rows of parked cars he took a piece of paper out of his shirt pocket. On it was a license plate number. He glanced down at it occasionally, pausing to check the plates on a blue Mercedes. The color was right, but the plates were wrong.

Gus would walk through three rows of parked cars before finding the one that belonged to Sam. Once he verified the license number, he put the piece of paper back in his pocket. He took another long look around the parking garage to make sure he was still alone.

After satisfying his concerns, he slowly knelt down, removing the device from his pouch. Balancing it in his hand, he lay down on his back and slid under the car. He took a second to look and make sure there was no better place to attach the device. As usual, his first thoughts were correct. He reached up and attached the bomb to the gas tank with a magnet that was strapped to the back side of it. Once it was in place, he removed the battery from his pocket and carefully inserted it between the two contacts. It snapped into place securely, and a single electronic beep signaled the device was armed.

The floor of the parking garage began to shake as a car made its way up the ramp. Gus slid under Sam's car as far as he could while the passing car drove slowly by looking for a parking space. The sound of the car's engine faded as it drove past him and down several more rows before finding an empty parking place. He listened intently as the engine was turned off and the car door opened then closed. He waited for footsteps but heard none.

Shifting his position, he looked along the floor of the garage between the cars, searching for a pair of feet. There were none. "Come on you son of a bitch" he mumbled to himself. Then he heard the door open and close once more, followed by the unmistakable sound of a woman's high heels making their way toward the elevator.

Slowly he slid out from under the car. He heard the bell, signaling that the elevator doors were about to open. He stood up and looked in the direction of the elevators just in time to see the doors closing and a woman wearing a bright red dress standing inside.

Quickly he walked back to his car, unbuckling his tool belt as he walked. When he reached his car, he threw the belt into the back seat through the rear window which he had left open. Gus opened the door and slid behind the wheel, starting the car as he pulled the door closed. In a matter of seconds he was on his way down the ramp and onto the busy city street. Sam's car sat in the silent parking garage bearing no witness to the death trap it had unwillingly become.

Arthur, Brad and Derek were sitting in their usual places in the lounge of the treatment center as they did every Thursday morning. Evan was late. Everyone took for granted it was a woman that made him that way, and they were usually right.

"Here we are without our women and Evan's at home getting laid!" Derek complained. "It isn't fair."

"None of this shit is fair!" Brad moaned.

"You know, it makes me feel bad sometimes that it's because of me and Katie that we're in this mess."

"It's not because of you and Katie." Arthur argued. "It's because of that low life that attacked her. It's his fault, not yours."

Brad laughed a little. "He did get what he deserved though. I can still see the look on his face when he realized he was wearing a Klan outfit and we were dumping him out in that part of town."

"Ya he got what he deserved and then some." Arthur agreed. "Maybe it was worth it."

"Well, it's elementary now." Brad sighed, looking down at his watch.

It was only a few moments after Brad spoke those words that Evan opened the doors and walked through the lounge. He was walking a little more slowly than usual.

Derek was the first to catch sight of him.

"Boy, she must have worn your ass out," he teased.

"She who?" Evan asked in an uncharacteristically dispirited voice.

"Are you feeling alright?" Arthur asked.

"To tell you the truth, I feel awful. I must have a bug or something."

"You do look a little green around the gills." Brad noticed.

"Whatever it is, I'm sure it will pass. I'll be fine tomorrow."

"Well I certainly hope so," Arthur added. "We're going to need you for the job. Think you'll be okay?"

"Ya, I'll be fine. Like I said, it's just a bug."

"I'll call tonight to check on you. We can't afford to have you out of the game at this point." Brad was a little concerned about Evan, but he had enough faith in his common sense and knew that he would take care of himself.

The treatment session that day made Evan feel one hundred percent better. That scared him, but he tried not to think about it. Maybe it was just a twenty four hour bug that worked its way out of his system coincidentally in time with the treatment. Just the same, he was grateful to be feeling better.

After a light snack consisting of soup and a piece of toast, Evan made the trip down the hall to check on Senator Edloe's phone calls. He flipped the light on in the den and could tell right away that there had been a number of calls made and received. He backed the tape up and began to play them back. The first was quite early that morning. It was a call to the Senator's office.

"Ya, it's me. You still need me to come over this morning?"

"Ya, I do. I'm going to call the stubborn son of a bitch again and try to reason with him. But if that doesn't work, he's all yours."

"Good. Then I'll be there in about twenty minutes."

The next call was the one made by Senator Edloe to Sam. It didn't take a rocket scientist to figure out that something was about to happen. Evan didn't even know who Sam was, much less how to get in touch with him. So he did the next best thing. He called Arthur. There was no answer on his private line so he tried his cell phone. Arthur answered it on the second ring,

"Arthur, I was playing back Edloe's phone calls and it sounds like he's about to make a move on Sam. You need to get a message to him and let him know that something's going to happen today."

"Like what? Could you tell who he was talking to or what they had planned?"

"No, but he did make it clear that he was going to give Sam one last chance to fold, but Sam didn't do it."

"The only way I've ever gotten a hold of him is on the internet but I'm not in the office to do that right now. I've just left a client meeting. It'll be another thirty minutes before I'm back."

"Then give me his e-mail address and I'll do it."

Arthur gave him Sam's e-mail address. He wrote it down as he reached for the switch on his computer.

"Let me know if he gets back to you."

"I will" Arthur replied then hung up.   He sat tapping his fingers nervously on the steering wheel trying to make a decision that would not take long to make. He changed lanes abruptly and made a right turn.

Sam had twenty minutes left in a recess he had called. Having finished a cup of coffee, he sat behind his desk in his chambers reviewing some transcripts. He was less than halfway through the last page when someone knocked on his door.

"Come in" he responded.

A young man, maybe in his early twenties slowly opened the door. He was clean cut and wearing a uniform bearing the letters 'MTD' on the pocket.

"It's me sir, Jim with Mid Town Detailing. I'm here to pick up and detail your car. You have an appointment to get it washed and detailed today."

"Yes I remember you, Jim. You're going to law school, aren't you?"

"Yes sir."

"How's it going?"

"It's hard. A lot harder than I thought it would be. But I'm managing to keep my grades up. I don't want to wash cars for the rest of my life."

"Good man." Sam encouraged. "I worked my way through law school cleaning stables on a horse farm. It made me work that much harder knowing that some day I wouldn't have to shovel manure anymore. I'm sure the same will work for you."

"Yes sir, no doubt about it."

Sam reached into his pocket and threw him the keys to his car.

"Please be careful with her. She's the only lady in my life right now."

"What about your wife?"

"She's out of town for a while."

"Well" the young man answered, "I'll treat her as if she were my own."

"Thank you" Sam replied.

The young man excused himself after telling Sam that the car would be finished and returned about an hour and a half. Sam kind of liked the kid. Maybe he reminded him of himself when he was growing up. He shook his head, considering how many years ago that was, and returned to his transcripts.

The further Arthur drove, the more anxious he became. He wasn't even sure if Sam was still in the same courtroom or not. He had no idea where his chambers were. But what he did know was that Sam's life was in danger, and he had to do whatever he could to warn him.

The traffic was getting heavier. People were beginning to get off work. Arthur weaved recklessly among them, hoping not to be noticed by the police. He ran several yellow lights and one red one as he rounded the corner in front of the courthouse. The parking garage entrance was in the back. His tires squealed as he turned onto the ramp.

The signs directed visitors to the upper level. That would be level five. He raced into the garage, through the first level up to the second. The way the parking garage was designed, you had to drive completely through each level to get to the ramp leading to the next. This made the journey seem endless.

Arthur rounded the corner and headed up the ramp to the third level. He was about three quarters of the way up the ramp when he caught sight of a pair of tail lights. At that same instant he saw a great white flash and felt the entire parking garage shake. The sound that followed was deafening. A huge ball of flames rose quickly to the ceiling of the third level, then billowed outwards, covering most of the parking level in a blanket of orange flame and smoke. He felt a jolt, and then felt himself drop. The ramp under him had collapsed, leaving the rear end of his car teetering over the edge between the second and third levels.

The flames had pushed their way through the level and out the sides of the parking garage setting numerous vehicles on fire in the process. Arthur jumped out of his car. He was stunned at the heat that still remained. He ran towards the burning shell of the car that had exploded. There was little left, and certainly nothing left of the driver. Arthur was sure that was Sam's car.

The intense heat forced him back along the perimeter of the parking garage, and even there it was nearly unbearable. A crowd of people had gathered outside the door to the stair well. Through the smoke he could see several building security officers and a number of what appeared to be office workers from the courthouse. Arthur began to make his way around the flames toward them. The faint sound of sirens could be heard off in the distance, growing ever louder. As he approached the officers, the stairwell door opened and a figure emerged that was strangely familiar. The closer he got, the more he was sure he knew that man. The man turned and looked at him. It was

Sam. Arthur felt a great, but brief sense of relief. If it wasn't Sam in the car, then who was it?

"Sam" he called.

Sam turned and looked in the direction of the voice.

"Arthur, what are you doing here?"

Arthur walked up to him then led him aside by his arm.

"I came here to warn you, but it looks like I'm too late."

"You knew about this?"

"Ya, Evan played the tapes of Edloe's phone conversations from this morning. He heard a conversation Edloe had with someone before he called you, then the one he had with you and it was clear something was going to happen."

"That fool, I can't believe he'd do something like this."

"Sam, who was in the car, it was your car, wasn't it?"

"Yes, it was my car. Every other Thursday I have a service come pick it up and wash it. Edloe killed a twenty one year old law student." Sam looked around at the police that had finally arrived. "Let's go down to my office. We need to talk some more."

The two walked down the stairs to the bottom floor of the parking garage then into the Federal Courthouse. They took the elevator to the second floor and walked down the corridor towards Sam's office.

It all looked strangely familiar to Arthur. It should have. It was the same hallway they all stood in after the trial of Katie's attacker. Sam opened a door on the left side of the corridor and held it as Arthur passed through. Sam entered behind him. Arthur sat in a chair in front of the desk and Sam behind it. There was a name plate on the front of the desk. Another question had been answered for Arthur. The name plate read, 'Gordon Samuel Hartfield'.

"Arthur, have you or anyone else gone to the police with this?"

"No, of course not"

"Strange as it may seem, you cannot; at least not at this particular time."

"But this might be the solution to the whole problem. There is enough evidence on the tape to link Edloe to the explosion."

"And how did you come by this tape?"

"Just like we always do; a transmitter and a relay. Evan is a genius at this stuff."

"It's called a wire tap, Arthur. Do you have a court order allowing you to tap his phone?"

"You know we don't."

"Then the information was obtained illegally and therefore it is inadmissible as evidence in court. Don't you see our position here? That information was of benefit to us and no one else."

"I see what you mean" Arthur reluctantly admitted, "but it was a nice thought though."

"Arthur, there's something else I wanted to talk to you about. Something you are not aware of that may be helpful to you in light of what has happened. Edloe is an uncommonly superstitious man. He has very definite beliefs in life after death, but more importantly, he believes that certain things happen to those who are taken before their time as well as to those who are responsible. He was almost killed himself not long ago, and came away from the experience with some strange beliefs."

"How does that affect us?"

"It's an opportunity, don't you see? He is responsible for a man's passing before his time. He's not aware of this yet but he soon will be. Then, by virtue of his own beliefs, he will become the recipient of whatever ill befalls one who is guilty of such a transgression."

"Well what does he believe will happen to somebody who's guilty of something like that?" Arthur asked.

"I know someone that can explain it better than I can. I want you to go and see her."

Sam took a piece of paper from his top desk drawer and began writing. When he was finished, he folded it then handed it to Arthur.

"Go and see this woman. She will give you all the information you need. Within this information will be the avenue that may end this for all of us. Once you understand what he believes, you and your friends will know what to do. And the sooner this is over, the sooner we'll all be re-united with our families."

"That's a nice thought" Arthur said as he stood up and turned toward the door. He stopped and turned back to Sam.

"Oh, I had Evan send you an email message. I guess you can ignore it now."

Sam stood up and walked around his desk to where Arthur was standing.

"It means a lot to me, your concern. I'm touched that you raced all the way down here because of it. My only regret is for the young man who had to die because of Edloe's greed."

Sam shook Arthur's hand then opened the door for him. Arthur made his way down the hall to the elevators. When he returned to the third level of the parking garage, he found the entire area cordoned off with yellow police tape. He walked up to the tape and motioned for one of the officers. The officer walked over to him telling him this was a crime scene and he was not allowed inside.

"That's my car teetering over the edge there."

"Oh, we've been looking for you. Where have you been?"

"I went inside the courthouse to call my wife. She worries."

"Well, we need to get a statement from you."

For the next forty five minutes, Arthur lied through his teeth about everything from why he was there to the part about his wife. He was convincing enough as nothing in his statement was questioned. When he finished, he was allowed over to his car, or what was left of it. He didn't remember it looking like this last time he saw it. But he had other things on his mind then.

The car was black. No trace of the blue paint was visible. The tires were gone, not flat or burned, but gone. They had completely melted them away. The headlights and windows had burst from the extreme heat. He opened the door to a wisp of smoke which served to forewarn him of the condition of his interior. The seats were burned so that nothing remained but the springs and the metal frame surrounding them. Arthur was dumbfounded by the damage. He walked back over to the policeman that had interviewed him.

"I don't understand it" he said in amazement, "when I left the car, it looked fine. Now it's burnt to a crisp. What happened?"

"The heat from the explosion set a number of other cars on fire." the officer explained. "Several of those other cars must have had full tanks of gas because they exploded too. One of them was parked on the end of the row, right next to your car. If it wasn't for that, you wouldn't be making that call to your insurance company tonight. Sorry."

"So am I" Arthur added. "Guess I'll call a wrecker and have it hauled out of here."

"Not just yet." The officer responded.

"Why not?" Arthur questioned.

"Your car is evidence. We're going to have to impound it. When we're finished with it, the insurance company can have it. It shouldn't throw you off more than a week."

"You're kidding?" Arthur said, as if things weren't bad enough.

"Sorry, police policy. Guess you were just in the wrong place at the wrong time."

Arthur gazed out over the smoldering parking lot. "It's not the first time that's happened." he mumbled.

Arthur made a call to Evan on his cell phone. It was a twenty five minute drive from Evan's house to the Courthouse. Then he called his office and explained to his secretary what had happened and that he would not be in for the rest of the day. A third call was placed to his insurance company. A much more detailed explanation would be owed to them.

After making the call to the insurance company, Arthur walked to the front of the building and through the doors onto the steps leading down to the street. How strange it felt being here, in the place where this all began; and the place where Arthur hoped it would eventually end.

The rush hour traffic was heavy as Evan and Arthur made their way through the downtown area on their way to Arthur's house. Arthur's face still had traces of the explosion and fire in the form of a light black film of soot around his eyes and nose. He sat silently in Evan's car contemplating the events.

You know" Evan began, "every time I begin to think that no one's life could get further into the dumper than mine, you go and prove me wrong."

Arthur, resting his head on the head rest, turned and looked at Evan. "Thanks, that makes me feel much better."

"Man, to lose your wife, your kids and your car all in the same week has to be some sort of record, don't you think?"

"It is for me." Arthur emphatically agreed.

Up ahead the traffic was stopped. Evan began to slow down. All he could see in front of him was an endless line of tail lights. He pulled up to a stop and put the car in park, anticipating a long wait.

"Great!" Arthur scoffed. "What a perfect end to my day."

"We're liable to be here a while." Evan concluded.

Arthur laid his head back against the head rest again. He stared off aimlessly into space for a few minutes before his eyes focused on a street sign at the corner just a few car lengths ahead. Something about it was familiar, but he couldn't quite place what it was. He'd seen that name before.

"Wait a minute" he said aloud.

"What are you talking about?" Evan asked.

Arthur dug around in his shirt pocket for the piece of paper Sam had given him. He took it out and unfolded it. On it was a woman's name and an address. The street was East Haskell Street, the same name that appeared on the sign just a few feet in front of them.

"Evan, pull around this guy" Arthur insisted, pointing at the car in front of them. "I want to go down that street, that one right up there."

"What's down there? It's a dead end street."

"Somebody we need to talk to, so back up and pull around."

Evan carefully maneuvered the car through the narrow space between the car in front of him and the cars parked on the street next to the curb. It took a little doing but he finally managed to get to the corner. He turned right. The street was short and dead ended into a barricade which backed up to the railroad tracks.

"What's the address?"

Arthur looked again at the paper.

"Eight eleven. It should be up here on the right."

Evan drove slowly as Arthur checked the house numbers. Eight eleven was near the end of the street. It was a fairly well kept house compared to the others around it. There was no driveway. Evan pulled up to the curb in front of the house and turned off the engine.

"Who lives here?"

"Somebody Sam told me to talk to."

"Why?"

"It's about Senator Edloe. He said the lady that lives here could tell us about some of the weird stuff he believes in, you know, life after death, spirits, that sort of thing."

"What possible good could that do us?"

"I have no idea. But Sam is never wrong, and besides, we weren't going anywhere anyway, right?"

"Well, you talk and I'll listen. That spirit stuff gives me the creeps."

The house sat close to the road. There was a small front yard, most of which had been trampled down to the dirt, probably by the neighborhood kids. It was a two story house. Across the front of it was a porch that spanned its entire width, which couldn't have been more than thirty five feet. Two chairs and a small table sat on the porch. In the middle of the table was a large candle. The wax had formed a giant ball at the base and it appeared to be melted to the table.

Thick curtains covered all the windows. The glass in the front door had aluminum foil covering the inside. As they climbed the steps to the porch Arthur turned to Evan.

"Why do people put foil in their windows? I never understood that."

"Beats me, maybe it keeps the spirits away or something."

Arthur looked around for a doorbell button. There was none. There was no door knocker either. So Arthur made a fist and gently knocked on the glass. They both listened for footsteps. Evan hoped no one was home. He was wrong. A sharp click sounded as the locks on the inside of the door began to unlock. There were four in all. When the fourth one had been unlocked, the door opened. A large black woman clad in a floor length house dress appeared in the open door. She was heavy, but not really fat.

She looked serious, almost to the point of being angry. Her hair was tucked under a tight fitting scarf. In her left hand she clutched a hard covered book, bearing no title or author, simply a star inside a circle. It was a symbol Evan recognized. She looked at them with curiosity and disdain at the same time. The wrinkles in her face became magnified as she spoke.

"Yes"

"Excuse us" Arthur began, "but we're…"

"I know who you are." she spoke in an assertive tone, her speech thick with a distinct accent, possibly Jamaican.

"Then you know why we're here?"

"You're not a believer are you?" she asked, as if knowing the answer.

"A believer in what?" Arthur asked.

The woman paused, studying them both for a moment. "No sir. You're not a believer. But before this day is over, you might well be."

The woman laughed aloud as heartily as a bar tender telling a dirty joke, then she stepped back and motioned with her eyes for the two men to come in. Arthur stepped aside to allow Evan to enter. Evan took Arthur's arm and pulled him in front of him.

"You go first. I'll be right behind you."

Arthur stepped through the door with Evan following close behind. "How did she know who we are?" Evan whispered.

"How the hell should I know?" Arthur snapped. "Maybe Sam called her."

There were a number of adjectives that could have described the inside of this house, but the one that stuck in Arthur's mind was aberrant. It was as if they had walked into another realm of existence.

They followed the woman down a short hallway to a locked door. She removed a key from the front pocket of her house dress and unlocked it. The hinges squeaked a little as the door opened. It was dark inside the room. Arthur and Evan waited outside the door for the woman to turn on a light, but there was no light in the room, only a candle, which she lit with a large fireplace match. When it began to burn, she raised her eyes to the two men outside the door. Having determined that this was as light as it was going to get, Arthur took a step into the room, but not before taking a long look around.

The black curtains covering the windows were reason for the darkness. Hanging on the wall between the two windows was an artist's rendering of what appeared to be Satan. It was a hideous looking thing. Arthur stared at it for a moment. Something about its eyes made him turn away. There were clumps of garlic tied into small tight bundles hanging from the bottoms of all of the pictures in the room, except the one he had just looked at. The other pictures appeared to be of family members. Some looked very old, and others as if they were taken only yesterday.

The woman sat in a chair and rested her hands on the small table in front of her. Across from her was an old couch covered with a faded red sheet. Arthur and Evan walked cautiously over to it and sat down.

"I'm told your name is Sheila. May we speak to you by that name?" Arthur began.

"My name is not important. But if you feel you must, you may call me Sheila."

"We need some information from you. We appreciate you taking the time to speak with us."

Evan pulled a small tape recorder from his jacket pocket. He sat it on the table in front of the woman, then asked, "Do you mind if we tape our conversation?"

"You cannot tape my voice with that." she replied.

Evan thought for a moment, and then asked mockingly, "Are you telling me that your voice, for some mystical reason, cannot be recorded?"

The woman looked at him with contempt.

"No. I'm telling you that you have no tape in that machine."

Arthur looked over at him, trying to suppress his laughter. Evan picked up the recorder. Sure enough there was no cassette in it. He took one from his other jacket pocket and quickly unwrapped it and put in.

"May we begin now?" she asked.

"Of course" Arthur replied apologetically. "I take it you are familiar with the beliefs and persuasions of Mr. Ryan Edloe, are you not?"

"I am" she answered. "What exactly is it that you want to know?"

"We need to know what he believes. Let me explain why."

"There is no need. I know Mr. Edloe is responsible for the death of someone whose time had not yet come. Once he is made aware of this, he will try to learn as much as he can about this person. The way this person lived his life will be very important to him."

"Why?" Evan asked.

"You two have no experience with those who have crossed over to the other side, have you?"

"We have no experience or knowledge of any of this, that's why we're here. Now please, tell us what Mr. Edloe believes." Arthur found himself mildly pleading with Sheila. She had the two of them in the palm of her hand and she knew it. They were at her mercy, and the intimidation that the house reeked of helped to keep them there.

"Not long ago, Mr. Edloe was in an automobile accident. A high-school boy showing off to his girlfriend hit him head on. The boy's girlfriend was killed. When they brought Edloe into the hospital, he had been clinically dead for several minutes before the paramedics brought him back. After he had recovered, he came to see me. He told me what he had seen during those minutes before his heart began to beat again."

"What did he see?" Evan asked, his fear diminished by curiosity.

"He spoke of an encounter with the one they call the beast."

"The beast, what is that?" Arthur questioned.

"Satan. Haven't you ever read the Bible?"

"Apparently not as often as I should have" Arthur answered.

"The beast explained to Edloe that if he were to die because of the actions of the boy, the beast would, in exchange for Edloe's soul, allow him to return to this world in a sub-human form and exact his revenge on the boy for what he had done."

"What do you mean a sub-human form?" Evan asked.

"A spirit; that which can neither be seen nor heard."

"Exactly how would a spirit take revenge against a human?" Evan's curiosity was now out of control.

"The spirit, through subtle acts would make its presence known to its victim. They would be little things at first like moving and even hiding some of the victim's personal belongings, or re-arranging household items that would be noticeable only to its victim. The spirit would make its presence known gradually, but unmistakably. As time goes on, the spirit's actions become less elusive and more explicit and daring. The spirit's victim would hear voices in the night. The spirit would control his dreams and turn them into nightmares. He would be awakened by the sounds of laughter, only to hear the silence. His life would cease to be his own. The spirit would make its intentions known, through recurring nightmares. The nightmares would be so hideous that the victim would shun sleep, fearing that he would be unable to awaken from the dream. As the victim's strength is diminished, the spirit will invade his thoughts. An overpowering feeling of helplessness would consume him. He would become a prisoner of his own mind. The total feeling of fear and hopelessness will eventually give way to madness, and that madness will cause him to take his own life as a means of escape. This is what Ryan Edloe believes." She stopped momentarily, looking straight into Arthur's eyes. "Now, what do you believe?"

"I believe that is the strangest thing I've heard in my life!" Arthur confessed. "Why did Mr. Edloe come to you instead of someone else?"

"He came to me for help and understanding of what had happened to him. I have had much experience with those who have crossed over, and then returned, but none as extreme as that of Ryan Edloe."

"How did you know he wasn't making this up?" Evan asked.

"His eyes; the essence of a man's being is revealed through his eyes. The fear I saw in his eyes as he told me of these things could only be from one who was telling the truth."

"Why is it so important that he know about the guy that was killed? What is it that he'll try to find out?" Evan seemed to be asking the questions at this point, which was fine with Arthur.

"He must know the nature of the man while he was alive to determine what he will be capable of after death."

"You mean if a person was mean and hateful during their life, they would be the same after death?"

"It's not their actions but their inner being, their sense of balance. There is much more to a man than his actions."

"So what sort of person would want to get even with the one who killed them?" Evan asked.

"The more a person has to live for, the angrier that person will be for being deprived of his life. Someone with a promising future, planning to marry, or someone with small children whose lives have just begun, has much to lose. Those are the ones who will choose to take action from the other side."

There was a pause in the conversation as Evan and Arthur collected their thoughts and tried to absorb all they had heard. After a few moments hesitation, Arthur asked the final question.

"Do you believe as Mr. Edloe does?"

"I have felt the power of those who have crossed over before their time. It is more frightening than death itself."

Sheila paused, looking down at the wax from the candle which had melted and was dripping off the table onto the floor. She moved her hand to the edge of the table and allowed a small pool of the melted wax to drip into her palm. She winced slightly from the pain. When the wax had hardened, she closed her hand around it. With her fist clenched, she looked back up at Arthur.

"But unless you believe, you will not be able to tell what is real from what is not." As she spoke she opened her hand, and the wax which had hardened in her palm had once again melted and ran in small streams across her hand and down her long thick fingers. The wax trails hardened almost immediately. Arthur and Evan looked at her hand in disbelief. Evan began to stand up.

"I think you've answered all of our questions." he said as he made his way briskly toward the door. Arthur was close behind him.

"Yes" he added, "thank you very much for your help."

Sheila leaned back in her chair and began to laugh that same cold, maniacal laugh that she had laughed earlier.

"I trust you can find the door?" she mocked, momentarily regaining her composure.

"No problem" Evan replied as he closed it behind him.

The bright sunlight made them squint as they ran down the porch steps and across the yard to Evan's car. They wasted no time getting in. Once inside, they took a moment to catch their breath and try to comprehend what had happened.

"How do you suppose she did that with the wax?" Evan asked.

"I'll be damned if I know." Arthur admitted. "Start this thing up and let's get the hell out of here."

Evan started the car and quickly pulled away from the curb. He drove to the end of the street and made a U-turn, heading back to the main road. As they passed the house, Evan took one last look at it. He noticed the curtains were pulled to one side in an upstairs window as if someone was looking out, but he could see no one.

"Well, now we know. So what's next?"

Arthur thought for a moment. "We need to get everybody together, and you need to wire us in to Edloe's home phone."

"That's easy enough" Evan said.

"I'll need to listen to the tape you made at Sheila's house. I'm sure there's plenty I don't remember. That had to be the strangest conversation I've ever had in my life."

Evan shook his head. "She was definitely different, wasn't she?"

"Different? She was nuts."

There was a long moment of silence.

"Was she?" Evan reluctantly asked.

"I'm not sure" Arthur confessed. "That's what scares me."

CHAPTER EIGHTEEN

The estate occupied sixteen acres including a house of some twelve thousand square feet, several out buildings and a stable. It was about what Sandy and Katie expected, knowing what they knew of Evan's father. Carol on the other hand, was astounded. She knew Evan had money and figured his dad must have as well, but she had no idea until now, just how much money Evan's dad must be worth to own something like this.

"Brad told me Evan's dad was rich, but I think this is what they call 'big rich'. Look at this place."

The ladies and their children stood huddled in a group in the middle of a vast entry way. The floor appeared to be inlaid marble. It extended the entire depth of the house, about ninety feet or so. There were many doors and several other smaller hallways branching off of the main hall. The walls on either side of the hall were painted with two large continuous murals. The work rivaled that of the sixteenth century artists. They were hand painted and signed. Giant brass chandeliers, dangling majestically, lined the ceiling of the hall.

As their eyes moved around the vastness of the house, a man perhaps in his late sixties and a woman, probably fifty, approached them from one of the rooms down the main hall.

"Welcome" the man said, "we are most happy to have you as our guests." His speech gave the slight hint of an English accent, and his words seemed carefully chosen. "My name is Karstens, and this is Mrs. Terrell. We will see to it that your stay with us is a most pleasant one. You may leave your bags here. I'll have them sent up to your rooms."

"How many people are there here besides us?" Sandy asked.

"There are just the two of us, a handyman and the security staff, but I'm sure you will find that the staff is more than adequate to meet your needs."

"That's very kind of you." Sandy replied. "Do you know why we're here?"

"Unfortunately, I do, and I can assure you that you will be safe here. This estate is extremely secure. There have also been certain other measures taken to insure your safety so please, just relax and enjoy your stay with us."

"I don't know about you two" Carol spoke, "but I'd sure like to freshen up a little."

"Of course," Mr. Karstens agreed, "you must be Carol."

"Yes I am. How did you know?"

"It was just a guess." He turned toward Katie. "You must be Katie, and this little fellow must be Derek Jr." Finally he turned to Sandy. "And you would be Sandy, and you two must be Todd and Angie, would you not?"

"We would." Sandy said.

"Let me show you to your rooms."

He turned to Mrs. Terrell. "Get Jim to bring the bags up, would you please?" She nodded and hurried off down the hall.

As they followed Mr. Karstens, Carol leaned over to Sandy. "This place is just like a hotel. Is this what you were expecting?"

"No, it wasn't. But I'm not complaining."

"We could never afford to stay in a place this nice." Katie added. "It's just a shame it has to be under these circumstances."

"Ya" Carol agreed, "and without the guys." There was a long pause in the conversation before Katie spoke.

"I hope they're okay."

"Of course they are." Sandy said, putting her arm around Katie's shoulders. "They know what they're doing."

"I have no idea what I'm doing!" Brad protested.

"You don't have to" Evan snapped, "Just hold that circuit board still for ten more seconds."

The four men had gotten together in Evan's den to discuss their conversation with Sheila and to determine where they were going from here. Derek was putting the finishing touches to a listening device for Senator Edloe's home phone. Brad was his reluctant assistant.

"What is that thing anyway?" Derek asked.

"It's a tap. We need to know who he is calling. But this one will let us see the number of the person he is calling and it will let us intercept the call."

"Why would we want to do that?"

"You'll find out shortly. Wait till Arthur tells you about the conversation we had with this 'spiritualist' woman this afternoon. Talk about weird."

"Damn, I wish I was there."

"No you don't!" Evan said emphatically.

While Evan and Brad were working on the device, Arthur sat at the bar, talking to Sam on the phone.

"We're as ready as we're going to be." Arthur said.

"Good!" Sam replied. "I'm going to call Edloe right now. He should still be in his office, so you'll be able to listen to the conversation. I'll plant the seed in his mind, but you'll have to put your plan into place very quickly in order for us to be successful."

"I understand. We have everything ready at this end, but it's important that he stay at his office for at least two more hours this evening. So tell him whatever you have to, but we need that much time to do what we need to do."

"I'll take care of that. Just let me know when you are finished."

"We'll be in touch with you then."

Arthur hung up the phone. How different their conversations were now. It was almost as if the roles had changed somewhat. Now it was Sam who was in the hot seat. Yes, things certainly were different now.

It was less than two minutes after Arthur hung up the phone that the large open reel tape recorder clicked on and began running, signaling a call on Edloe's office phone. Seeing this, they stopped what they were doing to listen.

"Edloe, this is Sam."

"Sam." There was a long pause. "I thought you were dead," Edloe said, his voice shaky and nervous.

"Edloe have you completely lost your mind? Do you have any idea what you have done?"

"I don't know what you're talking about." He answered quickly.

""Don't lie to me, Edloe. I know you too well. I also know about the bomb you had planted in my car. And I'm sure you're wondering right now, if I'm still alive, then who was in my car?"

Edloe refused to answer; still stunned by the fact that Sam wasn't dead.

"Well let me tell you what you've done. You have killed a young law student who worked for a car care service. Every other Thursday he came to pick up and clean my car. You screwed up Edloe. That young man was a straight 'A' student with a promising career ahead of him, and he was engaged to be married, but you took all that away from him because of your greed and your mistakes. How does that make you feel?"

Edloe sat in silent terror, unable to speak.

Then Sam's tone changed. "I know about your beliefs, Ryan. I know about the accident." he spoke quietly. "What are you thinking right now? What's going to happen to you for this? I know that different things happen to those who believe, and I know that you believe. I know that the young man you killed had a lot to live for, and if what you believe is true, he's probably very angry with you right now. What do you suppose he'll do about it, Ryan? Are you ever going to be safe again?"

Senator Edloe's eyes were wide and bulging. His face was chalky white as sweat covered his forehead. He had heard more than he wanted to hear. He slammed the phone down, only to have it ring again seconds later. He picked it up angrily.

"What?" he shouted.

"Edloe" It was Sam again. "You and I do go way back. What you've done is a terrible thing, but I'm going to make a few phone calls and try to help you. I don't know if I can, but I'm willing to try. I need you to stay at your office until I call you back, just in case I need to ask you anything. Will you do that for me?"

"Of course I will. What do you think you can do?"

"I'm not sure, but I will try. So remember, stay by the phone in your office until I call you back. Understood?"

"I will." Edloe responded obediently.

Sam hung up as did Edloe, and the tape machine in Evan's den clicked off.

"What was all that about?" Brad asked.

"We're going to talk about that in a few minutes." Arthur answered.

Evan grabbed the small tape recorder off the coffee table and took the tape out of it and slipped it into his pocket.

"You guys won't believe this when you hear it." Evan warned as he pulled on his coat.

Carefully placing all of the electrical gadgetry into an aluminum brief case, he announced they were ready. Once again the lights were dim in the den, and the beginning of something none of them could have been prepared for was at hand.

Senator Edloe's home was about five miles outside the city limits. It sat on seven acres with a large pond, a workshop and a gazebo. Giant trees surrounded the house and gently wrapped themselves half-way around the pond, then down the drive to the street. It was like a picture postcard. Evan pulled his black van up into the circle drive and stopped in front of the house.

As he opened his door, he reached under the seat and pulled out a magnetic sign, then attached it to the street side of the van. In a very formal looking print the sign read, 'DJ's Electric Service'.

"That's got to be the weirdest conversation I've ever heard." Brad spoke as he got out of the van. They had listened to the tape of Arthur and Evan's conversation with Sheila on their way to Edloe's house. "Is she for real, or is she just making this stuff up?"

"Oh she's for real alright." Arthur confirmed. "Nobody could be that convincing unless they believed what they were saying."

"Well I'm glad I wasn't there. This whole thing is spooky enough as it is." Brad hoisted a large green bag over his shoulder and slid the side door of the van closed.

As the four men approached the front door, Arthur noticed a sign, partially covered by the plants in the flower bed. It was the sign from a security company. Arthur stopped everyone and pointed it out to Evan.

"Looks like he's got a security system"

"I would have been surprised if he didn't." Evan answered, setting a large black duffel bag that he was carrying down on the sidewalk.

He unzipped it and pulled out a small leather pouch and a rectangular box with several switches and a pair of wires coming out of its side.

"Okay" he began, "here's the plan. Derek, I need you to hold this." he said, handing him the box. "I'm going to open the front door. You come in behind me and close the door. Arthur, you and Brad wait out here until I come back out for you. Derek, once we're inside, you just hold that box up so I can get to it and I'll do the rest."

"What do we do if the alarm goes off?" Brad asked.

"Trust me, it won't." Evan replied confidently."

With little reason to doubt him, Arthur and Brad stood back from the door and let Evan do what he did best.

Evan cautiously studied the lock for several seconds then unzipped the black leather pouch he was carrying in his hand. From it he removed two thin shiny instruments that looked more like surgical tools than something used to pick a lock. He slid both tools into the lock. Holding one steady, he moved the other back and forth ever so slightly until he heard the tell tale clicking sound. He removed the instruments from the lock and placed them back into the case. He slid the case into his pocket and turned to Derek.

"Ready?" he asked.

"As ready as I'll ever be." Derek answered with some degree of uncertainty.

Evan opened the door. Immediately a beeping sound began, signaling the alarm was armed and would go off unless the correct code was entered into the key pad. The two entered and Derek quickly closed the door behind them. Evan hurried over to a key pad on the wall and pried the cover off of it with a screwdriver.

"Hold up the box, hurry!" he snapped at Derek.

Derek held the box up next to the key pad. Evan took the two wires extending from the box and connected them to two points inside the key pad. He flipped on both of the switches on the box. A readout containing six digits lit up and began changing rapidly, as if counting down. One by one they stopped changing as each displayed a different number. Derek looked down at his watch, knowing that they had only thirty seconds to defeat the alarm or it would sound and notify the alarm company. Twenty seconds had passed ant there was still two numbers to go. Derek looked nervously at Evan.

"Are we going to make it?" he asked.

"We'll make it." Evan replied confidently.

With only two seconds to spare the sixth number appeared and the beeping stopped.

They both heaved a sigh of relief.

"What the hell is this thing?" Derek asked, looking at it in amazement.

"Nothing special" Evan remarked, unhooking and wrapping the wires around the box, "it scans the security system's memory until it finds the code that turns off the alarm. Once it finds it, it enters it then displays it on this read-out. So next time, all we have to do is punch it in."

Evan snapped the cover back on the key pad while Derek walked over to the door and opened it.

"All done?' Arthur asked.

"Of course" Derek answered confidently.

"How did he do that?" Brad wondered out loud as he passed through the door.

"Nothing to it really" Derek said casually in his best sarcastic voice, "that box scans the memory and figures out the code. I thought you knew that." He looked at Brad and smiled. Brad shook his head.

"You've been hanging around Evan too much lately. His bad habits are starting to rub off on you."

"Come on you guys" Arthur called out. "We only have an hour and a half."

But an hour and a half was more than enough time to set the wheels in motion, and mark the beginning of the end of Senator Ryan Edloe.

Morning came and brought with it a looming sense of uneasiness which awakened Arthur from a sound sleep. There was something about this job, hell it was everything about this job, that made him feel unsettled. Maybe it was this whole 'coming back from the dead' thing. There was a greater element left to chance this time. *That's what it must be*, he thought to himself. *The other jobs were clear cut. I knew exactly what to expect, but this stuff is different. Maybe that's why I don't feel comfortable with it.* He stared up at the ceiling until it became evident that he had slept all he was going to for the night, so he may as well get up.

The clock beside the bed read four fifteen. Arthur got up and walked slowly down the stairs and into the kitchen. His hair showed the signs of a restless night as he filled the coffee pot with water. The house was unnaturally quiet. Even the dog acted as if he knew something was going on. As Arthur passed through the living room on his way to see if the morning paper had been left, his eye caught sight of a picture in the bookcase. He stopped and walked over to it, running his fingers through his hair as he held it in his hand. It was a picture of himself, Sandy, and the kids, in what was most definitely a much happier time judging by their smiles. He sat the picture back down on the bookcase though still holding on to it. Arthur missed his family tremendously and at times his longing for his family turned to anger, as it was doing this morning.

Arthur opened the front door and was greeted by a rush of cool morning air. He looked down and sure enough, the paper had been delivered. He picked it up, looking quickly around to see if anyone else was up at this time of the morning. There were no lights on in any of the houses he could see. Closing the door behind him, he made his way back to the kitchen and sat down at the table. He glanced impatiently at the coffee maker which was barely halfway through brewing a pot of coffee.

The plastic wrapper on the newspaper was still cold from sitting on the front steps. Arthur pulled it off and pushed it aside, then spread the paper out on the table in front of him. There was a picture on the front page just under the headline. It was a picture of the parking garage he had been in yesterday. He could see his car, or what was left of it, in the background. The headline read, 'Bomb Attack at Courthouse Linked to Crime Family'. Arthur scoffed and mumbled under his breath, "Not quite."

The article went on to explain how the car belonged to the judge that was presiding over the trial of the three men accused of a gangland killing, thus establishing a motive for the bombing. Arthur shook his head.

"If they only knew." he said aloud.

By the time he finished reading the article, the coffee pot was silent. Arthur put the paper down and grabbed a cup.

The sun had not come up yet. Evan was still asleep. His den was dimly lit by the lights of the electronic devices that stayed on all the time. A distinct click sounded followed by several lights illuminating and the large open reel tape began to move on the recorder. Soon the ringing sound of a telephone was heard, and then an angry voice spoke.

"Edloe, this is Russo. Are you nuts or what?"

Edloe, who was obviously awakened by the phone, was slow to respond.

"What are you talking about?"

"I'm talking about the bomb you had planted in the judge's car. They're blaming that on us you stupid son of a bitch."

"Hey" Edloe shouted, angered by the fact that he had been awakened from what little sleep he had been getting lately, "you can't talk to me that way."

"I can talk to you any way I want. I own your sorry ass, and we wouldn't be having this conversation if you had brains enough to stand and piss at the same time. The cops are all over us trying to connect us to that bomb. You told me you could get this judge to throw out the evidence. Did you lie to me or what?"

"I didn't lie" Edloe answered abruptly.

"Bullshit, you're a politician. You probably wouldn't know the truth if it jumped up and bit you in the ass. Now I don't care how you do it, but you get that judge to throw that evidence out, or as sure as my mother bakes lasagna, you'll be in the same place as that kid that was in the judge's car. You got that?"

"Now just a minute" Edloe shouted, but Russo had hung up the phone.

The tape machine had shut off and Evan's den was once again silent.

Edloe knew he would never get back to sleep after the conversation he'd just had with Russo. He got out of bed and went to the closet. He emerged with his robe and slippers and walked downstairs to the kitchen. He filled a kettle with water and put it on the stove to heat, then reached up and opened the cabinet door to get a cup. There were none there. Instead he saw a stack of plastic bowls. *Where the hell are the cups?*, he thought to himself. They had been in the same cabinet for years.

He stood silent, staring incessantly at the stack of plastic bowls. Slowly, he walked over to the cabinet where the plastic bowls had been stored. He reached up and opened the cabinet door to reveal the coffee cups.

"How could this have happened?" he asked himself.

Deep down he knew, but he was trying to avoid what he believed to be the truth.

He began talking aloud to himself. "It must have been the maid. She must have cleaned out the cabinets and not put everything back where it was. That's the only thing it could be."

Edloe reached up and took a cup out of the cabinet. By this time, the kettle was screaming as the water boiled. He turned off the burner and put a spoonful of instant coffee into his cup, then poured in the water. He sat the kettle back down on the stove, all the while glaring with a look of shock and disbelief, at the cabinets.

He took a sip of his coffee then slowly walked over to the kitchen table. "It's just a coincidence" he kept telling himself, though he remained unconvinced.

An immense weight was beginning to bear down on him. He was in the midst of something now that he feared he would not be able to escape from, but he kept telling himself, "It's just a coincidence."

Edloe sat slowly down at the kitchen table, taking another sip as he sat. His eyes wandered back and forth across the face of the cabinets. In all the years he lived in this house, he had never rearranged the things in his kitchen. He didn't know why the maid would want to either, but he would certainly ask her when she came in.

His mind kept drifting back to a memory he held of a time when he was near death, and of an offer that was extended to him. He took a third sip and became completely immersed in his thoughts.

He recalled more than anything the stench, the utterly foul odor of the place. It was unlike any place he had seen or could have described. It was dark, yet he could see, though there were others there who could not and were calling out for someone, anyone, to come and take them from this place. No one did. They wandered about aimlessly as if in agony, but their bodies seemed normal and unharmed. Their faces gave but a glimpse of the terror that their screams revealed. And in the midst of all of this, was the beast.

The very sight of the beast reeked of intimidation. It stood tall, much taller than a man. Its feet were huge and certainly disproportionate for its body. Its eyes, looking down from that height glowed slightly with a greenish orange hue. Its nostrils flared as it would breathe. Its skin was as that of an old man, yet its muscles and its posture was that of a youth.

But more than anything else, Edloe noticed the horns. There were so many of them, at least ten or maybe more. One of them looked as if it had an eye of its own. It slowly turned its head until Edloe was directly in its line of sight. The beast studied him, its eyes piercing his flesh and penetrating his very soul. Then it spoke in a voice with the depth and tone of a growl, yet low like a whisper.

"It has been written, 'Vengeance is mine, sayeth the Lord'. Those words may have meaning where you were, but they mean nothing here."

Edloe remembered listening in disbelief as he heard those words. He didn't know how or even if he should respond. But his fear soon made that decision for him.

"Vengeance can be yours that is if you want it." The beast took a step towards Edloe and raised its voice far beyond that of a whisper. "Well, do you want it?"

Fearing for his life or whatever form of existence he currently occupied, Edloe nervously spoke.

"Vengeance for what?"

"For what?" the beast roared impatiently. "Don't you know what place this is?"

Edloe looked slowly around himself, and then returned his eyes forward.

"This is just a bad dream. None of this is real, not you or this place, none of it."

The beast growled, drooling as a dog in anticipation of its dinner, then took another step towards him.

"This is no dream" it spoke again in a whisper, "and I am not the product of your imagination."

Slowly he raised his hand, pointing his long index finger in Edloe's direction. The finger when extended must have been almost a foot long. On the end of it was a fingernail that looked as if it had been honed to a point, its edges razor sharp. As

Edloe looked at the finger, he felt his flesh rip under his shirt. He grabbed his arm in pain. After squeezing it for a moment, he slowly pulled up his sleeve to reveal a gash about four inches long. The beast hadn't touched him yet blood was streaming down his arm, dripping off the back of his hand.

He grabbed the wound, gripping it tightly so as to slow the bleeding.

"Tell me, Edloe" it spoke, "is that your imagination, or your blood running down your arm?"

He paused for a moment to laugh. Then he spoke in a voice sounding more of anger and impatience.

"I'm offering you something that only I can give; true revenge. The chance to exact your pound of flesh, to make the person who is responsible for your being here pay, and to watch his fear and to savor his pain and to witness the transformation, by your own hand, from sanity to complete madness."

The beast paused, its tone and manner changing. "I will give you these things, and all I would ask in return is the pleasure of your company as my guest."

Before Edloe had a chance to answer, he felt his vision begin to fade. It was as if he were moving backwards. The figure of the beast slowly became smaller as the distance between the two of them became greater. After several minutes, it was completely gone. Edloe was in complete darkness. He was beginning to feel more pain than he had earlier. He was beginning to feel alive again. Just as he felt himself trying to open his eyes, he heard the beast's voice one final time.

"This time it was not to be. But rest assured our paths will most certainly cross again."

Edloe could almost feel it's foul, hot breath as it spoke.

The coffee was cold. The taste of it brought Edloe back to reality. He sat the cup down on the table so hard that what was left of the cold coffee splashed out onto the sleeve of his robe. He took his hand and wiped it away as best he could. In doing so, he raised the coffee soaked sleeve, revealing his forearm and a four inch scar. As he looked at it, the pit of his stomach felt as if it were on fire. His hands trembled as he lightly brushed his fingers across the disfigured skin on his arm, the memory of it still as fresh in his mind as it was the day of the accident. He pulled the sleeve down. Then, resting his elbows on the table, he put his face in his hands.

"What have I done?" he whimpered aloud. "What have I done?"

Lenny coasted the rental car to a stop on the circle drive in front of Evan's house. He hated rental cars, but even worse, he hated bringing his own car on a job. His car was his pride and joy. A sixty eight Pontiac GTO, fully restored with an engine that was barely street legal. It was a far cry from this little four cylinder import that he had rented. He opened the door and squeezed out, locking it behind him. Walking briskly up the steps to Evan's door, he rang the bell.

It took a couple of minutes for Evan to respond. Lenny sometimes forgot that not everyone had the military background and discipline that he had. Some people actually do like to sleep in until after daylight. He heard the clicking as Evan fumbled with the locks. Soon the door opened and Evan's head poked out.

"Oh, it's you. I forgot you were coming."

"Don't sound so excited to see me." Lenny teased. He walked into the house and closed the door behind himself. "You look terrible. Do you feel okay?"

"Actually, I feel like shit. Some mornings are worse than others. It generally goes away by noon."

"What does?"

"The pain, I think I'm getting worse. The other guys seem to be in remission, but sometimes I feel like I'm going downhill fast."

"Is there anything more that the treatment center can do for you?"

"Ya, they've modified my program. It helped somewhat, but not completely. So, I guess I'll just take what ever I'm given."

"Do you think you'll be alright for this assignment?"

"Sure, I'll be fine. I'm calling it quits after this one though."

"I don't blame you."

Lenny followed Evan into the kitchen. The coffee pot had turned itself on an hour ago so it had been ready for some time now. Evan filled two cups and carried them over to the table, sitting one down in front of Lenny.

"So tell me again" Evan asked, "what is it that we are going to do here this morning?"

Lenny reached down and removed a file folder from the bag he had carried in and sat it on the table. He opened it, exposing a number of eight by ten photos of the Russo family. Shuffling through them, he found the photo of the old man, Mr. Russo. He lifted it out and placed it on the top of the pile.

"It's his turn now!" Lenny announced.

"Oh man." Evan groaned, "This guy is a crime boss. How are we possibly going to get to him? Especially now, with the explosion and all, he'll be protected like Fort Knox."

"Now Evan" Lenny said in a somewhat patronizing tone, "we would never do anything as boorish as a physical attack on the man. We're going to do what we've been doing. We'll give him enough rope and he'll hang himself."

"Ya, well who's going to hand him the rope? It's not going to be me I hope."

"No, you don't have the legs for it, and besides, you're too flat-chested."

Evan looked at him as if he were crazy. Lenny, sensing his confusion again shuffled through the photos until he produced one of an exceptionally attractive young woman. He slid the photo across the table to Evan.

"I think we'll let her do it. Let's just say, her qualifications out-weigh yours in certain areas, if you know what I mean."

Evan looked at the picture with a predictable amount of lust in his eyes, despite the way he was feeling this morning. Then slowly his expression changed to one of concentration.

"Wait a minute. I know this girl. She showed up here one day claiming to know me and planted a bug here in my house."

"Ya, she works for us. Sam was testing you, or trying to anyway."

"So what's the plan?" Evan asked with a little more interest, now that a beautiful woman was involved.

"It's an old but proven one." Lenny began. "Man meets woman. Man likes woman. Woman flaunts herself in front of man. Man assumes because of his money and power that woman is attracted to him. Woman fulfills man's expectations and in doing so, puts his balls in a vise." Lenny stopped to take a sip of coffee. "It happens all the time." he said, smiling at Evan.

"It's happened to me a few times myself." Evan muttered under his breath. He picked up the photo of the woman, remembering her in his den that day, and at dinner a few nights later. He also remembered planting a bug in a piece of jewelry he had given her. And now they're all playing on the same team. What a long way they'd come since then.

CHAPTER NINETEEN

The noise was deafening, but Derek had worked there so long that he barely noticed it anymore. Of course the ear plugs he was required to wear helped. His job, to an uninformed observer, would appear extremely dangerous. But the training and experience he had acquired made the job simple for him, almost to the point of being mundane.

For nine hours a day, Derek stood surrounded by a pallet stacked with flat pieces of steel shaped as a shovel, with a shank on one end and the other end rounding off to a point. To the right of the pallet was a blast furnace. The temperature inside the furnace was around two thousand degrees. To the right of that were two presses, one much larger than the other. Next to the smaller press was a large mesh container.

All day long, Derek would load up the furnace with the flat shovel pieces. Once they were red hot, he would remove one and place it into the first press which would squeeze the hot steel and form the curve into the shovel. From there, he would remove it from the large press, turn it around, and place the shank, the top portion of the shovel that the handle fits into, in the smaller press to be rounded. Once that had been done, the fully formed shovel was tossed into the mesh basket. The entire process, from the furnace to the basket took about fifteen seconds. Derek was paid on the basis of how many shovels he could produce.

Because of the intense heat from the furnace, Derek wore a long sleeve shirt to prevent his arms from blistering. He also wore safety glasses and a face shield which made him almost unrecognizable to those who only knew him personally and not occupationally. He worked a rotation system that allowed him a five minute break every hour to get a drink and take some salt tablets if necessary. On a good day he could make around a hundred shovels per hour. But lately, with all that had transpired, his average was much less than that.

About mid-way through the second hour, his supervisor approached him, followed by the man who usually relieves him at the end of each hour. He saw them, but the pace at which he must work did not allow him to stop and ask what's going on. The supervisor walked up behind him as he worked and spoke to him in an audible tone that his wife was on the phone and needed to speak with him. This set off an alarm in his mind. The company only allowed their factory employees to receive calls if it were an emergency.

The relief man took the tongs from Derek and continued the sequence. As Derek and his supervisor walked towards the office, he removed the foam ear plugs from his ears.

"Is everything alright, Derek? Your average has been down the last week or so. Now don't get me wrong, we're still more than satisfied with your output, but if our star player has a problem, I'd like to know about it. I guess what I'm trying to say is, can I help you with anything, not as your boss, but as your friend?"

"No" Derek replied unconvincingly, "everything's fine. Katie's just out of town for a while. She's....visiting relatives; you know, showing off the baby."

"Well I'm not prying. You know me better than that. But if there's anything I can do to help, just say the word. Okay?"

"Thanks, that means a lot to me."

By this time Derek and his supervisor had reached the office door. Jake reached in front of Derek and opened the door. The office was a small, somewhat dirty cubicle in the middle of the factory. It was nothing like the front office where the higher-ups worked. Jake pointed to the phone on his desk which lay off the hook waiting to be answered, and then walked over to a filing cabinet and began rummaging through it as Derek picked up the phone. It was Katie.

"What's wrong, are you alright?" he asked anxiously.

"We're fine." she said, but her voice told him otherwise.

"You sound like something's wrong."

"Well, I just found out that we're moving to another house."

"Moving, why?" he demanded.

"I don't know, but I think it has something to do with last night. We all thought we heard gun shots outside, but they told us it was just fire crackers or something. Now this morning, they told us to pack up our stuff because we're being moved."

"Moved to where?"

"I don't know. They didn't tell us. I probably shouldn't even be telling you this but I'm scared."

"Honey, don't be scared. Nothing will happen to you, I promise."

"I just wanted you to know what was going on. I don't know if Sandy or Carol has talked to anyone yet, but since I'm all packed, I wanted to call you. I guess I just wanted to hear your voice. I miss you so much. How much longer will we have to stay away?"

Derek began to feel an overpowering sense of guilt. "Not long, I promise, not long."

"Well I'd better go now. I think I hear the helicopter coming."

"The helicopter" Derek repeated, "you're leaving by helicopter?"

"Ya, it's landing behind the house on the other side of the pool right now. I have to go. I'll try to call when we get to where ever we're going. I love you."

"I love you too, and I'm so sorry for all of this."

"Don't be. It's not your fault. I have to go now. Bye love." The phone went dead.

Derek heard the muffled sound of the helicopter as Katie hung up the phone. He'd never felt quite this way before. It was an indescribable combination of anger and guilt. The rage that consumed him would not soon release its hold. It had begun to motivate and control his thoughts and his actions. His mind was speeding a hundred miles an hour in ten different directions. His eyes remained fixed on the glass that looked out over the department.

"Is everything okay?" Jake asked.

Derek had forgotten that he was even in the office.

"Not really, I have a bit of a problem. Do you think I can get some time off?"

Jake took a step towards him. "You've got two and a half weeks of vacation time saved up. You want to take it now?"

"I thought I had to give you two weeks notice to take any vacation time?"

"Don't worry about it. If you need some time, you take it. You'll always have a job here."

Derek got up from the chair and shook Jake's hand.

"Thanks Jake. This really means a lot to me." As he headed for the office door, Jake stopped him.

"Hey, you remember what I told you. If you need me for anything you call, understand?"

Derek turned to him, mustering up as much of a smile as he could. "I will, Jake. I will."

He pulled the office door closed behind him and walked to the time clock. Without hesitation, Derek punched out, gathered up his things, and left. He wasn't sure if he would have a job when he came back, despite Jake's assurances, but right now that didn't matter. What did matter were Katie and their son. A line had been crossed, and now the rules, if indeed there ever were any, had changed.

As he drove out of the factory parking lot and onto the street, his eyes stared coldly forward, giving only a hint of the determination and the anger that possessed him. He wasn't sure what he should do or even what he could do. But he knew he had to do something. So he began at the place that seemed the most logical; a gun store.

It took only ten minutes to fill out the forms and two hundred dollars to buy the gun and ammunition. He had never owned a gun before and was surprised at how easy it was to get one.

He had used one before though on several occasions. His father-in-law was an avid hunter and somewhat of a gun collector. He had taken Derek out to a pistol range a couple of times. Derek had fired the same pistol each of those times and was more familiar with that particular type. That was the type he bought, a semi-automatic pistol with a clip that slid up into the grip. Although he felt uncomfortable carrying it, he regarded it as a first step; a step in the right direction. No one was going to take his family from him. He would probably be gone from them soon enough because of his illness, so everyday was a treasure. He would not be cheated out of one day, not by Russo, or Edloe or anyone else.

Brad had been writing without a break for several hours when his concentration was broken by the sound of the door bell. He slowly began to stand up, though still typing on the keyboard. He slid his chair back with the backs of his legs trying to complete his thoughts. Having typed as much as his broken train of thought would allow, he walked over to the door and opened it.

"Derek, you have the day off today?"

"I took it off. We got problems." he said, wiping his feet.

He walked into Brad's apartment and pulled off his coat, laying it across the back of one of Brad's dining room chairs and sat down.

"What kind of problems?" Brad questioned, closing the door and locking it.

"I got a call this morning from Katie."

"What's wrong? Are they okay?" Brad's demeanor had abruptly changed.

"They're being moved to another place."

"Another place, why did something happen?"

"She wasn't sure." Derek explained. "She said they thought they heard fire crackers going off last night. But this morning they're leaving by helicopter. She didn't know where there were going, but she said she'd call when they got there."

"Somebody must have tried to get to them, and I bet I know who." Brad clenched his fists around the back of the chair, his knuckles quickly turning white.

"I know damned good and well who it was, and I'm ready for those sons of bitches."

"What do you mean, you're ready for them?" Brad asked, looking somewhat puzzled.

"I bought some insurance this morning." He lifted his sweater to reveal the gun he had just bought. The barrel of the gun was tucked inside his pants and a full clip was loaded into the grip. Brad looked at it in disbelief.

"What the hell are you going to do with that?" he demanded.

"Whatever I have to" Derek replied without hesitation.

"Look, there's better ways of doing this. We're no match for those gangsters, not with guns anyway. We've got something better." Brad took a step closer and leaned forward.

"Brains" he said, pointing to his head. "They're no match for us. So get rid of that thing before you shoot yourself in the foot."

Derek stared at the gun for a few seconds before slipping it into his coat pocket. He slowly raised his head up until he was looking at Brad. Brad looked at him, not knowing if he had convinced him or not.

"I'm not going to let anything happen to Katie." he said defensively. "I made that promise to her and I intend to keep it."

"I agree with you. As a matter of fact, old man Russo is going to have an encounter with someone today that will make sure that he never gets another chance. So, relax, and I'll make a call and see if I can't find out where the ladies are going."

Derek reluctantly took the gun from his coat pocket and popped out the clip. He laid them both on Brad's dining room table. Brad returned from the kitchen with two soft drinks. He saw the gun lying on the table as he slid a can over to Derek.

"Now, don't you feel better?" he asked, looking down at the gun.

"Not really. But tell me about Russo. What's going to happen to him today?"

Brad looked at Derek over his drink and smiled without speaking. Derek recognized that smile and knew whatever it was it would be good.

Eli Russo ate lunch in the same restaurant almost everyday. He ate there so often that the owners had a special table for him that no one else was permitted to dine at. It was a corner table by a window overlooking the street.

Each day at precisely eleven forty five, a black Mercedes would slowly pull into the restaurant parking lot. After a brief moment to determine that it was safe to do so, Mr. Russo, accompanied by a bodyguard, would get out of the car and make their way to the front doors of the restaurant. Once inside, they would be greeted by whichever of the owners happened to be there at the time, and then would be escorted to their table. Mr. Russo always sat facing the window, and his bodyguard, facing the restaurant, always vigilant and aware of everyone that came through the doors.

This day was no exception. By eleven fifty five, Russo and his body guard, affectionately referred to as 'Ox', were sitting at their table by the window. It was a picture perfect spring day. The sun was shining, the temperature was getting to a more tolerable level, and most importantly to Russo, the ladies were shedding their winter overcoats and displaying more of what he referred to as their 'real estate'.

Russo was a ladies man. He looked quite good for a man of some fifty six years. His looks, his money and his power were the tools he used to pursue his past-time. And although most of the time he displayed more passion for his past-time than for his profession (if what he did could be referred to as a profession), he managed to keep each of them separate from one another.

But this was lunch, and lunch was for pleasure. Pleasure in the form of looking out the window onto the street at all the lovely ladies passing by, hoping that one of them would drop her purse and afford him a glimpse of her 'real estate' while bending over to pick it up. This day however, his expectations would be far exceeded.

The waiter walked quickly over to Russo's table with two glasses of water and one scotch and soda. Ox didn't drink while he was working. The waiter knew he would be rewarded if he was efficient and chastised if he was not. His steps reflected his resolve.

He sat the drink nervously down in front of Russo first. Russo looked at him and nodded. This was as close to a thank you as he would ever get. He sat the water down in front of Ox, then turned and walked back to the kitchen. There was no need to take their order as Russo ate the same thing everyday. He thrived on consistency. It made him feel a little more secure in an otherwise insecure profession. He was indeed a creature of habit. Today though, his routine was about to take a diversion that would change his life.

He tipped the scotch and soda all the way back allowing the ice to slide forward against his top lip. Having drained the last drop from the glass, he sat it back down on the table. Feeling temporarily bored, his eyes wandered over to the window and out onto the sidewalk. The street was not too busy today, but there was the occasional passer-by, and even the occasional mildly attractive woman. But it was definitely a below par day for the ladies.

He was about ready to focus his attentions elsewhere when a particularly attractive young lady came into view. She was thin and very shapely. Her skirt revealed several inches of the most delicious looking thighs he had ever seen. Her blouse was snug and unbuttoned to reveal just enough cleavage to make him want to see more. Her long red hair blew back slightly in the balmy spring breeze. She was a nine or better on the 'Russo Scale'.

As quickly as she came into view, he began undressing her with his eyes. He hadn't gotten much past her skirt when he noticed she had slowed down. Her eyes seemed fixed on something ahead of her. Soon she had stopped completely. She stared incessantly ahead. Russo sat up a little straighter in his chair. Ox, seeing his interest, also looked out the window.

A look of fear began to overtake her as she watched a man approach. As he got closer, he began talking, almost shouting, at the woman. She cowered at his voice and his obvious anger. Russo and Ox looked curiously at the two for a moment. They both knew something was about to happen, but weren't sure what it would be.

The wait was short. After less than a minute of shouting, the man raised his hand in the air and slapped the woman, striking her hard enough to knock her off balance. She fell to the ground and her purse flew out of her hand, its contents spilling out on to the sidewalk. The man stood over her still shouting. Russo looked over at Ox. Ox, sensing his stare, looked back.

"Go out there and teach that dick head some manners!" he demanded.

Ox got up quickly for someone his size and made his way through the restaurant. Before he got to the doors, Russo barked out another order.

"Bring the girl back in here."

Ox raised his hand slightly into the air acknowledging the request. He walked out the doors and around the corner onto the sidewalk. He could hear the man shouting as soon as he rounded the corner. He took a few steps down the sidewalk then shouted himself.

"Hey, you got a problem?"

The man looked behind him to see Ox bearing down on him with as quick a stride as he could muster. He looked back at the woman on the ground. Gritting his teeth he spoke.

"This ain't over, bitch." Looking back at Ox, he confirmed in his mind that it was definitely time to leave and in an instant, he was gone.

Ox had no intention of chasing him. He walked over to the woman and extended his hand to her. Russo watched through the window as Ox helped her up off the sidewalk and gathered up the things that had fallen out of her purse. Then he pointed with his hand at the restaurant. Russo could only assume that he was inviting her to join them. After a brief moment of conversation, the woman smiled then accompanied Ox down the sidewalk and into the restaurant. As they came through the doors, Russo felt his heart race just a little. The closer she got, the more beautiful she looked.

Finally she and Ox arrived at the table.

"Boss" Ox spoke, "this is Christy. Christy, this is Mr. Russo."

The woman looked at Russo and reduced his demeanor momentarily to that of a quivering school boy with her innocent yet seductive smile. Christy however, was not her name. Her name was Rita, and she was quite proficient at melting men's hearts. She had done it so well to Evan.

"I can't tell you how grateful I am for your help back there. I feel embarrassed that you had to see it."

"Please, sit down. We were just about to have lunch and I'd be honored if you'd join us."

Russo pointed with his eyes to the chair next to him. Ox immediately walked around Rita and pulled it out for her.

"Oh, I don't want to impose. You've already done so much by saving me from that lunatic"

"In that case, I would consider your joining me for lunch to be repayment of that debt." Russo could be very persuasive when it came to the ladies.

"Well thank you." she conceded. "Thank you very much."

She sat down in the chair and Ox, who had been standing behind it, pushed it in for her.

"I guess I was at the right place at the right time, wasn't I?" she said, referring to the help she had gotten from Ox.

"Oh you certainly were." Russo agreed. "You certainly were."

Russo smiled a smile that reeked of self-confidence and lust. He motioned with his hand for the waiter, all the while keeping eye contact with Rita and fueling the fires of his own imagination.

The ground trembled beneath Senator Edloe's feet. He did not know where he was or how he got here. The only thing he was sure of was that he didn't like it.   It was sort of a tunnel, dark and damp, the sounds echoing; their origins unknown. He was walking, unsure of why or where he was going, but knowing full well that he must not stand still.

As he slowly walked into the darkness, he began to smell that stench that had occupied a place in his memory for many years. Then the sound of breathing, more like growling than any normal respiration. He knew what was ahead and was somehow drawn towards it.

Through the darkness, a pair of eyes glowed. As he approached, a dull light illuminated the form of a creature; the beast. As it opened its mouth to speak, a trickle of vapor rose up and dissipated into the damp, still air. It spoke in a raspy growl like a record played at the wrong speed.

"I told you our paths would cross again, didn't I?" Then it began to laugh the most evil and terrifying laugh Edloe had ever heard. "Do you think you're dreaming again?'

Edloe tried but he could not speak. The words would not come out.

"What's the matter Edloe, cat got your tongue?"

The insane, evil laughter continued and grew louder. Edloe tried to speak but still was unable. He couldn't make a sound.

"Well it's not the cat that's got your tongue" the beast growled, answering its own question, "it is I."

Slowly it raised its clenched fist towards Edloe. As the fist approached him, it began to slowly open revealing a tongue with a long root that twitched as if it had just been torn from someone's mouth. It was fresh with blood, small streams of which ran down the beast's fingers and dripped to the ground.

Edloe looked at it, and then it became clear to him why he could not speak. The tongue in the beast's hand was his. The sight of the tongue made him open his mouth and try to scream, but he could not. The hand of the beast moved closer to Edloe, the blood still dripping from his palm. Edloe tried once again to scream. The closer the beast came to him, the harder he tried until finally he felt a shrill, blood curdling scream leave his body.

Suddenly, his eyes flew open and he raised his head from his desk. He looked around himself and realized he was at his office. It had all been a dream, or had it? Thankfully for now, he was back to reality. He wiped the sweat from his forehead as he steadied himself on the edge of his desk, licking his lips as if checking to see that he still had his tongue.

Was this nightmare the result of his beliefs and anxieties, or was it the manifestation of what he feared would be his fate? He could not get the dream out of his mind; first the cups in his cabinets and now this. He was afraid to think what might be next.

Unable to keep his hands from shaking or his forehead from perspiring, the Senator decided to go home. He was not capable of functioning adequately and ran the risk of revealing this side of himself to his staff. So under the guise of being ill, he slipped out of his office and down to his car. He unlocked the door and slid in behind the wheel. As he fumbled with the ignition key he thought about the bomb that had been placed in Sam's car.

I wonder why I haven't heard from Gus Eastman. I think I still owe him money. Maybe he won't ask for it since he botched the job. It wasn't my fault that someone else got into Sam's car. He should have made some provision for that. That must be it. He didn't earn it so he won't ask me for it.

For the moment, Edloe was convinced, but only until the next wave of paranoia made him question himself even more.

"What if he's pissed? What if he thinks I'm trying to stiff him? Would he try to get back at me? Maybe I'm a lose end that needs to be tied up. I wonder if there's a bomb under my car. No, absolutely not. He has too much to gain from me and I have too much evidence against him. It's an unspoken agreement, he leaves me alone and I don't rat him out. That's it."

Edloe's eyes closed tightly as he attempted to start his car. He pressed slowly against the key until the contact was made and the starter engaged, starting the car. He drew in a deep breath as his eyes rolled slightly back in his head. There was no bomb. He had the strangest feeling though. Despite his relief, he couldn't help being a little disappointed. Although it would have been the coward's way out, he would have been spared what he feared may now be the inevitable.

Russo had dominated the conversation throughout the entire meal, and Rita was more than willing to let him do it. He spoke mostly of himself and his exploits. He was trying diligently to impress her with talk of his wealth and power, and what a sexual virtuoso the women pronounced him to be.

His long-windedness was more than welcome to Evan and Lenny who, while Rita and her hosts were enjoying lunch, were working feverishly under the hood of Russo's car.

"You know" Russo stated, taking a long sip of espresso,"you are the most fascinating woman I have met in a long time."

"Why, thank you." Rita replied, thinking it odd that he could make that judgment based on hearing very little conversation from her. After all, he had done most of the talking.

"Say, I'm having a little get-together out on my estate in the country tonight. How would you like to be my guest? It's a nice romantic drive from the city. What do you say? Pick you up about six?"

"Well, I don't know. I mean I just met you. I don't really know you." Rita paused to read his reaction, which was as predictable as the weather. "But you do seem to be a nice man, and you did save me from my crazy ex-boyfriend." She paused again, watching Russo's anticipation level rise almost to the boiling point.

"Oh, what the heck, I'd love to."

"Great" Russo replied. "Ox and I will pick you up around six."

"Oh, Ox will be there too? I thought you said it would be a romantic drive?" Rita winked at him and brushed her foot across Russo's ankle.

"You know, you're right. I'll pick you up myself."

Ox, not paying much attention to the conversation to this point, spoke up.

"Are you sure that's a good idea boss?"

Russo looked at him adamantly. "If I didn't think it was a good idea I would not have suggested it, now would I?"

Ox raised his hands as if to surrender, knowing full well that it was a bad idea. Disagreeing with Russo had been known to have deadly consequences, so he agreed and dropped back out of the conversation.

"My dear, I hate to eat and run, but do I have appointments this afternoon."

Russo lifted his napkin from his lap and wiped his mouth. He slid his chair back as if to stand up. Rita quickly grabbed her purse. She reached down into it, fumbling through its contents. Ox quickly reached his hand inside of his jacket taking hold of his gun, but not bringing it into sight.

"What are you doing?" Russo asked, concerned about what she might be reaching for.

"I'm getting you my address." she smiled.

Ox slowly eased his hand from inside his jacket.

Before removing her hand from her purse, she found what she was looking for. It was a tiny transmitter Evan had given her. She pushed the button on it, then removed a small pad of paper from the purse and sat it on the table.

At that same instant, a small receiver clipped to Evan's belt went off.

"They're on their way out. Are you almost done?" he asked in somewhat of a panic.

"Done" Lenny announced, as he reached to close hood, "Let's get the hell out of here."

The two gathered up their tools and quickly made their way back to Evan's car parked three rows back from Russo's Mercedes.

Russo drew a slight sigh of relief at the sight of the pad of paper and pen Rita had taken from her purse.

"You'll need my address, won't you?" she said, looking up at him with the same girlishly seductive look that she had been using so effectively. Russo looked back at her, infatuated and helpless, a slave to his own libido.

She wrote down an address and below it drew a small heart. Folding it, she handed it to Russo, who was standing next to her chair. He opened it, looking at it briefly. Smiling, he winked at her.

"I'll be there at six. Wear something sexy."

"Oh I've got just the thing." she said, winking back at him.

Unable to control himself, he bent down and gave her a kiss. She did not resist. In fact, she acted as if she enjoyed it. She was indeed a superb actress to accomplish a feat such as that.

"Can we drop you somewhere?"

"No thank you. My office building is just down the block. I was on my way to lunch when that lunatic stopped me, but I'm looking forward to seeing you tonight."

The three got up and left the restaurant. Rita thought it strange that they would leave without paying. Russo never paid for a meal at the table. The restaurant sent him a bill once a month.

Ox walked toward the car while Russo said one last goodbye to Rita. He did so only as an excuse to kiss her one final time. This time she pressed her large, firm breasts to his chest. She was an expert at seduction and he was a sucker for a pretty face and a great body. Barely able to keep his composure, he walked over to the car which Ox had already started, and got in.

Rita stood on the sidewalk in front of the restaurant as the car made its way out of the parking space and past her to the street. As it passed, she blew Russo a kiss. She had him hook, line and sinker, and she knew it.

Once his car was out of sight, Evan and Lenny pulled up to her and opened the door. She got in and the three sped out of the parking lot, leaving it once again silent.

"How did it go?" Lenny asked. Evan looked at Rita in the rear view mirror as she answered.

"Just like we planned." she replied. "He's taking me to his place in the country tonight for some kind of party. He's picking me up at six."

"Alone, or with his bodyguard?"

"Alone, of course. I've led him to believe that he could get lucky on the way, so you'd better do this before we get too far. I'm afraid I'll get sick if I have to kiss that man too many more times."

"No problem" Lenny continued. "Here's the plan."

As the car made its way through the lunch hour traffic, Lenny and Rita worked out the details. Evan kept looking at Rita in the mirror, waiting for her to say something about their encounter, but she never did. What Evan did not realize was that this sort of thing was Rita's job. It was simply what she did, and she did it so frequently that she seldom remembered one assignment from the next. She thought Evan looked somewhat familiar, but she wasn't sure from where. What she was sure of was that this assignment needed to go off without a hitch. If Russo ever learned her true identity, he would kill her without a second thought.

So, having satisfied himself that Rita was not going to recognize him, Evan focused his attention on driving. For the first time in recent memory, sex had taken a back seat to a more pressing issue. *What's the world coming to,* he thought to himself.

CHAPTER TWENTY

Timeliness was the only virtue that Russo had, if indeed it could be considered a virtue. At precisely six o'clock, his car pulled up in front of the building in which Sam's organization had rented an apartment for just such an occasion. Seeing him drive up, Rita left the apartment and headed for the lobby. She did not want to be alone with him in her room. She wanted him to save those thoughts for the trip. About half way across the lobby she saw him come through the doors.

"I saw you drive up." she said.

He looked at her with some degree of surprise. "I was hoping to see your apartment.

"Well, my roommate is up there with her boyfriend, and they're getting a little 'friendly', if you know what I mean."

Russo smiled, "I know exactly what you mean. Everybody needs a little privacy, don't they?"

"Absolutely" Rita agreed.

Russo was wearing a black Tux, and although she hated to admit it, he looked quite good. Rita wore a red evening gown, very tight and quite low cut. She watched Russo's eyes as they drifted down towards her ample chest. As she approached him she joined her hands together in front of her, using her upper arms to squeeze her breasts against each other making them look even larger than they were.

"You look absolutely delicious." Russo exclaimed as he tried unsuccessfully to divert his eyes from her cleavage.

"Why thank you. You look perfectly chic yourself."

Rita watched his expressions and reactions to her comments. She was above all else an expert at handling men, and this was a very dangerous one.

Regaining his prospective momentarily he extended his arm. Rita took hold of it and the two made their way through the lobby and out onto the street.

His car was parked in a red zone. No parking was permitted within the area outlined in red. As they made their way through the doors of the apartment building, they saw a traffic cop resting his right foot on Russo's front bumper. He was using his knee to rest his ticket book on while he wrote. Russo appeared unaffected by his presence.

They walked over to the passenger side of the car. Russo reached down and opened the door for Rita. She got in and he closed the door. He walked around the front of the car and approached the officer. Rita watched through the windshield as the two briefly spoke. Russo produced a small card from his wallet and handed it to the cop. The cop read it, and then angrily passed it back to Russo, almost throwing it at him. He flipped his ticket pad shut, all the while glaring at Russo. In a threatening tone he spoke a few words to Russo which Rita was still unable to hear, then stormed off. Russo smiled as one who had won yet another conquest, then got into the car.

"Problems" Rita asked.

He turned to her, glancing at the cop in his rear view mirror as his eyes passed him.

"No" he said casually, "no problem at all."

He looked one more time in the mirror as he started the car, smiling a more malevolent smile than before. Glancing over his shoulder for traffic, he pulled out into the street and headed west on his way out of town.

"So, did you get a ticket back there or something?" Rita asked in her best girlish fashion.

"No, but he did try."

"How did you get out of it?"

Russo smiled. "You see, me and the mayor, we have an arrangement. I do things for him, and in turn, he does things for me. Its business, you know, just business."

"Wow!" Rita did her best to act impressed. "You must be a pretty important man."

"You could say that." Russo answered, his words dripping with self consumption.

He was playing into Rita's hands so well he was almost making it easy for her. As she looked at him with her big innocent green eyes, what ever tad of caution he had towards her quickly disappeared.

Edloe had spent the day at home watching TV in the hopes that it would take his mind off of his problems. It didn't. The fourth movie he'd watched had ended and credits had started when he realized that he hadn't eaten anything all day. So, as much as he hated to, he got up and walked into the kitchen and over to the pantry.

Slowly he opened up the pantry door, expecting the worst. What he found was the same pantry he had opened for the past twelve years. He heaved a sigh of relief as he reached in and took out a can of soup.

Ryan carefully slid it under the can opener and with a dull hum the lid was removed. Again the fear swelled within him as he reached down to open the cabinet door to get a pot. After a moments' hesitation, he opened the door. To his surprise (and relief) he found a cabinet full of pots and pans.

His pace quickened and his confidence level rose as things appeared to be normal. He poured the soup from the can into the pot and took it over to the stove. He sat the pot down on the burner and turned it on. The familiar clicking sound began as the igniter sparked to light the gas. It sparked an unusually long time. No flame appeared. Edloe stared at it curiously, taking a step back to satisfy his apprehensions. Then his look turned from curiosity to fear as the spark ignited a bright green flame. With a loud rushing sound the flame rose up and completely engulfed the pot. The flame continued to rise, illuminating the entire kitchen with its blinding green glow. It roared up to the ceiling, and then spread outward. The heat became as an inferno, and the reflection danced across the cabinet doors. As it began to retreat back to the stove, a voice with no apparent origin, yet seemingly coming from everywhere, growled his name in a distinctively familiar low, raspy tone. Edloe stumbled backwards, stopped by the cabinets behind him. Then, as quickly as it appeared, it was gone. All that remained was the small blue flame that brushed gently against the bottom of the pot.

Edloe looked up at the black circle left on the ceiling above the stove, all the while trying to determine where that voice came from. His eyes were wide with terror. Beads of perspiration covered his face as he reached to turn the burner off. The pot had turned completely black from the flame. The plastic handle had melted and was dangling onto the stove.

What he had been denying all this time had finally become undeniable. He ran his fingers through his hair afraid to move for fear of what might happen next.

A loud metallic sound startled him for a moment until he recognized it as the sound of his mail slot door dropping closed after the postman delivered his mail. Welcoming the excuse to leave the kitchen, he scurried out through the dining room and into the hallway that led to the front door.

There was a larger than normal pile of mail on the floor under the mail slot. He could see the silhouette of the postman as he walked down the front steps. After watching him walk out of sight, Edloe bent down and picked up his mail. He walked slowly back to the den where he had been watching movies all day, sorting through the envelopes as he walked.

One of them in particular caught his eye. It had no stamp on it and no return address. *How the hell did this get delivered without postage,* he thought to himself. There was a red smear where the stamp should be. It almost looked as if someone had cut themselves and wiped blood on the envelope.

He turned it over and ripped it open. Reaching inside he pulled out an unusually thick piece of paper. It felt peculiar, as if it were wet but at the same time warm. As he slid it out of the envelope, the words Daniel 7:7 were written on it in the same fashion and color as the smear on the outside of the envelope.

"Who is Daniel?" he said aloud to himself. "And what does 7:7 mean?"

Edloe knew he had seen notations like this one before and it took only a few seconds for the answer to come to him. *The Bible*, he thought to himself. *It's a passage from the Bible.*

He raced into the library. Scanning the walls of book shelves, he spotted what he was looking for. On one of the upper shelves was a Bible, the family Bible which had never been read very much by anyone in his family, particularly him. He reached up and took it down, blowing off the dust of twelve years accumulation. He fumbled through it, unfamiliar with the order in which the testaments and books were arranged.

Finally, he found the Book of Daniel. He followed the pages to the seventh chapter, then down to the seventh verse. As he read, a cold chill began at the back of his neck and followed his spine until his entire body was shaking. He looked up, staring into the air with great intensity. Then he dropped the Bible onto the floor and ran out of the study.

The Bible lay on the floor open to the seventh chapter of Daniel. The seventh verse read: "*After this I kept looking in the night visions, and behold a fourth beast, dreadful and terrifying and extremely strong and it had large iron teeth. It devoured and crushed, and trampled down the remainder with its feet and it was different from all the beasts that were before it, and it had ten horns.*"

Getting to the edge of town took a long time even when traffic was light. Rita was doing her best to maintain the effervesce of a school girl despite knowing what was about to happen. The conversation went from his money to his houses to his sexual prowess. Rita knew all the right questions to ask to keep him talking and to divert his attentions to where she wanted them.

After forty five minutes of insipid narration of what seemed to her to be almost his entire life history, they were finally leaving the city. Fewer and fewer buildings cluttered the landscape as they drove into the countryside. The terrain soon became rural and somewhat desolate.

They rounded a curve and saw a car on the side of the road with its hood up. As they passed by, Lenny, Brad and Arthur glanced inconspicuously at Russo's car.

Rita reached down to the power seat control mounted near the floor on the side of the seat. She pushed the switch downwards causing the seat itself to be lowered. When it had moved down as far as it could it stopped, but Rita kept her finger on the switch continuing to push it. After no more than ten seconds Russo noticed the car was losing power. He pressed harder on the gas but it made no difference. Soon the car was coasting to a stop on the side of the road.

"Are you going to tell me that you've run out of gas?" Rita asked, smiling her best school girl smile.

"I don't know what's wrong with this thing. It was just serviced."

Russo tried to start the car, but it was completely dead. The engine turned over, but it would not start. It wouldn't even kick. He reached into his jacket pocket for his cell phone. It was gone.

"Where the hell is my phone?" he asked angrily. "I put it in my pocket, I know I did." He turned to Rita. "Let me use your phone." He asked politely.

"I don't have one." She said innocently. "My crazy ex-boyfriend took it and I haven't been able to get it back from him." That wasn't quite true. Rita did have a phone. She had Russo's phone. She had slipped it from his pocket in the lobby of the apartment earlier that evening.

"Shit!" Russo muttered under his breath as he let go of the key, trying again to start the car.

"Maybe we should take a look under the hood." Rita suggested.

"I don't know a damned thing about cars except how to drive them."

"Well I do!" she stated confidently as she opened the car door. "My dad is a mechanic. Come on, let's open the hood and see if anything looks out of place."

Russo reluctantly pulled the latch that released the hood. He was not in control of this situation anymore and he didn't like it. He opened his door and got out, walking slowly to the front of the car. Rita was bent over the grill looking at something on the side of the engine. Russo's eyes quickly became focused on her and he was in the process of 'appraising her real estate' when a car passed and slowed down, then pulled off the road. It stopped then backed up. Rita stood up and looked at the car as it came to a stop in front of them. Three doors opened and three men got out and walked back to Russo and his now deceased Mercedes. Russo folded his arms, reaching inside his jacket for his gun.

"You folks got problems?" Lenny asked in a friendly tone. Arthur looked curiously at Rita feeling sure he had seen her before. Brad stood silently, breathing heavily.

"Damned thing just quit on me." Russo replied.

"I'd be glad to take a look at it if you'd like."

"Go ahead." Russo said.

Lenny, Arthur and Brad approached the car and looked under the hood, pointing and commenting as they poked and prodded. After no more than a minute, they walked back to the spot where Russo was standing.

"I'm afraid you're going to need a mechanic buddy. It's dead as a hammer." Lenny remarked.

Russo, no longer feeling threatened, took his hand off of his gun and uncrossed his arms. "I figured as much." he answered. "You guys got a phone?

"Sure do." Lenny said, pointing to his car. "It's in the console, help yourself."

Russo walked over to Lenny's car. Lenny followed behind him at a close distance. Once again Russo reached for his gun.

"You'll need these." Lenny said.

Russo turned to look at him. Lenny held out the keys to his car. "I keep the phone locked up in the console. I have teenagers at home. Ungrateful little bastards ran my bill up to four hundred dollars last month"

Lenny tossed the keys to Russo and continued to follow him to his car. Russo got in behind the wheel and slid the key into the lock on the console. As he turned it he let out a yell that could have raised the dead. In an instant, his entire body went limp and slumped across the seats.

"What the hell was that?" Arthur asked as he and Lenny looked at his temporarily lifeless body.

"About the same voltage as a stun gun I'd say." Lenny answered.

Brad was still standing back by the Mercedes.

"Come on you guys, let's get going already." Brad felt like a sitting duck out there on the side of the road. "Russo's goons are liable to be tailing him."

"He's right." Lenny agreed. "He'll wake up in a few minutes. We'd better get moving."

He and Arthur ran back to Russo's car. Lenny opened the driver's side door and slid on his back onto the floor. He reached up under the dash and in mere seconds the car started.

"What did you do to his car in that restaurant parking lot?" Brad asked.

"Ya" Rita echoed. "The thing just quit when I pushed on that seat control."

"It was simple really" Lenny said as he closed the hood. "I just wired the fuel pump and the cigarette lighter up to the same circuit breaker the power seats were on. When Rita here put the seat motor in a bind by pressing the knob after the seat had moved as far as it could, the breaker got hot and tripped. When it did it shut down the fuel pump and the car died; nothing to it."

"Ya, nothing to it" Brad replied sarcastically. "Between Evan's electronics and your mechanical knowledge, you make the rest of us look like a bunch of know-nothings."

"We all have our cross to bear." Lenny smirked, closing the door to Russo's car. He and Rita drove off in the Mercedes. Arthur and Brad returned to their car and securely bound Russo's feet with nylon ties, and then slipped a pair of handcuffs on his wrists. After they gagged him and put him in the back seat, they took off. Once the dust settled, silence cloaked the landscape and there remained no trace of what had just happened.

The trip took only an hour and a half but as far as Russo was concerned it took much longer. Since darkness had begun to fall and he was blindfolded, his concept of time was skewed. He had been blindfolded to protect Brad and Arthur's identity. When he came to, his mood was less than pleasant.

"What the hell's going on?" he demanded.

"Shut up!" Arthur shouted back.

Russo's hands and feet were bound and with his eyes covered he was completely helpless. He lay sprawled across the back seat like a sack of potatoes. He was sure that a rival family had perpetrated this kidnapping, and Brad and Arthur were more than willing to let him think just that.

"You know you guys are dead men. My boy's won't rest until they find me, and when they do, I'll put a bullet in the back of your head myself."

Arthur laughed at him which only served to anger him more.

"That's awful strong talk for somebody that's tied up, blindfolded and hundreds of miles from where he belongs."

"Will you be quiet already?" Brad rebuked. He and Arthur had rehearsed their lines very carefully. They were setting up an argument between themselves that would lead Russo to believe that Brad was sympathetic towards him. It was a good thing that Russo was blindfolded as Brad and Arthur found it difficult to argue with each other like this with a straight face. They had been friends far too long.

"Quit telling me what to do." Arthur snapped.

"Well somebody has to. You certainly can't figure it out on your own."

"Are you trying to tell me I'm stupid?"

"Look, its bad enough you had to handcuff and blindfold him. So why don't you just leave him alone. Don't you know who he is for heaven's sake?"

"I don't give a damn who he is. We were paid two thousand dollars to grab him and that's what we did. It doesn't make any difference who he is."

"Man, you really are stupid."

"Hey, I've had about all of the crap I'm going to take from you, so why don't you just shut the hell up and drive?" Arthur knew they were about to run out of lines.

Russo had been silent in the back seat, listening to their argument. It was clear he had taken the bait, or at the very least, he was considering it.

"That's it!" Brad shouted. "How would you like me to stop this car and kick your ass?"

"You'd need a step ladder you little son of a bitch."

Arthur pressed his hand tightly against his mouth, trying to contain his laughter at their exchange.

Suddenly Russo felt the car jerking violently. He felt it swerve off one side of the road then the other. He could hear the bushes and tree branches scraping against the side of the car as they ran through a ditch and into what felt like a pasture. The ride became very rough. They were defiantly not on a road anymore. Russo was not in a seat belt. He was being thrown all about the back seat. His head had hit the roof then came down and hit the right window. With his hands still handcuffed behind his back, he was helpless to protect himself from the violent movements of the car.

All at once he heard both men scream and felt the car breaking at full force. Before it could stop, it struck something. It struck it very hard, so hard in fact that Russo felt the back end of the car rise off the ground at impact. Russo was thrown against the back of the front seat then down to the floor. He heard glass smashing, then the frantic cries of someone who had been hurt. Because of his handcuffs and the restraints on his feet he was unable to move. It took a second for him to realize what had happened.

Before he could completely regain his composure, he felt someone pulling him from the car. Every bone in his body hurt, but he did his best to help maneuver himself out of the car. Once out, he was propped up against the door. His knees were weak but they did manage to support him. He felt hands behind his head untying his blindfold. He squinted when it finally came off even though there was not much light. It was almost completely dark, but there was enough light for him to see that the car had hit a tree.

There was a large hole in the windshield and no sign of the other man who had been in the front seat.

"Come on" Brad urged, cutting the ties on Russo's feet with a pocket knife, "we'd better get out of here."

"Where's the other guy, the one with the mouth?"

"Over there." Brad pointed to a spot about twenty feet in front of the car. "He didn't make it." Arthur lay face down on the ground covered with blood.

"Serves him right, the rat bastard. I'd have killed him anyway when I got out of here."

Brad's knife finally cut through the ties that bound Russo's feet. "Come on, let's go."

"What about the handcuffs?" Russo asked, turning for Brad to see them.

"I don't have a key for them and neither does he. We'll have to try and find someplace where we can cut them off or something."

Brad grabbed his arm to steady him and the two began running across the open field towards a tiny light off in the distance.

Once the sound of their footsteps could no longer be heard, Arthur raised his head. He saw two tiny figures, little more than shadows against the evening sky, running away from him. He picked himself up and wiped the red liquid from his face and hands. His stomach muscles were sore. At the same moment the car hit the tree, Arthur had thrown a cement block forward through the windshield to create the hole. It was something his muscles were not used to doing. But then, in the past five months, he'd done a lot of things he wasn't used to doing.

CHAPTER TWENTY ONE

Sam glanced cautiously into the rear view mirror before turning into his driveway. As he made his way up the driveway, he pressed the button to open his garage door. The door slowly began to rise. He drove in, remaining in his car until the door had completely closed behind him. As he opened the door of the car he had rented, Sam noticed how light and flimsy it felt compared to the door on his Mercedes. He would eventually buy another, but a purchase like that had always been made by both he and his wife. Since she was away, the new Mercedes would have to wait.

Sam left the garage, walking though the laundry room and into the kitchen. Dropping his briefcase on the table, he walked over to the answering machine to check the day's messages.

He hit the playback button. There were three messages; one from his wife, and two from a young lady who Sam's organization had charged with monitoring his e-mail messages. One of the messages indicated that Arthur needed to speak with him.

Sam reached into his inside jacket pocket and pulled out a leather covered address book. Flipping through it he came to Arthur's phone number. He picked up the phone and punched it in. It rang only twice before it was answered.

"Arthur, is that you?"

"No sir. This is Evan."

"I thought your voice sounded a little different. Where is Arthur?" Sam asked.

"He's kind of out in the middle of nowhere right now. He called me a short time ago to let me know that they had successfully snatched Mr. Russo, so everything is going according to schedule."

"Very good" He replied, his voice sounding pleased.

"The reason that we had you contact us was to let you know that I'm ready to video tape the judge. Arthur said that you would get in touch with the judge when we were ready to make the tape."

"That is correct." Sam replied.

"Arthur did go over the plan with you, didn't he?"

"Yes he did. When do you want to make the video tape?"

"The sooner, the better" Evan said. "I will have to edit it and put it all together afterwards, so we need to do it as quickly as possible."

Sam thought for a moment. "I can have the judge there within the hour."

"That would be fine. I have all of the equipment set up at my house. If the judge could come over I promise to make it as short and painless as possible."

"I will get the message to him and he will be there within the hour."

"Do you need directions?" Evan asked.

"That won't be necessary" Sam said. "I know where you live. I'll provide the judge a map."

The two, having agreed on all of the details, hung up. Evan raced back to his house to get things ready to make a video tape of the judge. Sam found Evan's address in his files. Within fifteen minutes he was on his way to see him.

Brad was exhausted. This was the furthest he had run since he was in college. Russo was in even worse shape. He had stopped three times to catch his breath and the trip was only a mile and a half. Finally they were at the house whose light they had seen back at the car. Brad motioned for Russo to be quiet as they made their way around the side of the house. As they approached the back door, Brad removed a gun from his belt. Russo looked at him with a hint of surprise. He still wasn't sure who had kidnapped him but he was beginning to trust Brad for getting him away from Arthur.

Brad gently gripped the knob on the back door and turned it. It wasn't locked. He opened the door a crack, then drew back and hit it, causing it to fly open and hit the wall.

He and Russo stepped quickly through the door into what appeared to be the kitchen. It was a small room with a sink and a few cabinets. The walls were in dire need of paint and the floor looked as if it hadn't seen a broom since Disco was in style.

They stormed through to the living room where the lights were on. A predictably surprised Derek sat clinging to the arms of the chair he was sitting in.

"What the hell's going on here?" he shouted as Brad pointed the gun at him. It was the same gun that Derek had bought earlier that week. Brad had loaded it with blanks.

"None of your damned business" Brad yelled. "We just need to borrow your house for a while." He moved the gun towards Derek until it was resting against his forehead. "You don't have a problem with that, do you?"

"No" Derek replied nervously, "just don't shoot me."

Russo was somewhat surprised by Brad's aggressiveness. He was almost a little proud of him since it seemed Arthur had gotten the upper hand of the conversations in the car.

Brad grabbed Derek by the front of his shirt and pulled him towards a closet in the hallway. He slammed him against the wall and opened the door. Placing the gun back to Derek's forehead, he ordered him into the closet. Derek did so reluctantly. Brad slammed the door to the closet behind him. Looking around, he walked back to the kitchen and grabbed a chair. He pushed it back to the closet and wedged it under the door knob, making it impossible for the door to be opened.

While Brad was subduing Derek, Russo had been scouring the house looking for something to get himself out of the handcuffs. He found nothing. There were no tools whatsoever in the house, not even a screwdriver.

"What is this guy, a pussy? He ain't got a thing in here I can use to get these cuffs off." Russo's impatience was quickly turning to anger.

"There's got to be something here we can get them off with." Brad said as he started going through the drawers in the kitchen.

But there was nothing. Anything that could possibly have been used to remove the cuffs had long since been taken from the house.

Finally in desperation, Russo's anger got the better of him. "Son of a bitch" he screamed.

"Take it easy." Brad said, trying to calm him down. "There's nothing here to get you out of these cuffs. Let's just lay low tonight and in the morning, I'll go out and get something to get them off; maybe a hacksaw or something"

Russo was hot and tired. Laying low didn't sound too bad to him right now. He figured Brad was on the up and up. He'd had plenty of chances to kill him. Hell he could have easily left him in the wrecked car but he didn't, so he figured he was okay. Besides as Russo saw it, he had no other alternative but to trust Brad, at least for now.

Russo walked back into the living room and sat down on the couch. It was difficult to sit with his hands behind his back, so getting comfortable was simply not possible. Brad returned in a few moments with two cans of soda. He sat one down on the coffee table in front of Russo and dropped a straw into it. He looked up at Brad.

"It's the best I can do." Brad said in his own defense.

Russo was grateful. He bent down and took a long drink from the can. As he did, a thought struck him.

"A phone!" he hollered.

"What?" Brad looked at him curiously.

"Let's find a phone and I can call for help. I'm sure my boys are looking for me by now anyway."

"Great idea" Brad said as he got up and began looking for the phone.

His search went from the living room to the kitchen, then down a small hallway to a bedroom. He found no phone.

"Find one?" Russo shouted from the couch.

"Not yet. Let me ask our host."

Brad walked back down the hall to the closet door. He tapped on it with the barrel of the gun.

"Hey asshole, where's the phone?"

A muffled voice from inside the closet replied. "I don't have a phone."

"You don't have a phone? What, do you think I'm stupid or something? Everybody has a phone."

"There's no phone here, I swear." Derek pleaded from the closet.

Brad walked back to the living room. Russo had heard Derek talking from inside the closet.

"No phone." Brad said.

"Ya, I heard." Russo replied, sounding disappointed.

"Don't you have a cell phone?" Russo asked Brad.

"No, my dick head partner has it. If you want, I could walk back there and get it. I don't think he's going to need it."

"Forget it." Russo quickly answered. "I'm not sitting here by myself wearing handcuffs. What if someone showed up? I'd be defenseless."

"You're right." Brad agreed.   "First thing in the morning, I'll go get a hacksaw and get you out of those things. I guess we just lay low till then."

Russo took another drink from the straw then leaned back on the couch. He looked over at Brad curiously for a moment, and then asked him a question.

"Why are you doing this anyway?"

"Doing what?"

"Helping me, why are you doing it?"

"We were paid two thousand dollars to grab you and deliver you to an address in some two bit town three counties over. I had no idea who you were. The guy laying dead out there made the deal. I was just the wheel man. I recognized you as soon as I saw you and I knew right then that we were making a big mistake."

"Why do you say that?"

"Hey, I don't need somebody like you pissed off at me. I figured we were grabbing some rich guy to be ransomed off."

"Who was it that hired you guys?"

"I never met him, but I heard my partner call him Pedro or Pablo or...."

"Paco" Russo said with contempt.

"Ya, that's it, Paco. That's the guy."

Russo gritted his teeth. Brad watched him as he quickly became filled with anger. "Paco Reyes" he spoke through clenched teeth.

"You know him?" Brad asked.

"Oh ya, I know him. He's been after a piece of my action for years. I never thought he was stupid enough to try something like this."

"Look" Brad said, throwing his hands into the air, "all I want to do is to get you out of those handcuffs and walk away from this situation, and hopefully you can find it in your heart not to have me killed."

"Hey you got nothing to worry about kid. I take care of the people that take care of me. You're alright."

Brad heaved a noticeable sigh of relief, and then he got up and switched on the TV.

"Let's see if there's anything on. Maybe it'll help pass the time."

In the small hall closet, Derek found a flashlight and turned it on. Hearing Brad's cue, he turned on a small black and white TV and a VCR, and quickly, pushed the play button starting the tape.

As Brad flipped through the channels, he came across a news broadcast. He stopped to listen. The picture on the television in the living room was the same as that on the small TV in the closet. The news was nothing more than a tape that had been made as part of plan. But the news anchor soon captured Russo's attention as she spoke.

"And on the local scene, reputed mob boss Eli Russo is missing and feared kidnapped."

Russo sat straight up on the couch as the anchor woman continued.

"A rival family thought to be the Reyes family, is suspected of carrying out the abduction, however the word is Russo may have escaped. Since then, an all out war has broken out between the two families. Local police are doing their best to contain the situation but so far there have been at least twenty two deaths related to this incident. Sources inside the police department tell us the exact whereabouts of Eli Russo are as yet unknown, but a ten man hit squad is said to be combing the countryside looking for Mr. Russo, whose son and two nephews go on trial tomorrow for murder. We'll have the highlights of the first day of that trial right here on this broadcast tomorrow, so be sure and tune in. Stay tuned for sports and weather next."

Brad got up and switched the set off. This was Derek's cue to shut the video equipment down and make his way out a small door in the back of the closet. The door led into a front bedroom. Once he was out of the closet, Derek quietly opened the window and was soon winding his way across the field towards the woods.

"Sounds like we'd better stay holed up here until the heat dies down." Brad cautioned.

Russo leaned back in the couch once again. He was overwhelmed by what he had heard on the newscast. Brad could tell it in his eyes. As much as he hated to admit it, he agreed with Brad, they were safer right where they were. He raised his feet to the couch, trying to get comfortable.

"Can I get you anything?" Brad asked.

"No, just keep an eye on things while I get some sleep."

Russo rolled over and tried his best to get to dose off. Brad took the gun from his belt to give the impression that he was actually guarding Russo. Staying awake would not be a problem for him tonight.

Sam rolled down the window of his car and pushed the button on the key pad outside of Evan's front gates. Evan accordingly pushed a button to open them. Sam drove through and up to the house. Evan opened the front door as Sam got out of the car. He walked down the front steps to meet him.

"Hi, I'm Evan. I take it you are the judge?"

"Yes I am", Sam answered, shaking Evan's hand. "Gordon Hartfield."

As they walked up the steps to the door, Evan looked back at what Sam had driven up in. "Is that your car?"

"No, mine's in the shop."

"I thought so." Evan said, taking a second look at it before closing his front door.

They walked through the dimly lit hall past the den to a room where Evan had set up a camera and some lights. The walls of this room were oak, stained a dark color, similar to those in Sam's courtroom. A large pulpit like structure, resembling a judge's bench had been set up in front of the rear wall of the room and a flag on a short mast stood next to it. Sam looked at it for a moment, nodding in approval.

"I've taken the liberty of preparing some lines that will convey what we are trying to get across. Take a look at them if you would and tell me what you think we need to change."

Sam took the paper from Evan and spent a minute reading it while Evan turned on the lights and camera.

"It sounds fine to me." Sam said as he took his place behind the bench.

Evan brought the camera in so that only Sam's head and shoulders could be seen, along with the flag and a small portion of the oak wall behind him.

"Are you ready?" Evan asked.

"Anytime"

Evan turned the camera on as Sam began to recite the lines from the paper, placing a momentary pause between each sentence. So far as Evan knew, this was just the judge in the Russo murder case. Evan had no idea he was in the same room with the man who was responsible for him being in the middle of this mess.

Brad glanced down at his watch for the fifth time since Russo had drifted off to sleep. It was approaching nine forty five and time for the next phase of the operation. He pulled his sleeve back down over his watch and took the gun from his belt. Gripping the butt, he pulled back on the mechanism that loaded a bullet (or in this case a blank) into the chamber. The distinct clicking sound awoke Russo. Brad was already on his feet. He motioned with his hands for Russo to get down as he cautiously walked out of the living room and into the kitchen. Russo sat frozen on the couch, thinking the worst.

Moments later, he heard the back door squeak slightly as Brad opened it. Then he heard Brad shout and the familiar sounds of a scuffle followed. The sounds grew louder as the scuffle turned into a fight. Pots and pans hit the floor as the struggle continued. The sounds of breaking glass and furniture peaked Russo's curiosity as Brad and Arthur knew it would.

Russo got up from the couch and hugged the wall as he made his way down the short hallway towards the kitchen. Arthur, who had been creating these sound effects with Brad in the kitchen, saw Russo's shadow on the floor as he approached the kitchen door. That was their cue.

Arthur ran for the back door and burst through it with Brad right behind him. The two ran out into the darkness and disappeared into the trees behind the house. Russo walked to the door and looked out, unable to see anything in the darkness. Within ten seconds there was a flash, then the unmistakable sound of a gunshot. Russo crouched behind the back door waiting to see who would emerge from the trees.

Soon, a lone figure gradually came into sight, still unrecognizable in the dim reflections of the light from the kitchen window. Russo hurried back toward the hallway. He looked around for a place, anyplace that looked as if it may be even remotely safe. The closest thing to safety was behind the door that separated the kitchen from the hallway. Standing behind it, he did his best to pull it back against the wall to conceal himself. The handcuffs restricted his movement tremendously, but using his foot, he managed to get the door pulled as close to the wall as it would go.

Unable to see, he listened for the footsteps, which eventually made their way up the back steps and into the kitchen. There was several moments of silence as Russo's heart pounded, not knowing which man it was that had come back into the kitchen.

"Mr. Russo?" Brad called.

Russo exhaled so hard that he pushed the door away from himself. It slowly swung closed. As it did, it revealed Brad standing, gun in hand, pointed at Russo.

"It's me!" Russo screamed.

Brad dropped the gun down to his side and heaved a sigh of relief himself.

"What the hell happened out there?" Russo asked, walking back into the living room.

"I heard someone outside, so I got up to check it out. Some guy had pried the back door open and was in the kitchen. I jumped him and we struggled until he broke free and ran out the back door. I went after him and caught up with him in the woods. I figured he was one of Paco's men, so I popped him."

"Is he dead?"

"He's not moving." Brad said almost proudly.

A smile crept across Russo's face. "You know something kid, you're alright."

Brad smiled back. "Thanks." he replied, as the two sat back down in the same places they had been before.

"Listen" Russo spoke, looking more serious than before, "we'd both better lay low for a while. Don't worry about going out in the morning to get a hacksaw. You'd better stay here in case another one of Paco's boys shows up. I can stand these cuffs for one more day."

"Are you sure?"

"I'm sure. We'll both stay here tomorrow, and if nothing happens, we'll sneak out of here after dark tomorrow night."

"Whatever you say" Brad agreed.

Russo put his feet up on the couch and tried once again to get comfortable. It would not be as easy falling asleep this time as it had been before.

Sam left Evan's place about forty minutes after he arrived. Shooting the video took very little time. It was the editing that was time consuming, and that was what Evan was working on. There were three DVD machines connected to a large panel with rows of knobs, each row with several switches and a light. A TV monitor, split into three equal portions, displayed three different pictures as Evan merged various parts of them together. He had been working for about an hour when his phone rang. It was Arthur.

"Evan, are you done with that video yet?"

"Almost, I need about twenty more minutes."

"Well me and Derek are on our way to pick it up. If you only need twenty minutes, you should be done by the time we get there."

"Ya, I should be. So how did it go tonight?"

"It went okay, but it's been no fun at all. Derek has been locked in a closet for hours and I've been killed twice since five o'clock. I'll be glad when this shit is over."

"You and me both" Evan agreed.

"We'll see you in twenty minutes."

Arthur hung up and Evan went back to work editing the tape.

All of the lights were turned off at Senator Edloe's house except for the light in his den. That was the only room in which any measure of comfort could be found. Edloe had nailed the doors shut into the library where the family bible still lay open on the floor. A two by four spanned both of the hand carved panels in the double doors. Nails driven through the two by four reached all the way through the panels and came out the other side.

In the kitchen, all four burners on the stove were lit. A dull bluish glow illuminated the walls and cabinets. The cabinets themselves were empty, their contents maniacally strewn about the kitchen as if raked off of the shelves. The cabinet doors had been smashed off their hinges with a hammer and lay in a pile in the middle of the kitchen floor.

A clock hanging on the wall had become the final resting place for the hammer that had destroyed the cabinets. The handle of the hammer protruded from the face of the clock as a dagger in a corpse.

Edloe sat in a chair positioned against the back wall of the den. This location afforded him a view of both the door into the den and the two windows that overlooked the garden behind the estate. The house was deathly silent. Edloe sat listening as if he expected to hear something. His eyes were bloodshot from his lack of sleep. He was wearing the same clothes he had worn yesterday. He had not left his house for two days now. Edloe had become a prisoner not only of his own home, but of his own mind as well.

As he sat clutching a pillow on his lap, he heard a loud thud, almost a crash upstairs. He jumped, squeezing the pillow tighter. He waited, but no other sounds followed. He was past the point of trying to explain things away. He was convinced of what they were and felt powerless to do anything about them. So he sat helplessly waiting for the consequences, the inevitable retribution for his actions.

Suddenly the lights in his den flickered, and then went out completely for a second or two. When they came back on, they seemed brighter than before. Edloe's shirt was wet with sweat as was the pillow he gripped in front of him. The intensity of the lights continued to increase until they were almost blinding. Then a voice, low at first though gradually becoming louder rumbled through the empty house. It sounded as if it were off in the distance, maybe in one of the rooms upstairs. It was the same low, growling sort of slow motion sounding voice that was etched into his memory.

"Edloe!" it angrily called.

There was silence for ten or fifteen seconds. Then it called out again, this time much louder sounding much angrier. "Edloe"

Senator Edloe sat shaking, unable to speak. He pulled the pillow yet closer as if it would somehow protect him. Another crash ripped through the silence. This one felt closer and sounded much louder than the last. It was followed again by the voice.

"Edloe, you did this to me." it roared.

The sound of the voice was deafening, as was the silence that came after it. It sounded as if it were drawing ever nearer to the den. Edloe got up from the chair and stood with his back to the wall. He felt like a caged animal with no way to escape. His hands, shaking to the point that he could not hold the pillow any longer, let it drop to the floor. He had never felt more vulnerable or more threatened in his life. Again the voice roared.

"Edloe, you did this to me. Now you must pay."

A portrait fell off the wall from the vibration caused by the sheer volume of the voice. It sounded as if it were right outside the den. The look in Edloe's eyes gave but an inkling of the terror that now consumed him.

Then suddenly as if possessed, he bolted across the room towards the windows. Without slowing down he dove at the large pane of glass in the lower portion of the window. It smashed into many pieces as first his hands, then his head crashed through. He landed on his back in the flower bed, his arms and face full of tiny cuts from the shattering glass.

He sat up, shaking his head as he tried to regain his bearings. When he was finally able to focus his eyes, he stood up and ran out of the garden and around the side of the house towards the front gates. He continued down the long drive that connected his house to the street below. As he ran past the gates and into the street, his pace quickened.

He continued to run as fast as he could down the middle of the street. He had only been running for a minute or two when a pair of headlights from a car behind him cast a shadow on the road around him. He continued to run, oblivious to the lights, and the car they belonged to. Within a few seconds the headlights were coupled with the blue and red flashes from the lights on the top of the police car that was now following him down the center of the road. Still, he made no attempt to stop. His eyes remained fixed, staring straight ahead. He had a look of maniacal determination on his face.

The police car pulled around Edloe and stopped abruptly in front of him. Both doors opened and two patrol officers got out, their night sticks in hand. Edloe tried to pass the car on the left but was tackled by one of the officers. He brought Edloe to the ground and held him while the other officer put a pair of handcuffs on him. Then they brought him to his feet and leaned him against the car.

"Now just what are you doing running down the middle of the road at this time of night?" the first officer asked.

"It's after me!" Edloe replied, his face still white with terror.

"What's after you?"

"The spirit, the spirit of the boy. I didn't mean to kill him, it's not my fault, but he thinks it is."

"What boy? What are you talking about?"

"The boy that was killed in the judge's car, it wasn't supposed to be him. It was supposed to be the judge."

"Wait a minute" the second officer observed. "I know this guy. He's a State Senator. I've seen his picture in the paper."

"Looks like he's gone off the deep end." the other said. "Hey, Senator, have you been drinking tonight?"

"No, you stupid idiot, haven't you been listening? The spirit of the dead boy is after me."

"Oh, I've been listening." the officer said impatiently. "You need help, and we're going to get it for you. Get in the car."

The two policemen opened the rear door of the patrol car and pushed Edloe inside. He resisted, kicking his feet and screaming about the 'spirit' he claimed was after him. The officers slammed the door behind him and looked at each other.

"What a wing nut." One of them remarked.

"Ya, I guess he finally cracked. He's being investigated you know."

"Ya, I heard." the other said as they got back into their car.

They switched the blue and red lights off and made a left turn at the next intersection, and headed for the city operated mental health care facility. The officer behind the wheel looked up through the windshield at the stars, then sighed and shook his head.

"I knew it!" he said.

"What?" the other asked.

"Full moon"

"Oh shit. All the crazies will be out tonight." He looked back at Edloe in the back seat. "All but this one"

CHAPTER TWENTY TWO

The morning sun gently warmed the air as the last remaining traces of winter melted into little trickles of water on the sidewalk. Evan paused for a moment to enjoy the sunshine before entering the office building. He walked through the doors and into the atrium. As he pushed open the door to the Senator's office he was greeted by a familiar face. It was the receptionist who he'd had lunch with right after tapping the Senator's phones. She looked up at him with curious anticipation.

"Well hi there stranger." she said, putting her phone call on hold. "What brings you to this seething snake pit today?"

"Why, you of course!" Evan could see that things around the office were a little stressed, to say the least. "What's going on around here today?"

"Haven't you heard? The Senator got himself arrested last night. They've got him in a mental hospital for observation."

"Really" Evan said, trying his best to act surprised.

"It's true. He's been acting really strange the last week or so, almost like he was off in another world. He didn't talk much, but when he did, he was as grouchy as a bear, you know, yelling and screaming for no reason at all. The joke around the office was that he had PMS."

"Well I've never met him" Evan admitted, "and from the sounds of things, I think I'd like to keep it that way."

"You're sure not missing anything. You know he chewed me out for not checking your ID when you came to fix the phones that day?"

"My ID? I was in my phone company uniform and wearing a badge with my picture on it." Evan laughed.

"I guess he doesn't trust anyone. I'm sure no one trusts him either." She paused for a moment, just long enough to realize that Evan had said he was there to see her. "Are you really here just to see me?"

"Absolutely, I was wondering if you were free for lunch today."

"Are you kidding? I'll do anything to get out of this mad house for an hour."

"Great, I'll pick you up around noon?"

"I can't wait," she said, smiling a smile that she knew he couldn't resist.

Evan smiled back, then turned and took a step towards the door. He stopped abruptly, as if he'd forgotten something. At least that's what he wanted her to think.

"Oh, I almost forgot. I found this on the floor next to the atrium out there."

He reached into his pocket and removed a watch. Not just any watch, but a watch that he himself had worn for the past three years; a watch that had been given to him by a lady from his past. But more importantly, a watch that had been captured by the security camera outside of Jerry Kinson's apartment, a photograph of which was still in Katie's research files.

The receptionist reached out and took the watch from Evan.

"I've never seen him wear this before. How do you know it's his?"

"Look on the back. It's engraved."

She turned the watch over and read aloud the inscription on the back.

"To Senator Edloe: Thanks for your help. I owe you one. V. Russo." She looked up at Evan, puzzled at what she had just read. "Who is V. Russo, I wonder?"

"Eli Russo, the organized crime boss. You'd better go and put that in the Senator's desk. It won't do anyone any good for the wrong people to find it."

Evan headed for the door as she walked towards the Senator's office. She turned and called out to him as he opened the office door.

"See you at noon."

Evan turned and winked. This assignment did have its moments.

Sam sat silently in his chambers reviewing the material in file folder that lay in front of him on his desk. He had rearranged the entire court docket in order to begin the trial of Russo's son today. He knew Russo would know nothing of this since he had been out of touch with all current events except those that were provided to him. So far, things seemed to be working out as planned. But there was still a lot that could go wrong.

A light knock on his door drew Sam's attentions from his work.

"Come in." he called.

"Excuse me sir" asked a rather soft spoken man. "My name is Andrew Weeks. I'm a doctor, a psychiatrist actually, at the West Side Mental Health Facility."

Sam stood up and the two shook hands.

"What can I do for you?" Sam asked.

"We had a patient brought to us last night. He is extremely delusional and his behavior is paranoid. After an extensive psychological evaluation, we feel that this man does indeed pose a threat to himself as well as those around him." The man took a few steps forward, as one who felt awkward with what he had to ask. "Normally, we would simply submit a written petition in a case like this, however this case is a little different."

"What exactly is it that's different?"

"The man I've been talking about is a State Senator. His name is Ryan Edloe."

Sam looked up at him with a haunting intensity.

"Anything I file with the court in this matter will become public information. I see no good coming from this type of publicity, especially in terms of Mr. Edloe's psychological needs." the doctor explained.

"I understand and appreciate your coming here personally to take care of this. I assume you feel a mandatory stay at your facility will be beneficial?" Sam appeared to be genuinely concerned.

"Yes, we feel he needs to be observed for at least seventy two hours. As I said, he has completely lost touch with reality."

"Do you feel confident that you can help him in seventy two hours?"

"Not really, but it will be a start." the doctor answered.

He produced a three page document from his brief case and put it on the desk in front of Sam. Sam studied it intently for a few minutes then, having determined everything to be in order, signed it in two places and handed it back to Dr. Weeks.

"Thank you, sir. I know this is a very delicate situation and I feel it would be in no one's best interests to have this smeared all over the newspapers."

"I totally agree." Sam said, standing to shake the doctor's hand once again. "If you find that an extended stay is in order for the Senator, get back in touch with me and we'll handle it as discretely as possible."

"Thank you for your understanding, your honor."

Dr. Weeks closed the door behind him as he left Sam's office. Sam sat back down. Momentarily distracted, he thought about Edloe and what Arthur and his friends must have done to him to make him a candidate for such a place. But with much still to do, he re-focused his attentions to the matter at hand.

Brad hadn't slept a wink all night. In spite of that fact, he was wide awake. Russo had been asleep off and on since about midnight. Brad expected him to wake up anytime, although he hoped he'd stay asleep.

His stomach was growling, and for good reason. He hadn't had anything to eat since yesterday afternoon. With everything that went on last night there was hardly time. Brad got up out of the chair and walked to the kitchen to see if any food had been left there.

The house and thirty five acres around it were part of a hunting lease that Arthur's company used to court new clients. Arthur had made sure that no one was using it this week.

But Arthur was a forward thinker as Brad soon discovered when he opened the refrigerator. In one of the bins was several pounds of deli meats and cheeses, a loaf of bread, some mustard and a bottle of hot sauce. Brad looked at it all with lust in his eyes. He loved hot sauce. He ate it on almost everything, and this morning he would eat it on a sandwich.

He reached into the refrigerator and grabbed the bread and meat and the two bottles out of the door. He sat them up on the counter and began to make a sandwich. After making what to most people would be just a sandwich, but to him was a feast, he walked back down the hall, stopping briefly at the living room door. Russo was still asleep. He continued on down the hall to the front bedroom from which Derek gained access to the closet. As he walked into the room, he noticed the small door to be open a few inches. He walked over to it and peered in through the cracked door. The closet was empty. He pushed up his sleeve and looked at his watch. Derek should have been back by now.

Brad turned and walked over to the window looking out towards the woods. In the distance, he saw a lone figure running toward the house. As the figure approached, Brad heaved a small but noticeable sigh of relief, realizing it was Derek.

Within minutes, Derek was climbing through the window into the front room. Brad grabbed his arm and helped him through.

"Did you get it?" Brad asked. His concern was evident in his voice.

Derek reached behind him and pulled a tape from his back pocket.

"Right here." he said, holding it in the air.

As Derek passed by Brad, he quickly grabbed the sandwich off of his plate. "Thanks" he said, taking a huge bite, "I'm starved."

"You're welcome." Brad said reluctantly. "Now, you remember your cue right?"

"Ya, I remember. It's not like I have anything else to do in this closet but listen for it."

"Good." Brad whispered. Then, thinking about who it was that gave the tape to Derek, he felt compelled to ask another question.

"Evan didn't give you any movies from his porno collection to help you pass the time, did he?"

Derek stopped mid-way through the tiny closet door, backing out slightly. "Evan has a porno collection?"

"He's probably got a copy of every one that was made." Brad scoffed.

"Really, I'll have to ask him about it. Hell, if I'd known, I'd have brought one back with me."

Derek crawled into the closet. Brad began to close the door behind him."

"Remember, twelve o'clock."

"I got it." Derek assured him as he pulled the door closed.

Brad slowly walked back to the living room. As he walked through the door, Russo was awake and sitting up on the couch. He was rubbing his eyes, one at a time, with his shoulders as if he had just awakened. His hands, still secured behind his back were numb from his laying on them. He looked up at Brad as he walked over to the chair and sat down.

"Sleep okay?" Brad asked.

"I thought I heard you talking to someone."

"I was" Brad said, thinking fast, "I was asking the kid in the closet how far it was to the nearest town."

"So how far is it?"

"Sixteen miles"

Russo didn't seem to have as much trust in Brad as he did last night when he thought Brad had saved his life. But then maybe he just wasn't a morning person. Nonetheless, Brad tried to keep up the same front to make sure Russo believed that he was on his side.

"There's some bread and meat in the refrigerator. Can I make you something to eat?"

"How the hell would I eat it with my hands cuffed behind my back?" Russo responded angrily.

Brad got up and walked over to him.

"You know, I've been thinking about that. Lets try pulling your knees up toward your chest, and maybe we can slip your hands past your feet and get them in front of you."

"What are you talking about?" Russo asked in a foul tone.

"Just try it. Here, I'll help you."

Russo bent his knees and moved them up as far as they would go towards his chest, which wasn't very far. Brad pushed against the front of his ankles and at the same time, pulled the handcuffs and his hands literally out from under him. The chain that connected the two cuffs dragged snugly across the bottoms of Russo's shoes. Russo began screaming like a child with his fingers caught in the car door.

"Keep pushing!" Brad shouted as Russo's hands slipped past his feet. "There you go."

Russo dropped his feet back to the floor. His hands, though still handcuffed, were now in front of him. This posed a much greater risk for Brad, but he felt he had to do something to regain Russo's trust.

"Hey, this is much better. Thanks kid."

Russo stretched his arms out in front of him, enjoying his new found but limited freedom. There were two deep impressions on his wrists where the cuffs had pressed hard into his skin. But his hands were out from behind his back now, and that was a step in the right direction as far as he was concerned. His temperament had suddenly changed.

"Now" he said in a much more upbeat manner, "I'm ready for that sandwich."

The courtroom was filled to capacity and people were still lined up outside to get in. Most of those already seated were reporters and family members. A few curiosity seekers did make it in as well, but the majority of them would not get a seat.

It was very noisy. The air was thick with voices speculating not only the outcome of the trial but on how the judge would rule on the evidence that would make or break the case.

Russo's family and friends sat somberly in the first row behind Russo's son and two nephews. The district attorney had decided against separate trials for the three men, so all of them were together this morning in Sam's courtroom.

At precisely ten thirty, a voice spoke up above all the others.

"All rise. Court is now in session, the honorable judge Gordon Samuel Hartfield presiding."

Sam walked through the door behind the clerk's desk and across the front of the courtroom and up the two steps to his bench. He stood for a moment, his eyes scanning the crowd of on-lookers.

Sam sat down behind his bench, and when he did, everyone else followed suit. Sam took hold of his gavel and brought it down soundly on its base, then spoke with confidence and determination.

"This court is now in session."

As he spoke, he looked down at the three defendants. They did not share his confidence, nor did their attorney. The trial had been unexpectedly moved up, Russo was nowhere to be found and there had been no verification until now, as to whether the fix was in on the admissibility of the evidence.

But the defense attorney knew. He could tell from the look on Sam's face and by the way he spoke. He leaned over to Russo's son and whispered, "We're in deep shit."

Arthur and Lenny had taken up positions outside of the small house where Brad and Russo were hiding. They knew sooner or later, that Russo's men would stumble on this place in their search for him, and they weren't about to take any chances. Besides, their lives and the lives of their families were at stake here. Arthur thought it rather ironic that he was standing guard over the same man who had threatened his family, but he knew things would find a way of equalizing themselves. They always did.

The clump of bushes provided cover but little comfort for Arthur. It reminded him a little of the war, except nobody was shooting at him, at least not yet. He settled in, resting his back against a tree that grew out from the middle of the bushes. It was quiet, except for the occasional bird. The house was far enough from the main road that there were none of the usual traffic sounds. Arthur saw this as an advantage. He kept his eyes peeled and listened for even the slightest sound, but soon became bored.

He was checking his watch for the fourth time when he heard a rustling sound off in the distance. He ducked down further into the bushes, gripping tightly on the hunting rifle in his hands. His eyes were fixed on a clearing where he expected the sounds would emerge. It seemed a shame now that he and Lenny had decided to split up and each watch opposite sides of the house. The sounds grew louder as two figures appeared in the clearing. Each of them carried a gun although neither of them looked like hunters. *Who goes hunting in a suit?*, he thought to himself.

He watched the two for a couple of minutes trying to determine their direction. When it was clear that they had spotted the house and were heading towards it, Arthur stood up from the bushes. He startled the two men. They quickened their pace towards him. Arthur figured the best defense was a good offense, so he fired the first verbal shot.

"Hey" he shouted, displaying a noticeable thread of anger in his voice, "just what the hell do you two think you're doing? This is private property."

The two continued towards him, their guns pointed in his direction.

"Who the hell are you?" one of the two asked.

Both men were larger than the average man, over two hundred pounds for sure. They both wore suits and white raincoats. The guns they were carrying were not hunting rifles.

They looked more like automatic weapons. Arthur was out manned and out gunned and he knew it.

"I live here." Arthur barked back. "Who are you?"

"We're looking for somebody." the other man replied. His tone revealed some degree of resentment and impatience at having to explain what they were doing to some 'nobody' out here in this field.

"Well he's not here!" Arthur snapped.

"Is that your house over there?" he asked, pointing to the house where Brad and Russo were hiding.

"Ya, so what?"

"So we're going to go and have a look inside." Both men raised their guns towards Arthur's head. Arthur froze. "You don't have a problem with that, do you?"

Before he could answer, a distinct thud interrupted the conversation. It sounded as if something had fallen from a small clump of trees to their immediate left.

Both thugs turned at the same time, their guns still pointing at Arthur. Arthur too had turned to see where the sound had come from. As he turned his head, he caught a glimpse of the soles of Lenny's shoes as they flew through the air towards the two suits.

By the time their attentions were drawn from the noise in the woods, Lenny's feet were making positive contact with the chest of the man to the right of Arthur. He hit him with such force that he pushed him into the other man and the two hit the ground. The larger of the two let go of his gun in an attempt to keep his balance, but the other held tightly to his. The fight was on.

Arthur grabbed the barrel of his assailant's gun and raised it up into the air, struggling with him as he was much stronger than Arthur. The man scrambled back up to his feet. Arthur pushed upwards on the barrel of the gun with all his might. As he did, it drew the man closer to him. Arthur's military training, though years ago, taught him that there were no rules in a situation like this. Not that any rule would have stopped him anyway, he jerked his knee upwards and struck the man in the groin. The man loosened his hold on the gun but didn't let go of it. His knees buckled slightly as he cried out in pain. Arthur had expected him to fall and was surprised when he didn't. He pulled the gun free from his hands and took a step backwards. The man, still in pain, was slow to react. He showed no sign of surrender as he took a step towards Arthur. Arthur, not wanting to arouse Russo's suspicions with gunfire, flipped the gun around in his hands and struck the man soundly on his head.

This was more than the man could endure. He dropped to his knees as a trickle of blood ran down his face. He was unconscious before he hit the ground.

Catching his breath, Arthur looked around for Lenny. In the midst of the struggle, Arthur had become oblivious to everything but his assailant.

Lenny and the other man were twenty feet or so away from the spot where Arthur stood. Lenny was poised to attack but was waiting for his opponent to make the first move. While Arthur secured his unconscious attacker's hands and feet with nylon tie straps, Lenny continued to bait the man who would soon join his partner in a state of unconsciousness.

"Come on tough guy." Lenny taunted. "Give me your best shot, or are you a pussy like your friend over there?"

"I'm gonna kick your ass!" the man growled.

"How" Lenny mocked, "your momma's not here to help you."

The man became enraged. He lost his temper, which was exactly what Lenny hoped he would do, and charged at him. Lenny grabbed his arm as he approached and threw him over his hip into a tree behind them. The man was dazed, but still aware enough to fight. He got up and extended his fists, hesitant to get too close to Lenny. Lenny ridiculed him further.

"Is that the best you got? My sister could kick your ass and put her make-up on at the same time."

The man gritted his teeth, but resisted the temptation to charge Lenny again. He reached down and pulled a switch blade from his left sock. With the push of a button, the blade was extended and locked into position. He began waving it though the air as if he had the upper hand. Lenny soon dispelled those thoughts.

"Ooh, I'm scared now!" Lenny continued to challenge and taunt him, waiting for him to make another move. "Remember", he scoffed, pointing at the knife, "the sharp edge faces this way and the dumb end goes in your hand."

"You're going to be talking out of the other side of your ass when I rip you a new one."

Lenny laughed at him. "That's awful strong talk for someone as stupid as you."

The man became enraged again and charged toward Lenny waving the knife wildly in front of him. Lenny seized the opportunity to end this nonsense. He grabbed his arm as it approached him and bent it back until the pain forced him to drop the knife.

The talk was over. Lenny was the aggressor now. With the man's arm still in his grip, he raised his foot and kicked him three times very quickly in his chest. The man doubled over. Lenny brought his right knee up, striking the man in his face. Blood was dripping from his nose as Lenny delivered a final blow with his foot to the side of the man's head, and he fell unconscious to the ground.

Arthur quickly rolled him over and secured him with some of the same ties he had used earlier.

"I hope these two are it." Arthur said, wrapping the tie around the man's wrists.

"Don't count on it." Lenny replied. When these two don't come back, they'll send out two more. Hopefully we'll be done and out of here by then."

"That would suit me just fine." Arthur muttered.

After catching their breath, they both returned to their original positions. Once again the woods were silent.

The mood in the courtroom was somber. The preliminary proceedings moved quickly as the attorneys for both sides made their opening remarks and pleaded their cases as to the admissibility or lack thereof of the most crucial piece of evidence in the trial. By eleven thirty, it was in the hands of the man who would decide its fate; Sam.

Sam had long ago reviewed the circumstances, weighed the evidence and had determined what should be done, but he listened attentively as each side made their best attempt to convince him that they were right.

With that formality behind him, it was time to make the decision that had so impacted their lives for nearly a month; the decision that he had agonized over for even longer than that. It was time for it all to be over with. Sam began.

"Having reviewed the evidence and the manner in which it was gathered, it is the decision of this court that this evidence, pursuant to the laws and statutes governing the collection of such evidence, shall be deemed admissible, and will be entered as such in this proceeding."

A roar of mumbling filled the courtroom. Sam pounded his gavel in vain to silence the courtroom as the reporters feverishly began sending text messages to their respective publishers. Two of the three defendants sat with their heads cradled in their hands. The third, Russo's son, could be heard screaming at his attorney above the noise.

"You stupid son of a bitch, you told me this was in the bag."

The attorney did his best to silence his client but the enraged young man was not to be silenced.

"I'm going to have you killed, do you understand that? I'm going to kill you and your family, and then I'm going to kill him." He pointed directly to Sam. Their eyes made contact. Sam looked at him coldly for a second, before summoning the bailiff. Both the bailiff and the clerk approached the bench.

"Bailiff, this court is leveling additional charges against Mr. Russo."

"What charges sir."

"He threatened both me and his council with death."

"I heard him say it as well," the court clerk said, "and I'll gladly testify to that fact."

The bailiff walked over to young Mr. Russo and informed both he and his council of the charges that the court was filing against him. The noise in the courtroom refused to yield to Sam's demands for silence, so the on-lookers were removed. The only people allowed to remain were the immediate families of the defendants. When the dust settled, Sam pounded his gavel again.

"Let's get on with this" he shouted.

He glared for a long moment at young Mr. Russo, whose demeanor had changed significantly, and the trial resumed.

"Let's see if we can catch some news." Brad suggested as he walked over and switched on the TV.

He had just finished making himself and Russo another sandwich. Derek had been waiting for the signal to start the video, and quickly did so upon hearing Brad mention the news. As the picture began to appear on the screen, the logo of the news cast was just coming up.

"Good timing!" Russo remarked.

If you only knew, you stupid shit, Brad thought to himself.

As expected, the top story on the news this mid-day was the Russo trial. Brad reached over and turned the volume up as the newscast began.

"In an unusual turn of events that began with the trial date being moved up a week, the judge has just ruled that the evidence in question may not be admitted and will not be used in this trial."

"I don't believe it." Russo exclaimed. "The son of a bitch actually did it."

"Did what?" Brad asked as innocently as he was able.

"Shh, just a minute." he said as he listened to the rest of the story.

"The district attorney commented earlier that without that evidence it would be almost impossible to get a conviction. It remains to be seen now if the charges will be dropped or a plea bargain will be attempted. This is Pamela Grissom reporting live for channel six news at noon."

Russo got up and turned the TV off himself. As he walked back to the couch, Brad could see in his eyes that he was both relieved and surprised. He sat down, and then offered Brad the explanation he had been waiting for.

"I had this politician on my payroll for about five years. He was a State Senator; Edloe was his name, Ryan Edloe. You know him?"

"I've heard the name before but I don't know that much about politics." Brad admitted.

From the hall closet, Derek watched the needle on the VU meter move back and forth as Russo spoke and the tape recorder captured his conversation.

"Well, Edloe was just another tin horn politician until I started pumping money into his campaign. He got some legislation through that helped me so I kept funding him and his bad habits."

"His bad habits" Brad questioned.

"Ya, the Senator had a gambling problem. I pulled his narrow ass out of the fire a couple of times from people that wanted to break his legs. So, when my kid got in trouble I called on him to help, you know, to return the favor. He said he could get to the judge and make him change his mind. I was beginning to think he was blowing smoke up my ass, but the little bastard actually did it."

"What kind of connection did he have to the judge?" Brad asked.

"I don't know. He never would say, but he gave me a list of people that needed to be leaned on. So we did, and I guess it worked."

Brad's fingernails dug into the arm of the chair as he listened to Russo. He and his friends were on that list, and he had not forgotten about that. But he had a job to do and he would not let his feelings get in the way of that.

"Well it looks like things are working out for you. Your son's off the hook, you dodged a kidnapping and after dark tonight, we'll get the hell out of here and back to civilization.

"You bet." Russo said raising his hands and placing them behind his head. "This just goes to show that when you're a nice guy, nice things happen to you." He smiled as if pleased with himself.

What a crock of shit, Brad thought.

CHAPTER TWENTY THREE

Detective Mo Harris thought he had put the 'Kinson' and 'Dugay' cases to bed. He was wrong. As much as he hated being wrong, the outcome of this mistake would prove to have a very positive effect on his career. Although both cases were officially listed as 'unsolved', from the standpoint of justice they were both closed. In fact, Mo had forgotten all about them. But his memory was about to be jogged.

It was unusual for Mo to be sitting behind his desk at this time of the day, but he had been delinquent with his monthly reports. So in the absence of any life or death cases, he had resigned himself to the task of completing the dreaded reports by day's end. But as usually happened, after an hour or so of filling out forms, Mo was looking for a reason to quit. Today he wouldn't have to find a reason, the reason would find him.

The sound of ringing telephones and typewriters were often drowned out by the multitude of different voices all talking at once in the precinct. Mo had learned long ago to tune them all out whenever he had paper work to do. The one voice he could not tune out was that of his captain.

"Hey Mo" he called from his office.

Captain Sidney Voss had held that position for some eight years now. He ran a tight ship based on the simple principal everyone does their very best, not just their fair share. His stature didn't hurt things either. He stood six foot two, and at two hundred forty pounds, most everyone took him seriously, like Mo was right now.

"Ya, what's up?"

"Didn't you and Findley handle the Kinson case a while back?"

"Sure did, why?"

"Someone sent us some new evidence that may help you to close it."

Mo muttered, not thinking his captain could hear him, "As far as I'm concerned, it's already closed."

"What?" Captain Voss yelled.

"Be right there." Mo answered, not wanting to explain himself to his captain.

Mo got up and walked through the maze of desks scattered about the large squad room and over to his captain's office door. Captain Voss was sitting at his desk in a small office wrapped on two sides with glass walls. This afforded him a view of just about everything that went on in the squad room, but little privacy for himself.

"What have you got?" Mo asked from the doorway.

"Come here and I'll show you."

Mo walked into the small office and sat down in a single chair in front of the captain's desk. The captain threw a large brown manila folder into Mo's lap.

"This was on my desk this morning. It's from an investigator for the newspaper. Check it out. You might want to re-open the cases."

Captain Voss put his reading glasses back on and returned his attentions to the papers on his desk. This was Mo's signal that the conversation had finished and it was time for him to leave. He reluctantly took the envelope and went back to his desk.

Mo pulled a photo and a short letter out of the envelope as he sat back down at his desk. It was a picture showing a man, whose identity could not be determined, wearing a most unusual watch. The watch was very clear and detailed. It was obvious to Mo, having been a detective for a number of years that the watch was the reason that the photo was sent. Then he flipped the letter over on top of the photo and began to read.

'In the course of my investigation into the similarities in style of what happened to Jerry Kinson and Vince Dugay, I obtained this photo taken by a security camera. Although the faces are unrecognizable, the watch has proven to be otherwise.

After some extensive investigation, I traced the watch as belonging to a State Senator by the name of Ryan Edloe. Through sources that I am not willing to reveal, I obtained a copy of the inscription on the back of Mr. Edloe's watch. Once I learned who had given it to him, I determined it to be time to involve the police. The watch was a gift from Eli Russo, the reputed head of an organized crime family.

I have a husband and a young child and would prefer not to become directly involved to any further degree in this matter. However, in exchange for the information I have just given you, I will expect to be kept informed so that I may break this news as it happens. It is my understanding from my source that the watch can be found in the Senator's desk at his offices downtown. I will be out of town on a story for a few days, but I will contact this department upon my return.'

A name was typed at the bottom of the letter, that of Katie Williams. There was no signature. This made Mo a little skeptical, the fact that this 'Katie' person was not willing to sign the letter. Anybody could have written it. Nonetheless, he was obliged to check it out. Besides, he was looking for an excuse to get away from the paperwork that had been a nuisance to him all morning.

It took only an hour and a half to get a search warrant based on the letter and the accompanying photo, but one was finally signed by a judge from the county court building. Mo and his partner, Patrick arrived at Senator Edloe's offices twenty minutes later. They approached the receptionist who by this time had lost not only her patience, but her resolve due to the absence and apparent mental condition of her boss.

"Afternoon Miss, I'm detective Harris and this is detective Findley. We have a warrant here to search these premises for evidence in an assault case."

"Fine, go ahead."

Mo was surprised at her attitude. Usually there is some degree of resistance to his exercising a search warrant, or at least an attempt to stall so as to hide or dispose of certain evidence. But this woman looked as if she could care less whether they carted off the whole place or not.

"His office is through that door" she offered, "and if you know what's good for you, don't answer the phone if it rings. It's been brutal. I've never talked to so many pissed off people in my life."

Mo looked at her curiously before he and Findley proceeded to Edloe's office.

It didn't take long. The watch was in the pencil tray in the front of the center drawer. Patrick picked it up and turned it over. There was indeed an inscription on the back and it was from Russo. Patrick turned to Mo.   "Looks like we're back in business on this one."

As Patrick spoke, Mo's cell phone rang. He looked at it to check the number. It was the precinct, more specifically, captain Voss.

"Ah shit!" he jeered. "He's probably going to jump my ass because the monthly reports aren't done."

Mo pushed a button and answered the phone.

"This must be your lucky day." the captain said.

"Why is that?" Mo asked.

"We just got another piece of evidence, anonymously."

"What is it this time?"

"Are you sitting down?"

"I'm afraid to in this place." Mo answered.

"Someone sent us a cassette tape of Eli Russo. He implicates Edloe and places himself in the middle of the scam that Edloe's being investigated for. He also implicates Edloe in an extortion scheme to make the judge in his son's case throw out some evidence. We got him dead to rights."

"And we don't know who sent it?"

"It was signed, a concerned citizen."

"We got the watch, and it is engraved just like the letter said it was."

"Well pick Edloe up and bring him in."

Mo paused a second. "He's not here."

"Well find out where he is and bring him in." the captain snapped.

Mo took the phone from his mouth and called out to the receptionist.

"Hey lady, where's your boss?"

She looked back at him in disbelief. "Don't you read the newspapers? He's been locked up in the nut house. He went wacko yesterday. Why do you think it's such a zoo around here?"

The receptionist did not mince her words. Her frustration was evident.

Mo raised the phone back to his head. "You're not going to believe this captain, but he's in a mental hospital."

"What?" he barked. "Well find out which one and go see him."

"Right away sir" Mo answered.

"And while you're at it, try to find Russo. He's missing too." The captain hung up the phone, then spoke aloud to himself. "We get all the evidence dropped in our laps and now we can't find either one of them. Shit."

The audio tape now in the captain's possession was the one that Derek had made of the conversation between Brad and Russo after the phony news cast convinced him that the evidence had been disallowed.

Thanks a million, whoever you are, Mo thought.

The drive from Edloe's office to the West Side Mental Health Facility took about forty five minutes in the early afternoon traffic. Mo called ahead on his cell phone to let them know what was going on and that he and his partner would need to talk to Edloe. He spoke with Dr. Weeks, the same doctor that had sought out Sam for his signature on the forms to have Edloe held for observation.

"Ya doc, my name's Harris. I'm a detective. I'm working on a case that a patient of yours may be involved in and I need to ask him some questions."

"Which patient is that?" the doctor asked.

"Edloe, Ryan Edloe. Are you familiar with him?"

"Oh yes" Dr. Weeks confirmed. "But I don't know that you'll get anything from him. He's extremely paranoid and completely out of touch with reality."

"What's wrong with him?"

"He thinks someone's spirit is after him. He's completely obsessed with it."

"We'll be there in about fifteen minutes."

"You should know that I've sent for a judge to sign the papers to keep him here indefinitely. He's that far gone."

"Be there as quick as we can." Mo assured him, and then hung up the phone.

"He's flipped out." Mo said to Patrick. "I don't know how much we're going to get out of him."

It took a little longer than fifteen minutes for Mo and Patrick to get to the hospital, but it really didn't make much difference. They identified themselves to a nurse who took them to Dr. Weeks' office. He was just hanging up the phone as they walked through his door.

"Doctor" the nurse spoke, "these two gentlemen are detectives. They said you were expecting them."

"Yes I am. Thank you."

The nurse smiled, then turned and walked away. Patrick followed her with his eyes for a moment. She looked as good walking away as she did when she approached them. Once he realized that he was standing alone in the doorway and that Mo had entered the office, he snapped back to reality and to the matter at hand.

"Before we go and see Mr. Edloe, I must warn you he's not rational. Don't expect much, and take what he tells you with a grain of salt."

Mo looked at him curiously, but somehow believed him.

The doctor got up from his desk and led Mo and Patrick down a long corridor. They passed by the seemingly endless lines of locked doors. Mo glanced through some of the windows into the rooms. Many patients were strapped to their beds and some were just sitting there looking off into space. Some had their faces pressed maniacally against the glass in the door, their skin rubbing and squeaking on the window, distorting their expressions. He noticed more than anything their eyes. Their eyes had a look of utter terror, as if something was inside them and they were trying to escape their own bodies.

Finally they reached the end of the hallway. An orderly unlocked the door which led to yet another corridor and another row of closed doors. They walked down to the third door on the right. Dr. Weeks motioned for the orderly to unlock the door. He did so with some amount of apprehension. He pushed the door open by the knob, stepping in with it as it opened and remaining there it until all three men were inside. Then the orderly entered the room, closed the door and stood in front of it.

Edloe lay strapped to a bed, his hands and feet restrained with wide leather straps. His vital signs were monitored by an array of electronic devices mounted on the wall above his bed. His eyes had the same look that Mo had seen in other patients' eyes as he walked down to Edloe's room. He approached the bed and quietly spoke.

"Mr. Edloe, my name is detective Mo Harris. I need to ask you some questions."

The Senator stared up at him, seemingly unaffected by his presence.

"Do you know a man by the name of Eli Russo?"

"Eli Russo" Edloe said, not as a question, but more as if he were repeating what Mo had just asked.

"That's right" Mo continued, "Eli Russo. Do you know him?"

"Ya, I think I know him. He gives me money when I need it."

"Has he given you a lot of money?"

"Yes" Edloe answered without emotion, "Yes he has."

"Does he ever ask you to do things in return for this money?"

"He wanted me to fix his son's trial by threatening the judge."

Mo's eyes grew large at the information that Edloe had just given them. But before anyone could continue, Dr. Weeks spoke up.

"Detective, I don't know if this will affect your investigation here, but Mr. Edloe has been given a drug to slow down his thought processes. This allows him to rest. One of the side effects of the drug manifests itself in much the same way as sodium amytol, you know, like a truth agent."

"Shit!" Mo snapped.

"What's wrong?" Patrick asked. "We're on a roll here."

"We can't ask him anymore questions, and we can't use what he just told us."

"Why?"

"Because of the drug, that's why. He's not answering of his own free will. So what ever he tells us, and any other information we get because of it will be inadmissible in court. We're violating his civil rights by questioning him while he's under the influence of that drug."

"You mean we got to stop?"

Mo flipped his notebook closed. "Ya, we're out of business here."

As he and Patrick turned towards the door it opened, bumping the orderly's back who was still standing in front of it. He moved out of the way as a nurse entered, followed by Sam.

Edloe looked up at him and his demeanor immediately changed. He became hysterical, screaming and pointing at Sam.

"That's him!" Edloe screamed. "That's the man!"

"What man?" Mo asked.

"I thought we weren't supposed to ask him any more questions," Patrick said.

"Shut up." Mo snapped, and then returned his eyes to Edloe.

Edloe was becoming even more impassioned. Sam looked at him with a fatherly sort of concern.

"He runs a network of vigilantes." Edloe screamed. "They go around punishing people for beating the system, and he's one of the head men in the organization."

Mo looked up at the doctor, who slowly shook his head. Then he pointed to Sam.

"Detective Harris, this is Judge Hartfield. He is a federal judge. He's also the one that signed Mr. Edloe into our facility. I contacted him personally due to the delicate nature of this case."

Mo looked over at Sam and extended his hand. Sam reached out and shook hands with him.

"So you run a team of vigilantes, huh?" Mo said.

"It's sad" Sam spoke, shaking his head, "how a man can be perfectly normal one minute, and like this, the next." He pointed over towards Edloe then looked back at the doctor. "You have papers for me to sign?"

"Of course" Dr. Weeks replied.

Mo took one last look at Edloe as he slipped his notebook back in his inside coat pocket. Then everyone but the nurse left the room. Mo thanked the doctor for his help and expressed his pleasure at meeting Sam. Patrick scanned the hallway for one last glimpse the nurse that had led them to the doctor's office.

"Come on" Mo snarled, "Let's get the hell out of here."

On their way back to the car Mo's phone range again. And once again it was the captain.

"Great" Mo complained, "It's the captain again. Probably just another wild goose chase." He flipped open the phone.

"What can I do for you, captain?" he asked.

"How did it go with Edloe?"

"We crapped out on Edloe. He's gone completely nuts. They got him locked up. Hell, he even accused a federal judge of being a vigilante."

"Well maybe this will cheer you up." the captain said excitedly. "We got an anonymous tip on Russo. The caller said he's holed up in a house about thirty miles outside of town. I got uniforms on their way, but I want you two to meet them there."

"We're on our way." Mo replied as he made a U-turn and headed back in the opposite direction. "Who the hell's doing this?" Mo asked his captain.

"Beats the hell out of me" He admitted. "But I'll take all the help I can get."

Before Mo had a chance to hang up, Captain Voss added, "Russo is with a federal informant, so separate them as quickly as possible, but go through the motions of arresting the informant if you have to so we don't blow his cover. You got that?"

"Got it" Mo answered, the roar of the car's engine growing ever louder in the background.

Mo hung up. Maybe this thing would turn out alright yet.

It was four thirty in the afternoon. Brad paced nervously across the kitchen floor, checking his watch at what seemed ten minute intervals. Russo sat watching TV in the living room. He figured Brad was standing guard as just another of his hired help would do. Brad knew that Arthur and Lenny had left thirty minutes ago and that he would be unprotected until the police arrived. According to the timetable they had worked out the police should have been there by now. They should have been here twenty minutes ago.

He looked, for the sixth time, out the kitchen window at the woods that separated the house from the road that passed in front of it. And for the sixth time there was nothing.

He looked away but stopped, then looked back. Something was different, but he wasn't sure what it was. He looked back out the window and studied the view for a moment. Then he noticed it. As the sun peeked in and out from behind the clouds, it was being reflected off of something that had not been there the last time he looked. He studied the reflection for a few seconds. It was a car bumper. *Must be the police*, he thought to himself. *It's about damn time, too.*

He scanned the woods around the house, but saw nothing. *Where the hell are they? They must be going to storm the place. That's what it is. Maybe they're waiting for back-up. I think I'll just get out of they way and hope they don't shoot me.*

The back door burst open before Brad had a chance to find that 'out of the way' place he had thought about. Three men rushed in, each carrying a large hand gun. They looked at Brad and the first to come through the door pointed his weapon at him. Brad raised his arms into the air. Although it was just a formality, Brad was scared. This was the first time anyone had pointed a gun at him. He didn't like it.

Russo, hearing the commotion, got up from the couch and ran into the kitchen. He looked with shock at the three men standing there, who immediately trained their weapons on him. There was a slight moment in which Brad became very confused. Then it all became painfully clear.

"Boss!" one of the men yelled.

"Hey Harry, you found us." Russo cheered, raising his still handcuffed hands into the air.

Oh shit, Brad thought. *What the hell do I do now?* A gun was still pointed at him.

"Leave him alone." Russo shouted. "He helped me escape. He's looked out for me the whole time we've been stuck here."

Brad looked nervously at the man who took an incredibly long time to lower the gun. When he did, he glared at Brad for a few long seconds before turning away. It was as if he didn't trust him. That seemed fair since Brad didn't trust him either. Finally the man walked over to where Russo was standing. Brad exhaled and leaned back against the kitchen sink.

"Hey Luke, get me out of these handcuffs, will ya?"

"Sure thing boss. I'll go get a tire iron from the car and I'll be right back."

Russo and the other two men walked slowly back to the living room and sat down. Brad could hear them talking.

"What the hell happened, boss?"

"It was a set-up. That bitch outside the restaurant set me up. She talked me into picking her up by myself and her pals were waiting for us on the road. They must have done something to the car 'cause the damned thing just quit."

"Well we've been looking for you ever since you didn't show up at the party."

"Now that you've found me, we're going to teach Paco Reyes some manners," Russo said indignantly.

"Paco Reyes? What the hell's he got to do with this?" Harry asked.

"What are you talking about? I saw the news. How many of his guys have we capped so far?" Russo was beginning to feel uneasy.

"None of them," Harry said, "we got no beef with Reyes."

"But I watched it on the news. They said that we killed a bunch of Paco's men and that his family had admitted to kidnapping me." Russo moved closer toward the edge of the couch.

"We never killed any of his men. What channel were you watching?"

Russo and his two men looked at each other for a moment, then over at the door.

"Son of a bitch" Russo muttered, "That little shit set me up." He became enraged for a second, and then looked at Harry again.

"The news said that the judge threw out the evidence. Is that bullshit too?"

"The judge allowed the evidence. Junior went nuts right there in court and ended up getting more charges filed against him."

"He set me up good." Russo repeated angrily.

The three stood up. "It's time to find out just what the kid knows, the hard way." Russo smacked the palm of his hand with his fist as much as the cuffs would allow.

Brad heard the whole thing from the kitchen but had nowhere to run. Luke was on his way back from the car and

Russo and the other two goons were on their way in from the living room into the kitchen.

Brad maneuvered himself into the corner by the cabinets. Luke walked through the back door a second before Russo and the other two got to the kitchen.

"Grab him!" Russo shouted to Luke.

Luke looked behind him out the back door, not knowing who Russo was talking about.

"The kid, the kid" Russo yelled, pointing toward Brad.

Luke hadn't trusted Brad from the beginning and took pleasure in being right. He raised his gun and walked over to Brad and rested the barrel of it against Brad's temple. *This is it,* Brad thought, *all those treatments, all of the shit we did for Sam, all of it, for what? To be shot in the head here in the kitchen of this shack, just my damned luck.*

Russo looked with contempt at Brad. "Alright you little prick you're going to come clean with me right now."

Brad remembered Arthur speaking those words to Jerry Kinson. He never dreamed someone would be uttering them to him.

"Who the hell are you? Who do you work for?"

"I told you, Paco Reyes made a deal with my partner to snatch you. Look, I helped you, remember? I'm on your side." Brad felt perspiration forming on his forehead. His hands were shaking and his knees felt weak. He thought about the gun he had in his belt under his shirt, but it was loaded with blanks.

Russo began looking around the kitchen, as if searching for something. His men looked at him, not knowing what it was he was doing.

"What are you looking for boss?" Harry asked.

Russo looked over at the sink. "This" he said, pointing down at the garbage disposal, "stick his hand in that garbage disposal and we'll find out if he's telling the truth."

"Bullshit!" Brad yelled and bolted out of the corner. He was quickly seized by Luke. Harry grabbed Brad's arm and rolled up his sleeve. Brad struggled violently, but to no avail. They drug him over to the sink by his arm. Russo stood by with his hand on the switch.

"One last chance to come clean" Russo warned.

"I already have." Brad yelled. "If you're too stupid to believe it then that's your problem."

"Stick his hand down in there." Russo demanded.

Brad thrashed and fought for his very life, but he was no match for the three men who had a hold of him.

Slowly they forced his hand down into the disposal. Brad pushed against the front of the cabinets which allowed him a little leverage. The three men pushed furiously on his arm.

"Turn it on." Harry yelled.

Russo flipped the switch and turned the disposal on. Brad could feel the air rushing against his knuckles created by the spinning blades. He could feel his hand sinking further into the disposal. As hard as he fought, he couldn't stop it. Russo stood there smiling, waiting for the inevitable. He felt the blades tearing at his knuckles and soon he felt the pain.

Suddenly there was a crash. Glass broke and little bits of wood flew through the air as the back door literally disintegrated. Everyone's head turned towards the noise. Six men, weapons in hand, charged through the door.

"Freeze assholes!" the first one yelled.

Brad felt their grips loosen and then finally released as all of them, Russo included raised their hands. A seemingly endless stream of police officers and SWAT team agents poured through the door and descended on the four, immediately binding them in handcuffs. Russo had yet to have the cuffs removed that he had been wearing for the past two days.

"This is handy." One of the officers laughed as he grabbed Russo. "This one's already cuffed."

Brad slowly raised his hand out of the disposal. Blood was dripping from his knuckles which had just begun to come in contact with the blades when the cavalry arrived. He reached over and turned the disposal off, when a hand carrying a handkerchief reached over and began to wrap Brad's fingers. Brad looked up. It was a detective.

"Hi, I'm Mo. I take it you're not one of them?"

"No, I'm not one of them, and if you'd been ten seconds later getting here, I wouldn't have been one of me either."

Mo chuckled as he tightened the handkerchief around Brad's fingers, then led him outside.

"You need an ambulance?"

"Naw, I'm fine."

"I'll need a statement from you."

"Sure. Just let me get some air. I'll be outside whenever you want me."

Mo turned and walked back into the house as Russo and his three goons were led out to a fleet of waiting police cars. Brad looked over the sea of flashing lights and noticed one car that looked as if it didn't belong. It looked strangely familiar, though he couldn't put his finger on just whose car it was.

He walked slowly towards the road. As he did, the door of the car opened and Arthur stepped out. Brad saw him and quickened his step towards him as the passenger door opened, then one of the rear doors. Lenny and Derek stepped out as well. Brad broke into a run. Arthur walked around to the other side of the car, noticing the blood soaked cloth wrapped around Brad's hand.

"You okay buddy?"

"Ya I'm okay." Brad looked over at Lenny. "I could have used you back there."

"I'm sorry I wasn't here to help you." he said.

"I'm just glad it's over." Derek added.

"I can't wait to tell the ladies. I'm sure they're ready for this to be over too." Brad said, holding his hand that was now beginning to throb.

"I already have." Derek announced. "They're on their way back as we speak."

Brad looked over at Arthur. "It's finally over, isn't it?"

"It's over." Arthur said.

Brad looked out at the swarm of police officers milling around the house. "You'd better get out of here before they spot you."

Brad turned and slowly walked back toward the house. Arthur got back in his car and the three left, not wanting to create suspicion. Brad spent twenty minutes concocting a most prolific collection of lies and giving them as answers to Mo's questions. Mo seemed satisfied with them and when he was through, he directed a patrol car to take Brad to the hospital to get a tetanus shot and to have his hand looked at.

The sun was setting as Brad pulled away from the house, and a chapter in his life that was more inconceivable than anything he had ever written, was about to close.

CHAPTER TWENTY FOUR

It was almost two in the morning when the skilled hands of the pilot brought the small jet gently down on the far left runway of the airport. When the nose wheels had touched down, he reversed the thrust, bringing the aircraft quickly down to taxing speed. Arthur, Brad and Derek watched as the plane's lights approached and the steady whine of the engines slowly grew louder.

It seemed to take forever for the jet to get to the hanger where the three very anxious men were waiting. Eventually it did taxi to a stop. An airport employee walked under the plane and placed blocks in front of and behind the wheels as the pilot shut down the engines. The cabin lights came on and soon the door opened and the staircase extended itself to the ground. Katie and Derek Jr. were the first ones out the door and down the steps. Derek ran to meet them. He hugged Katie at the bottom of the stairs, long and tightly as he used to when they were dating. Then he took his son in his arms. He felt as if he'd grown since Derek had held him last.

"I missed you so much." Katie said with tears of joy in her eyes.

"I missed you too." Derek kissed his son on his forehead.

Sandy was the next one down the steps, followed by Todd and Angie. Arthur was waiting for them at the bottom of the stairs. Sandy ran to him with open arms.

"I'm so glad to be back." she told him. "I don't do well when we're apart."

Arthur hugged Sandy and the kids.

"You two enjoy your little vacation?" he asked.

"You bet." Todd answered. "That plane is neat. The pilot let me come up to the cockpit while we were flying. You should see all those lights and buttons. That's what I want to be when I grow up dad, a pilot."

Arthur squeezed him again then looked over at Angie. She looked back at him and he knew that Sandy had told her everything.

"I'm glad you didn't get hurt dad. Mom told me what was going on. I think it's pretty cool that you'd go after the guys that threatened us like you did."

"It wasn't that big a deal really." Arthur said. But she knew better, and Arthur knew she did.

Carol was the last one out of the plane. She walked cautiously down the steps to Brad's awaiting embrace.

"It feels so good to hold you again." he said, not ever wanting to let her go.

"It felt like we were gone an eternity. I missed you a lot." She hugged him a while longer then reached for his hand as they walked toward the van. Feeling the bandages, she stopped and looked down at it. His hand was bandaged from his finger nails to his wrist.

"What happened to your hand?" she asked, her voice filled with all the concern of a loving spouse.

"Just a little mishap in the kitchen" Brad scoffed, winking at her as they continued on to the van.

The baggage had been loaded and the van was well out of the airport complex before Derek got up enough nerve to talk to Katie about what had happened while she'd been away that directly concerned her.

"There are a few things I need to tell you before you go back to work." he began.

"What's that?"

"Well, you probably have a message on your desk from the police."

"The police"

"Ya, it's a long story, but I think you'll like the way it turns out. You may even get a promotion out of it before it's all over with."

For the next twenty minutes, Derek explained to Katie the letter to the police, the picture of the watch and the engraving on the back of it. Although she was a little uncomfortable telling stories, there was really no way she could tell the truth here.

Everyone was so glad to be home that no one realized Evan, who had driven them all to the airport when they left, hadn't come along. It wasn't until the van was pulling up to Derek and Katie's house that Sandy asked, "Where's Evan?"

"He said he wasn't feeling very well." Arthur told them. "We're all getting together for dinner tomorrow night so he said he'd see you all then."

"Well I hope he's okay." Sandy said knowing Evan was afflicted with the same illness as Arthur.

But everybody's entitled to have an off day, including Evan, and they figured that's all it was.

Arthur had decided to take a few more days off, and although it was unusual for him to be in bed at eight thirty in the morning, the past few days had been exhausting. Besides, it felt good to have his wife back and to have her next to him. The phone rang as he lay there thinking back on the events of the past few days. He knew who it was before he picked it up.

"Good morning Arthur." It was Sam.

"Good morning Sam." The ringing phone had woken Sandy up, but it was the mention of Sam's name that captured her attention.

"What can I do for you this morning?" Arthur asked.

"I just wanted to call and express my gratitude as well as that of our entire organization. We couldn't have asked for a more equitable solution to our predicament."

"Well I'm glad it's all over. This was certainly a tough one."

"I trust Brad is alright. I understand he had a close encounter with a garbage disposal."

"Ya, his knuckles are skinned up, but he's okay"

There was a pause in the conversation before Sam spoke again.

"Well Arthur, I'm a man of my word. I told you going into this assignment that it would be your last. You have kept your part of the bargain and I intend to keep mine. So, you may all consider yourselves retired that is if you want to."

There was again a pause.

"Do you want to Arthur?"

Arthur thought for a moment. "Do you need an answer right now?"

"Of course not" Sam replied.

"I'm sure I speak for the others when I tell you they are ready to retire."

"I felt quite sure they would be. You on the other hand, I wasn't sure about. Arthur, you have a talent for this work. I think you know that. And I also think you know what you're going to decide, you just haven't come to terms with it yet."

"Maybe you're right."

"Well Arthur, my door is always open. I do hope I hear from you soon."

"I have a feeling you will." Arthur smiled and told Sam good bye, then hung up the phone.

"Was that who I thought it was?" Sandy asked.

"That depends. Who did you think it was?"

"Sam?"

"Yes, it was. He was calling to say good bye and to thank us for what we did."

"He didn't ask you to keep on doing it?"

"No, our agreement was that this would be the last one."

"Good." Sandy said as she snuggled up close to Arthur. "I'd never be able to sleep knowing that you might be out there somewhere in a shoot out with some criminal."

Arthur lay staring at the ceiling. This is just what he needed, another decision.

Brad sat quietly in the lounge of the treatment center reading a book. He had gotten used to Arthur getting there early these last couple of months and found himself a little lonely this afternoon. But Arthur did finally arrive and shortly after him, Derek. The three talked a while of the events of the past week. Evan was still conspicuously absent.

"I didn't figure he'd be here this afternoon anyway." Brad said.

"Ya, he's probably still trying to recover from last night." Derek laughed.

"I'm afraid you're wrong." a voice answered from across the room.

The doctor had slipped through the doors unnoticed by anyone.

"We are?" Arthur asked.

"He's here in the hospital, room three ten."

"What's wrong with him?" Brad asked in disbelief. He had talked to Evan just two days ago.

"He came in last night in a great deal of pain. We admitted him and ran some tests. He asked me to come down here and talk to you before you went up to see him."

Derek was visibly upset. "Is he going to be alright?"

"No, he's not Derek. He's dying."

"What?" Arthur stood up face to face with the doctor. "How could this happen so fast?"

"It didn't happen as fast as you might think. Evan has been slipping for some time now. I have increased the intensity of his treatments three times in the past six weeks. There were even occasions that he came back here in between his regular treatments. No, I'm afraid this has been coming on for some time now."

The three men were shocked. They had been so close, so very close for so long. It just didn't seem possible that one of them was going to be gone.

"If you like, you can go up and see him before the treatments. I won't be ready for you for another fifteen minutes or so." The doctor looked at his watch, and then walked out of the lounge into the treatment room.

The three headed for the elevators. They were silent, not knowing what to say. They had all known that one of them would have to be the first to go, but none of them wanted to think about who it would be.

They arrived at room three ten and gently pushed open the door. Evan was lying, his eyes closed, in a bed with an IV bag to one side and a line of electronic monitoring equipment on the other. They quietly entered the room and walked over to the side of the bed. Arthur put his hand on Evan's shoulder. Evan opened his eyes and looked up at Arthur, then smiled and closed them again.

"Did we do it? Are we off the hook?" Evan asked in a whisper.

"Ya, we did it." Arthur said.

Evan looked past him to Brad and Derek. "Looks like the gang's all here." Again a whisper was all he could muster.

"We're here" Brad said, fighting back his emotions. "We'll always be here for you."

"You know, you three guys are the best friends I ever had. I don't know if I ever told you that, but it's true." Evan's voice was becoming weaker though his face showed a look of contentment.

"Arthur" he said softly, "if I don't make it out of here, tell my father what we've been doing for the past few months. I always wanted to make him proud of me. It looks like this is my last chance."

Evan drew in a deep breath, then exhaled and momentarily drifted off. The three stood watching him, their hearts aching for their friend. Evan's eyes opened again.

"Listen" he whispered, "I'm a little tired right now. Why don't you come back and see me after your treatments."

"Sure" Arthur assured him, "we'll come back."

Arthur patted him on his shoulder. They all stood quietly for a minute, looking at Evan, and silently wondering why it was he and not one of them as Evan had drifted off to sleep.

Arthur looked down at his watch. "We'd better get downstairs."

They walked slowly down the hall toward the elevator. No one could speak. No one knew what to say. Before they made it to the elevator, they heard a loud beeping sound coming from the nurse's station at the opposite end of the hall. The three men stopped, not wanting to think about what was happening. Brad turned to look as three nurses, one pushing a cart, rushed into Evan's room.

It was no more than a minute before two of the three nurses walked slowly out of Evan's room. Brad knew what had happened. Soon after, the cart was pushed back out and down the hall. Brad lowered his head and closed his eyes tightly. He knew he had just lost a very dear friend. Arthur, Brad and Derek stood motionless in the hallway, looking back toward Evan's room. As they watched, the door opened one final time, and the bed was wheeled out. A sheet was pulled up over Evan's face. Although he had put up a gallant effort, Evan had finally lost. Each of them felt as if a little bit of them died along with him.

It rained the day of Evan's funeral. Those at the grave site were not many in number. Arthur's eyes remained fixed on Evan's father. He was unable to judge his expression. Maybe it was because he didn't know him very well, or maybe it was just the way he showed his grief. Nonetheless he stood, unaffected by the pouring rain, being the father he now wished he had been while his son was still alive.

As the mourners filed by the casket, Arthur took it upon himself to speak with Evan's dad.

"Mr. Marshall, my name is Arthur Jensen. I knew your son very well. He was a fine young man who spoke very highly of you. You should be very proud of him." Arthur paused as Mr. Marshall wiped a tear from his eye. "Sometime, when this day is behind us, I'd like to talk to you about something Evan was involved with just before he died."

Mr. Marshall looked at Arthur. It was obvious he was trying very hard to control his emotions. "Thank you, Arthur. I'd like that. I'd like that very much."

Arthur shook his hand, and then turned to walk away. A figure caught his eye as he began to walk to his car. He turned his head and found himself making eye contact with Sam. He looked to see where the others were. They had already made it to Arthur's car as they had all ridden together. Sandy was unlocking the doors to get in from the rain. Arthur walked over to Sam and stood umbrellas distance apart.

"It was good of you to come, Sam."

"I do hope that the activity Evan was engaged in during the past few months were in no way responsible for this." Sam had a worried look in his eyes.

"No, this would have happened whether we'd ever met you or not."

"Thank you Arthur. Thank you for everything." Sam smiled ever so slightly, then turned and walked away.

The rain continued as Arthur made his way back to his car. Sandy had started the engine from the passenger seat and turned the heater on. Brad and Derek were sitting in the back seat.

"How's Evan's dad?" Brad asked as Arthur got behind the wheel.

"Not too good right now, but he'll be alright eventually."

"Who was that guy you were talking to back there?" Derek questioned.

"You didn't recognize him?"

"We didn't see him." Brad replied.

Arthur closed his car door then looked back at them. "That my friends, was Sam." Arthur smiled then shifted the car into gear.

Brad and Derek both looked at each other, then frantically over the line of cars for the man Arthur had been talking to, but he had blended in with the others and was nowhere to be seen. They both looked at each other.

"It's probably better this way." Brad said as he and Derek buckled their seat belts. They both took one last look at the casket as it was slowly lowered into the ground, and silently bid farewell to their friend.

It had been a week since the funeral. Arthur was contemplating what to eat for lunch when his private line rang. He picked it up, half expecting it to be Sam. It was Brad.

"Hey, what are you doing for lunch?" Brad asked.

"I don't know. Do you have something in mind?"

"As a matter of fact, I do. I'll pick you up in ten minutes."

Brad picked him up as he said he would. They drove for nearly twenty minutes before Arthur began to get curious.

"Just where the hell is this restaurant anyway?" Arthur complained.

"Who said it was a restaurant?" Brad asked.

"I'm totally confused."

"You won't be for long." Brad assured him, as they pulled to a stop across the street from a high school.

"What are we doing here?" Arthur complained. "This is where Angie goes to school.

"Come on, let's get out."

They got out and walked around the front of the car and leaned against the fender.

"So now what?" Arthur asked, feeling he had wasted his lunch hour.

"See that young man over there?" Brad asked, pointing to a teenager standing next to a red sports car in the school parking lot.

"Ya, I see him, so what?"

"Remember the night you called me because Angie's date had thrown her out of his car when he couldn't have his way with her?"

"Ya, I remember, why?"

"Well, that's the little prick that did it, right over there."

Arthur looked at him again, and then almost lunging, took a step towards him. Brad grabbed his arm and pulled him back.

"What are you doing?" Arthur snapped. "I owe this kid an ass whipping."

"Relax. That's not why I brought you here. Now let me finish."

Arthur was already pissed off. He'd wanted to teach that kid some manners ever since Angie told him what had happened.

"Now" Brad continued, "see that pretty young, dark haired girl walking into the parking lot from the sidewalk?"

Again Arthur looked. "Ya, I see her, what about it?"

"Well, he did the same thing to her that he did to Angie. Only this time, someone caught the whole thing on video tape and gave the tape to that man right over there." Brad pointed to a man just getting out of a van on the street side of the parking lot.

"So who is he?"

"He is that girl's father. He has just viewed the video tape and he is extremely upset." Brad paused for a moment, and then added, "Did I mention that he's a Martial Arts instructor?"

Arthur looked over at Brad with a million dollar smile on his face. "You devious son of a bitch, did you do this?"

Brad just smiled.

The two watched as the girl's father made his way through the parking lot to the young man by the sports car. There was a brief exchange of words, before the boy made the mistake of pushing the girl's father. The boy stood a full head taller and some thirty years younger than the man which made him a little over confident. The man grabbed the boy's arm and quickly twisted it behind his back. Then in an instant, he used his right foot to kick the young man's feet out from under him and the boy fell to the ground.

Embarrassed by how easily this older man was getting the better of him, the boy jumped to his feet and ran at him with his hands extended in front of him. The girl's father let him get close enough, then dipped down and grabbed the boy's arm. He threw him angrily, but effortlessly over his shoulder. The boy became airborne, crashing into the car he had been standing next to. He bounced off of it, landing hard on the gravel in front of his friends. The man stood poised and ready for more, but the kid got up and ran off in the other direction as fast as he could while his friends taunted and laughed at him.

"See, I told you." Arthur said. "You got a knack for this stuff. Maybe you should stay with it."

He was wasting his time trying to talk Brad into continuing on with Sam.

"No thanks!" Brad said, brushing his hands together, "This was my last assignment."

"You know what?" Arthur asked as they got back into the car.

"What?"

"This is the best lunch I've had in a long time."

It was dark, probably close to eleven o'clock when Brad switched on his computer. He slid a disc into it and entered a pass code. Once the file was open, he looked at it for a few moments before pressing a button on the key board. The file was Brad's day to day diary of what he and the others had done since they began working for Sam. Brad paused again before hitting the button to remove the disc from his computer.

He held the disc indecisively in his hand for several seconds before slowly walking over to the fireplace. After moments' hesitation, he tossed it in.

Brad watched it melt and burn for a few moments before sitting down on the couch. He picked up a glass that he had been drinking from and took one last sip. As he sat the glass back down on the coffee table he heard Carol's voice calling out to him from the bedroom.

"What are you doing out there?"

Brad got up and walked toward her. "Just taking care of some unfinished business." he answered. The fire was dying down and the disc had melted into little more than a puddle of unrecognizable plastic. The rest had drifted up the chimney with the smoke. Brad walked out of the living room and switched off the light. It was indeed, over.

Made in the USA